SONS

OF

SORROW

SONS

OF

SORROW

A Novel

Jerry
Fagnani

AVENTURA
PRESS

Cover painting "Winter in Coaltown"
by Colleen Mondics
cemondics@webs.com

ISBN-13: 978-1-936936-07-6

Published by
Avventura Press
133 Handley St.
Eynon PA 18403-1305
www.avventurapress.com

First printing July 2014
Printed in the United States of America

Dedicated with love to my wife Elaine,
and my daughter, Kimberly,
and my grandchildren, Ryan and Garret

FAGNANI
MAIN ST,
N, PA. 18403
e: 570-604-2681

We are the sons of sorrow, and you are the sons of joy.
We are the sons of sorrow, and sorrow is the shadow
of a God who lives not in the domain of evil hearts.

We are the sons of sorrow, and sorrow is a rich cloud,
showering the multitudes with knowledge and truth.
You are the sons of joy, and as high as your joy may
reach, by the laws of God it must be destroyed before
the winds of heaven and dispersed into nothingness,
for it is naught but a thin and wavering pillar of smoke.

Kahlil Gibran— *We and You*

DEAR MR. PRESIDENT,

THROUGH THE KIND
INTERVENTION OF OUR MUTUAL AND
WONDERFUL FRIENDS, ROB & KIM FLYNN,
I AM EXCITED AND HAPPY TO

INTRODUCE YOU TO MY NOVEL,
"THE SONS OF SORROW."
I HOPE YOU'LL FIND IT
INTERESTING AND ENJOYABLE.
GOD BLESS YOU, SIR.
RESPECTFULLY,
Jeff Faansn

PRELUDE

Joseph Flynn was sure he was in the middle of a nightmare, a haunting illusion where a minute is eternity. But the blood that dripped into the back of his throat was real, mixing with the bitter taste of vomit. It was choking him.

Hesitantly, he opened his eyes. The bizarre contortions were still there—images flashing across his brain like the stuttering movement of celluloid and the sounds were growing to thunder in his ears. It would all come at him, garishly, only to ebb and fade and come again.

The sounds were loud, now. "I don't need you! I'll throw you out!" The moment stopped like a frozen frame. It was a familiar voice. The image became focused: The sound and the face behind it belonged to Joseph's father.

Suddenly Joseph heard his own voice, clear and screaming, "I'll kill you, you bastard!"

His father's words and leering face taunted him. "Let him go. Let's see how tough he is."

Joseph tried to attack, but he couldn't move. He was being held fast.

The ugly laughing voice cut at him. It made him bleed. "Let him go. Let's see how tough he is. Let him go. Let him go."

Slowly, the viselike grip released and Joseph found himself free. He glared at the evil, challenging face of his father. But now there was a new image. He saw the face of his mother. He saw the face of his brother. That same ugly voice was taunting them. It was defiling them.

He saw his father's body in front of him, and Joseph lunged toward it, furiously trying to still the voice and its filthy, degrading words.

Joseph tried, but he was grabbed by a powerful force and thrown about. Punches pounded against the back of his head and against his kidneys. He could barely catch his breath, but he hung on.

There were more punches, more pain. He felt himself crumbling, but in a feverish moment he called on a deep reserve of fury and moved forward.

He felt the supreme pleasure of driving his fist against the flesh and bone of his father's face; he saw his father's blood. The taunts became grunts, wheezing animal whimpers. Joseph kept punching, striking again and again. There was blood everywhere

Finally, his father fell, but Joseph suddenly felt another flash of pain. Another figure was striking at him. Raging and cursing, Joseph lashed out at it. His fists pounded in violence, until this figure, too, collapsed in blood, until Joseph Flynn stood alone, in a triumph he couldn't understand.

And then the vast, clear image grew hazy again, and Joseph felt himself fading with it. The feel of nightmare returned and reality became unreality.

The stutter was building again within his skull, crashing and reverberating into the deepest cavity of his brain. The flashing returned in bursts of images that brought his body warmth, to be suddenly removed by visions containing the touch of death.

He was drifting in a depersonalized realm, and he saw his broken self, writhing and bleeding. He heard the strangled cough that brought the blood up from his throat.

He watched it spill from the corners of his mouth in jagged, crimson paths to the edge of his jaw.

He tried to understand the nightmares—the contrasts of beauty and ugliness, pleasure and terror. And now he was struggling, desperately, to return to his body; struggling to turn the switch that would bring him back to his life...to quiet the scream of revenge.

HANWAY

It was called Underwood, in the beginning, and surely the land had something to do with it; five thousand acres of lush valley enjoying the protective shadow of its proud mountains.

John Hanway was the President-Judge of a judicial district near this village and was the first to recognize the hidden treasures of its land. Within the bowels of this vast, green surface, where the vegetation had died and layered itself from the primordial hour, the peat had become coal and this interior had evolved into a part of the rich, Pennsylvania coal seam known as anthracite.

The Judge bought up huge parcels of the territory and by 1856 had several coal shafts in operation. More and more land was mined and its industry flourished, and eventually Underwood became a thriving community.

Thirty years later, the land was incorporated into a borough and the petitioners named it Hanway, in honor of the man and his vision.

The English were the first to enter the pits...and then came the rest—the Irish, the Italians, the Poles; all of them coming to raise families and to build lives.

The flush of activity in the Hanway coal fields produced different levels of wealthy but with the wealth came blights—mountains of culm, the worthless byproduct of the digging, humped their way across the valley like giant stalagmites on the land.

Eventually, new forms of industry came to Hanway and the pervading influence of the coal mines withered; but the attitudes they had sown and the personalities they had tempered, remained. The fabric of that labor had produced conflicting effects; its fruits a puzzling blend of pride and anger, acceptance and resentment.

The generations that would come from all of this were to bear these conflicting banners of the new order, a collection of contrasts that would paint the flickering images on the face of a continent. A collection of contrasts that would become the breathing substance of America.

In altering its guise, Hanway would change…and it would not change. Images would endure. Culm dumps would remain, standing on the periphery, paying testimony to the history and the legacy; the memory of men who tore their bodies in that fevered labyrinth beyond the shafts, and the memories of dreams that were either smashed and abandoned or brought into a rewarding reality.

Like all Hanways everywhere, the town would always be there, containing everything that had gone before as well as all things coming…all of the memories past and all of the dreams behind the shadows in men's eyes.

APRIL, 1946

Joseph Flynn would never forget that Saturday morning in Hanway. It was warm and the sky was overcast, suggesting the possibility of rain. The sparrows chirped nervously on the wires above Moosic Street. All through the day, Joseph Flynn was obsessed with thoughts of his father.

The war ended months before, but Patrick Flynn's return had been delayed by wounds sustained during the last days of fire in the Pacific. But now he was coming home, and his young son found himself struggling in a confusion of joy and fear. Joseph Flynn had been born while his father walked in the jungle of that conflict, so far away. He didn't know Patrick Flynn; he had never even seen him.

The morning moved on to early afternoon. Joseph and his brother Larry, along with their energetic band of friends, went about their usual business. They watched as Mr. DeFazio's old red truck labored to a stop in front of Palumbo's Saloon. The boys moved quickly. They scurried up the two-step ladder at the rear of the truck and ran along its open back. They scrambled about, grabbing slices of ice that filled numerous pails on the truckbed. They heard the expected voice, "Ya dirty bastards!" Mr. DeFazio yelled, as he lumbered out of the cab. He waved his fist, as the boys moved, in a burst of excitement, across Moosic Street and up the hill that led to the railroad.

With pieces of ice protruding from their mouths, they climbed in and out of abandoned coal cars and crept under their huge bulk. Finally, they went up to Main Street, taking their innocent brand of mischief with them. Joseph took part in all of it, hut he was somehow removed. The obsession remained locked in his five year old brain: He couldn't stop thinking about Patrick Flynn.

In the late afternoon of that homecoming day, Joseph and his brother made numerous trips from their house to Main Street, happily running errands in preparation for the party. They helped

JERRY FAGNANI

their Aunt Gena tie streamers of crepe paper from one kitchen wall to the other, until the room was filled with the hue of celebration. Their mother, Anna, prepared the food and directed the men from the neighborhood, who had come to help, in the placement of tables and chairs on the front lawn.

It was five o'clock and Uncle Tommy's car was expected. He had gone, almost two hours earlier, to pick up Patrick at the train station. Before he had left for Clarkson City, Tom Conroy waved his finger and teased Anna, "I'll bring him home drunk," he had said with laughter.

Anna had laughed in return, "You'd better not, you devil."

Gena smiled at her husband's good natured teasing. She opened the car door and kissed Tom on the cheek. "Hurry up, Tommy," she whispered. "Come right back. Don't fool around."

Joseph waited on the front sidewalk. His eyes searched the street for Uncle Tom's car. He felt the softness of his Aunt Gena's hand on the back of his neck. She crouched down alongside of him. Her voice soft and reassuring, "Everything's going to be wonderful now. Your Daddy's coming home, and everything's going to be fine."

Joseph shuffled his feet on the sidewalk and dug his hands into his pockets.

"Aren't you excited, Baby?" Gena whispered.

Joseph was very excited. He nodded and looked at her.

Joseph thought of his father's picture on the parlor coffee table, the same picture that had been on the front page of the local newspaper when he was proclaimed a hero. His name was all over the streets, then. It was Patrick Flynn this and Patrick Flynn that, and they had all been so very proud.

Gena was Patrick's sister, and the resemblance to him was pronounced; her lips were full and wide over square, white teeth. She was tall and imposing, with a lean, perfectly cut body. Gena was beautiful.

Joseph ran his fingers along her luxurious, auburn hair.

He wanted to say something, but he knew that he couldn't. His throat was full and he felt as though he would cry. Gena pulled him close and pressed her lips against his warm cheek.

"Don't you worry. You're gonna be so glad," she said. "Your dad'll show you his medals and tell you just how he saved that whole company."

Joseph bowed his head.

"I'll bet you can hardly wait to hear about all that? Right?"

"Yes," Joseph said.

Gena picked him up and cradled his hips. "All right, then. Let's see a smile."

Joseph felt his lips tremble.

"Ah, c'mon," Gena said. "Let's see a little old smile."

Joseph swallowed hard and stretched his lips.

Gena laughed. "That's better, ya sonofagun. Perk up and don't be nervous, because you're gonna be so glad."

Joe wrapped his arms around her neck and hugged her.

"Your Daddy's wounds are all better now. He's all right. He's perfect again," Gena said, pulling her head back to look at Joseph. "We can all thank God for that." She kissed him again. "You're seeing your Dad for the first time, but there's nothing to be nervous about. You're gonna love him."

The minutes crept by. Joseph and Larry stood holding hands on the back porch. Larry looked down at Joseph and smiled tenderly. "It won't be long now." At last, Uncle Tommy's car pulled into the driveway. Tom was out of the car in an instant. Laughing and yelling, he ran over to the passenger's door and eluberantly swung it open.

And then, a man got out and walked toward the brothers.

Patrick Flynn, a duffel bag across his shoulder, walked slowly along the driveway. He walked up onto the back porch. He tried to say something to the boys, but his voice choked. Anna Flynn and Gena ran from the kitchen to the porch. They wanted to see him, to touch him. They stopped when they saw Patrick standing there, looking at his two sons.

Larry, eleven and nearly grown, rushed to the father he hadn't seen for so long. Joseph's eyes followed his brother. Larry, the brother who was always there through those lonely years without a father. The brother who did all the household chores—shoveling sidewalks, painting, carrying coal up from the cellar with his thin arms straining. Larry, who throughout that long void, protected Joseph with understanding and love. It was Larry who laughed and struggled to comb his brother's stubborn cowlick on Sunday mornings before Mass. It was Larry who sang Joseph to sleep with soft bedtime songs, and it was Larry whom, at the moment, Joseph loved with a passion that made him tremble.

Patrick Flynn knelt down and squeezed his son. Larry was crying; huge tears formed streams as they cascaded down his face. Joseph stared at his father. He was huge, a giant. His jaw was square and proud in a solid face of muscle and skin, set perfectly over bone. Brown curls fell over his forehead and his eyes were blinking and wet.

Joseph's heart pounded. He wanted to scream, he wanted to shout, but in the raging tumult of his soul, he stood mute and waited.

Finally, Patrick Flynn turned, and his eyes pierced Joseph's face. He looked at his youngest son with a gaze that was intermingled with all the things of the heart. His hands went to Joseph and in an instant they were tight on his son's shoulders. Joseph was unable to utter a sound, his voice contained by the chains of panic.

"Joseph," his father whispered.

Joseph thought his chest would split. Patrick Flynn held the son he had never known. He held him so tight, his muscles bulged against the inside of his sleeves. He picked Joseph up and kissed him, feeling the wetness of his son's tears and his own.

In all of his young life, Joseph had never known such a surge of pure pleasure. He planted his hands against the large curves of his father's shoulders. Joseph smelled the freshness of his father and the roughness of his face as it pressed against his cheek.

And then Joseph heard the joyful, sobbing whisper of his mother's voice. Patrick gently set Joseph down and turned to look at Anna. Patrick saw the wonderful look of anticipation on her face. He rushed to her, and suddenly she was in the air, in his arms. They kissed and cried and spun about the room.

The others were so touched, they couldn't speak, until Patrick and Anna reached for them, beckoning them. Gena ran to her brother and threw her arms around him. And then, they were all together in a mixture of laughter and tears.

The party went on all night. Almost everyone in Hanway came to welcome Patrick Flynn back home. Joseph watched everything, swallowing and digesting every moment.

Later that night, Joseph and Larry were finally sent to bed, but Joseph couldn't sleep. He stayed awake all through the noise and hilarity coming from the front lawn. He was still awake after all the people had gone. Joseph heard the quiet voices of his parents and their soft steps coming up the stairway.

He stayed awake through the quiet of the early morning hours. He heard the milkman's arrival and the clicking of glass on the front porch. Joseph rubbed his hand along Larry's back; he was fast asleep beside him. Joseph lay there, his eyes wide, the rush of eIcitement still within him; the same lingering feeling of panic and joy that had gripped him on the evening before, when his father finally came home.

Joseph would never forget the days that followed his father's homecoming, golden days that were slowly transformed into long, ugly years. In the beginning Patrick Flynn was busy, drawing the designs that would outline his future and his power.

He would go up to Main Street, with Larry and Joe often tagging behind, and talk to an assortment of men in Billy's Pool Hall, explaining the ways and means that were to eventually control the politics of the county. The men listened intently as Patrick convinced them to follow him and become part of the takeover. Before long the design became reality and Patrick Flynn spread out his talents, successfully moving into politics, beer distribution and real estate.

But it wasn't always business. There were good times: the festive holidays when family and friends would crowd into the house, as Joe and Larry ran laughing and shouting through all those heedless and bright hours; the summer church parties and the glitter of colored lights along the stands erected on the sidewalks, Patrick and Anna Flynn walking with their sons, smiling and talking amongst the friendly crowd that so typified the town of Hanway; the many nights that Joseph lay upstairs, listening to the happy voices of his parents in the parlor, safe in the warm cocoon of his bed. He would wait and listen for the sound of the locomotive as it would churn past his backyard, its familiar whistle, pleasant and reassuring to his ear. Joseph Flynn loved his family and he loved Hanway. He could never be without them. It was unthinkable. Impossible.

But times would change. Eventually his parent's warm relationship would erode, becoming one continuous argument. Joseph began to resent the attention his father showed Larry, the brother whose face was the image of Patrick Flynn. Joseph was annoyed that he looked so much like his mother—wanting to look like his father, wanting to be like his father, desperately wanting to be the favorite son.

For all his later trying, Joseph could never put his finger on the exact moment where it began, but he knew it was during those years when all their lives took a fateful turn into despair.

It was then when he recognized his father's detachment from him, and his torture in wondering why.

All through that period, he struggled diligently to be his father's son, and was filled with rage and disappointment to know he was failing. He began to blame his brother for his father's rejection. Joseph drifted apart from Larry and all the warmth began to slip away. The noose that was to throttle all their lives began to tighten around their throats.

Joseph would never completely reweave that tender fabric of memory, but he knew that it was during those early years that the chasm cut through the mountain's bulk. It would always come out of the past, in an intermittent tattoo of vagueness and clarity, like sweaty morning dream fragments trying to connect the lost events of the night before.

BOOK
ONE

1

January 1958

JOSEPH walked swiftly across his bedroom. He stopped before the mirror hanging from the wall above his bureau. His reflection in the mirror offered him a surge of pride. He was dazzling in the starched pink and white shirt, with its high collar hugging his muscled neck. He stood proud in his uniform of youth—the bright shirt and the black pants, pegged tight at his ankles; the white buck shoes, framed by a rubber heel and sole of soft red.

He had forgotten, long ago, the resentment of looking like his mother His hair was now the raven black of Anna Flynn's. His large eyes, black and deep, as well as his full perfect mouth were hers. He was almost seventeen and at full growth; in shoes he was over six feet, and as tall as his father. He had Patrick Flynn's broad, ceiling beam shoulders, and the same abdomen, flat and rock-hard. Everything about his young body bespoke power. His clothes hung perfectly from a frame of splendid symmetry.

He carefully brushed the thick, black hair, allowing some curls to fall upon his forehead, arranging them carefully, in neat ringlets. He doused himself with a final handful of aftershave lotion. After examining himself one last time in the mirror, he left the room.

He stopped at Larry's doorway across the hall. Larry was sitting at his desk. He brooded over a large textbook, and was totally oblivious to Joseph's presence.

"Hey. egghead!" Joseph said,. "Don't you ever take a break?" Larry looked up. His face was in no way similar to his brother's. He was typically Irish in appearance, containing not a nuance of his

23

mother's dark, Italian heritage. Except for discrepancies in color, he looked very much like his father.

His hair was also full, and curled, but instead of being black, it was auburn, with highlights of bright red. He was fair-skinned in sharp contrast to the dark flesh tones of his younger brother. Larry's eyes were blue and hooded by heavy brows. It was unusual, the way the genes had mixed, leaving each son with a facial content that almost eerily captured the image of the mother in one case, and the father in the other. However, the bodies reversed the inheritance. Joseph had the strong, powerful lines of Patrick Flynn's structure, and Larry had the narrow shoulders and short, frail development that was so reminiscent of Anna.

Larry contorted his mouth in disgust, "Don't bother me, Joe, I'm busy," he said.

Joseph half leaned into the room, "Yeah," he said. "I know you're always busy with that studying shit."

Larry's eyes went back to the book. "You ought to try it sometime," he said,

"What!" Joseph laughed derisively, "and wind up like you, a friggin' pantywaist."

Larry pushed his chair back from the desk, and glared at his antagonist, "Goddammit, leave me alone, " he scowled. "I told you I'm busy."

Joseph turned away laughing. He jauntily ran down the stairs to the kitchen. As he entered the kitchen, he heard his mother's voice.

"What is Larry shouting about?" she asked in a quiet voice.

She was scrubbing the top of the huge coal stove. Beads of sweat dotted her forehead. as she brushed back strands of dark hair, damp with labor. "What is Larry shouting about?" she repeated.

"Aww, he's up there with those books again. "

"You should try imitating him once in a while, it'd do you good. And watch your mouth."

"Whaddya mean it'd do me good? I make out pretty good in school without all that nonsense!" Joseph said.

Anna tiredly returned to her scrubbing.

Joseph removed a cookie from a tray on the table. Ha wolfishly chewed it and swallowed it almost simultaneously.

"Where are you going?" his mother asked.

"I've got a date!"

"Who with?"

"What is this—the third degree?"

Anna turned and faced her son. "I don't know, Joe. This wise guy attitude of yours is getting on my nerves," she said.

She wiped her hands on the soiled apron. She began to smile. "You're keeping steady time with Carol, aren't you?" she asked.

She crossed her arms over her chest and continued smiling. A wet, dirty cloth hung loosely in her hand. "I'm getting to think it's serious," she said.

"Just a friend, just a friend," he said mockingly. He put on his jacket and zipped it tight to his throat. He mumbled a goodbye and left the house.

Joseph walked hard into the January night. The wind was frigid, against his face, He moved fast, trying to neutralize the frigidity of winter. The street lamps attached near the top of the telephone poles along the street, offered a glimpse of a steady stream of snow. It moved slowly in soft flakes past the hooded illumination.

When he reached the wide expanse in front of Mickey's gas station on the corner of Main Street, the wind intensified.

It caused his hair to become disheveled. Joseph cursed to himself and carefully arranged it with his hand.

"Oh my, don't we look pretty!" Mickey laughed as he walked away from the old Ford pulling slowly away from the pumps. Mickey Clark was an old and dear friend. Joe could not count the days and nights he spent leaning over hoods in Mickey's garage, asking interminable questions on cars and repairs. It was a relationship that he deeply respected.

"How ya doin', Mick?" Joseph said.

"Not bad, kid. How's yourself?" Mickey smiled. "You look like a guy with a heavy date."

"Yeah, yeah. Sure I do," Joe laughed as he continued walking. He couldn't stop to fool around. He was already late and could easily imagine Carol's anger.

"Be a good boy now," Mickey yelled. Joseph waved and continued on his way up Main Street.

He saw Carol from a distance. She was standing in front of the drugstore. She looked expectantly in his direction. When she saw him, she waved and began to jog down the neon-lit street to meet him. When she reached him, her breath was fast, forming small clouds of condensation around her face. "Hi, Joey. You're late!" she said smiling.

Joe was relieved to see that she wasn't angry, "I know, babe, I got tied up," he replied. He looked at that face, the most gorgeous he had ever seen. Her hair was dark and abundant, full and hanging free to her shoulders. For a girl of fifteen her body was devastatingly curved and voluptuous, obvious even through her thick coat. She had glittering blue eyes framed by an oval face containing sensuous, wide lips. Her nose was tiny, flaring at the sides whenever she laughed, and she laughed often. She was of medium height, her forehead on a level with his chin.

"What are we going to do?" she asked, as she slipped her arm through his.

"I don't know," he said.

"Well are we just going to walk or what?" she smiled.

"Whatever you think," Joe laughed. "As long as it doesn't take too much money."

Carol looked at him, her eyes dancing. "Let's just walk then, okay?" she asked,

"Yeah, okay," Joe replied as he squeezed her hand.

They walked for hours, talking quietly, holding hands, and occasionally bursting into soft laughter. After a long while, they stopped before a large lot on the north side of town. An old, ramshackle, abandoned house was profiled in the darkness, about fifty yards back from the street.

"Do you think your father will really buy this place?" she asked, as her eyes gazed over the immense, dark terrain.

"It looks that way," Joseph scowled.

Carol's eyes grew large as she turned to Joe. "Why do you seem so annoyed about it? My god, Joe, anyone would love to live on a piece of land like this."

"I like Moosic Street!" Joseph said.

"Oh, wait and see, you'll probably love it. It'll really be something with a new house on it and everything. You'll probably love it." She hesitated for a moment, "Is he really going to buy it?" she asked.

Joseph's voice grew in annoyance. "I told you he probably will. I don't really know and don't care," he said.

Carol's face was pink from the wind, and long strands of hair drifted across her cheek. She looked at him. and smiled. "Wouldn't you like it, Joe?" she asked earnestly.

His anger spilled over. "Oh, I don't give a damn what he does!" he replied.

Carol was shocked by such an unexpected burst of venom.

"My god, Joe, you shouldn't talk, like that. If he ever heard…"

"I don't care if he hears or not, I don't care what the bastard thinks!" His voice was still, filled with anger. "All he worries about is impressing everyone, just as long as everybody thinks he's a big deal!" Joseph's voice grew more quiet. "That's what it's all about, that's all he worries about."

A look of pain crossed over Carol's face. "I'm sorry I brought it up, honey, I'm sorry." she said.

"You've got nothing to be sorry about." he said. "You don't understand the situation." Joe's lips trembled and his jaw muscles tightened. He squinted his eyes and thought about all the years behind him as well as those coming. "You couldn't understand, baby," he said. He wrapped his arms around her waist. "I'm sorry for yellin', I'm really sorry. You have nothin' to do with all this."

Carol wanted to ask a thousand questions, but it wasn't the

right moment. She leaned against him and brushed the softness of her mouth against his. For a moment, they hungrily kissed each other. Finally, they walked to the corner and disappeared into the darkness.

Later that night, Joe lay in his bed and thought about his conversation with Carol. Outside his window the thunder from the railroad slowly died away, as the freight train rumbled off into the distance. He knew every line and contour of his room—the walls, the furniture, the pictures. Everything contained deep, personal attachments. He didn't want to leave his home.

There was too much to leave behind. Somehow, Joseph's mind always managed to obscure any bad memories of the house; he loved it in the same way he loved the street and town outside, his window, the familiar places that served as the supporting columns of his life.

Joseph could no longer bear thinking about it. In desperation he closed his eyes and fought back all thoughts of leaving. He twisted and turned. Finally. after long. troubled hours, he temporarily avoided the torture by escaping into a fitful sleep.

2

THE front door slammed loudly. and Joseph instantly heard the angry, resonant voice of his father. "Joseph...Joseph," the voice wailed angrily. "Come down here!"

Joseph heard his mother move quickly from her room down the hall. She was suddenly framed in his doorway. Joseph reached over and switched on the lamp.

"Joseph, you stay right here. Do you hear me?" she said. "You stay right here!" Her face was strained and wretched. Her dark circled eyes looked frightened.

"He's drunk again!", she said in a scared voice. "I can tell by the sound of him. Please, honey, stay here." She had her old blue robe wrapped around her, and her hands nervously tied and untied the sash.

Joseph felt the anger drive unyieldingly through his body. His mouth trembled and his lips stretched tight with menace. "I'll go down there and kill the sonofabitch!" he said.

"Oh, Joey, please stay here, stay here!" she cried.

Joseph quickly made up his mind. "Sorry, Ma. I'm going down." Joseph leaped from the bed and ran past his mother. As he rushed past her, she made a pathetic effort to stop him.

She held him for a moment before he broke free and ran to the stairs leading to the kitchen.

Larry emerged from his room and ran to his mother. "What the heck is wrong?" he asked in a shrill voice.

Anna reached out and desperately grabbed the front of her son's undershirt. "Your father is drunk, and he's yelling for Joey, oh good God he went down there. Larry, go ahead quick, and help him, quick, help him. Help him!"

Larry touched Anna's disarrayed hair with a concerned tenderness. "Don't worry, Ma," he said, "Don't worry. Everything'll
be all right."

Anna, unhearing, looked past him to the stairs, "Quick!" she
said. "Get down there and help him...quick!"

Patrick Flynn leaned heavily against the kitchen sink. His eyes
were tired and red rimmed. conveying a silent message that confirmed his drunkenness. For a man in his middle forties his structure was admirable; straight, lean, powerful. His face was almost
unlined, ignoring the thousands of nights of drinking and lack of
sleep. There was only a touch of gray at his temples.

Joseph looked at him hatefully. "Whatta ya want?" Joseph said
in a mean, irritated voice.

Patrick answered slowly, menacingly. "Put on some coffee,"
he said, "And put it on now." He squinted, trying to keep Joseph
in focus.

"Ya mean ya woke me up for that?" Joseph said loudly. "Can't
ya make it yourself? Goddammit, ya woke up the whole house!"
Joseph reached to the stove and wrapped his hand around the
empty coffee pot. For an instant he was compelled to throw it at
his father. At that moment. Larry stepped into the kitchen.

When he saw Larry, Patrick let out an affectionate burst of
laughter. "Larry, boy. I didn't know you were awake," he said in a
slurred voice. "Gimme here." Patrick lurched across the kitchen
and wrapped his son in his huge arms. "C'mon, siddown here, boy,
right here." He half-pushed Larry into the chair at the table. He
grabbed another chair and slid it next to him. Patrick stumbled
into the chair.

"Your brother there is goin' to make us some coffee."

As he sputtered the words, thick, cottony saliva filled the edges
of his mouth.

Larry sat stiffly at the table, his face reflecting the fear that
traced itself through his body. His hand, lying along the table's
edge, trembled imperceptibly. He softly cleared his throat. "Dad,"

he said, "I think we should all go to bed now. Okay...?"

Patrick turned away from Larry, almost toppling over the chair in his sudden, twisting effort to look at Joe's face.

"No, not yet," he said as he stared contemptuously at Joseph.

"I said big shot there is going to make us some coffee!" Patrick leaned drunkenly in his chair. "Go upstairs and get my wife down here!" he shouted.

Joseph just stood there. His pajama top hung loosely on his torso, his chest showing under its unbuttoned front. He was leaning against the stove, his hands tightly grasping its edge. "Leave her alone," he said, "She's tired. Whatta ya think she does all day, play games like you!" The words dripped from his lips like poison.

Larry immediately knew what to expect. He suddenly bolted from his chair and heavily placed both his hands against his father's chest. "Dad, please," he whispered hoarsely.

With very little effort, Patrick removed Larry from his path and lunged at Joseph. He struck his son with all the force his drugged fist could muster. Joseph caught its full impact with his abdomen. Expecting his father's attack, he had moved away from the stove, geared to defend himself. But the punch, in its quickness, caught him by surprise. He reeled back hard against the metal edge of the stove. The pain took his breath away. He vainly attempted to remain upright, but the force of the punch and the impact of the stove behind him caused him to bend forward. The second blow fell heavily between his shoulders. Joseph crumpled to the floor. Patrick kicked wildly at his son, smashing him violently on the arms and shoulders. Larry tried with all his energy to restrain him, reaching his arms around his father's waist, vigorously trying to hold him back. It was useless. Joseph crawled like a wounded animal along the floor. Near the door, on the far side of the kitchen, he was finally able to get back on his feet. For a moment, he thought of flight to escape into the darkness of the Hanway night. He made up his mind almost instantly. He flew at his father, grabbing his hair and punching wildly, trying to make contact, trying to destroy him in any way possible. He felt the power of his father's fist against the back of his skull, and his vision blurred. He felt himself bounce off the kitchen wall. Another punch sent him to the floor, once again, beaten and dazed. He felt the warm thickness of blood slipping down the back of his neck, soaking the inside collar of his pajama top. From a long way off, he heard the wounded cry of his mother. There were sounds and shouts. A grappling was taking place above his battered head. Finally, the barrage ended. Joseph heard the vile thunder of his father's voice. as Larry and Anna half-dragged him upstairs.

Joseph pulled himself to a sitting position against the wall. After a short while, he felt the sharp coldness of a washrag move slowly across his pained face. He opened his eyes and saw the ravaged countenance of his mother.

"Oh, baby, my baby," she whimpered. "Are you all right, Joseph? 0h God, my baby, are you hurt? Are you all right?"

3

Gena heard the soft rapping on the back door. She heavily lifted herself from the soft parlor chair and quickly made her way through the rooms that led to the kitchen. She opened the door. Joseph stood silently in the late shadows.

"Joey, come in, honey." she said.

She pulled him into the harsh light of the kitchen, and jerked back in shock at the sight of his swollen, wounded face.

"Oh, God" she whispered. She led him to a chair and sat him down. Joseph said nothing. Gena examined the cuts and bruises carefully. She touched the cut with its dried up blood near the base of Joseph's skull. She tenderly ran her finger over it. "I think everything's okay." she said in a strained voices as she desperately tried to hold back tears. "Your mama fixed up that cut on the back of your head pretty good. She fixed it up fine, just like she said."

Joseph felt sick. His stomach was sore and upset, and he felt the vomit rising in his throat. "Aunt Gena. I want to lie down," he said.

Gena helped him to his feet. She pulled the jacket slowly from his shoulders and set it on the back of the chair. "Okay," she said in an emotion-filled voice. "Okay, baby, come into the parlor. You can lie on the couch. C'mon."

Joseph was relieved to feel the soft warmth of the cushions under him. "Thank you." His voice was distant and alien to him, as if it were coming from another place, far away; like an echo coming down a long tunnel.

Gena knelt down on one knee beside him, lovingly running her palm over his bruised forehead, "Are you able to talk? We've got to talk, honey." she said.

Joseph propped himself up on his elbows. For a long while he

33

stared at nothing in particular, "Yeah. I guess we can talk if you really want to," he said.

This wasn't a first experience for Gena. Many times Joseph came in the darkness of the night, fresh from an ugly argument with his father, to sleep in the safe confines of her home.

"God, Joe," she said, "He never beat you like this before. For Christ's sake, this is getting way out of hand." She grasped her nephew's arm. "We've got to do something. We've got to figure something out. None of us, especially you, can go on like this!"

Joseph looked at her through his swollen eyes. "There's nothin" to figure," he said, "Nothin' at all. He hates me. That's all there is to it."

"Oh, no, no, it's not as simple as all that, Joey," Gena said as she stood up. "There's a hell of a lot more to it. You've got to understand. There's a hell of a lot involved here!"

Joseph felt the familiar swell of anger in his chest. "Understand!" he said sarcastically. "Understand! That's a joke." He slowly ran his hand over his face. feeling the lumps and dried blood. With each breath he felt the searing pain in his chest. "My father just beat my head in for no goddamned reason and you're telling me I've got to understand!" He looked directly at her and his voice raised to a shout. "Understand what!" As he spat the words out at his aunt, he immediately felt guilty, "I'm sorry, Aunt Gena, honest to God I'm sorry," he said. "I'm hurtin' so bad, I don't know what I'm sayin'." He reached out and lightly squeezed her hand, "I'm sorry, honest to God I am." Gena knelt back down beside him and hugged him carefully.

"I know, baby. Don't you worry, I understand," she said in a sympathetic voice, "You've been through hell, I understand. You don't have to apologize." Her tears finally came. She sobbed quietly against her nephew's face. "We've got to talk now, honey. We've got to," she said, in a voice breaking in quick sobs.

Joseph slowly pulled away from her and sat up. He rested his hand on the top of her head, "It's just that right now my head hurts."

He smiled. "Come on now, please stop crying."

Gena walked over to a box of tissues that rested on the arm of the parlor chair. She blew her nose softly. After a short while, she looked at Joe. "Uncle Tommy will be home in the morning," she said. "And I'd rather say what I have to, right here and now."

Joseph looked at her. She still had that beautiful face. but her hair was cropped too short, emphasizing the streaks of grey. In the dim light of the parlor, he studied her face and was surprised at the lines that were deeply etched around her eyes and mouth. She was staring at him, her eyes begging for conversation.

He smiled at her. "What is it, my love?" he said, "What do we talk about now?"

Gena smiled nervously and walked across the room. She picked up a pack of cigarettes from the coffee table and fumbled about until she had one between her fingers. She lit it, carelessly throwing the wrinkled pack into a large ashtray. She walked back to the couch and sat next to Joseph.

"There's one thing we never did enough of in this family," she said. "We never talk things out. We never try to understand the problems that bother us. We never do anything but sit back and hope they'll go away." She took a deep drag from the cigarette and ran her fingers through her hair. The smoke curled above her and Joseph's head. "You and your daddy just can't seem to get together," she said.

Joseph stood up and immediately felt a hot stabbing pain in the small of his back. "That goddamned stove," he muttered.

"What, honey?" Gena asked.

"Nothing," he replied. "Let's get on with it, okay?" He pressed the tips of his fingers against the ache in his spine.

"It's not going to do any good, anyway," he said. But go ahead and say whatever it is that you think is so important."

Gena reached up and gently grabbed his arm pulling him back onto the couch. "Joey, do you ever wonder why your father seems to hate you so much?" she asked.

Joseph turned his head and looked at her, his eyes filled with sudden interest. "Why?" he asked.

Gena wrung her hands, unsure about approaching the subject.

"He resents the way your mother feels about you." Her voice was barely audible.

"What?" Joseph said. He squinted his eyes and looked at Gena as if she were crazy.

She caught the insinuation, "Well? Did you ever think about that, Joe? Did you?" she asked defiantly.

"No, I never did, " Joseph answered in a smiling. sarcastic voice, "I suppose he's jealous."

"Yeah, maybe he is," she said, "That's it exactly. Maybe he is."

"You've' got to love someone to be jealous of them," Joseph said, his voice ringing with sarcasm,

Gena's hands jerked in animation. "Well, that's it. Joe. That's what I'm trying to say. That's it!"

Joseph stood up, "Ah c'mon," he said in disgust. "He doesn't love, anyone but himself and Larry."

"No, no, you're wrong, Joe, You're wrong and I'm telling you what it is."

"What!" Joseph said loudly, "What is it? What the hell are you talking about?"

Gena's eyes widened as she bit her lip. "It's your mama!" she half-whispered.

For a long moment, Joseph was silent. He turned and searched his aunt's eyes. He saw their desperation, their hurt. He knelt down before her, "How could that be?" he said, in a gentle voice. "He doesn't care about her. If he isn't yelling at her, he's ignoring her or hurting her. It doesn't make any sense. God. Him jealous of me and Mom. It's ridiculous."

"Not if you knew your father the way I know him."

"I don't know what the hell you're talkin' about."

"Listen to me, then. Just listen to me."

"All right," Joe said. "Go ahead."

"Your Dad is a strange guy, Joey, and he loved Anna in a way none of us can really understand."

"He doesn't love her now."

"I told you why," Gena said.

Joseph smiled sarcastically. "Oh, that's right. He's jealous of me."

"Don't be a wise guy, Joe."

"Well for Christ's sake, Aunt Gena. What did we ever do to him? Why should he wind up hating us?"

"He resents the way she cares for you."

"Why? "

"He's blamin' you for taking her away from him."

Joseph laughed. "Oh Jesus," he said. "Will you make some sense? How did I take Ma? What the hell do ya mean?"

"You gotta understand something. Your father never cared for anyone before he met your mother. Not me. Not anybody."

"Why?"

"Because he never had anything, that's why. He never had anybody."

"He had you, goddamn it," Joseph said.

"Oh yeah, but I wasn't enough. Ma and Pa were gone when he was only a kid. I was nineteen. I tried to give him things, but it was hard."

"If I know you, you gave him enough."

Gena shrugged. "He was in the coal mines when he was sixteen. He never had time to be a boy. It was always work, work. Shinin' shoes, peddlin' papers. Always something. And then it was the mines."

"Well, what about it," Joseph said. "A lotta guys hadda do that."

"Not too many, Joey."

"Anyway, what's the point?"

"The point is that the whole thing changed him. It put a distance between me and him. He got mad at everybody; the people, Gena, the town."

"The town? This town has been pretty damn good to him."

"That's not the way he saw it. He thought everything was against him."

"That's bullshit."

"Maybe so. But that's the way it is."

"A lotta guys hadda go to work."

"Yes. But certain things effect people in different ways. Patrick felt used. He thought he was pushed around."

"That figures," Joe said in disgust.

"But when he met Anna, things got a little different," Gena said. "She was alone too. No family. No nothin'. He loved her so much."

"That's hard to believe."

'Well, it's the truth. He was so jealous of her. It was like he owned her."

"He doesn't give a damn about her now."

Gena didn't seem to be listening. Her voice rambled on. "Your father changed after Larry was born. The kid was like an intrusion."

Joseph laughed, sarcastically. "Oh, c'mon. He loves Larry. Everybody knows that. You're all wrong there."

"Am I wrong? Am I? Was he lovin' Larry so much, when he went into the service, leaving a five year old kid behind?"

"He hadda go."

"He didn't hafta go. He wouldn't have been drafted. He had a family. He was workin' in the mines. He joined up! And went because he wanted to."

"I don't get it," Joe said.

Gena's voice sounded tired. "Your father had a plan. He told Uncle Tommy all about it. He figured there'd be a lotta green kids in the service. Little lambs, ya know. Your father knew all the tricks. He gambled. He loan sharked. He grabbed them, just like he figured. Like I said. Your old man was never a kid."

"He grabbed them?"

"Yes. He grabbed them," she said, as she stood up and walked nervously about. "He made a small fortune. He cheated them, but your dad never worried too much about scruples."

"So that's where the money came from!"

"Yeah. I don't think he thought he'd get caught up in a war, but what's the difference," she shook her head and smiled. "The sonofagun came back a hero. Can you imagine?"

Joe walked over to where Gena was standing. "He's not that good an actor," he said.

"Actor? What do you mean?"

"He loves Larry. Anybody can see that."

"You just won't let that go, will you?" she asked.

"You're damn right," he said. "Your judgment is way off on that."

Gena's voice was pleading. "Can't you see that he's just using Larry to get at you, to aggravate you?"

"No, I can't see it!" Joseph shouted.

Joseph stuffed his hands into his pockets, causing the muscles in his back to send a quick ripple along his shirt. "If he thought kids were an intrusion, why did he have me?"

"I don't know. Anna got pregnant during one of his furloughs. Just remember, when your father went into the service, he left a wife who adored him. He was everything to her. That's the way it was. He was her whole world. Oh sure, she loved Larry too, but Patrick was really her whole life and he knew it." For a moment Gena grew quiet and remembered. "He never paid much attention to poor Larry back then. There's no way you could know that, but I knew it, and I damn well know it now. My heart ached for that kid, and it still aches for him. But you just can't understand that."

"No! No, I can't!" he said.

Gena's voice grew more and more agitated. "While he was in the Army, your mama just seemed to fall apart. Larry was practically disregarded." Her voice grew suddenly soft. "Your mom was always a little unstable, Joe," she said. "She's always, known it and feared it, and I've always felt sorry for her. When you were born, she centered her whole life around you. Those years changed her in a lot of ways, and when your father came home, he was aware of it. She was never totally his again. He blamed you and he's still blaming you. It's not so hard to understand if you just think about it."

Joseph remained silent as he stared and listened to Gena.

Gena placed her hands on her hips and shook her head in disgust. "I don't know if he loves your mother anymore, but if he doesn't, that means he doesn't love anybody—not you, me, poor Larry or anyone else."

"Poor Larry my ass!" Joseph said.

Gena went on as if she didn't hear him. "I know you've had it tough, but don't blame your brother. He's got the worst deal of all. The kid doesn't know if he's comin' or goin' and it shows. He's as unstable as your mother and he's getting worse every day." Tears were glistening on Gena's eyelashes. "The kid's killin' himself with all his studyin', and why? I know he's doin' it to satisfy your father, to make him proud and release some of the rotten tension in that house. Deep down, Larry knows what your father is doin'. He knows that he's being used."

Gena's voice grew harsh. "And you," she said. "With all your hate, you're breaking your brother's heart." The sound of her voice was tender now. "He's always been so good to you, Joey. He's always done so much for you. Give him a break, for your sake and his."

Joseph didn't answer.

"Maybe if the two of you get together, things'll straighten out. Maybe you can help your father. He needs help. I could never do enough for him." Her face relaxed and her gaze drifted far away. "That's why I'll always love him. His life was so rotten, and I could never do anything about it, but love him."

She touched Joseph's face. "Maybe you and Larry can straighten things out, honey. Right now, maybe you're the only chance you father has, to learn how to care again."

"I couldn't do it."

"Yes you can. Just try."

"It wouldn't do any good. He doesn't give a shit about me."

"You can try," she said.

"I couldn't be bothered."

"For God's sake Joe. Help him. He is your father."

"Fuck him!" Joseph said. He was horrified at himself for using such a word in front of his aunt. but he didn't apologize.

Gena ignored the word. She went on talking as if she hadn't heard. "Your mama still loves him. I know that," she said, "While he was away she almost couldn't cope without him. She's been afraid ever since, afraid that he might leave her again. But she still loves him the way she's always loved him."

She stared at Joe. "She loves all of you, but most of all she needs her husband. She's sick with insecurity and fear. Maybe your father and mother can be the way they used to be, but your hating him won't bring them together. You've got to forgive him!" She shook Joseph's shoulder, "Do you hear me? You've got to!"

Joseph felt the anger building in him like a mounting storm. "Go to bed, Aunt," he said, "It's getting late. You must be tired." He put his arm around her. "Go ahead."

His voice was gentle as he tried desperately to hide the hurt and anger that pressed against his skull.

"All right, honey." Gena said, "But we will talk again about this, won't we?"

"Yeah, we will." Joseph replied in a controlled voice.

Gena kissed him and pulled her bathrobe tight. She walked laboriously across the room to the archway. She turned and looked at her nephew's back as he stood peering through the window into the fathomless night,

"Maybe you do love him," she half whispered.

Joseph heard her and he turned around. His gaze, deep and foreboding, formed a direct path to his aunt's eyes. He couldn't deny his feelings any longer. "I hate him!" His words were furious. Tears of rage and pain filled his eyes.

Gena lowered her head and sighed. "Goodnight," she said as she slowly left the room.

Joseph listened to his aunt climb the stairs to the floor above For a moment he sat on the couch and then slowly stretched his long. taut body over its entirety. He rested his head on the armrest, dangling his feet from the other end. For a long while he remained motionless, except for an occasional nervous tic that caused his mouth to suddenly twitch into a quick, meaningless half smile. For a while his mind was blanks but then, inexorably, inevitably, the torrent began. His mind climbed and tumbled over the long, rambling conversation with his aunt. "So that's what the bastard did." he thought to himself. "Robbing and hustling young kids a thousand miles from home." Nevertheless, Joseph was forced to give his father one grudging credit; considering the poverty of his youth, he had achieved the impossible. He had pushed and driven himself to be the most powerful man in the history of Hanway. He owned a real estate office that practically controlled all the land in the county, and a beer distributing business that was worth a fortune. Politics—he was in the center of its whore's world. His money influenced every political! office in the county. Joseph could almost see the poor, pitiful faces that wandered through their little house on Moosic Street begging his father for favors, a job—anything that might give them a break. He thought of all the sycophants who hung on Patrick Flynn's every word. Yes, in his father's own weird sense of the possible, he had achieved a great deal. And now, in a short time, he'd be dragging all of them into the huge mansion he was building—a sick castle, swelling from within with the callousness of the man who built it.

Thinking of his father caused Joe to mutter and curse to himself. He began to toss and turn. The back of his head was stinging and irritating him. He could stand it no longer. He walked into the kitchen and threw his arms into his windbreaker. He had to breathe, to walk and once again form a communion with the one constant in his life...Hanway.

4

HE was inevitably glad to feel the fresh coldness of the winter's night. It had snowed continuously through that Hanway winter, but in the freezing, pre-dawn morning the streets had melted dry, and the sidewalks and asphalt had, once again, donned their dull coats of grey and black.

He walked for hours on the familiar streets. Through the veiled mist, his eyes scanned Main Street rising before him as he approached the summit of the railroad crossing, with its old, battered station profiled in the eerie darkness and the striped gates pointing toward the sky. He loved that street.

His eyes swept its distance to where it disappeared on the top of the long hill that led to the uptown district.

He stopped on the corner of Elm Street, the heartland of Hanway. He stood on terrain he knew as well as he knew himself.

It was lonely and quiet in the shadows! devoid of the familiar, blinking nighttime neon. The sidewalks that passed the plate glassed store fronts were empty. The two-story buildings were silhouetted against the black, winter sky.

He stood there for long minutes in his deep, intangible reverie. He heard the heartbeat of the town and felt strong again; a town that remained his strength through all times, good or bad. The milieu of the streets was the wellspring of his life.

He was always revitalized by the atmosphere, always offering him a better world than the world of his nightmares and personal demons, always backing him away from the abyss of his darkest fears.

He forgot the biting January cold and just drifted from here to there. He walked down to the river and watched the quick water hump and hurtle in the blackness. He stopped at the bocce alley. His mind, digging and reaching, recalled the laughter and gentle cursing of the old men of spring. He could smell their tobacco-stained breath and see the soft rustle of their excitement. It filled him with a yearning and hope that they would be there again, in the first flush of flower and green through all the years that would ever exist in his life, in his world.

He sat for a long while on the small porch of Mickey's gas station. He heard the howling wind rifle past him and into the hills. As dawn began to creep its way into the cold sky, he squinted to see the peaks of the culm dumps in the distance, and even those ugly black giants that overlooked Hanway day and night with the eyes of a thousand good men caused his chest to fill with pride. The town of his birth, about a mile wide and perhaps two in length, was all of the world and eternity Joseph Flynn ever cared to see.

Finally, he saw the unyielding arms of the beginning sun. The horizon far beyond the boundary of Hanway became discernible. He smiled as he watched the bright crimson reaches of dawn send its red glow through the brightened sky.

Joseph stood up and pulled his jacket tight. He felt the cold now, piercing and chilling his body. He was tired and aching. It was time to go home.

Through the parted curtains of the kitchen window,, Joseph saw Larry hunched over papers on the table. As Joseph walked through the door Larry quickly turned around, startled by the unexpected interruption.

"What are you doing here?" Larry asked.

Joseph walked tiredly to the sink and ran hot water over his hands.

"I thought you'd stay at Aunt Gena's for a couple of days." Larry said.

"Never mind me," Joseph said. "What the hell are you doing up so early? Jesus. I don't believe how a guy could be up studying this goddamn early!"

"There's a lot of stuff I've got to catch up on. What are you doing back here already? I'm telling you, Joe, Dad is really pissed off!"

"You should be in bed." Joseph said. "Not looking at those goddamned papers."

"Let's not make a project out of it. All right? I told you there's
a lot of work I've got to catch up on."

"No wonder people think you're half nuts." Joseph sneered.

"What do you mean?"

"Just what I said. Some people think you're a little wacko."

Larry looked blankly at the papers propped before him.

"What is it with you, Joe?" he said, "You're on my back all the
time." His voice was barely audible. "I can't figure it out."

Joe removed a box of crackers from the cupboard and carelessly
opened them. He took a handful of saltines and shoved them into
his mouth. He pulled a chair over to the table and removed his
jacket. His curly black hair was in wind blown disarray, his dark
face the color of burnished gold.

"C'mon, what's the problem, Joe?" Larry asked. "Why are you
always hounding me, for Christ's sake!"

"Do you know the bullshit I've been listening to from Aunt
Gena?" Joe said.

"What bullshit?"

"I can't believe how she figures things."

"Why? How is she figuring things? What did she say?"

Joseph stood up and looked at the ceiling. His jet-black brows
were close together in a frown. "Did you know I've been breaking
your poor little heart?" he said sarcastically. "Do you know what
a horrible time you've been having and how confused you've been,
you poor, poor thing?" He angrily spun on his heel and walked
across the worn linoleum and leaned against the stove. Larry sat
quietly, staring at him. "What was it she said, Joe?" he asked.

Joe went through the entire conversation of those black and
punishing hours, his voice cutting Larry with its sharp edge of
sarcasm. When Joe finished his mouth was twitching and his eyes

were blazing dangerously.

Larry tried to ignore the sparks of violence that Joe's fiery eyes were shooting across the room.

"She didn't mean to hurt you," Larry said. "She's just trying to help out, that's all."

"What she means isn't in question here, you bastard!" Joe's words were grinding and faltering in his throat. "I know she meant well. I don't need you to tell me that, you fuckin' punk!" He tried to keep his voice lowered. for he knew only too well that his father lay asleep in a room directly above him. "I just can't figure how you got such a bad deal," he said.

Larry attempted to answer, but Joseph burst through his words, continuing his interrupted tirade. "It was always you who went to the ballgames, wasn't it?" he asked.

Larry sat quietly, not daring to reply in that atmosphere of blood.

Joseph's anger was expanding to a feverish level. "You were the one he always did everything with." Joe said. "You were always the good boy, right? If it wasn't for Ma and Gena I'd never get a god-damned dime for anything. But you—you always got whatever the hell you wanted." Joseph was having a harder time keeping his voice down. "But look at you," he sneered, "What does he think he's got that's so great? You're a goddamned sissy. You can't hold a baseball bat without looking like a friggin' girl."

Joseph walked over to him, Larry felt the sweat filling his forehead and the ugly fingers of fear grip his heart.

"You've never had a girl and you're twenty-two years old," Joseph growled, "Look at you. You're scared shitless of me. You're not worth a shit."

Larry moved out of the chair slowly, cleverly keeping it as a barrier between them. "Oh, never mind, Joe," he said in a quiet voice, "Let's just drop it. Okay?"

"No, I won't drop it. You've taken everything all your fuckin' life. You never gave a shit for me and you know it." Larry felt the fear inexplicably slip away from him.. It was replaced with an anger of his own. "Who are you to talk," Larry said, his voice shaking with emotion. "You're the one who takes and never gives. Aunt Gena is right. Dad is using me to get at you. He doesn't really care about me, I know that."

Joseph was stunned by his brother's vigorous response.

"But I try," Larry continued, "Damn it, I try. Maybe if I become a doctor like he wants, things'll change around here. It'll get better for Ma. At least I try to keep peace for her in this madhouse. You and Dad don't help with your arguments and fighting," Larry lowered his eyes. "Sure, I never played ball or dated. I was too busy watching out for everybody here, especially you. But what do you care? You're too selfish to care about anything."

"You goddamned liar!" Joseph snarled.

"No, I'm not. No, I'm not lying and you know it. Ma always worried about you and your selfish tantrums. She always catered to you. She never had time for me. But I understand that. What do you understand?" Larry hesitated a moment before he continued. "Sure he took me around with him, I just never thought it bothered you. Maybe I didn't know any better, I was a kid."

"You're not a kid now, " Joseph said.

"No, I'm not and I do understand it now. But what happened when we were kids, don't hold me to blame for that. Honest to God, Joe, I didn't know it hurt you. Honest to God I didn't." Larry pressed his back against the wall. "I've been trying to make him see that it's wrong what he's doing to you. I've been trying, but it just doesn't help. What am I supposed to do? I try to help. I try to do things to make him happy and release some of this tension."

"Anything you do makes him happy," Joseph said. "Now you're in medical school. Big deal."

"That's what he wants, Joe."

"That's right, you jerk. You just do everything he wants."

"That's right. I will. If it'll help things out around here, I will."

"How can you help anybody by kissing his ass all the time," Joseph said. "You're doing for yourself, you bastard."

"Joe, please," Larry said, his voice pleading. "Father doesn't care about me. He's just trying to aggravate you by pretending. God, I know that. Aunt Gena knows it. But you won't let yourself understand. You've never listened to anybody."

"Well, then, why don't you just walk away from the rat," Joseph said.

"What good will it do to walk away? If I do what he wants, maybe, things will change. It's not likely, but it's possible."

Joseph felt disgust seep through his body. His anger receded. "Larry, if you believe everything you just said, you really are nuts."

Larry was offended by the inference. His anger burst through. "Listen!' he said, "I'm sick and tired of your insults and your complaints about how bad it is around here. You ought to think about somebody else besides yourself." He walked to the sink and nervously rinsed a glass over and over. He finally filled the glass and drank the water. He turned and looked at Joseph. "Let me tell you how selfish you are. You've been so busy trying to aggravate Dad that you've ignored Ma and treat her like hell. You're the end of her world and you can't deny that. But you hurt her as much as Dad does."

Joseph felt his body and every muscle in it spring to life. "You better shut your fuckin' mouth!" Joseph said.

"Look, Joe, you do hurt her. Maybe you don't know it, but you do hurt her. Think about her for a change and forget about Dad. Let me deal with that problem. I think I can straighten it out."

Joseph walked over to Larry and stood directly in front of him. His teeth were clenched and his fists hung at his sides in two tight rocks of fury.

Larry felt once again the grip of cold fear. "Joe, please don't start. Can't you see I'm trying to help?"

"You dirty bastard!" Joseph roared. "What do you mean I've hurt Ma? I'll kill you, you fuckin' punk. I'll kill you."

His hands were on Larry's neck, pulling and pushing in a vicious rhythm of violence. The glass fell from Larry's hand and crashed on the floor. The room was suddenly filled with Larry's cries and the dull pounding of fist against face. Larry reeled from one side of the kitchen to the other. Joseph, in madness, pursued him and punched him unmercifully. His huge fist drove Larry over the chair that sat at the kitchen window. Larry hit the floor with a pitiful thud. Joseph dragged him upright and began smashing again. Blood ran from Larry's nose and mouth, spraying Joseph with its pink wetness. Larry fell again.

Joseph, his powerful body poised to inflict more damage, paused to catch his breath. At that moment he only knew the destructive rage sweeping through his body in a blazing. bounding convulsion; deaf and blind to all else except the burning passion that told him to destroy his brother, his enemy.

He never heard his father's quick footsteps behind him. The thundering power of Patrick Flynn's fist smashed against the back of Joseph's skull and sent him hurtling and spinning through the splintered crashing of the window. His body came to rest on the cold hardness of the back porch, his unconscious face pressed hard against the floorboards. The same porch where approximately a decade before he waited with a brother he loved for a hero he had never seen.

5

THE first thing Joseph was aware of when he opened his eyes was the warm, safe atmosphere of his bedroom. Someone stood at the edge of his bed. He had to squint his eyes to bring the figure into focus. Doctor Benson smiled. "How're you doing, boy?" he said. "You've had quite a long sleep for yourself."

Joseph stared quietly at the tall, stately figure and his bald head, gleaming under the bedroom's light. Joseph vaguely remembered the tremendous impact that sent him drifting in a dazed nightmare. He recalled Larry beaten and bloody on the kitchen floor.

"What hit me?" Joseph asked.

"Your father had to do something, son. He thought you were going to kill your brother."

"I thought so. He could've killed me."

"You could have killed your brother."

"Yeah. I heard you the first time."

Joseph tried to lift himself to a sitting position. He felt the stabbing pain rush down the back of his skull. My goddamned head feels like it was hit with a sledgehammer," he said.

Doctor Benson surveyed Joseph's face. "You received some nasty cuts. But you're lucky, I didn't have to apply any stiches. I managed to stop the bleeding without them. Your father thought it best to fix you and Larry up here at home and I agreed with him. It was the best thing to do."

Joseph's eyes narrowed, "He's afraid he might have his reputation hurt. That's why he thought it was a better idea."

"Now, Joseph," Dr. Benson said.

"That's why you thought it was better," Joseph said.

"Take it easy, Joseph."

"Don't give me your shit, doc. He owns you like he owns everybody else in this town."

Doctor Benson stood up, "Here, here, young man. Watch your mouth."

"Yeah, he owns you like he owns everybody," Joe said. "Everybody but me."

Doctor Benson picked up his bag and walked to the doorway, "You'll be all right," he said. "I suggest you stay in bed for a while. But you'll be all right. Your ribs aren't broken and those cuts will heal up fine in a few days."

"Get the hell out of here," Joseph said.

Doctor Benson in a flurry of anger and embarrassment turned around and disappeared through the doorway.

After a while Anna Flynn came into the room. Her face was filled with torture and pain. But there was something new added. Her right cheek was swollen and discolored.

"What happened to your face?" Joseph asked.

She walked over and sat down on the bed. Her eyes were red-rimmed and swollen from crying, "You were unconscious for a long time," she said. "When you came to, you were like a madman. Doctor Benson gave you a shot to make you sleep, Oh, God, I was scared. He says you'll be okay. You won't have to go to the hospital."

Joseph looked at the small clock on the bureau. It was almost ten o'clock. "Jesus," he said. "It's been almost five hours. I can't remember any of it." He looked at his mother with concern. "What happened to your face?"

Anna carefully ran her thin hand over her purple cheek.

"Oh nothing, honey. Nothing," she said. "Daddy was just angry. My screaming and crying didn't help. He just got mad. That's all."

Joe's eyes turned to ice. "Goddamn. Goddamn he hit you. Didn't he? He hit you!" Joseph looked at her slight, hunched form, and felt his heart tear.

Anna was taking quick breaths. "Oh, Joe, please," she said, as she began to cry. She sobbed loud, heartbreaking sobs.

Joseph felt his eyes grow wet. He watched the large, glinting tears squeeze out of the corners of her dark eyes and stream down her cheeks. "Don't cry, Ma, don't cry. I won't say anything. I won't do anything to cause any trouble here, but please don't cry."

After a while her tears and sobs subsided. "Larry's okay too," she said. "I won't ask what happened, Joey. I don't want to know. But oh, God, your brother's face is a mess. Why did you have to hit him like that?" She half-turned and looked toward the doorway. "I begged your father not to come up here. He's liable to kill you if he comes up here."

"What did stop him? I figured he'd do a worse job on me than this," Joe said.

Anna didn't answer.

He looked at her injured face, "You stopped him," he said.

He reached out and caressed the side of her head with his large hand. "Thanks," he whispered.

She slowly stood up. Her fragile hands through a lifetime of habit smoothed the covers that lay over her son's torso.

"I'll go and lie down now," she said. She smiled at Joseph.

"You do that, Ma. Go ahead." He shifted his position on the bed. "I'll be okay. Everything'll be okay. Go and get yourself some rest."

She walked slowly out of the bedroom. Her too-large shippers made a familiar flapping sound. Joseph's heart and soul cried for her. He dropped back onto the pillow. His own great tears began to come. He muffled his sobs so she couldn't hear. He felt battered and torn. His hands trembled as he covered his face. Eventually he regained his composure and lay still on the bed. He lay quiet for a long time, until he felt someone watching him. He opened his eyes and saw Larry standing in the doorway, Larry's face was swollen and covered with welts. He stood there, almost afraid to breathe.

Through puffed lips, he finally spoke to Joseph, "Are you all right, Joe?"

Joe surveyed the damage inflicted by his fists. He felt no remorse, no regrets.

Larry shuffled from one position to another. "Dr. Benson says you'll be fine."

"You better get your ass out of this room."

Larry began to say something, but changed his mind. He knew there was nothing he could say to his brother. He forlornly turned back to the hallway. Before walking to his rooms, he turned around. His eyes ran over Joe's face.

"Get outta here!" Joseph warned.

Larry quickly left. The room was quiet once again.

Sometime around noon Joseph left his bed. He half-staggered to the mirror. He closely studied his reflection. There were numerous small cuts covering his face. There was an angry bruise on his right cheekbone. "Nothing serious," he thought.

The back of his head throbbed where his father's fist had smashed him. Molten fire crawled over his skin. He thought of what his crumpled figure must have looked like. "I never knew what hit me," he muttered. But as he stood before his bedroom mirror in pain and ferment, his mind pounded with what he knew at that moment. He very well knew now, and like everything else in his life, he would never forget it.

6

THE months came and went. Joseph was glad to see spring drift into simmering summer. Since that feverish January morning, the family affairs had grown worse. His mother grew more and more distant. She ignored even those things that brought her a small measure of enjoyment. She stopped knitting. She stopped taking her nightly strolls to Gena's house. She seemed to stop everything.

It was the same with Larry. He retreated into a shell that became a fortress against Joseph's fury. And, as always, Patrick Flynn's presence provided the haunting spectre of hate and evil. On the first of June, Joseph's birthday passed without fanfare. But summer seemed to breathe some life back into the family. Anna Flynn and Larry were excited about moving from Moosic Street into the new house. Patrick was very excited. He had never been happier. His dream was finally coming true; he prepared to surround himself with the opulence of the mansion on Jessup Avenue.

Joseph appreciated the tremors of life the relocation was providing. But in the deepest reaches of his heart, he was torn with the thought of leaving the neighborhood he loved.

He tried to wrap himself in the adventure of his coming graduation. It was now only several days away. He spent many hours at the school preparing for the big event. As usual, he was glad to be involved in anything that recalled the lingering camaraderie of his childhood. The boyhood games. The friends. The adventures.

Joseph watched as Ray Walton came toward him with his quick. familar sprint. He sat down alongside of Joe on the auditorium steps. He was huffing and gasping, trying to both laugh and talk.

Joseph smiled, "What the hell are you choking about now?"

It seemed to Joe that Ray was forever running and excited about something. He associated everything. even the mundane, with the heady rush of adventure.

"Jesus, Joey, I forgot about the damn singing rehearsal."

Joseph laughed. "So what's the big deal?"

Ray's long legs stretched out over the steps. His body, like Joe's, was lean and hard. His wild red hair was wind-tangled and sweat-soaked in the noon heat. The freckled, friendly face broke into a smile. "Well, what the hell. We want to sound good on Wednesday, don't we?"

"Well, pal, you didn't miss a thing. Just the same old business, singin' the same old songs. Don't worry about it."

Joe suddenly remembered he was expected at Carol's house for lunch. He stood up and tucked his shirt into his jeans, "I've got to get going, my man," he said.

Ray looked up at his friend, standing in the white glare of the sun. "What're you doin' here all by yourself anyway? Everybody else is gone."

"Oh, I just thought I'd sit around for a minute, that's all. Look, I've gotta get going. I'll talk to you later. Okay, buddy?"

"Okay, man. Don't let me keep you." Ray quickly bounded to his feet. The old madness enveloped him once again.

"See you tonight." he said. Ray ran down the short hill to the basketball court. Joseph watched him as he ran full gallop across the courts, spinning and faking shots at the baskets as he ran. "Good old crazy Ray," Joe laughed to himself.

He was still thinking of Ray when he arrived at Carol's house. He knocked softly on the large door. In a moment Carol opened it. "You're a half hour late, but that's okay," she smiled.

"Sorry," Joe murmured.

In the presence of Carol Granahan apologies from Joseph Flynn were ludicrous. She loved him wildly, doing everything possible to soften the hardness that constantly welled in his eyes. Mr. and Mrs. Granahan weren't home. They walked through the parlor.

There was a large round mahogany table, and straight-backed chairs were carefully positioned along the flowered wall.

Joseph sat in the kitchen and devoured a huge sandwich.

Carol bustled about in excitement. She handed him a dish of ice cream, surrounded by strawberries and covered with a cloud of whipped cream.

"Oh, wow. Hold it," Joseph said, "What're you trying to do, put me to sleep with all this? Hold back, girl." He was amused. "I'll be too filled up to be able to do anything tonight, "

"Oh, God, aren't you excited, Joey? Can you imagine? It's your class night tonight. Can you believe it! Oh, how I wish it were mine."

"It's no big deal."

Carol sat on his lap. He felt the underside of her thigh press into his groin.

"Oh, c'mon, you big grouch." she said. "Why can't you be happy like everybody else?"

Joseph thought about Ray and his mouth broke into an amused smile.

"What are you smiling about?"

"Oh. I just saw Ray a while ago," he said. "Dammit that guy is forever excited about something."

Carol laughed. "He's a good boy," she said.

"I can just see him tonight," Joe said. "He'll be all over everywhere, just like a maniac,"

Joseph removed Carol from his lap and stood up. "I'd better get going," he said. "I've got a lot to do before tonight."

They walked together to the front door, "We'll have a good time tonight. Won't we, babe?" she asked.

"Sure, we'll have a blast. Don't worry."

She grabbed him behind the neck and pulled his thick lips toward her face. The erotic softness of her mouth touched his. He felt the familiar arousal of his instincts,

"Not now, hon," he said, "I told you I gotta go."

Carol feigned a pout. "Boy, what an insult," she said. Joseph squeezed her body against him, "I'll make it up to you tonight." He began to laugh. He opened the door and backed out onto the porch. She playfully tried to restrain him, but finally let go.

"I'll hold you to that."

Joseph leisurely jogged toward Main Street. As he reached the corner of Moosic Street he quickened his pace. When his house was finally in sight, his legs ground to a halt. From that distance he saw the large truck in the driveway. Men were hauling furniture into the trailer. He stopped and watched for long minutes before moving on.

When Joseph entered the kitchen, his mother was standing at the window. "I thought we weren't moving anything until next week," he said.

His mother looked at him and forced a weary smile. "They're just taking out the larger pieces."

Joseph stood annoyed and staring at her.

"Don't worry, honey. We're not leaving yet," she said.

"I'll never understand why you want to leave here, Ma."

Anna Flynn stared silently at him. When she spoke her voice was filled with weary disgust. "Oh, stop it, Joey!" she said. "I feel as bad about it as you, but we're going and there's not a thing we can do about it."

Joseph moved about the kitchen in a burst of nervous animation. "No, there's never anything anybody can ever do in this house, except him."

His mother stood there in her long brown print dress. She began to wring her hands. Her eyes followed Joseph as he continued his furious march around the kitchen. He raised and dropped his muscular arms in frustration, as he raved and growled to himself. Anna's eyes filled with large tears, Joseph saw them.

His rumbling came to an immediate halt. He walked over to her and enveloped her frail shoulders with his arms. "I'm sorry," he said.

Anna released a long sigh.

"I'm really sorry, Ma. Forgive me, I know I promised not to do things like this."

His mother looked at him and smiled. "You've been doing pretty good, I must say. I'm proud of you." She patted his face. "I know how you feel, honey. But you've got to face up. We're moving out and that's it." Her shoulders sagged at the thought of Joe's heartache. "Maybe you'll like it. Why don't you wait and see?"

"No, Ma. I'll never like it. But I'll learn to tolerate it. I'll do that much for you." He smiled and squeezed her. "You'd better get ready for tonight," she said,

"Yeah, you're right, I've got a lot to do." He bent over and kissed her head. "Is he coming?" he asked, in a tight, dry voice.

Anna looked up but avoided her son's eyes. "He can't, Joey. He's got some kind of business tonight."

Joseph emitted a sarcastic grunt,

"C'mon, Joey, You've got to realize that your father is a busy man." She reached up and softly touched his cheek, "After all he is involved in a lot of things, honey. He really does have a lot of business to attend to. But he'll be there for graduation. I'm sure of it." There was a hint of desperation in her soft voice." He promised me. He'll be there for graduation. Wait and see."

"Yeah, right. I'll wait and see." Joseph walked to the stairway and went upstairs.

It was the kind of June night Joseph had always associated with Hanway. There was a heavy scent of magnolia drifting from the large bushes alongside the auditorium. The stars, glinting and alive, filled the night sky. A breeze moved across the large green lawn, carrying the gentle, sweet fragrance of freshly cut grass.

People were milling about, smiling and shaking hands. Proudly, the parents stood next to their sons and daughters. The program was over. The whole affair had moved along with just the right amount of formality. But now the youngsters were outside, and quickly loosened ties and removed jackets.

Joseph and Carol piled into the back of Ray's old Ford.

Ray was pulling his date comfortably tight to his side, He was screaming and laughing, "Let's go," he said, "Let's goooo!" Joseph and Carol waved at Anna Flynn as she stood smiling on the sidewalk. Ray squealed his car on to the roadway and just as suddenly braked it to a halt. In one crazy jerk the car lurched back to the curb. Joseph had remembered that he forgot to say goodbye to Gena and Tom. They were delayed by the crush of people in the auditorium hall. Joseph rushed from the car and into the throng of people to find them. He reached them just as they were exiting the hall, stumbling and laughing in the crowd, He pulled them to an empty spot on the sidewalk. He kissed Gena and shook Tom's hand, "Sorry I can't talk now," he said. "Everybody's leaving. We'll talk tomorrow."

In a moment he was back in Ray's car as it roared away. Carol nestled comfortably against his shoulder. "You think the world of your aunt and uncle, don't you?" she asked.

"You bet your ass," he said, "Along with my mother. They're all I've got."

She sat up straight and her eyes widened, "What about me?"

"Oh, yeah. Don't worry, I love you too." He started to laugh at her perplexed expression,

"Hey, Joe. I really mean it. I'm beginning to wonder if you care or not."

Joseph leaned over and kissed her parted, wet mouth.

They were still caressing and kissing when Ray's swerving car braked to a screeching halt, Joe looked out through the back window and saw the blazing red neon traversing the roof of the long. one storied building. It was Kay's Place.

The bright lettering lit up the darkness. This was the place for parties, the place where the high school kids could always cajole old sly, sexy Kay to fill their bellies with beer. Once inside all hell broke loose. The class had cleverly and secretly pilfered money from the class treasury. They had the entire place rented for the night. The party would go on for hours. In the middle of the hilarity, Joe and Carol escaped to an empty quiet table near the wall. They watched Ray, as he ignored all the annoyed and tired stares, race like a madman from one table to the other. One minute he was pulling someone onto the dance floor, the next minute, he was off by himself performing wild, crazy dance steps to the blaring music of the juke box.

All the while he was shouting and screaming. His eyes were wild and laughing. He raced about, spilling the contents of his glass in one hand, while he used the other to drag his poor, hapless date from one table to the other. In the middle of his nervous convulsion, the corner of his eye caught his friends sitting alone at their table. In an instant he was all over them, laughing and spitting. He tried to say so much, his mouth couldn't keep up. Ray's date, relieved with a moment of rest, collapsed on a nearby chair.

Ray looked at Joe. His smile filled his whole face. "Man this is it," he yelled. "This is really it. This is almighty jumping up and down it. Jeeeesus, Jeeesus, Joey, let's go. Let's get on with the shooooow."

Ray was soaked with perspiration. His new suit was in ruin, covered with stains of beer and whiskey. "Why are you two sittin' there like two old asses? Let's get it moooving, baby. Let's get it moooving." His breath, saturated with alcohol, whistled across the table.

"Hey old buddy," Joey said. "Slow down. Take a break before you have a heart attack. We'll never get you home tonight."

Ray ran over to the half-conscious girl on the chair. He tore her to her feet. "Let loooose, baby. Let loooose, you bastard."

Joseph was forced to chortle to himself as he watched his friend dash back onto the small dance floor. In an exaggerated shuffle, bumping everything out of his way. he cruised along the floor, legs jumping and jerking completely out of time with music or sanity.

Joseph turned to Carol, who was staring in amazement at what Ray Walton was doing. "He's crazy," she said.

Joe squinted across the room to where Ray was about to irritate an unsuspecting couple. "Oh, it won't be long now," he said. "In just a little while he'll be throwing up all over the place. I know him well. It won't be long now." Joe tried to be serious, but he couldn't resist a broad smile as he watched Ray.

It was only a few minutes before midnight. Joseph carried the full burden of Ray Walton's weight across his shoulders. The slow-moving parade—Joe, Carol and Mary, Ray's, date, marched across the parking lot toward Ray's old Ford. Inside the building the party roared on. Music and gales of laughter emanated out into the warm June night. Joe set Ray on the front seat and then turned to Carol. "Wow. He was really sick," Joe said.

Ray had paid dearly for his needless drinking. He had vomited violently behind Kay's building for a long time with Joseph's standing by helplessly.

"I've gotta' take him somewhere to sober him up."

Carol's face dropped at the news.

"I'm sorry, honey," he said. "I'll take you and Mary home."

In a moment Joe was behind the steering wheel and negotiating Ray's car out onto the highway. He drove across the miles to home. The car was unusually quiet except for Ray's deep snoring.

Ray constantly tossed and twitched in the seat. Joseph watched the dark asphalt with its white snake ahead of him. The wind whistled past the open windows. The car smelled heavily of beer. Joseph kept driving, the woods and trees along the roadside hovering like a dark, silent wall. The headlights reflected off occasional signs along the way.

Finally the car moved through the Hanway streets. Joe pulled up before the Granahan residence. Carol sat heavily forward, opened the door and got out. She walked to the front window. Joseph leaned his head out of the window and softly kissed her. "I'll call you tomorrow," he said.

The disappointment was stamped across her eyes.

"I'm really sorry," he said.

The truth rang in his words. Carol knew he had planned a big night. "That's okay, Joey," she smiled. "Don't forget. Call me tomorrow. I'll be waiting."

Joe watched her run up the long walkway to her porch.

Before entering the house she turned and waved. Joe blew her a kiss. He turned and studied poor wiped-out Mary on the back seat. Her eyes were closed in a deep sleep. A few minutes later he was in front of her house. She got out of the car without even looking at Ray.

"Good night, Joe."

"Good night, Mary."

Joseph drove directly to Petry's Restaurant. At that hour it was a good place to sober up a friend.

The harsh fluorescent lights of the diner's interior hurt Joe's eyes. He helped Ray to a booth. They sat there for a long time with Mr. Petry running back and forth with steaming black coffee. They forced it down Ray's throat. After almost an hour of dry heaves and long, embarrassing burps Ray began to feel better. Mr. Petry returned to the far end of the gleaming counter and continued the pleasant dozing that Joe and Ray had earlier interrupted. The rest was well deserved. It seemed like his entire life was spent in the restaurant. Joe always wondered how Mr. Petry's black, Italian eyes were able to twinkle with such kindness and energetic life. He was always there. Rest was seldom available; the breakfast crowd of puffy-eyed factory workers sitting hunched over the counter always saw him starched and ready for good service and good talk. He was one with the smell of frying grease and the sound of dishes sliding down the counter. Between the hours after school until well after midnight. the diner was the high school kids' domain. After midnight the hawklike old man would find maybe a moment or two for dozing, until the late couples and the nighthawks would come starving and eager. He would close around three, he'd be back at seven, and it would start all over again.

Joseph watched him and wondered what the little old man thought of behind his quivering eyelids. But he was no longer able to concentrate on Mr. Petry's plight. Ray was now fully recovered and as boisterous as ever.

He couldn't find enough to do. He irritatingly rapped his fast knuckles against the formica table top.

"Oh, stop it, Ray. Will you?" Joe said.

"Thanks for the good help, baby. Where do we go from here?" Joe didn't answer.

Ray's eyes were filled with the familiar excitement. "Let's take a drive or something." he said.

"Naw. Nothin' doing." Joe answered.

"What were you thinkin' about today?" Ray asked suddenly.

"When?"

"You know. At the school this afternoon. What were you doin' there all alone?"

"Nothin'."

"Ya know, sometimes I worry about you, man. You're always brooding. You've gotta laugh once in a while, kid. You know, laugh. What the hell. Is something the matter with your brother or what? He wasn't at the ceremony tonight."

Joe let loose a low, derisive laugh, "Oh Jesus, Ray," he said, "I don't give a shit if I ever see him. He did me a favor by not show-ing up."

"Well, where the hell is he keeping himself? I never see the guy at all anymore."

"His nose is so far up my father's ass it's hard for him to get around." Joe could see that Ray was confused. "No, seriously," Joe said, "the jerk is always studying. He's lookin' to be a doctor, you know. He'll do anything to satisfy the old man."

"Where was your dad? I didn't see him either."

"Who cares?"

"Jesus, you really hate your old man. You oughta get over that. I wish I had one. If you were in my shoes you'd know what I was talkin' about."

Joe looked at his friend and understood. Ray never even knew his father. He disappeared when he was just a baby. Ray would generally laugh about it. "My old man went out for a beer and never came back. What a drunk that must have been," But now it was different. Ray's laughing eyes were distant and clouded. "Could you imagine," Ray said in a quiet voice. "He left. Just like that. He just upped and left. I was two years old."

He looked over at Joseph, "What could've made him do a god-awful thing like that, buddy?"

Joseph didn't reply. He just sat there, surprised by his jovial friend's seriousness.

"Oh, I know why he went," Ray said. "Yeah, I know. He and my mom never got along. At least according to her. Do you know that she never tried to find him or find out what happened? Jesus, that's really somethin', isn't it? She musta really hated him. She never even tried to find him."

As Ray talked on, Joe thought about Lila Walton. She was a big, fantastic looking woman. She had dyed blonde hair and a sexy face, She had eyes that saw everything. Whenever she walked past him in Ray's house, Joseph always averted his hungry eyes. Her hips always undulated, and her ass always beckoned under a flimsy house dress, Whatever she wore it always emphasized her magnificent body. Everything about her sent out a message of sensuality and desire and she knew it. She enjoyed men and men obviously enjoyed her. In her own way he was a woman of mystery, coming and going as she damn well pleased, leaving her son Ray to run his careless way. Joe often saw her in the morning, riding straight-backed on the dirty commuter bus on her way to her job in the city. She would return late at night.

Ray was left on his own, an independent madman running up-roariously along the Hanway streets, or rummaging through the cluttered house with record players and radios blasting simultane-ously in a cacophony of sound that rocked Elm Street.

"I know he was a real good guy."

Ray's words dislocated Joseph from his thoughts of Lila Walton. He looked at Ray and blinked.

"My father," Ray said, "I heard he was a real good guy. Everybody who ever talks about him tells me that, except my mother. I just can't understand why he left like that."

"Well, you just said he and your mom couldn't hack it."

"Yeah, but all the guys at the pool room who knew him, they even say they can't figure it. They didn't think he was the type to leave his kid. He was too good a guy for that. That's what they said." Ray stopped talking for a moment while his eyes drifted over his personal enigma. He turned his head and quietly looked through the large window.

Ray's conversation in Petry's, on that pre-dawn June morning, was the first and last time Joseph would ever hear his friend discuss the subject. Catharsis wasn't the life style of Ray Walton.

"Forgive me for forgetting the business at hand, my man," Ray said with mock seriousness. "But as I was sayin', you've got to stop takin' things out on your old man, I mean, what the hell. He is a busy guy. Maybe he just can't get free for a thing like class night. It's a crock of shit anyway."

"Fuck him," Joe said.

"No. I really mean it, Joe. I'm not kidding. Jesus, the guy is tied up in everything. You gotta give him credit. He owns the county for Christ sake. Wow! Talk about real estate. And what he doesn't own he sells. Shit man, that's somethin'. Jesus, he's made a fortune. He's up to his ears in politics, and then the beer business. Jesus. Just think about the new house you're movin' into. I saw it the other day. It's a goddamn mansion. I heard you're goin' to have gardeners and everything. Holy shit that's what I call livin'. Jeeeesus..."

Ray was bouncing and clapping in the booth. "Jeeeeesus, it's the Ritz. It's the ever-lovin' good goddamn Ritz."

Joseph said nothing. Ray bounced out of the booth and headed for the back of the long shining counter. "I'm for coffee!" he yelled,

Mr. Petry was shocked out of his reverie. "I get it for you," he said.

"No, never mind," Joseph said. "You sit there. We're leaving."

Joe lifted himself out of the booth,

"Oh, shit man. Let's stick around," Ray said.

"C'mon," Joe said. His voice was insistent.

Ray bolted from around the counter to the door. "You're right, baby. Let's go driving. Let's tear the old ass off my Ford. Let's go! Let's goooo!"

Joe studied his friend. The long talk had told him something about Ray's nerve-wracking hilarity; it was a masquerade hiding his torment. Even crazy, happy-go-lucky Ray had his demons. Maybe the people in Hanway saw it too. Maybe that's why they always tolerated Ray's wild mobility. Without thinking or solving, maybe they saw it too. Maybe long before that morning. Joe, in the furthest depths of his gut, was well aware of Ray Walton's lonely game. Perhaps when all was said and done the catharsis wasn't necessary; the story was always there, in Ray's wild eyes.

A moment later, in a cloud of dust, the old car rushed off into the shadows.

7

ANNA was standing at the sink. Joseph walked over and kissed her.

"It'll start about seven," he said. "Make sure Tom and Gena have the right time or they might not get a seat."

Anna dried her damp hands on her apron. She placed them on Joseph's chest and looked at him sadly. "Don't feel bad, Joey, Please don't feel bad." She turned away from him and leaned on the sink. "I know your father meant to come. He didn't expect the business to tie him up this long. He never expected to be in Clarkson three days."

Joseph felt the rage rise in his throat. The city was only a half hour away. *How busy could he be?* he thought. Joe knew his father was staying away on purpose but his mother would never believe anything.

Joe was careful to keep his voice under control. "Yeah, Ma. Don't worry. I don't really care."

"Okay. Okay. But I want to you to know that he really expected to come. He wanted to come."

"Just make sure you get there on time. Okay? Otherwise none of you will get a good seat."

As Joseph walked the distance to the school, he thought about his graduation. He knew it was going to be a sad event. Joseph Flynn had always relished the adventure of being a kid on the streets. Graduation had a way of ending all that.

Carol had waited for this day with a building excitement, and now, she couldn't be there. She was sick in bed with a fever. Joe was vaguely surprised at himself for being so upset about her not being there. But, most of all, he was enraged about his father's refusal to come and amazed at Anna Flynn's failure to read through her husband's deceptions.

Larry was sick in bed too. Joseph was at least relieved about that; now he wouldn't have to force himself into any displays of false cordiality with his brother. Nevertheless, he was beginning to really wonder about Larry. He was becoming more and more withdrawn, and Joseph was concerned about its effects on his mother.

Several hours later, after many speeches and much singing, Joseph found himself walking up the long auditorium aisle. The melancholy group walked along with their flowing black gowns and their tasseled caps. They all felt sad in that cadenced line, leaving childhood behind forever.

As he marched along, Joseph saw his family in the middle seating section. They were desperately trying to catch a glimpse of him. Gena, with her proud, smiling face, saw him first. Tom was straining his neck and waving. Joe's eye caught the ebony of his mother's hair. And then their eyes came together. From a distance of thirty yards, Anna's look sent its message, a message of love and pain, A message of apologies and pride.

He wanted to rush from that aisle, and crawl over the heads and bodies separating them. He wanted to touch her, that woman of his life, that buffer of bruises and blood, that mother, that queen. He strained to resist the tears that threatened to explode from his eyes. His legs went numb and his heart thumped. His throat was sore and filled with love for her.

When he reached the lobby, people were bustling about in the excitement, excitement and pleasure interwoven with grieving smiles and heavy hearts.

Later out on the lawn, he hugged and kissed Anna. She held him tightly, as if preventing him from escape. For a long time he held his friend Ray close to him. He smelled Ray's clean, young manhood and felt the respect and friendship of his sinewy arms wrapped about him.

But through it all, the gnawing image of Patrick Flynn cut and tore at Joseph's brain. His father's face rolled over and over in his thoughts. The father who never cared. The father who never came. The father Joseph Flynn so desperately yearned for. His thoughts howled in rage at his father's callousness and hate.

Standing there on that graduation day, during a milestone event he had no stomach for, surrounded by kisses and congratulations, Joseph thought of Patrick Flynn.

8

MR. GRANAHAN peeked his head into his daughter's bedroom. His head was bald and shining like new plastic. Carol was sitting up in bed. Her auburn hair was pulled back into a pony tail. Some of the wavy strands fell loose and hung like heavy silk against her temples. She matched her bedroom perfectly; all soft and feminine, carrying a fragrance of the freshness and glory of young womanhood. She sat cross-legged on the bed, deeply interested in the magazine she was reading.

The little man quietly watched her. Finally he walked over to the bed. "What's my princess reading?"

Carol looked up in surprise., "Oh, daddy!" she exclaimed happily. "When did you get home?"

Mr. Granahan sat down next to her and placed his palm on her forehead.

She smiled, "Oh, don't worry. The fever is just about gone. Mama just took it. and it was almost normal." She placed the magazine down on the fluffy, flowered bedspread.

"She called Dr. Benson and he said if it's normal tomorrow I can go out."

"Don't worry, I'm sure you'll be out by tomorrow," he smiled. He leaned over and puckered his lips against her soft cheek. "Okay, get back to that story now. By the looks of things it was mighty interesting."

"Oh, just the usual true story stuff," she laughed.

He squeezed her shoulder and. walked to the doorway. "Is your mom in the kitchen?" he asked, with his back turned,

"Yes, Dad," she replied. Her eyes followed him out of the room, and then she returned her attention back to the magazine.

Frank Granahan kissed his wife and sat down at the kitchen table. "Carol says her fever is just about gone," he said.

He untied his shoes and kicked them from his feet. He hunched over the table and began to stir the hot chocolate his wife placed in front of him.

"Oh, yes. Thank God," Mrs. Granadan said. "Thank God the darn thing is finally going. Fevers always worry me." She looked at her husband and smiled. "Dr. Benson said it was just an ordinary grippe. She should be fine by tomorrow."

"Good. Good." he said. "Three, four days is just about what something like that lasts."

He looked preoccupied, Mrs. Granahan noticed, always sharply aware of his every mood. "Something on your mind, honey?" she asked.

He looked up from the steaming cup. "Come over here, Elaine, and sit down. I want to talk to you."

"Oh my," she smiled. "It sounds like something serious."

She sat down and looked at him across the table. His eyes were troubled, Suddenly, she grew very serious. "What is it, Frank?"

"The factory's moving out."

"What does that mean?"

"It means the factory's moving out. Just what I said. They told all the workers today. Word came down from management and they're moving out. It's as simple as that."

"What's going to happen? What about your job?" she asked. She felt frightened and unsteady.

"Well, they're moving," he said. "I might be able to go with them. But it's not sure. Nothing is sure."

"Where are they going to relocate? How can we just leave here like that? Even if there is something, how can we leave?

"Everything depends on them now," he said. "If they've got something for me everything will be okay. If they don't..."

"Well what did they tell you exactly?" she persisted. "Jesus, tell me!"

"Look, it's very simple. They're moving out to Ohio. I'm not sure why, but that's where they're going. Mr. Rupp told me it's possible that I might relocate with them. If it works out it'll probably be a real good break. He said my rate out there will be a lot higher. The company will cover all the moving expenses and everything, and they'd find us somewhere to live. He said it's a nice place. The way things look, we'll be a hell of a lot better off in Ohio."

"Well, what do you think?" she asked.

"I just told you what I think, honey," he said, "We don't have much of a choice anyway, the way I see it. I'll never find a decent job anywhere else—not at my age." He leaned back in the chair and emitted a long, troubled sigh. "Will it bother you to leave here, honey? I mean if the relocation works out. It doesn't matter to me, but I'm worried about you and Carol. You've spent your lives here and I know you love it." His voice trailed off.

She rushed to him and placed her hand firmly on his shoulder. She bent over and kissed his wet forehead. "Good God! If that's all you're worrying about, forget it. Carol and I will go anywhere you want. As long as we're all happy and together, as long as you're happy, that's what counts. Now stop your worrying for Christ's sake. Stop it!"

He stood up and wrapped her in his arms. "I knew it would be all right," he said in a happy and excited voice, "I knew it. God-damn, I knew it. You're the best there is." He kissed her and spun her in his arms.

"Jesus, honey, do you know what this might mean? They'll move us at their expense. Holy God! I know Mr. Rupp will get me that raise. He says he'll be the Ohio manager. He promised, me if he found anything for me there, he'd get in touch with me immediately. He said I'd wind up a supervisor. He means it. I know he does. I'm the only guy in the factory a relocation was even offered to, I mean if it's possible. That says something right there. Doesn't it?"

"Yes, I think it does," she said.

"I really believe you're going to be glad with all this, once we get there and everything." Suddenly his voice lowered. "But what about Carol? I'm worried about the way she'll take it."

"You let me take care of that," she said, with a knowing smile. "At first I know damn well she's going to be upset. But I'll convince her it's all for the best. Let me worry about it. She's young. It'll be easy for her to adjust. Don't worry. Just let me take care of it."

"Okay," he said. "Now all I have to worry about is Mr. Rupp coming through. He couldn't guarantee anything. I know he'll do everything he can but he couldn't guarantee anything."

He walked to the screen door. He looked at the back yard, and the railroad tracks on the bank behind the yard. The clothes pole, standing like a weather-beaten cross, was silhouetted against the sky. "Well, we're lucky we didn't buy the old place after all. Now we won't have to worry about selling it." He let out a low laugh, "Listen to me," he said. "You'd swear I already had the job."

His wife walked over to him as his eyes drifted over the grey sky.

"Don't you worry none, You'll get the job. They'll never find another mechanic like you."

Frank Granahan smiled. Maybe it wasn't much, but he was proud of his job. He was a machine mechanic in a lingerie factory but he was proud of his expertise in dealing with it; he had worked long, hard years, and had won the respect of everyone who worked with him. He had a fast mind and fast hands. He was a damn good mechanic and proud of it. He smiled at his wife, "Well, if I don't get it I'll have to sign for relief."

"Don't worry. You'll get it," she said. She walked to the doorway. "I'll go in and talk to Carol. There's no use putting it off. Even if you don't get it, I'm not going to have you worrying about her. I'll talk to her right now, Don't worry. Everything will turn out fine."

Frank looked at her and his heart filled with pride. "Thanks," he whispered.

As she approached her daughter's bedroom. Mrs. Granahan paused. She was in a frenzy. Her brain, usually coherent in such matters, was spinning. "I must remain calm" she thought. "God. I must remain calm." She thought about leaving Hanway. She thought about what it might mean. Even though her heart might break, she knew if they got the word to leave, she'd leave in a minute. For her dear husband's sake, she'd leave in a minute; no questions no fears. She would force herself to adjust to anything for his sake. As long as the only man she'd ever loved remained laughing, strong and whole, there'd be no scenes. She would make Carol understand. She had to. She had to do it and get it over with.

She explained the situation to Carol. Carol sat wide eyed, and listening. When her mother finished. Carol began to cry. After a while her mother quieted her. She felt the wetness of Carol's eyes against her shoulder. She held her daughter's back as it heaved with sobs. "All right, all right, honey," Mrs, Granahan crooned. "He might not even get the job." She instantly flinched at her betrayal. Her mouth and voice grew firm, "Carol, you have to think of Daddy. What's he supposed to do if he doesn't go? What are we going to do, live on relief? He'll never find another decent job around here. You've got to understand, honey. He can't hear us crying and complaining. We can't hurt him like that. He doesn't deserve it. The way it is, I know he's already worried sick about us feeling bad." She felt her own strength give way. The tears slowly made their way down her cheeks. "We have to be strong, honey. For him, we've got to be strong," Her voice was disjointed with soft sobs.

"How long before we'll know for sure?" Carol asked in a tortured whisper.

"Oh, don't worry. It'll be a while—a couple of months anyway." Mrs. Granahan had no idea when it would be. It might be tomorrow but she chose to lie.

Carol lay back on the bed. Her mother patted her forehead and wiped her eyes with a tissue. Carol just lay there motionless, her mind filled with the face and body of Joseph Flynn.

9

Joseph looked at Carol's red, swollen eyes and her face disfigured with confusion and worry.

"Jesus, honey, you're making too big a deal out of this," he said.

Carol looked at him. "Too much of a big deal. You've got some nerve, you jerk. Oh, how would you know the way I feel? Nothing ever matters to you."

Joe pulled her face to his chest. They were both sitting on her bed.

"Look." he said. "In the first place your father might not even get the job. What the hell, he won't get the job. It's not likely that they'll go through the trouble of moving him and everything. They just said that to make him feel good."

He smiled at Carol. "Naw, no way. You won't be leaving here. Now c'mon, stop crying and perk up, will you?" It was difficult for him to arouse any joy in Carol. He had been sitting there for over an hour listening to her cry and sob over the possibility of her father's new job.

"But what if it does happen?" she asked. "Oh, God. I won't be able to live without you. I'll die. I know it. If I can't see you... ."

"No, you won't die, and besides you're not even going. so forget it. Now I'm telling you, stop it. I don't want any more crying or I'm going to walk out. So c'mon for Christ's sake. stop it."

Joe was annoyed and Carol knew it. She forced herself to regain her composure. After a while she sat quietly on the bed, staring at Joe. He stood at the window looking out onto the street.

He turned and looked over at her. "Now I hope that's the end of the goddamn crying." He sat next to her. His voice changed to a soft affectionate appeal. "You're going to wind up sick if you keep this up. Promise me this is the end of it. C'mon now, promise me."

Carol sniffled and her shoulders moved in a soft shudder. "Okay," she said, "but if I do leave, you'll be sorry."

Joe laughed and hugged her. "Tomorrow you'll be able to go out. Everything'll be okay, wait and see. When you get out there traveling with old Joe, everything'll be okay." He tenderly kissed her. Before long the tenderness transformed into passionate hungry loving. The heat of their embraces drove Carol to a wild abandon. Joe's eyes watched the foreboding doorway, where any moment her mother or father might appear.

He reluctantly pulled his lips from Carol's hot mouth, "Look, babe, we'd better not fool around in here. Somebody might come in."

Carol rolled on her side, turning her back to him. He rubbed her leg. "I've gotta get going anyway. We're moving tomorrow and there's a lot of things I've gotta pack." He stood up and straightened his shirt and pants. His groin was wet and aching for her.

"I'll call you tomorrow," he said.

As he made his way home, he smelled the fresh June night. There was a hint of rose and lilac. He waved at familiar faces on the porches he passed. The bark of alerted dogs came from the back yards. He walked slowly along the tree-lined sidewalks, running his fingers over hedges and fences. The nervous sounds of crickets punctuated the summer lawns.

Joe was surprised at Carol's carrying on. He never thought her feelings for him ran so deep. He felt good about it; she was beautiful and desirable. He smiled to himself thinking of her trembling and tears. All for nothing anyway. That job would never come off. And even if it did, so what. He'd adjust to her leaving, and she'd adjust too. He knew she was misgauging her feelings. *She's more in love with love than she is with me.*

What Joseph Flynn was unaware of on that splendid summer night was the fact that Carol Granahan did love him. He didn't understand the ugly beauty of such a love, but he would, very soon, understand it, all of its passion and heartbreak. All of its beauty and tears. He would soon feel the searing sharpness of its blade and the burning longing of its wound.

His thoughts drifted away from Carol Granahan to the pressing desolation of what awaited him on Moosic Street.

After all the time spent avoiding reality, the terrible truth of leaving his home poured itself over him. I don't want to leave. God in heaven, I don't want to leave.

Joseph lay awake in the bare and quiet house, the blood of his life. He stared into the darkness and thought of all that had happened there. He listened to the groans and creaks of the walls and floorboards. In the distance was the familiar rumble of the night freight as it made its way through the valley. Soon its whistle and the locomotive would be at his window.

As he mercifully fell off to sleep he was a little boy again, hearing quiet steps and whispers on the stairs. They would sound as real as when he first heard them so many years before, the sounds of a man and woman, breathing hope and life into a young receptive soul. It all came back—the standing at the stairway on that homecoming night, the drinking and laughing, the dreams and prayers, all of the memories that were locked in the furthest reaches of Joseph Flynn's heart.

BOOK
TWO

1

ON A SIMMERING June morning Joseph finally saw his new residence. He hated it as he knew he would. Everything about it was too large and opulent.

The property was enormous. There were yards and yards of rolling grass and small hills and dales, with a small forest of elms, oaks and birches covering its surface.

A large black metal fence surrounded the property. A driveway led from the front gate to the house and back, forming a wide U-shaped stretch of macadam. There was a fountain in the center of the driveway directly in front of the house. On that morning. its spouting water glinted like crystal in the sun.

Over the months the contractors and landscapers had worked feverishly to get things ready. There were freshly planted flower beds along the walkway that led from the front fence to the mansion. The house was unseen from the street, obscured by leaves and distance.

The house itself was a large, antebellum-type mansion. It stood dead center on the land, like a white colossus. Its portico was huge, containing high round pillars that supported an ornate balcony. The windows were high and framed by green shutters. The interior was composed of oak paneled, high ceiling rooms. All the furnishings were plush and brand new. A wide spiral staircase led to an upstairs hall that overlooked the first floor.

Joseph watched his father rush about and heard his authoritative voice echo through the halls, as he shouted orders at the nervous painters who were applying the finishing touches to his castle. Joseph never hated his father more than he did at that moment. He wondered if the ugly ego of Patrick Flynn was, at long last, satisfied.

The house was too big. Joseph was nauseated to see his family dwarfed by its ridiculous dimensions. His mother, standing in the foyer, looked like a lonely, haunted bird. His heart ached for her, for like him, she belonged in that simple home they left behind, the house that throbbed and pulsated with the beat of their blood.

That evening Joe visited Tom and Gena. For the first time in that long feverish day, he enjoyed an atmosphere that allowed him the freedom to relax. He and Tom sat on the back porch, while Gena busied herself in the kitchen. As they talked, the sun hovered like a blazing, red sphere over the distant mountain.

"How do you like the house?" Tom asked.

"I don't," Joe replied. "I don't like it at all. As a matter of fact, I hate it."

"Jesus, it's big!" Tom said.

"That's just it. It's too goddamn big. Too rich and too big."

"Most people would love living in something like that."

"Maybe most people, but not me. I went over, hung my clothes and got the hell out of there."

"Gena told me that today was actually the first time you really saw the place. Is that right?"

"Yeah."

"You mean you never saw the place at all before today? That's hard to believe."

Joe smiled and nestled, himself into the long chaise. He was proud, knowing he resisted the bite of curiosity, refusing to be driven to that hated location any sooner than he had to. "If it wasn't for Ma I'd never live there."

"Do you mean that?"

"Yeah. I looked at the place once or twice before they even began working on the house. Things were just being planned out. I don't consider that an actual visit, you know," Joseph smiled.

"You're welcome here anytime, you know that," Tom said.

Joe looked at him and nodded his head. "Uncle Tom, you know

how much I hate my father, and I think you're the one person who can understand it."

"Why?"

"Because I think you hate him too. I've thought that for a long time. Am I right?"

"Well, Pat and I haven't seen eye to eye for a long time. We're not the same kind of men. I don't understand him and he doesn't understand me."

The screen door suddenly opened and Gena carefully made her way on to the porch. She was carrying a tray with two glasses of lemonade loaded with ice, and a small basket filled with pretzels.

She was oblivious to their conversation and she was wearing a smile that wrinkled the corners of her eyes and lit up her face. "It's hot! Here, this should quench your thirst," she said. Tom passed a frosty glass to Joseph. He walked over and set the tray on a small table. He took a long thirsty gulp from the glass. "Joey was just telling me that he's not too crazy about the new house."

Gena smiled, "He'll get used to it. Once he's there a while we won't be able to drag him out of the place. He's got to get used to feeling like a rich boy."

Joe pretended to be amused.

"I'll come out and talk later, I've got a lot to do inside," she said.

Tom's eyes followed her as she left the porch, "She loves your father," he said.

"Yeah, I know," Joe replied as he poured the sweet icy liquid into his throat. He set the empty glass down on the table and wiped his mouth with the back of his hand. "But you don't."

"He's a selfish man," Tom said, "But I guess nobody knows that better than you. He'll do any damn thing he has to but he'll always wind up getting what he wants. He doesn't care who he hurts. That's the kind of man he is."

"The two of you used to be good friends, I remember," Joe said.

Tom sat down. Remembering pained him. He looked up at Joe. His face was a blend of sadness and hostility.

"I thought a lot of him once, but that was a long time ago, before I knew what he really was. He used me like he uses everybody."

"What do you mean?"

"Well, he just used me, that's all. He never gave a damn about me, but in the beginning I thought he did. I was a fool," Tom closed his eyes and rested his elbows on his knees,

"How did he use you?" Joe asked,

"I got to really know your dad after he came back from the service. Like everybody else I admired him for his war record, you know, the medals and all. Everyone in town thought a lot of him back then."

Joe's eyes gleamed with the sharp recollection of those long past years. "Well what happened? What changed things?"

"Well, the way it turned out proved he was nobody to admire. He was never the best guy in the world, the way some of us thought. He just deceived everybody until he got what he wanted, And then all of us, especially the ones close to him, found out what he really was all about." Tom turned and looked toward the kitchen, making sure Gena was out of earshot, "Except her," he said, as he nodded his head toward the kitchen. "She overlooks all his faults. But she is his sister. I guess that's why she feels about him the way she does."

"But why does she feel that way? Can't she see him for what he is?" Joseph asked.

"Well, what the hell, like I said, she is his sister. Another thing is that she has always felt guilty where he's concerned."

"She has no reason to feel guilty," Joe said.

"Well, there's no telling her that. She feels that she never offered enough to him when he was growing up. It's always that old story, and it's stupid. Goddammit, I know my wife, and I'm damned sure she did everything for him that she could," Tom sighed. "She refuses to see his faults. There's no use talking about it. There's no use trying to make her understand," Tom leaned back against the porch railing and rubbed his hand across his chest. "Before the war, I didn't know Patrick, but I knew that he was just a kid and everyone in town was scared shitless of him." Tom quickly shook his head back and forth. "Wow! What a temper. He was one mean bastard. When I started taking Gena out I tried to get to know him. but we never really got close back then. Not even after me and Gena got married. He was a tough guy to get close to."

"Did everybody feel that way about him back then?"

"Yeah, just about. But after he married your mother he seemed to mild out a bit. Everybody always liked Anna. It seemed as though they accepted him a bit more after he married her. It was that more than anything else." Tom's eyes drifted, "Hell, everybody felt bad for her when Patrick went into the service. I remember it like yesterday. She was so alone without him, so scared. She straightened out a lot after you were born. There was a big difference then," Tom said. "When he got back home most of us felt different about him. A lot had to do with his war record. but most of us were glad for Anna."

Joseph sat mute; his eyes and ears honed to every word.

"I don't know if you can remember when he got back. We had a hell of a party. And Jesus, he was happy and nice to be around, genuinely nice to be around. I was so glad for you and Larry and Anna. Jesus, it was nice. Honest to God, it's just like it was last night. Do you remember it at all?"

"Yeah, I remember."

"Well, I'll tell you. We were glad he was back. We felt real happy to have him home. That hero bullshit might have had something to do with it, but I'll tell you right now, it was mostly for your mother." Tom stood up and walked in a tight circle on the sidewalk below the steps. He squinted as he looked into the light of the kitchen, "I don't want her to hear," he said.

"She can't hear you."

Tom moved closer to Joe and spoke in a low voice. "For a while there he was a different man. He enjoyed his family. But the old Patrick soon took over. He was on the street conniving and scheming just like before. It wasn't long and everyone was fearing him all over again. Brother, he was always on the road. That's when he started to build up the money. That money was never meant for any of you, but I know you already know that."

Joe leaned forward in the chair, "The only two people his money ever took care of were himself and Larry," he said.

"Yeah, kid, I have to admit it. He just seemed to cut you and your mother out of the action. I can't figure it, but that's just what the bastard did. There's no doubt about it. I couldn't get into the service," Tom said. "I had an ulcer, can you imagine that, an ulcer. Goddammit, I still have it. The pain comes and goes, you know. Well, anyway, I couldn't get in. I had quite a few bucks saved so I got into the hardware business, and shit I did real good, real good." Tom's eyes clouded over in memory. "But I gave it all up when Patrick came home. Jesus, what a story this is, Joe. Your father convinced me to get into the beer distributing business. I went in. It cost me all the dough I had. Three months later Patrick told me the whole thing was coming apart. I believed him. The business was gone, he said. I believed him; never checked a goddamn bill or anything.

"I believed him just like he knew I would. I got out broke, not a pot to piss in. A coupla' months later he formed the business over, by himself this time, only with all my friggin' money, the bastard, and in a year he was on his way to the big money. I couldn't get to see any of the old books. He threatened me. He said I was callin' him a crook, and Gena was another one, blaming me for condemning her brother. Goddamn, she's so sonofabitch blind when it concerns him, and here I am, a good many years later, still broke, workin' my ass off in that shoe factory, not able to save a dime. Jesus, he never offered any explanation, nothin' at all, not even a job in the business when it got big and he had trucks all over the friggin' county. Not even a job or any explanation. That was it, kid. I knew what he was made out of then. I stayed away, just as far as I'm able. If it wasn't for your aunt, I wouldn't go near him at all."

Joseph was shocked, "You mean you let him take you over like that, he just got away with it?"

"Yeah, that's what I mean, kid. It was a comedy. I was a fool or maybe just plain scared or what, but that's the way it went. I'll tell you, Joe. there's a lot of stories like that one in your father's life. You can bet on that."

"Christ," Joe said.

"Nobody ever messed with Patrick too much," Tom said.

Joseph stood up and leaned against the porch banister.

He felt sick in his stomach, sick for his Uncle Tommy and sick of his father's cruelty.

Tom looked up at Joseph. "Ya see this house we're living in. It ought to be Gena's. It was hers in her mother's will. But what did she do? She signed it over to Patrick right afterwards. She wanted to make sure he got something. That's a laugh. How does he repay her? He owns so many goddamn houses and properties now he can't count them. Does he give her this place back?" Tom let out a low hate-filled grunt. "No way. No way. He doesn't give away anything. When he went out on his own he turned the house over to us. He would've taken it back when he married Anna, except the house her parents left her was bigger and nicer. But goddamn, he made sure he charged us rent and he still does. Won't fix a rotten thing here. Any painting or repairs done, it's me and Gena that foots the bill."

"Why the hell don't you move out?" Joe asked.

"Because your aunt loves it here. She grew up here. All her life she's been here, and to tell you the truth, I like it myself. It's my home now too. Screw him. We'll pay the rent and keep the place up ourselves, doesn't matter a damn anymore anyway."

Joseph walked to where his uncle was standing. He placed his hand on his shoulder, feeling the tight muscle beneath.

He was taller and heavier than Tom, but his uncle was solidly built and heavily muscled, a short handsome man with a face that was usually happy and smiling, but he wasn't smiling now.

He turned to Joe. "Do you see what he did with your old house?"

"What?" Joe asked.

"He had it rented out in a day," Tom replied, "In a goddamn day, with furniture and all."

"Oh yeah, I know," Joe said.

"Doesn't it bother you?" Tom asked, "Doesn't it bother you that people are sitting and sleeping on things that have been yours all your life? I'd sooner burn the damn thing down."

"What?"

"I said I'd rather burn the damn thing down," Tom said.

"What?"

"My house, I'd rather burn it down than turn it over, furniture and all to somebody who has no business touching things that involve all the things in my life," Tom said.

"Oh," Joe said.

"Do you know what I mean, kid? I mean all the things are personal. Your father should have burned all that furniture before turning it over to strangers like that. Do you see what I mean?"

"Oh, yeah, yeah. I know exactly what you mean. It kills me to think about it so I don't. It's as simple as that. I just don't think about it," Joe said.

"Well I guess when you've got a business mind like Patrick's you don't think in terms of sentiment. It's more a matter of business. He manages to get more rent by throwing in the furniture so he throws it in. For a guy like him it's a simple matter of mathematics Maybe I'm the fool—I don't know. I just couldn't do it, that's all," Tom said.

"Neither could I, I guess. I've got the same kind of mind as you. I'm proud to feel like that. If I felt any other way I'd be ashamed. Honest to God I'd be ashamed," Joe said.

Joe was standing so close to Tom he could hear his breath.

He had always admired his uncle, and he was silently glad that Tom was the man he had always imagined him to be.

"Tom, me and you, we should talk more often. This talk was a nice thing. I appreciate all you told me. It's important to me."

Tom turned and put his arms around his nephew. He held him only for a moment, feeling somewhat awkward in holding another man so close. Tom wasn't used to such shows of affection.

"You're a good old kid, Joe," Tom said. "A good old kid. You sure as hell haven't deserved some of the deals you've been getting, but you're tough. You'll pull through. I'll bet on it."

Joseph smiled. "Oh? I'll pull through all right. I've pulled this far, I don't think it can get much worse."

Tom twisted into a long lazy stretch. While he and Joe had talked, the shadows of night had silently stretched its black cloak over the yard. "I think I'll take me a walk up to the corner," Tom said. "Tell Aunt Gena I'm going up the bar for a while. All this talk has given me a helluva thirst."

"Yeah, okay Tommy," Joseph said, "I'm going in to talk with her for a while anyway. I'll see ya." Joseph jauntily ran up the steps to the back porch. The screen door sharply snapped shut behind him. Gena was just entering the kitchen from the parlor archway.

"Tom's gone up the road a minute," Joe said.

"He's gone for his nightly beer, eh?" Gena smiled.

Joe walked to one of the chairs near the table and sat down. Gena was perspiring and tousled.

"What the hell are you doing now?" Joe asked.

"Oh just straightening out some things out here. There's not enough time in a day," she said.

"Me and Tom had a nice talk," Joe said.

"My God? what were the two of you talking about all this time?" Gena asked.

"Oh this and that."

"How do you really like the new place?" she asked.

"Lousy."

"Oh c'mon."

"No, I really mean it. I think it's lousy."

"You're being stubborn, Joe," Gena said.

"I don't think so, I think a house that size is a joke."

Gena was exhausted from a long trying day of housework. She chose to drop the subject.

"I saw Mickey Clark today. He's giving me a job at the gas station," Joe said.

"The gas station!" Gena's voice was filled with surprise. "You mean you're definitely not going to see about college?" she asked.

"Yep, I'm going to work at his station. I'd rather do that anyway," Joe said.

"Joey, sometimes you're a fool. Why in Jesus do you want to work up in Mickey's when you have a chance for college? Sometimes I don't believe you, What's your reason? Is it your father again? I know damn well it's not that you're afraid you couldn't make it through. Your grades in school were great. You're every bit as smart as your brother. You know that and so does everyone else. It must be the bullshit about your father again."

"Oh, I don't know, That might be it, but I don't know. I really don't think I'm cut out for that college business. Anyway, I'm not gonna have Ma kissing his ass to go for the tuition money. I don't need that and I don't need him." Joe's eyes were filled with a familiar fire.

"Bullshit, Joe!" Gena said, "Bullshit and you know it. Your father would pay the money without a word. You know that damn well."

"Yeah, he probably would," Joe said.

"Then what is it?" Gena asked.

"He'd give the money all right, only after he'd have Ma begging, and the only reason he'd finlly come across is so people won't talk about him. So the hell with it."

"He'd give the money," Gena said. "I think he'd do it to make her happy. All right I agree with you. Maybe he wouldn't do it expressly for you, but he'd do it for her."

"Yeah? well maybe that's right, so the hell with it," Joe said.

"You think you're spiting him, Joe, working in a gas station. And him with all that money. You want to embarrass him. That's it, isn't it?" Gena asked.

"I don't know. Maybe it is, I don't want to think about it." Joseph read the irritation on his aunt's face and simultaneously decided to terminate the conversation. He moved toward the door.

"Don't leave. I don't want to scare you off," Gena smiled.

"I can smell it in the air. It's time to go, Auntie babe," Joseph said.

Gena was still smiling, "Ya know sometimes you're a regular punk. You know that, don't you?" she said.

Joseph laughed quietly as he pushed open the screen door.

"1 know sometimes you're a regular punk, Aunt. You know that, don't you?" he said.

"So long, Joey," Gena's voice was quiet but her eyes gleamed with the love that surged through her soul.

"See ya, Aunt Gena. I'll probably stop by tomorrow. I'll see ya then." The door slammed shut and he was gone.

2

BY MID-SEPTEMBER the last vestiges of summer had all but disappeared from Hanway. The night breeze was cold and the afternoon sky was a sheet of iron grey.

As always, in autumn, Joseph could feel the presence of sadness. He leaned against the hood of the old Chevy, as the gas pump shot its liquid fuel into the car's belly. The wind moved cold and fast off the mountain, sending his hair into a flurry of black curls. As Joe approached the station with the customer's five dollars clutched tightly in his hand, he noticed the forlorn creature standing near the office door. It was Lobo Pagnozzi.

Lobo just stood there, in his raggedy, oversized coat; his hair was straggly, covering his ears, and sticking out in all directions. He had at least a week's growth of beard covering his sad, tired face, but the face was also handsome, with its proud Italian nose and high, striking cheekbones. As Joseph passed him, he smiled at the large, stooped figure.

"How ya been, Lobo?" Joe asked.

The man didn't answer.

As Joe opened the door to go inside, he spotted a flash of green in Lobo's tight fist.

Mickey looked up from the desk, "Did you say somethin', kid?" he asked.

"Naw, I was talkin' to Lobo," Joe replied.

"Oh yeah. Lobo, good old Lobo," Mickey said. "He just stopped by for a minute."

"He comes around here an awful lot. Doesn't he?" Joe asked.

"Naw, not so much kid, not really," Mickey said,

"Did you give him money?" Joe asked.

"Yeah, just a few bucks. The guy could use it," Mickey said. Joseph walked over to the battered red coke machine and inserted a coin. The caramel-colored bottle slipped into his hand. Joseph guzzled the contents of the bottle and walked to the desk. He rubbed his lips dry with the back of his arm, as he half-sat on the desk facing Mickey.

Mickey leaned back in the wooden swivel chair. "You can call it a day, kid. It's almost five o'clock," he said.

"Yeah, right. I'm just takin' a little break before I clear out," Joe said.

Joe's eyes rested on Mickey's weather-worn face, with his healthy sparkling eyes and his hair abundant and black. It was a strong man's face sitting on a wide neck, bounded on both sides by cords of muscle.

Mickey smiled showing a perfect set of white, large teeth. Everything about Joe's boss and friend bespoke of health and strength.

"He musta been a good friend of yours," Joe said.

"Who?" Mickey asked.

"I mean before he got sick and everything," Joe said.

"Who?" Mickey asked, "Are you talking about Lobo?"

"Yeah," Joe said, "Loho, he musta been a good friend."

"Do you know Lobo's story, kid?" Mickey asked.

"Well, yeah, you know," Joseph replied, "Only the things everybody's heard. He got hurt in the war or somethin', right?"

"Yeah, right," Mickey said, "He got hurt all right, the poor bastard. He got hurt all right. He was a tail gunner during the war." Mickey went on, "His plane was shot up somewhere over Germany. It crash landed but nobody was killed. I guess there were a lot of injuries. Nobody was captured or anything, but Lobo came but of it the way you see him now. He wasn't always this way, kid. Before the war he was a bright guy and a goddamned good car mechanic." Mickey's eyes wandered as he laughed a long, nostalgic laugh. "Yeah, he was a hell of a guy. Jesus, what a sense of humor! He was a hell of a guy. He worked here with me for a coupla years before he went into the service. Hell, he was a better mechanic than me, and boy how he loved cars. He was either workin' on them or drivin' them, and Jesus he drove good and fast. I'll tell ya he used ta scare the hell outta me, but that's all over now. After he got outta the hospital and came back home, just a few days before your dad as a matter of fact, but Lobo didn't have a party or nothin'. His family never had much and no one was all shook up about poor Lobo, so there was no party or nothin'. Anyway, since he got back, he's been the way you see him. He never recovered. He just lost his mind and stayed that way. His old man died a few months after Lobo got back. I think the old man's heart was broke, you know. Now it's just Lobo and his mom. She's real old now and stays in the house all the time. Have ya ever seen her?"

"No," Joe answered.

"Well, ya see, she's real old and she's almost always alone. Lobo's out all the time, constantly walkin' the streets. I feel real bad for the old gal, ya know. I'll tell ya somethin' kid, when Lobo got back home that time after he got outta the hospital, I went over to his house. Like I said there was nobody there except them, and ya know my heart damn near broke when I saw what happened to the poor guy, and my heart broke for his parents too. I'll never forget it, it was a goddamned awful sight."

Mickey stopped talking and just sat there. He was suddenly a million miles away. He momentarily broke from his reverie and looked at Joe, "Well, take it easy, kid. Have a good time tonight, okay?"

"Yah, sure Mick," Joe replied,

Joseph slowly slid from the desk and left the building. As he made his way home he thought of Lobo Pagnozzi; through all the years of Joseph's growing up, he and his friends antagonized and teased Lobo. They imitated him and laughed at him, always hoping for a chase. But Lobo never chased or even responded to them, except for his sad defensive face and his quick walk away from their torment. Joseph had never meant harm, and neither had Ray

Walton or any of the rest of his friends. All the way home, Joseph thought about Lobo Pagnozzi.

As Joseph finally lumbered up the long walkway, he looked at the shrubbery, containing the last hint of the season's color, and his vision enveloped the elaborate mansion ahead of him and the numerous trees of varying types that covered the property. The leaves were beginning to change color and the view was speckled with a kaleidoscope of color and beauty. It amused Joseph to imagine what he must have looked like. He was dirty and his clothes were grease-covered. He carried the workingman's traditional lunch pail, and there he was approaching the essence of opulence. He laughed to himself, knowing he felt as out of place in such surroundings as he might have looked.

Joseph entered the kitchen through the back door of the house. Before he was able to rest his pail on a nearby chair, he heard the feared, resounding voice.

"You should change in the cellar, boy." His father was standing in the large archway that led to the dining room. "You're going to make the place here a mess. What the hell is wrong with you?"

"Okay, okay, I just got in the house. Give me a chance, will ya?" Joseph said in a quiet voice.

"Well, Jesus Christ, that's what I'm saying. You shouldn't be in the house with that goddamn grease. You'll soil everything, you ignoramus," Patrick said.

"It's honest grease," Jospeh said.

"And what's that supposed to mean?" his father said.

"It's honest grease and honest dirt and I'm damn proud of it. I worked hard today. I work hard every day and if I get dirty and greasy I'm proud of it." Joseph's voice was raised and his face was masked with hurt and anger.

"Now I know damn well what that's supposed to mean. You're hinting that maybe I don't do honest work. That's it, isn't it, you little bastard. That's it, isn't it?" Patrick's color turned to flame as he spoke.

"No, I didn't mean that at all. Don't be so nervous. Maybe you got a guilty conscience or something," Joseph replied.

Anna Flynn's spare, hawklike figure appeared through the archway. "Quick, Joey. Go ahead. Go upstairs and change now. Go ahead." Her words were fast and nervous.

"Goddammit, I just told him to go down in the basement and change. What the hell is wrong with you? You're making a goddamn habit out of contradicting me," Patrick said.

Before his father could speak any further, Joseph interrupted. "I'll go downstairs, Ma, I'm goin' right now," Joe said. As Joe hurried down the steep stairs to the basement he could hear his father's voice rising in its tirade.

Joseph sat on the floor and began to remove his heavy work shoes. He stopped working the laces and wearily rested the back of his head against the cool cinder block wall. From above the thundering lecture of Patrick Flynn continued. Joseph waited for the welcome silence before he returned to the kitchen.

Anna Flynn scurried about preparing dinner. As always her hunched shoulders showed her tiredness, even in the midst of energetic activity. The enormity of the house was too much for her. Joseph put his arm around her. "Why don't you let Mrs. Davis do the cookin', Ma?" he said.

Mrs. Davis was a tall, gentle woman hired by his father as a maid of sorts. She was a childless widow and a long-time friend of Anna's. She came in three times a week to clean up following the entertainment his father provided for business friends.

Joseph was certain her presence was only to heighten the image of luxury, rather than being a genuine effort by Patrick Flynn to offer assistance to his beleaguered wife. Nevertheless, Anna Flynn insisted on doing most of the housework and all of the cooking, and her strength seemed to ebb, day by day.

His mother's answer was edged with annoyance. "Don't get into that again, Joey, I'm all right, so if you don't mind I'll do the cooking in my home. Leave me that much, okay, at least that much," she said.

"His goddamn parties have you worn out. You're supposed to relax and get some enjoyment out of them, but he's got you runnin' around like some scullery maid! Wise up and let Mrs. Davis come in here to serve and cook the goddamn dinners. You oughta sit around and talk to the people, not be a servant, Ma."

Before Joseph could finish, Anna turned and pressed her finger softly against her son's lips.

"Shhh," she said.

Joseph looked down at her and his heart broke to know how uncomfortable she was in this new life. She moved through her husband's party atmosphere like a small, frightened bird with her wide black eyes showing the discomfort of trying to be a socialite. "If it wasn't for you I wouldn't stay in this mausoleum for another minute," Joseph said.

"Go ahead. Go ahead. Sit down and eat and stop worrying about me," his mother said.

"Where's everybody?" Joseph asked.

"Your father's gone out. He's got some business in town and Larry says he's got some work to do on some school project so he's staying up in his room. I'll send something up to him later," she said.

"Well, I'm glad Dad's gone. I didn't feel like listening to any more of his bullshit. But what is it with Larry? He never comes downstairs, for Christ's sake. I'm going to have a talk with that guy," Joseph said.

Anna became very agitated and walked to the large kitchen window. She looked out over the expanse of land that surrounded the house. "Now Joey, please don't say anything to him. I'm worried about him, he's not the same boy anymore. I don't know what it is. Maybe it's the pressure at school. I just don't think he can handle the work, and he's so worried about disappointing your father. He's just coming apart at the seams. He's just not the same boy anymore," she said.

Joseph watched her as she rubbed the linen curtain nervously between her fingers.

"Okay, Ma, I won't say anything. I was just wondering why he was playing the hermit, that's all. Jesus, if he's having trouble with school, why doesn't he forget about being a doctor and do something else, and the hell with what Dad thinks."

"Oh, never mind. Never mind. Sit down and let's just eat. All right honey?" she said.

Joseph sighed. "Okay, Ma, let's eat."

3

THE LARGE black Cadillac slowly eased its way out of traffic and pulled to a stop in the lone parking place in front of the huge hotel. The name "Hotel Clarkson" blinked in a steady throb of neon across the hotel's brick façade. Patrick Flynn looked from the car window into the busy evening of the colored, blinking city. The huge man behind the wheel looked at him.

"What time shall I pick you up, Boss?" the man asked.

Patrick continued to look out the window. "About nine, nine thirty, Bill. Somewhere around there. I'll be waiting at the entrance," Pat said.

"Okay, Boss," Bill Manley was Patrick Flynn's closest confidant. They had been together from the beginning of Patrick's business life. He was one of the men who had listened in the stuffy heat of the pool hall many years before. He had helped Patrick arrange the political empire that spread throughout Clarkson County.

"Anything that you want me to do in the meantime?" Bill asked.

"No, nothing. Just drive around. Do whatever you want. Just pick me up about nine thirty. That'll be fine," Patrick said. Patrick squeezed Bill's arm and got out of the car. As he approached the entrance to the hotel, Bill called to him. Patrick turned, "What's that, Billy?" he said.

"If you need me, I'll be in the home office."

"Okay, buddy," Patrick replied. He disappeared into the hotel.

Bill Manley pulled the car back into the Clarkson city traffic and took a slow ride back to Hanway. Patrick Flynn existed as Bill Manley's whole family. He was a completely dedicated slave who moved at Patrick's whim and fancy. Manley was one of the strongest and meanest men ever bred on the streets of Hanway.

No one could ever beat him or intimidate him; no one, except one man, and that was Patrick Flynn. Their battle was legend and discussed over and over, in the whiskey-tinged, huddled reminisces of the Hanway saloons. It happened one evening prior to Patrick's war hitch. An argument developed in Stanley's, a favorite Hanway saloon in the shopping district of town. Before it was over both men nearly tore each other apart, but it was the legendary and feared Bill Manley who wound up bleeding and defeated on the linoleum, with Patrick Flynn bloody and triumphant above him. A grudging respect had been won by both men, and their friendship was to develop into a union as enduring as the memory of the fight itself.

When Patrick returned from the war, it was Bill Manley he looked up first to help construct the plan that would result in Flynn's complete takeover of the political reins that would control future county candidates and elections. Patrick knew there would have to be blood spilled in any such takeover, and he was well aware his own image had to be spared. It was Bill Manley who became the strongarm; never questioning the word of his boss, just constantly prepared to do whatever had to be done in order to advance the fortunes of Patrick Flynn. In the process, they both became rich and powerful, but there was never any doubt who was the commander; Patrick remained supreme in the relationship as he did that bloody night so long behind them. As it turned out, Patrick Flynn became Bill Manley's saviour and hero. Manley never married or fathered. His dedication was total and permanent. Patrick Flynn was his god.

Patrick entered the hotel lobby and quickly made his way to the side staircase that led to the row of business offices on the second floor. He ran up the stairs and walked directly to a door midway down the musty corridor. "Flynn's Real Estate Brokerage" was emblazoned in deep black on the white opaque window. He unlocked the door and entered a large room of office furniture. He walked to another door that led to a far more private room.

He closed the door softly behind him. There was a small bar on the far side of the room in front of a huge, solitary window with its Venetian blind pulled tightly closed. There were soft, leather easy chairs carefully placed throughout the area. Along one wall a great sofa served the purpose of both couch and bed. The room was softly illuminated by the dull glow from a lamp. There was another light that escaped from the slightly open door to Patrick Flynn's right that led to the bathroom. Patrick listened to the gurgling sound of running water and smiled as he walked over to the sofa. He removed his jacket and tie and fell heavily on to the leather and waited. He closed his eyes as he lay back, feeling the sharp coldness of the leather against his neck. He rested his powerful forearm across his forehead. A few moments later he heard her voice.

"I thought you'd never get here." Her voice was soft and teasing.

Patrick smiled and looked across the half-lit room. Lila Walton stood in the doorway of the bathroom. Her delicious, nude body was in a pose that best displayed the artwork of her pulsating figure. She ran across the room and fell into Patrick's arms. He kissed her neck and mouth. She whispered to him and they both began to laugh. Patrick ran his hand over nakedness, touching all the softness and hollows.

Their lovemaking was feverish. Patrick hungrily moved his body over hers; Lila responded with a wild passion of her own that rushed both of them into a storm of lust and sensuality.

When they finished, Patrick sat above her on the leather sofa. "You are somethin', babe," he said.

Lila sat up and lit a cigarette, "Did you miss me?" she asked. "It's been over a week, you know."

"I think I showed you how much I missed you," he said.

She ran a long fingernail down his bare back. "I missed you real bad, baby," she said.

"Well, we can't get together too often. It's bad for business, I've got to watch myself."

"Oh, screw your reputation," she said, "I've got to see you more often. I can't stand it this way, meeting here twice or three times a week like horny kids hiding from their parents. There's got to be something we can do."

"Now what's this all of a sudden?" he said. "For ten years we've been doing it this way. and now it's not good enough. What the hell are you complaining about all of a sudden?"

"It's just that sometimes I feel you just use me like some kind of whore. You make love to me like I was some side alley bang," she said.

Patrick stood up. "Hold it, hold it," he said. "You're not exactly a princess in the sack. You use me the same way I use you."

"No matter what I do or how I do it," she said, "you know damn well how I feel. I love you! I've always loved you! So don't stand there and pretend anything else." Her eyes were filling with tears.

Patrick, sat down and pulled her into his arms. "Okay, baby, okay," he said. "I love you. C'mon, don't tell me you believe anything else. You know you're my woman. C'mon, tell me you know that," he said.

Lila softly ran her soft, wet mouth along the muscle of his neck. Patrick grabbed her wild hair in his hand and pulled her face near his.

"You know what I did for you. Isn't that enough? What more could I ever do to prove that I love you?" he said.

"You mean Bill did it, not you, honey," she said.

"It's the same difference." Patrick said. "Bill or me? it's the same difference."

Lila's voice grew hard. "The hell it is," she said. "If you cared enough you would have done it yourself."

Patrick said nothing in reply. He stood up. His mind wandered to the memory of Sara Walton. He knew in his gut that the whole thing had been a crazy mistake. Patrick had come home in 1946 and found his wife Anna engulfed with the welfare of their son Joseph. The thought of Joseph caused him to clench his teeth with rage. "It was that little bastard," he thought. "He was the one who ruined everything with Anna." He was convinced that it was Joseph who drove him away from the woman he had once loved. Patrick had been Anna's whole life, but she betrayed him with her devotion to their second son, and he couldn't forgive her.

He wouldn't leave her. He couldn't leave her. But he would make her pay; he saw her turn into an old woman before his eyes. He tortured her by hating Joseph, her precious son. He made them both pay for their crime against him. He would no longer make love to Anna, but he found others for that purpose; and when he found Lila Walton, she became the ultimate answer to his hungry passion. Unfortunately, Lila's husband had found out about them and threatened to expose them. It would have wrecked Patrick's reputation. Between his desire for Lila and his selfishness, there had been only one solution. Bill Manley was the executioner. It started off as a simple beating, an understanding, nothing more; but things got out of hand, and Sam Walton wound up dead under the power of Bill Manley's fists. They buried him in a lonely field a few miles outside the town limits. It had been a foolish mistake. Sam Walton would never have said anything; he loved his wife and son too much. It was a mistake, and it was compounded when Patrick made the mistake of telling Lila. She never let him forget it, and she never let him get away—holding her to him, always with, the unspoken threat of exposure.

"Hey, c'mon, honey, what are you thinkin' about there? You're a million miles away," Lila said.

Patrick snapped back to the present. "Oh nothin', Lila, nothin'. I'm just tired I guess," he said.

She pulled gently at his arm. "Come down here with me. I'll make you forget about being tired."

Patrick looked at her splendid nakedness as she languorously stretched her body on the leather. In spite of himself, she aroused him; no matter what, she never failed to arouse him. He would keep her in the necessary money. He would put up with her sniveling, and he would even lie, and tell her he loved her. He would continue to use her.

4

URING the autumn of 1957 Joe Flynn desperately needed something or someone to fill the void that was crippling his life. Carol Granahan was there, eagerly waiting to help make him whole. Joseph never wanted to fall in love. It occurred in such an insidious fashion, he was never really aware of his feelings until the torch of jealousy and possessiveness set his soul on fire. Suddenly, he found himself awakening in the morning with a tingle in his body just to think of her. In spite of himself he saw her constantly, and when he wasn't with her he burned the telephone wires with his words of love and commitment, his demands and orders.

Nothing was simple anymore. He had to control her life—what she wore, what she said. He smothered her with an affection he thought she was incapable of. In the center of a memorable October, he and Carol Granahan moved into a love story so profound, they were both stunned by its intensity.

He bought an old Chevy with some money he had managed to put aside. The two of them spent almost all their time driving through the countryside, while they talked and planned their coming futures. He told her things about himself he had never told anyone; speaking from his heart, he talked and reminisced about the old men of Hanway, men like Mr. DeFazio—dear old friends that the years had taken away. He explained his love for the town he could never leave. He told her of his burning hate for Patrick Flynn, his hate for the mansion he refused to recognize as his home. He told her everything and she understood; loving him all the more for his fears and sensitivity, two commodities she never thought he possessed.

On a Saturday morning they had driven deep into the hills all the way up to the dam that sat high above Hanway. They spent the whole morning laughing and eating and making love. Later they lay on the browned grass and watched the sun move toward the lip of the horizon.

Carol ran her fingers through the thick unruly black curls that filled the top of Joseph's head,

"I love you. You know that," she said.

Joseph cupped her face into his hands and kissed her softly. "Yeah. I know that," he whispered.

Joe suddenly sat up. "Jesus, if your father gets that job..."

"Oh, please. Joey. Not now. Please," Carol said. "He never talks about it anymore and mother never mentions it..."

"That doesn't mean a damn thing," Joseph said. "They know talking about it upsets you. That's why neither of them mention it. I have a feeling that something's going to happen. He's going to get that job. I just know it. Why don't you come right out and ask them? One way or the other, we've got to find out."

"Well, I do ask them, I ask them all the time. They evade the whole thing. I don't know what else I can do,"

"Well, dammit, I do!" Joseph said. He stood up and walked to the shore line, letting the water touch softly against his shoe. "Dammit, I know what to say," he said, "I'm just going to ask your old man point blank if he's going or not going, that's all. I'm going to lay it straight out at him."

Carol got up and walked over to him, placing her arm along his shoulder. "No, Joey, don't say anything," she said. "It's just better if we let it go. We're not leaving here—it's impossible, it can't happen. Please just let's forget about it, okay? Please."

"Yeah, sure, that's right. We'll just forget about it. The hell with you and that friggin' job," Joe said in a voice trembling with anger.

"Oh, Joey, honey, please...."

Joseph shoved Carol away from him and walked quickly to the large blanket spread over the cool ground. He picked it up carelessly, and threw it into the back seat of his car. Carol just stood quietly and watched him. For a moment Joseph stared into the trees that surrounded them. He turned suddenly and faced Carol, Tears were blinding him and his voice was shaking and cracking.

"Why don't you just tell them you're not going, not matter what they do. You better tell them tonight, I'm warning you, tell them tonight or stay the hell away from me. If you love them more than me, that's all right. Just say so. Tell me!" Joseph screamed.

He ran to her and began to shake her violently. He slapped her hard on the face, causing her cheek to redden immediately.

Carol bowed her head and began to cry. Joseph pulled her to him and felt her tears soaking his face. He rubbed his hand through her hair and whispered to her as she reached her arms around his neck. "I'm sorry," he whispered, "I'm sorry."

"Don't worry, baby," Carol said, "everything'll work out. Wait and see. It'll work out." Her voice was riddled with sobs.

"You can't leave, Carol, You can't," Joseph said in a hoarse voice. Slowly they slipped onto the cool grass. Joseph felt his desire burning and filling his loins. He rubbed his hands over the softness of her breast and tasted the salt of her tears. His lips and mouth explored her face. Their breath became fast and in a moment all trouble and pain were forgotten.

Joseph dropped Carol off at her house and drove straight home. When he entered the large foyer of the mansion, the afternoon had faded into the long shadows of dusk. Anna Flynn lay asleep on the long couch in the elaborate parlor. Joseph walked over and stood quietly, looking down at her for a time. She was in a restless, fitful sleep and he wanted to wake her and reassure her but thought better of it.

He retreated to the staircase and began to slowly climb the steps. Halfway in his ascension, he caught a quick moving shadow in the corner of his eye. It was Larry. He was pacing almost unobtrusively near the archway that led to the hall. Joseph walked back down the stairs and approached him.

"What are you doing?" Joseph asked.

Larry didn't answer.

Joseph studied him closely. It was the first time in weeks that he had managed to see him close up. Larry ignored Joseph's presence as he continued to silently walk back and forth.

"What in the hell are you doing?" Joseph said, his voice a loud whisper.

Larry stopped and stared. His face was a silent mask. He continued to stare. Joseph began to feel the icy fingers of fear grip his throat.

"What the hell is wrong. Larry?" Joseph said.

Once again Larry ignored him and began to pace back and forth. Joe turned and went back to the stairway. He didn't look back as he went upstairs.

Joseph sat for a long time near the large window in his bedroom and looked out at the rolling land of his father's estate. The autumn wind rattled the tiny, square panes and sent the drying, colored leaves from the countless trees into a playful scramble across the grass, until they finally came to rest in a scattered piece of twilight beauty.

For a while his brain was numbed, but eventually he gave way to thoughts of Larry, He knew it was unquestionable; his brother's personality was dangerously changed. *He deserves misery*, Joseph thought, *he deserves it*. Joe believed with all his heart that it was himself and his mother who absorbed all the violence of his father's personality, while Larry had basked in the ill-gained glory. Joseph held no personal concern for Larry's strange condition, but his mother was becoming more and more miserable. Something had to be done.

Joseph went downstairs and awoke his mother. Her eyes opened slowly. She looked up at him. "What's the matter? What is it, honey?" she asked, her voice quivering in alarm.

"Nothing, Ma, nothing," Joe said. "I just want to talk to you for a minute. I'm sorry I woke you up, but I don't think it can wait."

Anna sat up. "What is it, Joe?" she asked.

Joseph slowly rubbed his fist over the dark stubble of his unshaven face. "Maybe we ought to have a doctor look at Larry," he said.

Anna looked at him in surprise, "Why, Joe," she said, "I've already had it done. Doctor Benson saw him this afternoon."

"What?" Joseph's voice was sharp with surprise.

"Yes, yes, just today," Anna said. "You were out. I was going to tell you."

"Well, what happened?" Joseph asked. "Why did you call him? Did Larry get out of hand or what?"

Anna leaned back into the couch. Her voice was tired and weak. "No, no, I just felt the way you're feeling right now for the same reason you must have woke me up," She rested her arm on Joe's shoulder. "What was it, Joe? Did you see him when you came in or something? You must've, that's why you woke me up. Isn't it? You were scared by what he looked like." Anna's voice was tight and shaking in her growing panic.

Joe saw the anxiety in his mother's eyes. He reached out and pulled her near to him, "Yeah, Ma, that's it exactly, I saw him, and honest to God, he scared me." Joe ran his hand along his mother's forehead and softly kissed her cheek, "But don't get upset," he said. "It's not your fault. Everything'll be okay. Don't worry,"

Anna emitted a long sigh and quietly nestled in the strength of her son's arms.

"What did the doctor say?" Joseph asked.

Anna carefully set her hands in her lap. For a moment she said nothing. She watched her fingers move slowly against her colored apron. "He didn't say much, Joe, just that your brother's nervous and needs some rest. He said it was no big deal." Anna tried to keep her voice from revealing the fear that filled her heart, "It's no big deal. That's just what he said."

Joseph stood up and began to pace about the room. The anger of his dark, liquid eyes was glinting in the fading light of the parlor, "Goddammit! No big deal!" he half-shouted. "What does he mean? No big deal, where does he get that crap?"

Anna was afraid Larry might hear. "Shh, Joe, for God's sake, your brother might be listening. Where Is he? Have you seen him?" she asked.

"No, not in about an hour anyway," Joe replied, "I don't know where he is now, probably up in his room. That's where he usually hides."

"Joe, don't," Anna said, "Not now, please! He might hear you."

"Well, where does goddamn Benson get off saying it's no big deal. All you have to do is look at Larry to know something is wrong," Joseph said in an angry voice. "No big deal," he muttered.

Anna stood up and walked over to her son. "He's a doctor, Joe. He ought to know," she said.

"Doctor, shit," Joe said. "He doesn't know the first thing about medicine, the goddamn quack. What made you call him? What does he know about something like this?"

"Your father..."

Before Anna could finish. Joe interrupted, "My father! Jesus Christ Almighty. he knows less than anybody about anything. Why did you even bother?" he said.

"Well, who could I tell? Who could I call?" Anna asked. "Larry was acting so strange and he scared me so bad. I didn't know what to do. He was walking around the house, refusing to talk, acting like he didn't know I was here, and talking and whispering to himself. I called your father at his office." Her voice was shaking and tears began to well in her eyes, already reddened from prolonged crying. "He told me to call Doc Benson and I did," she said.

"Did Dad come here?" Joseph asked.

"Yes, he got here just as Doctor Benson was leaving."

"What happened? What did he say?"

"Nothing, We just listened to what the doctor said, that's all. Your father agreed that Larry is probably just overworked. Oh Joe, that's got to be all it is," Anna began to cry.

Joseph made no attempt to stop her. "Look, Ma," he said. "Doctor Benson doesn't know anything. He'll say anything Dad wants to hear anyway, and you know damn well he doesn't want to hear his number one son is cracking up. That'd look bad for the record." Anna's sobs caused Joe to release himself from the anger that was choking him. He rushed to her and tried to calm her.

After a short period the sobs subsided.

"Mom," Joseph whispered, "It probably is no big deal. I didn't mean that it was. It's just that someone better should look at him, that's all," he said.

"Oh, Joey, he's gotta be all right," she whimpered. "He's gotta' be."

Joseph held his mother close as he sat her back down on the couch. "Don't worry, Ma. Everything'll be okay.... Shhhh," he whispered.

Joseph held his mother with a feigned calm, but his mind was raging. Joseph was sure that his father would want only the best for Larry, and he was just as sure that if it were he instead of Larry slipping toward the edge Patrick Flynn would be totally unconcerned. He spoke softly to his mother. "Mom, I know that Dad thinks he's doing the right thing by listening to Doctor Benson, but he's believing what he wants to believe, and Benson is just telling him what he wants to hear. Joseph's voice grew more firm. "But you gotta understand one thing. He's so concerned with his and Larry's image, he's going to continue to believe that Larry's all right."

Anna listened intently to what Joseph was saying.

"We've gotta have someone look at him and give him the attention he needs before it's too late," Joe said. "That's all I'm saying. I don't really care about him. It's you I'm concerned with. If Larry does get worse it's going to upset you. That's what I'm concerned about."

"Thank you, Joey," Anna said. "I'm happy you feel that way about me, but you shouldn't be so callous about your brother. He's sick, and if he's sick bad, he needs your help and understanding Don't be so cruel. He loves you. He always loved you!"

Joseph knew it wasn't the proper time for an argument concerning Larry's love or hate for him. He smiled at his mother.

"Okay, Ma," he said, "Maybe he'll snap out of it.... I'll do all I can."

Anna smiled and squeezed his hand, They sat quietly in the darkened room for a long while, neither of them saying anything; both of them lost in the reverie of their own private thoughts.

5

OVER the subsequent several weeks Joseph diligently tried to help Larry. In the light of the hatred he felt for him, his effort was extraordinary. He stayed home far more often than usual, forcing conversations and using his imagination to activate his brother out of the strange lethargic state that enveloped him. Larry's condition appeared to improve and Anna Flynn noticed the developments. It created a new energy in her and she was laughing again.

It was a late afternoon in December. Snow was falling, heavily coating the countryside in a cloak of brightness.

Christmas was barely a week away and a spirit of holiday filled the Flynn household. Patrick was thrilled with Larry's improvement and was constantly reiterating how he always knew everything would work out. He even found occasion to speak to Joseph and discuss Larry's condition. Those conversations were generally one-sided with Joseph playing the role of listener, unable as always to find any common ground with his father.

Joseph intently read the afternoon newspaper and was unaware of his father's presence in the parlor.

"I want to talk to you a minute," Patrick said.

Joseph looked up at the powerful figure before him. His father looked handsome and impressive in a business suit, a frame that belied his middle age. Joseph put down the newspaper.

"What is it?" Joseph asked.

"I've got to go downtown, Your mother is busy with dinner, so I'd like you to go up and sit with Larry a while."

"Yeah, okay," Joseph said.

Patrick sat himself on the arm of the chair. "I'm having people over tonight, so count on staying home and keeping Larry company. If someone's not with him, he might get irritated, and I don't want any problems here."

Joseph's face mirrored his annoyance, "Look, I have a date with Carol tonight. We planned—"

Before Joe could finish his statement, his father interrupted in a low, harsh voice. "Look, don't give me any of your goddamn plans or bullshit. You're staying home and that's it!"

Joseph realized that an improvement in Larry or his mother's happiness, and the holidays, together couldn't masquerade for long, the ugly truth of his father's personality.

"Your mother will be down here with the guests all night and there's not anyone else to stay with him. Larry seems comfortable with you. So that's it. That leaves you and you're staying. I don't want to hear any more about it." As far as Patrick Flynn was concerned the conversation was over. He got up and walked toward the front door,

"Wait a minute," Joseph said, "I want to say something."

Joseph stood up and walked toward his father, Christmas music hummed from the radio, and the distant chattering of his mother and Aunt Gena faintly drifted into the room from the kitchen. Patrick's eyes were hard and squinting as he watched his son approach.

"We've gotta straighten something out," Joseph said.

"Like what?" Patrick asked.

"Like I'm tired of playing Larry's handmaiden." Joseph said. "I've gone as far as I'm going to go, being his nursemaid. It's time to stop babying him and treat him like a man."

Patrick reached out and grabbed Joe's arm. His grip was tight with his building violence.

"Listen! I don't need any advice from you. Just do what I said and shut up!" Patrick said.

Joseph jerked his arm away. "Oh yeah, I forgot. I'm supposed to shut up, I'm supposed to screw up my life for that baby upstairs." Joseph's words were quick, one stumbling over the other, trying to say everything that had to be said. "For one thing, Larry's not comfortable with me. We can't stand each other, and the only reason he wants me around is the same reason he wants anybody around, so someone is there to cater to him. As long as he thinks someone is feeling sorry for him, he's satisfied."

Patrick was stunned at his son's sudden verbosity. He remained quiet and clenched his teeth allowing Joseph to continue. "Yeah, that's right," Joseph said, "Leave him alone for a couple of hours and he's right back to his whining self. Well, I'm telling you, I've had it. I'm finished with this nonsense. He wouldn't do it for me if the situation were reversed, so I'm through with this hypocrite shit."

As Joseph spoke his voice grew louder. His father shoved him, indicating an order for quiet. Patrick listened to the murmur of discussion coming from the kitchen. When he was certain the women weren't listening he turned back to Joseph.

"Listen to your mother in there. She's happy. Do you want to spoil everything for her?" he said, in a quiet voice that carried a nuance of warning.

"Oh Jesus, don't give me that!" Joseph said. "Since when are you concerned about her? Cut the shit! All you're concerned with is a successful party to impress your phony friends. If you were worried about Ma you'd knock these rotten parties out. They only upset her and she's not up to runnin' around and catering to those bastards."

Patrick roughly grabbed Joseph's neck and jerked him close to his face, "Listen, boy, I'm warning you," Patrick said, "I'll break you in half."

It was difficult for Joseph to speak. His father's grip was like a vise on his neck, but he managed to spit out the venom. "That's right, Break me in two. That's it. Break me in two. It's always bust me up and kiss the pansy's ass." Joseph emitted a derisive laugh, "And you expect me to nursemaid him? Hell. No goddamn chance." Patrick continued to hold Joe tightly at the neck. "If you cared a damn about him or Ma you'd have a half-decent doctor look at him, instead of your goofball Benson."

Joseph said, "You know damn well he'll say anything to make you satisfied. Get a goddamn psychiatrist or somebody to look at Larry. That's what the jerk really needs ..."

Patrick opened the front door with his free hand. He yanked Joseph toward the porch and softly closed the door behind them. The clean coldness of the air rushed Into Joseph's face. The outside grounds were filled with grey, leafless trees, and all vestiges of green were hidden by the snow's blanket. There was no one present, except Joseph and his father. and except for Patrick's heavy breath there wasn't a sound.

The momentary silence was broken by Patrick's threatening voice, "You sonofabitch," he said. He pushed Joseph's back against the house. Joseph felt the frigid contact as it passed sharply through his thin shirt, "I'm not listening to any more of your garbage," Patrick said, "If you're not home with Larry tonight, I'll kill you."

His father's strength was building in an even flow with his mounting anger. "Now I'm tellin' you," Patrick continued, "be here. Just be here. If you value your skin, be in this house with your brother tonight." He shoved Joseph free. "Now get back in the friggin' house before I kill you right here and now." Joseph held back an overwhelming desire to attack him. Turning his back to his father he reentered the house. He stood for a minute in the foyer, trying to compose himself. Perspiration dotted his forehead and upper lip. His face was pallid. He trembled as a violent chill passed through him.

Joseph picked up the phone and dialed Carol's number. When she realized it was Joe speaking to her, Carol's voice grew in excitement. "What's up, honey?" she asked,

"It's about tonight," Joseph replied. He went on and explained what had happened, Carol tried to hide her disappointment. "Would you like me to come over to your place tonight?" she asked. He felt sick in his stomach, "No. No. I'll call you later." Carol was disappointed to the point of tears, but she carefully camouflaged her feelings by managing to keep her voice light and pleasant, "Okay, hon," she said. "Okay, I'll be waiting."

Joseph appreciated her understanding. Carol always understood. "I love you, baby," he whispered.

"I love you too," she softly kissed into the phone.

Joseph hung up and walked slowly across the parlor. He had just sat down when his Aunt Gena entered the room,

"Supper's almost ready, baby," she smiled.

"Yeah, okay," Joseph replied, "but I'm not hungry," He closed his eyes and tiredly leaned back into the chair,

Gena could sense trouble in Joseph's attitude, "What's the matter, honey?" she asked, as she crouched down near him, resting her hand on his arm.

"It's nothing, Gena, I'm just not too hungry, that's all."

"Where's your father?" she asked, immediately sensing the root of her nephew's problem. "I heard his voice just a while ago. Where is he?"

"He just left," Joseph replied. "I guess he walked down to the front gate. Manley must be picking him up. He mentioned something about the office; I suppose it's business as usual."

Joseph's voice was spiced with an edge of sarcasm,

"Why that ingrate!" Gena said, "Your Ma and I are in there slaving to prepare dinner and he just leaves without as much as a word." Her voice was angry. "Didn't he say what was so important?"

"No, he didn't," Joseph said, "He just left, that's all. And I'm glad he did."

Gena looked at Joseph. Her eyes were filled with a lifetime of understanding. "C'mon, Joe," she said. "What happened? I know damn well something happened. Tell me. Maybe it'll help." Joseph abruptly stood up and walked over to the huge stone fireplace. Resting his elbow against the edge of the mantle, he turned his head and looked at Gena. "He ordered me to stay here with Larry tonight, you know. It's the usual garbage. He's having friends over." The side of Joseph's mouth twitched. "I had plans but that doesn't make any difference. You know how he is," he said. Joseph walked back to where Gena was standing. His face was burning with anger, "It's not my damn plans I'm pissed off about. I'm just sick and tired of letting goddamn Larry and his lousy problems run my life."

Gena was about to say something but Joseph didn't stop. "Look! He's okay now, and whether he is or not, I've had enough," He looked at Gena with eyes begging for some measure of understanding. "Gena, if Larry needs anymore help, none of us in this house can give it to him. Personally, I don't care. I never did and I never will. It's only Ma I care about. If he's not permanently over this thing, then he needs professional help and it isn't going to come from a jerk like Doc Benson."

"But Joey!" Gena's voice contained a nuance of surprise. "Larry seems to be a hundred percent better. How can you say none of us has helped him, especially you. All the attention you've shown him has worked. He's like a new kid," she said. "Anyone can see that."

"Sure, sure," Joe replied, his arms angrily waving in the air, "as long as we're all kissing his ass and feeling sorry for him. Look, Aunt Gena, that guy just likes pity. I'm pretty well damn sure there's nothin' wrong. Whenever we let him go for an hour or two he's back to the same nonsense, so you've got to wonder sometimes if it's really on the level." Joseph's voice went on with its rising and dropping inflections. "The only way to find out is to send him somewhere or bring a decent doctor in, or some goddamn thing." He disgustedly sat back down in the chair.

Gena looked at him with concern. "What do you have against Doctor Benson?" she asked. "He's a good doctor and he's been with the family for years. What is it that bothers you so much about him?"

Joseph rested his forehead on his hands. His voice was a monotone and displaced as if he were speaking to himself. "I've heard a hundred stories," Joe said, "a hundred lousy stories about him. I've overheard the guys say that he's one of Dad's lackeys." Joseph looked up at Gena. "C'mon, Aunt Gena," he said, "you're not going to tell me you haven't heard the stories."

Gena didn't reply.

"How did Larry stay out of Korea?" Joe asked. "Answer that for me. How did he stay out?"

"Well, I ..."

Before Gena could finish, Joseph interrupted, "You know damn well how," he said. "It was Doc Benson making up that phony story about Larry's ear drum. That was a crock, wasn't it Gena? Wasn't it?" Joe's voice was loud and demanding.

"Shhhh, for God's sake, Joe. Don't let your Ma hear." Gena's eyes darted toward the kitchen.

Joseph rubbed his hands over his eyes and looked toward the kitchen with concern. He lowered his voice to a whisper. "Well, c'mon. Level with me. You've heard them too. Haven't you?"

"Yes, I have and so what?" Gena's voice was defiant. "Your father did what a lot of others did. He had money and connections and he kept his son out of it. So what?" she said,

"So what!" Joe replied in an incredulous, loud whisper. "So what!" He shook his head in disgust.

"Yeah, so what!" Gena repeated. "Stuff like that is done all the time. Your father did enough for his country and their wars. I don't blame him for keeping Larry out of it,"

"Does Larry know?" Joe asked.

"Of course not, it would kill him," she responded.

"I don't know about that," Joe said, "He was always a coward. I don't think knowing about it would upset him that much." Joseph went quiet and for a moment was lost in thought. "No, I really don't think it would," he said.

"Did anyone ever say that in front of him?" Gena inquired,

"No, I don't think so," Joe replied. "At least he never mentioned it to me."

"Well, it doesn't matter if they did or not. There's no way they could know about it for sure. We can always disregard it as a stupid rumor," Gena said.

Joseph stood up and looked squarely at his aunt. "Do you think he would've done the same for me?" he asked.

"What ...," Gena said.

"Do you think he would've tried to keep me out of Korea?" Joseph paused and waited. Gena didn't answer. "You bet your ass he wouldn't!" Joseph said. "You goddamn bet your ass." He turned around and looked out the window.

Gena walked up behind him and wrapped her arms around him. Joseph's voice continued in a low, dull tone, "And there were other things, like Dad seeing to it that Benson became county coroner, and getting his stupid son into medical school. That's how father returned the favor."

Gena smiled softly against her nephew's neck. "Joe," she said, "your father is the political boss of this county. He made Dr. Benson coroner because it was good politics."

"Was it good politics to make him wealthy in real estate too?" Joseph asked in a sarcastic voice. "Was that part of good politics too?"

"No," Gena whispered. "That was just good investing. My brother is as sharp in real estate as he is in politics and beer distributing. It's just part of the good genes he's got."

Joseph was annoyed with the note of amusement that ran through Gena's voice. "Look, Aunt Gena," he said, "This is no joke. My father's a crook and he's surrounded with parasites like Benson, who's no better than he is, and he's got a son upstairs who's half nuts because he's driven him to it by trying to make him something he's not. It's no joke."

"Joe, honey," Gena said, "Larry's upstairs, a little sick because he's tryin' a little too hard to accomplish something he wants real bad." Gena's voice was low and steady. "He's tryin' to make your father proud and everybody else proud, and I told you before, he knows damn well that his father doesn't hold him in any special light." Gena's tone turned gentle in thinking of Larry. "The poor kid knows the story pretty damn well. It's time you tried to understand a little bit."

Joseph broke away from Gena and walked a few steps away. "Don't start," be said with his back turned. "Don't start with that nonsense about Dad being jealous of me and Ma. Just don't start, I don't want to hear any of it," he said. "It's time you faced it and realized that he hates me. That's all there is to it, and he thinks Larry is hot shit. That's it and I don't want to hear any more of that other garbage about Ma and me."

Gena heard Anna's voice as she loudly called them to dinner. Soon Larry would be coming downstairs, and it was not the time to continue the conversation. She walked over and gently touched Joe's arm. "Let's go in and enjoy your mama's dinner," she smiled.

Joseph allowed some of the tension to recede from his taut muscles. As they both approached the archway, Gena was silently thankful for the radio's Christmas songs that surely prevented Anna from hearing their conversation. Gena tried to change Joe's mood, "By the way, pretty nephew, have you heard the news?" she laughed.

"What news?"

"Tom got rid of our old stinkeroo car. He found a nice used one. We should have it any day now," she said. "We had that Buick for over ten years."

For an instant Joe's brain whirled back to his first memory of that bright black Buick on the evening of his father's return from the Army hospital. The taste in his mouth went bitter, as he remembered the first time he saw him walking that long ago driveway. Gena's laugh intruded on his thoughts. "I'm goin' to learn how to drive it and take you and our gang to midnight Mass. How about that!" she said in a happy voice.

Joseph looked at her, one of the saviors of his life. He reached out and tightly swept his arm around her. he laughed. "You bet, babe," he laughed. "You bet."

6

IT HAD SNOWED heavily all through the month of December. On the twenty second of the month, another snowfall was threatening.

Hanway road maintenance couldn't keep up with the elements and layers of thick ice coated the roads. The roar of racing car engines and the squeal of tires spinning on the slick streets disturbed the evening quiet. Many of the homes were dressed for the holiday celebration. Colored lights surrounded by artificial holly framed windows and doorways. Front yard evergreens, heavy with snow, blinked in a rhythm of red and green, gigantic icicles hung from the eaves, and in every home, Christmas trees were lit up and the fragrance of pine filled the parlors.

Tom Conroy walked back from the window and poured himself a shot of whiskey. "Did you see it out there? That's what winter should always look like."

Gena hugged him, "But it's freeeeezing," she said.

"What the hell. It gives you the holiday spirit."

"Brrrrr, it's freezing."

Tom laughed. "Ah, you're like a baby. You don't know what cold is." He sat down in the chair near the window. He looked out onto the street as he sipped his drink.

Gena placed herself in his lap. "C'mon, honey, you promised" she said.

"But you said it's freezing."

"C'mon," she laughed.

"You mean you don't think it's too cold?"

"C'mon. I need the practice."

"Naw, it's nice in here. Let's stay in, You can drive tomorrow.

"I'm going to look like a monkey on Christmas Eve trying to park that car in front of the church."

"Don' t worry about it. I'll drive."

"No, you won't. I promised the kids and Anna that I'd drive to Mass. Now don't ruin it."

"Drive them next year."

"C'mon, Tommy. I'm serious. It's only three days away. I need the practice."

"Okay, okay. Tomorrow you'll practice. I promise."

"Oh, bullshit. Then tomorrow it'll be something else. You'll be too tired. God, you've only had me out two or three times. We're wasting my permit. C'mon."

Torn placed the empty glass on the floor and wrapped his arms around her. "Okay, you spoiled brat. Let's go out and freeze our asses off."

Gena let out a whoop and jumped off his lap. "Where's the keys?"

"They're in my coat pocket. I'll get them," he said.

"No, I will! I will!" She ran in the direction of the hallway like a happy child. Tom stood up and stretched. "You picked a beauty of a night. It's slippery as hell out there."

"Don't worry about it. Nobody'll be on the road and you'll be in the hands of a pro."

Tom smiled to himself as Gena's words, filled with excitement and delight, drifted in from the hallway.

Lobo Pagnozzi shivered in the face of the freezing wind.

He stood on the sidewalk in front of Bill's Pool Room. He bent his head and tried hard to hear Mickey Clark's voice coming from the den of shouts and noise. He walked up onto the porch and stood on his tiptoes, enabling him to look over the window's painted sign.

His eyes quickly scanned the interior. Mickey wasn't there.

Lobo began to walk toward the railroad station and its old, battered entrance which would offer some protection against the cold. His hands were numb and his threadbare overcoat provided little or no protection from the battering winter night. He stopped for a moment and looked at the late-model car parked a little down the road from the pool hall. His freezing fingers worked at the door handle. The car wasn't locked. Lobo quickly moved himself onto the front seat and slammed the door, feeling instant relief from the frigid wind that swept the length of Main Street. He rubbed his hands together and the steam escaping from his mouth coated the inside of the windshield with a covering of mist. At first he didn't see them, but finally his eyes caught the glint of metal hanging from the steering column. He leaned over and touched the keys. He laughed to himself. "He left the keys." He laughed again. Without thinking about it, Lobo slipped behind the wheel and turned the key. The engine of the car coughed once or twice before emitting a steady, soft hum.

Many years had passed since Lobo felt the steering wheel of a car in his eager hands. At first, he negotiated the car slowly around town. As he drove, he thought about years long behind him. His mind was filled with a mental picture of himself at twenty-one.

Cars, cars. He lived for them. He was the best man behind the wheel he ever knew. His hands were magic on an engine. He could do anything with an automobile—fix it, drive it, command it. He saw himself on the race track near the lake up in the mountains: the dust, the swerve and screeching cars. the trophies and respect. He could handle any turn and move ahead in the straight-aways. He could feel the dust and sweat, the satisfaction. "Lobo, you were on two wheels!" "Unbelievable!" "How did you run it up so hard?" "You're the best!" "You're the best!" "You're the best!"

The words drummed in his head and he felt the swell of his heart. He rubbed his hands along the steering wheel and his foot applied mere pressure to the accelerator.

He brought the car around the curve of Birch Street. He saw the macadam stretched out before him, three hundred yards of straight road. He pressed his foot to the floor. The car swerved on the ice but Lobo's deft hands, even after years and years of idleness, brought it under quick control. The machine had barely moved at full throttle for fifty yards and he saw the needle pointing at seventy-five. With his left hand he rolled down the window and listened to the freezing wind roar past his ear. He felt real again. He belonged again. The stop sign loomed ahead and the car was pushing one hundred. He expertly worked the brake and wheel as he approached the sign. The wheels locked, but the car slid quickly forward, past the corner and out onto Hill Street. He saw the snow-coated sidewalk and house looming before him. Again he quickly worked the brake and steering wheel and the car fish-tailed to a halt in the ditch before the sidewalk.

He gunned the machine and wildly pulled his arms to the right. The car jumped out of the ditch, sweeping in a complete circle. Exhaust gusted from its tail and it pushed, in a jerk, straight ahead. For a moment, the back wheels spun. The front end of the car turned back toward the sidewalk. Lobo hit the clutch and spun them again. He hit the clutch and shifted fast and the car went forward in a straight line. He slammed the gas pedal, and once again he was at breakneck speed.

Tom and Gena slowly walked out to the front sidewalk. Tom buttoned the top of his jacket and took a long. deep breath. "Ah, it smells good." He flexed his muscles.

"Jesus, don't get carried away," Gena laughed. She put her arm in his and shivered. "Brother, it's really cold. Maybe we should have waited until tomorrow."

"What?"

"I'm only kidding. I really do want to drive."

"Let's go back in."

"No, c'mon, you know I was only kidding."

Tom turned around. "Let's go back in."

"Don't you dare, Tom Conroy!"

Tom gave her a slap on the butt. "You go back in. I'll warm the car up for you."

"Well, well. Aren't you considerate? You sly bastard. If I go in the house, you'll be right behind me."

"Well, goddamn it. It's too cold!"

"Once we get in the car and get moving, everything'll be fine. Let's go. Let's go."

Tom put his arm around her waist and they walked onto the street. Tom stopped and looked at the car parked on the other side. "Isn't it beautiful?" he said.

Gena looked at the dark sleek lines of the late model Pontiac. "It is, it's gorgeous."

"We waited long enough to get it," he said.

"I'll only drive it once in a while."

"Oh, c'mon, honey. You'll drive it as much as you want."

"Which key is it?"

"The long one."

Gena fumbled the keys in her hand, They slipped from her fingers and fell on the road.

"Clumsy bitch," Tom laughed.

Gena crouched down to pick them up. She looked up at him. "Clumsy my ass. Before I'm finished, I'll make you look sick driving that car."

"Oh shit, that'll be the day." Tom's laughter rang out into the quiet night.

Lobo Pagnozzi's eyes were wide and wild as they locked on the street before him. He ran the car from Hill Street and took the Moosic Street corner clean. The car was moving fast. It slid a little to the right before he managed to point the hood straight ahead. As he brought the machine over a little hill, he saw the viaduct some four hundred yards ahead of him. The streets and sidewalks were still. His excitement reached mind-burning height. "By the time I hit Palumbo's, I'll hit a hundred," he thought. "I'll have this baby's ass out as hard as it could move under that viaduct." He never slowed down for the stop sign across from Mickey's Gas Station. As he passed the station his mind raced back to what seemed like another world, another place. He remembered Mickey standing on that same corner, screaming at him to slow down, to stop. On that winter afternoon, he wasn't racing to the viaduct, but was determined instead to cut the corner at Bridge Street, with his brand new Oldsmobile at full throttle.

He'd done it, too. He remembered. He cut that corner clean. Maybe a little skid. Maybe a little shaky, but he cut it. He remembered Mickey's face when he got back, white, perspired, scared, "You stupid nut." That's what Mickey said. "You stupid nut." Lobo laughed out loud as he remembered. Good old Mickey. The corner of Bridge Street was just ahead. "I could still do it," Lobo thought. "I could, I could." The streaking car was approaching Palumbo's bar. The corner was directly ahead. "I could, I could." He adjusted himself quickly in the seat and held his breath. He swung his arms and hit the brake hard. The car flew around the corner. It began to slide toward the sidewalk at furious speed.

He waited the necessary second and floored the pedal. The car straightened. Its speed was blinding. Lobo smiled and his heart pounded. "I could, I could, I knew it. Goddamn, I knew it."

He gripped the wheel with all his strength. The road ahead was a blur in the excitement. Suddenly the machine's tail went into a skid on a solid long patch of ice. Lobo worked the wheel wildly. First to the right. To the left. He braked hard. The car couldn't stop. He couldn't control it. The brakes sent out a loud screech. Lobo's mouth went dry as the automobile began to go into a violent spinning circle. Lobo couldn't see anything.

He couldn't do anything. The car kept spinning and spinning in a forward motion.

Tom was laughing and Gena was still crouched, picking up the keys, when they heard the whining, ugly screeching. Tom turned quickly to the sound and almost slipped on the ice. Gena looked too, but saw nothing, Tom's body blocked the view of what was coming.

"Jesus Christ!" Tom screamed. He turned back to Gena and in

one movement grabbed her arm and pulled her upright. She saw it then. The large car, like a whirling hulk, was coming at them. She tried to scream but no sound came. Tom jerked her toward the sidewalk. There was no sound. except for the screaming menace at their heels. Gena slipped and fell, bringing Tom down on top of her. Before they could move again a ton and a half of metal smashed over them, crushing them against the iced pavement. The car kept spinning, spinning. It collided with the Pontiac and drove it up onto the sidewalk, a pile of shredded metal. It continued to spin and severed a telephone pole and rammed over a metal fence like it was butter. Finally, it came to a grinding battered halt in the Conroy's front yard.

7

THE SNOW began to fall in lazy, large flakes. The wind drifted them in waves across the Flynn estate. Patrick sat staring into the flames of the fireplace. His head rested against the back of the chair as he absentmindedly took deep drags from a cigarette. His arms hung like two oaks along the armrests. There was a perceptible chill in the room, but even in the thin undershirt that covered his torso, he seemed not to notice.

Bill Manley applied the bellows to the flame. "It's gettin' a little chilly, Boss."

"Throw a log or two on."

Bill added one of the chunks of wood that rested against the fireplace. "Boy, I can't get over this place. It's really something."

"Yeah, it's nice. I deserve it."

Bill smiled. "Yeah, you do."

"Bet your ass."

"The committee meeting is set for nine. Ya gonna get ready?"

"Relax. We've got time. Let's just relax a while."

Patrick listened to Anna rustling about upstairs. "That goddamn lady is always doing something."

"She's a good lady."

"I suppose."

"Shit, Boss, you're awfully rough on her. I mean she's a good lady. She's a good wife."

"She's no wife at all."

"Whadaya mean?"

"Never mind what I mean, Bill. Just shut up. I don't need your opinions on it."

"Okay. I sorry. I just meant…"

137

"I know what you meant. Now shut up."

For a moment there was an embarrassing silence. Patrick walked over and patted Bill Manley's shoulder.

"Forget what I said, buddy. I just don't like talking about it, you know."

"Yeah. Right."

"I don't tell you everything, Billy. There's a lot I don't talk about."

"Yeah, okay. Let's forget it, Boss."

"No. let me tell you something as an example. I haven't made love to the lady in over ten years."

Bill Manley poked at the flames, pretending he hadn't heard. "Ten lousy years. No, she's no wife to me. She hasn't been in a long, long time."

Bill turned and looked at him. "Then why do you keep her? I mean why do you stay with her?"

"I don't like the idea of anyone else having her," Patrick replied.

"Oh shit, Pat. She'd never ..."

"Bullshit! No woman would never do that. Don't shit yourself. My youngest kid has had her for a long time."

"Oh Jesus, Boss. Goddamn, don't say a rotten thing like that."

"I don't mean that, you goddamn idiot. I mean in other ways."

"Whadaya mean?"

"There's a lot of ways you can have somebody, not necessarily sex all the time. He has her in other ways. He's her number one boy."

"You don't like the kid, Boss. Why?"

"That's why! That's why! On account of him, she's different. Has been ever since he was born. I don't know what he's got, but she's wrapped herself around him."

"Jesus, he's her kid."

"The other goofball up there is her kid too. She's not wrapped around him. Never was."

"Larry's a good kid."

"He's a pain in my ass. That's what he is."

"Larry?"

"Yeah, Larry. He's upstairs sulking right now, like a goddamn screwball."

"Shit, you always liked him."

"The hell I did. I put up with the little bastard."

"Let's forget it, Boss."

"No, you brought the subject up. Now I'll talk about it for a while, I'll fill your newsy ears."

"I didn't mean…"

"He's a pain in my ass. That's what he is, with his crying and nerves. What I'd like to do is go up in that goddamn room and kick his ass down the steps. The goddamn sissy, I'd love to kick his ass."

"Maybe you'd help him if you did."

"Help him, shit. I can't stand a pantywaist punk like that. I'd kick him in the ass real good."

"Well, what's stopping you?"

"The other jerk. That's what's stopping me."

"Joe?"

"I wouldn't give him the satisfaction, I've been bugging his useless ass for years by being nice to the other one. I wouldn't give him the satisfaction."

"Why? Boss, what the hell is wrong?"

"Look, Bill, I'm screwin' ten different broads a week. I screw Lila inside out. But don't kid yourself. It don't mean nothin'. The woman upstairs is the only one who ever got to me and I'll never get over her. Goddamn it, I'll never get over her but we're dead. You know what I mean?"

"Yeah, but why? I mean, shit."

"She gave it to me good. Joe? Joe, well she could have him, but she'll never have me now. A cold day in hell. She'll never have me again."

"Well, why didn't you clear out a long time ago?"

"Coupla' reasons. One, in this town, if you get divorced, you're marked. I can't afford that. Business is too good.

"Two. I just couldn't do it. Shit, man, I've gotta' have her around.

I've gotta see her."

"You've got a real problem," .

"No problem at all. No fuckin' problem. I've got all of them screwed up. They're under my thumb. Before I'm finished with them, they'll be worn down. I'll kill them all."

"You don't want to do that."

"Shit, I don't but I'll do it my own way. I'm doin' it every day. Are you blind?"

"I don't see the point, Boss. Honest to God, I don't."

"Ah, frig it. Don't tell me you're getting soft. Listen, Billy. None of 'em are any good. I tried, I did. Shit, when I got home I was a good father, a good man, but what did it get me? Anna never straightened out. She didn't give me enough time but I paid her back. I paid her back. What the hell, I tried. But it was always Joe this and Joe that. Well, now she's got the little punk but she doesn't have me. Never will."

"She didn't mean nothin', Boss."

"Shit. Shit, she didn't mean nothing. Your man is your man. You don't pass him by for kids or anything else. Oh, what the hell, I never gave a shit for the kids anyway, they got in the way all the time, I mean I don't have time for kids and their fuckin' two-bit problems. At first it was nice, I was glad to be home. I had big plans. In the beginning the kids were all right but I got over it fast. They were in the goddamn way. And then her waitin' on Joe hand and foot finished it. My nerves couldn't take it."

"But Larry. You …"

"Shit, he was in the way too, but he was useful. I bust the other guy's balls every day with him."

"He's a nice kid."

"Nice! Take a look at him. He's a piss-eyed sissy, for Christ sake. Are you blind?"

"Anna loves the kids. That doesn't mean that she doesn't love you too."

"Ah, what the hell, A friggin' lamebrain like you can't figure nothin' out. Shut up and let's forget it."

Bill Manley didn't like insults but he silently swallowed them.

"She thinks a lot of Larry too, doesn't she?"

"Oh, Jesus yes. She likes him. She caters to him, too. But nothin' like the other one. Nothin' like that. One of these days I'll punch his..."

Patrick's voice was interrupted by the shrill ring of the phone. He walked over and lifted it off the receiver. "Pat Flynn here." After the greeting he held the phone to his ear and said nothing.

Bill Manley looked at him. Pat remained silent. His jaw locked and his eyes shifted from one position to another.

"What's up, Boss?"

Patrick slowly raised his hand to indicate quiet. A full minute passed before he uttered any sound. Finally he said, "Uh huh. Right. Yes. Yes. We'll be there in a little while." He slowly set the phone back into its cradle. He stared at the floor for a moment before looking at Bill. "That was the Clarkson Hospital," Patrick said.

"What? What's the matter?" Bill Manley knew there was something terribly wrong.

"It's my sister. She and her husband were hurt. Hurt bad."

"How bad?"

"They're dead."

"Jesus Christ. How?"

"They were run down by a car right in front of their house. Call Anna downstairs."

After he told her what happened, she began to scream.

Patrick and Manley forced her onto the couch, She continued to scream.

Joe burst from the basement and ran into the parlor.

"What's the matter? Jesus Christ, what's wrong?"

Patrick told him.

The impact of his father's voice staggered him. He lurched over to the couch and fell into a sitting position alongside his mother. His mind was in such ferment he no longer heard her screams,

JERRY FAGNANI

Anna's eyes rolled back and she collapsed into a lopsided position,

"Jesus, Pat, she fainted." Bill said.

Joseph didn't notice his mother's condition. He just sat there staring at nothing,

"Go in the kitchen! Get some water!" Patrick said.

In a burst of excitement Bill Manley rushed toward the kitchen.

"Go up and get your brother!" Pat said in a hoarse voice.

Joseph didn't answer.

Patrick pulled him by his shirt and tore him from the couch. "Goddamn. I said get your brother down here!"

Joseph pushed his father away and ran up the stairs.

When Joe rushed into his brother's room. Larry was lying on the bed. "Joe, what's wrong? What's wrong down there?"

His voice was shaking. In the dull light of the room Joseph saw the tears filling Larry's eyes.

For once, Joe's voice lacked its usual sarcasm. "C'mon, get up. We're going to Clarkson."

"Why?"

"Aunt Gena and Uncle Tom were in an accident. C'mon."

"Are they hurt bad?" Larry was beginning to sob.

Joseph couldn't tell him. The words wouldn't come, "I don't know. Just c'mon."

8

THE HOSPITAL corridor was a bustle of activity. Nurses and doctors moved quickly under the harshness of the fluorescent lights. Patrick and Joseph were rushed into a side room off the hall. The room was small, containing a desk and two chairs. Joseph looked around the tiny space; a bulletin board with old, yellowed, edge-curled papers taped to its surface, hung on the wall behind the desk. He saw a telephone, a desk calendar; sheets hadn't been torn away from the calendar in months. July 1 was emblazoned in large, black letters across the top sheet. He looked over a work schedule pasted to the stained blotter on the desk. His eyes scanned the room again and again. He refused to think of the corridor activity or what was held in the rooms beyond. Instead he attended to schedules that meant nothing, names he didn't know, notices he didn't care about. He read everything. He looked at and touched any tiling in reach, anything that might blot out the horror of the moment.

The nurse walked into the room and softly closed the door behind her. She looked at Patrick. "Mr. Flynn," she said quietly.

"If you would please identify them."

"Yes."

They walked out of the room leaving Joseph alone. Bill Manley, earlier, had returned both Anna and Larry to the house. Patrick had told Larry just prior to entering the hospital that Gena and Tom were dead. Upon hearing that he refused to go inside; he cried, he screamed. His carrying on caused Anna, who was doing her best to compose herself, to collapse in Bill Manley's arms. Patrick ordered Bill to take them back home. "Stay with them!" Patrick ordered. "Stay with them!"

At the time the words had almost escaped Joseph's mouth before he managed to smother them. "Call Gena! Call Gena! She'll take care of things. Call Gena!" But there was no Gena and now the words pounded in his temples.

He stood fidgeting in the room. He looked at the notices again, but he could no longer block it out. The thought of her, her and Uncle Tom. He fell against the wall and his knees buckled. The sobs came, harsh and violent. He wanted to scream. He began punch the hard, plaster wall with all his strength. He punched until the pain turned his arm stiff. He sat behind the large desk and rested his forehead on his arm.

He stood up when his father returned.

"Do you want to see them?" Patrick asked.

"No."

"Well, if you do ..."

"I don't! Goddamn Jesus Christ, I don't."

"Okay. C'mon."

Outside the hospital two of Patrick's friends waited behind the wheel of an enormous black sedan. The car was as quiet as stone all the way back.

"Anna will be all right. Both of them will. They're sedated and sleeping." Dr. Benson's voice was tense.

"Yeah, okay," Patrick said.

"My wife will stay with them. She's a nurse. She's going to stay the night," Benson said.

Patrick emitted a long sigh. "Yeah, okay."

Joseph went into the downstairs bathroom and threw up for the third time. When he returned to the parlor, Patrick Manley and Benson were putting on their coats.

Joseph looked at Manley. "What's up? Where you going?" Patrick walked to the front door.

"Where are you going, goddammit?"

Patrick stood before the door, not turning around.

"We won't be long, kid. Your dad's got a meeting. It's important and he's late. We won't be long," Bill said.

Joseph looked at his father's back. "Fucker!" he shouted.

His father turned around. "Somebody else'll be dead tonight if you don't shut up."

"Fuck, fucker!"

Patrick moved quickly toward Joe but Bill intercepted him.

He held on tight to Patrick's shoulders. Doctor Benson stood with his head down and said nothing.

"C'mon. Boss. We've all had enough tonight. Let's go," Bill said.

Patrick clenched his teeth and glared at his son. "Lousy little bastard! You lousy goddamn little bastard!"

Manley and Benson half-shoved him out to the porch. Joseph stood alone for a long time looking at the door after it slammed behind them. "Fuckin' dirty fuckin' fuckin' rat!" A wave of nausea struck him again. He turned and quickly walked to the bathroom.

9

HE THREE men walked slowly into the large, one-roomed
building. The room was filled with men. No one was sitting.
Wooden chairs lined the walls. A long table, with chairs
neatly arranged alongside it, stood in the center of the hall. An
immense framed picture of Franklin Roosevelt overlooked the assembly. On the wall facing the main entrance, an old sign, tattered
and fading, identified the Third Ward Democratic Club.

Patrick Flynn was immediately separated from Manley and
Doctor Benson. The news of Gena and Tom's deaths had spread
quickly. Each individual member of the group offered their con-
dolences to Patrick. He grasped their hands and shook his head,
speaking to each of them in a hushed voice. Patrick waited for what
seemed like a reasonable period before calling the meeting to order.

He took the floor and went over the excellent results of the past
November election, but he wasted little time in getting to the real
reason of the meeting. "I've got the list of the May primary candidates in front of me," he said. "It's a strong list and we're going
to be in great shape with it. Bill will give you all a sheet with the
names I've chosen for the available offices."

He nodded to Manley, and Bill quickly moved along the table
handing a typed sheet of paper to each member. The men perused
the infomation before turning back to Patrick's voice. "I would like
a unanimous agreement here," he said.

The assembly raised their arms in unison, giving him the time-
worn sign of unity.

Patrick Flynn smiled. "Thank you. Thank you," he said.

The group stood up and gave their chairman a ringing salute
of applause.

"Okay, okay," Patrick yelled in a happy, loud voice. "Our secretary will see that it's all made official. Now we'd better get to the booze at the back of the room." Once more there was applause as the men pushed back from the table.

In a den of noise, Patrick made his way to Bill Manley. "Bill, take Benson on the side and get that problem straightened out."

"Yeah, Boss,"

"Now! Do it now! "

"Yeah, Boss. Okay."

In a moment Bill Manley and Benson were making their way through the crowd as they headed for the front door. Once outside the men bundled themselves against the cold.

"Now this is the way to get sick," Benson said. "Coming out of a sweat box like that into a night like this."

"Pat wants me to get somethin' checked out with you," Manley said.

"What?"

"There's goin' to be a girl comin' around to your office one of these days, ya know."

"Oh, Jesus, Bill."

"C'mon, Doc, No bullshit, Pat told me to tell you. He doesn't want any problems."

"But I told him last time I wouldn't do it again."

"I know what you told him but the girl will be comin' around and he wants you to take care of her."

"Well, why didn't he tell me himself?"

"Maybe he figured you wouldn't like the idea. He's not in the mood for arguments."

"When did he tell you?"

"Tonight at his place. Not long before he heard the news about Gena."

"I can't go through with it."

"Cut the shit, Doc. Just do it."

"The last time I aborted one of his pigs, she almost bled to death. I mean I'm not good at it. Goddamn it, I'm afraid."

"You've done it enough to be a pro. Whadaya mean you're afraid?"

"I've done it five times. I remember each one. I haven't forgotten any of them. Every time I'm shitting in my pants. Pat's gotta understand. It's not my style. I had bleeding trouble with all of them. Jesus Ohrist, why doesn't he leave those whores alone?"

"What he does is his business. The girl will be over. You'll take care of it then."

"I don't like it. I told him I'd never do it again after the last one. Jesus Christ."

"You'll take care of it, right? I'll tell him everything will be okay, right?"

Benson stared down the long dark street. The steady, frigid wind caused his eyes to smart and tear. "Yes, all right. Tell him I'll take care of it, but Jesus Christ I don't like it."

"I'll tell him." Manley said. "You don't have to say anything about it. You'll only make him nervous if he sees your attitude."

"Well, what in the hell do you expect? How would you like it?"

"Never mind. Doc. I don't feel like hearin' your complaints. We all have to do things we don't like, so cut the shit."

"We don't all have to, you know."

"Don't we?"

"No, we don't."

"Pat wouldn't like hearin' that."

"That's too bad about Pat."

"Oh, is that so?"

"Yes, that's so! I'm sick of putting up with this nonsense. I've repaid him for all his favors. I've more than repaid him."

Manley reached over and harshly grabbed Benson's shoulder. "Shut up! I'm warnin' you, pal. Shut up!"

Benson saw the fury in Bill's eyes. "Well, for God's sake, Bill. You can see my point..."

"I said shut up! I don't see your fuckin' point. I just see that Pat wants you to do somethin' for him and you're goin' to do it. You hear me! You hear me good!"

Benson sighed. "Yes, I hear you."

Manley moved back toward the entrance. "All right, then. Let's get back inside before Pat gets nervous."

Once back in the hall, Manley caught Pat's eye. He gestured to him, confirming that everything was taken care of. Flynn smiled and winked back to Bill before he returned to his conversation

10

THE FUNERAL was held on the day after Christmas. A large throng of people gathered under the tent on the hilltop of St. James Cemetery. It was a biting cold December morning. Joseph was bundled under his thick grey overcoat, and still he shook in the face of the wind. He only half heard the drone of Father Kane's voice as it continued in the prayers for the dead. His eyes scanned the width and breadth of the large cemetery, its headstones grey and white against the winter morning, the frozen snow thick on the ground. And then his eyes moved to the incongruous color of spring—the bright flowers, roses, chrysanthemums, lilies, their bright and various shock of colors lining the two coffins. He felt his mother tremble as she sat in the folding chair before him. None of them were crying now, not Joe, not Anna, not Larry. They had cried and grieved so deeply over the past several days, there was nothing left within them except a silent cry of heartbreak, so profound, it was beyond the description of tears. Joseph felt as if he had been beaten; his body ached with pain. He felt feverish. As hard as he tried, he was unable to attend to the words of the priest, or the stillness of the coffins, Something in his heart refused to accept the evidence of the graveyard's finality. "How in God's name could they be dead?" he thought. "For all eternity, dead and gone." He couldn't imagine. Their voices and laughter forever stilled.

When it was finally over, Joseph supported his mother as they made their way back to the cars lined along the narrow cemetery roadway. He watched his father as he moved down the icy hill. His back was huge and straight. He was surrounded by a swarm of people; they were patting him on the shoulder and whispering to him, their eyes and gestures filled with sympathy. Joe was rushed with a compulsion to attack and destroy that figure of his discontent; for never once, through the entire trauma, had Patrick shed a tear, or show emotion of any kind. Instead, it was the old story of political glad-handing and phony nods of understanding. Even the death of a sister, a sister so fine and decent, it made Joseph's heart tremble. It was the same old Patrick Flynn, the same sad, ugly story. Joseph pulled his mother close.

All of the mourners returned to the Flynn mansion. Patrick hired a caterer to fill the kitchen and hallway with piles of food. A bar was set up in the parlor. The house was filled with people. Joseph sat and watched them eating and laughing; the mourning suddenly passed. The talk was loud now, the phonies had removed their masks and were themselves once again. Except for Anna, who sat immovable as a statue on the couch, and Larry, who predictably ran up to his bedroom fortress. Carol, unable to stand the frozen pain of Joe's face, had gone directly home from the cemetery. The depth of that pain, however, was unable to remove him from the low level of hilarity around him, his father and Manley in the dining room, laughing loudly with their cronies, the animals stuffing themselves with drink and food, almost all of them, friends and intimates of Patrick Flynn. Most of the people from town, as always, uncomfortable amidst the power and wealth of Patrick, had also gone straight home from the burial ceremony.

Those that came to the house sat reverently and quiet, as Joseph knew they would. But the others, they turned his stomach. Gena and Tom wouldn't have even known them, those disciple bastards to his father.

Joe went up to his room and changed his clothes. He slipped into old faded dungarees and a heavy, red, plaid wool shirt. He threw on the brown leather wind breaker. No one noticed as he walked past the noise in the parlor and left the house.

The old Chevy stopped at the base of the hill. Joe looked from the window to the silent summit. There was no one there.

The cemetery was still. The tent had already been removed,

and even from the distance, he discerned the mounds of fresh earth that were piled over the graves. The flowers were absently thrown over the gravesite. As his eyes swept the landscape, he noticed spots of brightness where families had set holiday bouquets against the headstones of loved ones. Around the Flynn plot, there were hundreds of dark footprints in the snow where the crowd had stood and walked only an hour before. But now they were gone, and Gena and Tom were alone; walled away forever from the breath and life of Hanway.

Joseph slowly walked up the hill and sat heavily in the snow alongside the ugly mounds. He thought about what their lives had meant; he would force himself to think about it now, now that it was over and finished. Since they were killed, he was unable to think of their lives. The heartache was too great. His grief so terrible, he could think of nothing but their deaths.

But now, he thought of Gena, and her laugh, and the quick turn of her head whenever she was excited. Her laughter that would turn the worst moments into something tolerable. Her infinite goodness. Her warmth. The decency and magic of her mind. He would miss her. God, how he would miss her. Who would he turn to now? Not Anna. Although Joe loved her more deeply than he had loved his aunt, he knew, from his earliest youth, that his mother could never possess the quiet power of his aunt, for in the worst times of trouble for his family, it was Gena who consistently remained as their savior. He could picture her as she was when he was a child, so beautiful, so fine. The soft touch of her hand on his neck and forehead during all those past, painful hours. He thought of her, and once more, he cried.

From where he sat he could see a panorama of Hanway in the distance. He watched, through misted smarting eyes, the smoke ascend from the chimneys. Far off, he saw the freight train moving past the valley and even at that great distance, he heard the clank and rumble of its journey, the sound of its lonely whistle filtering through the wind. Joseph swallowed hard through the pain in his throat. Gena was dead, and her brother, the man she loved and defended, was alive and laughing, safe and sound in his obscene world. Thinking of such an injustice stilled Joe's sobs and transformed his heart to violent stone. He remembered what his Uncle Tom had said, "He's a selfish man. He doesn't care who he hurts. That's the kind of man he is." The words came as sharp and clear as the night he had heard them, that hot June night that seemed now to be a world ago, when he finally came to really understand the goodness and wise perspective of Aunt Gena's husband. Joseph felt ill, knowing that there would never be such moments again; he would not grow old enjoying his Uncle Tom's companionship and wisdom, not now. Not ever. He remembered more of the conversation from that simmering summer night. "Why the hell don't you move out?" Joseph had asked him, in reference to the house Patrick had practically stolen from Gena.

"Because your aunt loves it here," Tom had answered. "She grew up here. All her life's been here, and to tell you the truth, I like it myself,"

Joseph remembered the words, every word,

Joseph idly ran his finger through the snow as he recalled the conversation and wondered what would happen to the house now, now that Gena and Tom were gone. But he need not have wondered, for in his heart he knew. His father would sell it to the highest bidder, the same way he sold the house on Moosic Street that Joseph so loved. He'd sell it all with no recognition of memories or love. The last vestige of Tom and Gena would be sold off in its entirety, like unwanted chattel.

"I'd sooner burn the damn thing down," Tom had said, during that evening. "I'd rather burn it down than turn it over, furniture and all, to somebody who had no business touching things that involve all the things in my life. I just couldn't do it, that's all."

Joseph turned and looked hard at the graves. He walked over and lifted two roses from the large accumulation of flowers, and tenderly placed one on each grave. He placed rocks against the stems to help secure them against the wind. He said a prayer, and roughly brushed the remaining tears from his eyes. He had business to attend to.

11

JOSEPH drove directly to Mickey Clark's station. He walked into the garage and saw Mickey's clodhoppers sticking out from under a large maroon Buick.

"Hey Mick!" Joe said.

"What's up, Joey?" Mickey replied, immediately recognizing Joe's voice.

"I need some gas. I'll pump it."

Mickey slid out from under the car. He rested his weight on his elbow as he looked up at Joe. "Okay kid. I didn't expect to see you around today."

"Well, I need some gas,"

"I was at the funeral,"

"Yeah, Mick, I saw you. Thanks for coming."

"I came here right afterwards. I wanted to finish up Mr. Moran's starter. Once I finish I'm closin' shop for the day."

"How come?"

"I don't know. I just don't feel much like workin', you know."

"Well, thanks for taking the time to come up to the cemetery. I appreciate it."

"I know you do, kid. But hell, I wouldn't think of not goin'. I wanna tell you, you handled yourself real well. I know what Gena meant to you."

"Yeah. Well, I'II go out and get the gas. I'll take care of the register."

"Okay, kid. Listen, if you have a minute afterward, I'd like to talk to you. I'm just about wrapped up. Do you have a minute?

"Sure, Mick, I'll be right back in."

Joseph pumped five dollars of gas into his tank. He opened

the back door of his car and pumped an additional dollar's worth into an old battered can he had removed from Mickey's junk pile on the side of the station. He covered the pail with his jacket and slammed the door shut. After placing the six dollars in the register, he walked back into the garage.

Mickey slid out from under the car, "Well, that's that!" he said. He walked to the sink and washed his grease-matted hands and forearms, "Pull the doorshade, will you, Joe? I don't want any more customers."

Joe pulled the long green shade down over the door's window. He turned and walked back to the office desk where Mickey was sitting.

"Pull up a chair," Mickey said.

Joe sat down and looked at Mickey questionably, "What's up, Mick?"

"I didn't get a chance to talk to you much about Tom and Gena. I want you to know how sorry I am, but I'm sure you already know that."

"I sure do, Mick, I do,"

"There's something else though," Mickey said. "I want to know how you feel about Lobo."

"Ah, Lobo," Joe said, "For a minute there, I thought about killing him. But I mean what the hell, what did Lobo know. I know damn well he didn't mean it." Joe stared silently for a moment at the worn desk. "Jesus Christ, Mick, what made him take that car? I wouldn't figure it in a thousand years. I mean he was so scared of everything."

"You never know what goes on in a mind like Lobo's."

"I never thought I'd be able to forgive anybody for something like this, but I guess Lobo's a special case. As a matter of fact, I haven't given him a thought in the last couple of days. How is he?"

"They transferred him to a V.A. Hospital near the state capital. I understand they had to cut his leg off."

"Oh Jesus!"

"Yeah, the poor bastard will never come back now. He belonged in a hospital like that from the start. Maybe he'd be all right if they just took care of him a little bit. Sometimes the government pisses me off. The guy destroys his brain tryin' to defend his country, and they cast him aside like garbage."

"Yeah, you're right there."

"I know damn well I'm right. His old lady won't last a year without him. That accident was her death warrant."

"Yeah, she'll be all alone now."

"Kid, I was wonderin' if you might go to see her. Show her that you don't blame Lobo. Maybe it'll give her some peace."

"Oh Jesus, Mick, I can't. I mean, I can't really blame Lobo for what happened, but goddammit, it was him that killed them, I couldn't do it. It'd be like committing a sin. Honest to God, it would."

"Okay, Joey, I sure understand that. I expected that answer, but would you mind very much if I went up to talk to her? It'd mean a lot to the old lady. I'll tell her nobody really blames Lobo, that everybody understands the situation. I know damn well it'd mean a lot to her."

"Sure, Mick. Go ahead and do it." For a moment Joe reflected on the time-worn face of Mrs. Pagnozzi. "The poor old broad," he half whispered.

"Thanks, kid. Thanks a lot."

"No problem, Mick," Joe lifted himself out of the chair.

"Wait a minute, Joey. Sit down."

"What?"

"I wanna tell you somethin'."

Joe sat back down and leaned his elbows against the desk.

"Ya know I love you, kid. It's like you're my own son," Mickey said.

Joe smiled.

"Yeah, you're a good, good kid. Man, I'd love to see you get straightened out with your old man and your brother. By the way, how's Larry doin'? I don't see him at all."

"He's a creep. Honest to Jesus, Mick, he's a fuckin' creep."

"Ah c'mon, Joe. Don't be like that. I mean, after all, he's your brother. He used to take care of you all the time. I remember when you were just little kids. Shit, he took care of you like gold."

Joe's eyes grew clouded. "You know," he said, "Gena used to say the same kinda thing, I can hear her saying it like it was this morning." Joe felt the tears rush to his eyes, and the tightness grow in his throat.

"Well, why don't you do it for her?" Mickey asked.

"I can't, Mick. There's no chance in hell. Too much, too much has gone by."

"What about your old man?"

"The same fuckin' thing. They match up as a team. I don't want anything to do with either of them."

"But why?"

"Mickey, c'mon. I know right well you know the situation. I was always in their way. Well, I'm finished with it."

"I think you're wrong, kid, especially about Larry. I don't care what you say. You've got it all screwed up."

It was the touchiest of conversations, but Joseph felt no anger toward Mickey. He understood his purpose. He was trying to look out for him, trying to help.

"We're both entitled to our opinions, Mick. I'd sooner not talk about it."

"Shit, kid, you're a hell of a lot bigger than that. I know you. You've got a good heart. The tough guy act doesn't fool me. Can't you even try?"

"No, I can't."

"Ya know, Joey, you and I, all of us, we're lucky people."

"How do you mean?"

"I mean being born and raised in this town. We're damn lucky."

"This town is the best. Right there, we're in full agreement," Joe said.

"But why is it the best? Did you ever think about that?"

"The people. It's the people."

"That's right. The people. I'll tell you, this is the most unique place in the world. The back road here, our neighborhood, it's the most cosmopolitan in the world."

Joe leaned back in the chair and smiled. "Wow! Listen to the vocabulary."

"You know what the word means?"

Joe's smile grew broader. "Yeah, Mick, I know what it means."

"Well, okay then, that's what this neighborhood is, the most cosmopolitan in the world. We've got Irish, Italian, Polish, Hungarian, Jewish, all piled together over four or five streets. Never an argument or a misunderstanding around here. It's a remarkable melt of people. I mean, I've been around, I'm fifty years old. In my time I saw a lotta people, a lotta towns."

"What's the point?"

"The point is, you're part of it. The whole thing has rubbed off on you, and me as well, and everybody else. We're special people. We really are."

"All right. What's the point?"

"You should be able to forgive your old man and your brother. Even if you're right about them, you should forgive them. You've been taught to do that by your mama, by this town."

"It's not that easy."

"Sure it is. If you pull yourself together and think a little bit. You've got a bad chip on your shoulder. Okay, maybe you got a bad deal in some ways, but your carryin' it too damn far."

Joseph laughed sarcastically. "Too damn far, huh. Mick, you don't know. Take for instance, my father making us move outta here. There's nothing up there on Jessup Avenue, nothing but that rotten house. What'd he make us move for? There's nothing up there. It's like living in another town."

"Well, Jesus, you ought to be proud to live in a mansion like that. What the hell's the matter with you?"

"I'm not proud. We don't belong there. I know the people up that way are as good and decent as everyone else in this neighborhood. But it's different. I miss it. My mom misses it too. I know she does. She's all alone up there. The people she knows feel funny about visiting. They think my father resents them being around, and they're right. All he wants around are the big names, the big shots. Naw, Mick, he never should've made us leave Moosic Street. It was wrong and selfish, like everything else he does."

"I think you've got it wrong, kid."

The skin tightened over Joe's face and the hostility glinted in his eyes. "Ya know Mick, I'm surprised at you, I really am. You're a sharp guy. I thought you'd figure out my father real easy."

"He's a tough man, Joe, an aggressive man. That's just the way he is. I can't say he's all that bad. I know he's been rough here and there, but that's life.

"Is it life? Is it life the way he acted during the last few days? The lousy prick went to a meeting on the same night Gena died. His sister, she would've done anything for him, and that's the respect he showed her. He's no fuckin' good and that's all there is to it."

"You don't know, Joe. Maybe he had to go. He's a politician. Gena would've understood."

"Yeah, sure she would, because she was blind to all his faults. Her own husband knew that. The fact is, my father didn't give a shit about her dying. He doesn't give a shit about anybody except Larry, and that's a fact."

"And what about Anna? You mean you're sayin' he doesn't care about your mother?"

"You're damn right. That's what I'm saying. You ought to live with him, then you'd know."

"That's real hard to believe, Joe. I remember them when they were courtin'. No one was ever more in love than your father. Why, he'd break somebody's neck if they as much as said a curse in front of Anna. He worshipped her and she felt the same way about him. That's what I mean when I say you've got things wrong. He's gotta care about Anna."

"Well, he doesn't."

"Let me say just one more thing, Joey. I know damn well Patrick has been hard on people when it comes to business and politics. But maybe he had to be hard to get where he is. He's a millionaire. And that's really somethin'. You don't get a million bucks by being a sucker. Maybe he had to be hard. He didn't have a picnic growin' up. I remember the thirties weren't easy times. Your dad had to pick here and pick there for every buck he ever got. He'd shine shoes, run errands, clean up in the bar rooms. It wasn't easy. With no mother or father, he had to fight all the way. He had to win respect from people. There was no other choice. No money, no nothin' and a young sister beatin' her brains out to raise him. He had to be tough and Jesus he was. Nobody played games with him. Not if they didn't want their teeth knocked in. I've gotta give him credit."

"Well give it to him then, but I won't. This town has been damn good to him and what does he give it back? He screws them in real estate. He screws them politically. He'd rob the gold right out of Hanway's teeth. He doesn't deserve respect from this town or anything else. I've got him figured right. He's a fuckin' bum of the worst kind."

"Jesus Christ!" Mickey said.

Joseph got out of the chair.

Mickey also stood up. "I hope you're not sore."

Joe looked at his friend and the anger slowly dissolved.

"Mad! How could I be mad at you?" He walked over and put his arm around Mickey's shoulder. "Let's drop the subject, okay? I've gotta get going anyway."

Mickey smiled and playfully punched him on the shoulder. "Okay, hardhead," he said, "but try and think about what I said."

"Yeah, sure I will," Joe said.

Joseph left the station and walked quickly to his car. Before getting in, he checked the full gas can on the back floor board.

His eyes moved to the clock in Mickey's window. It was three o'clock. In not too many hours It would be dark. Joseph gunned the engine and drove away.

1

B Y EIGHT O'CLOCK that evening, the weather had once again grown violent. The temperature had dropped to zero. The snow began to fall and blow in swirls through the streets. Joseph had left Carol's house much earlier than usual, on the pretense that he was tired and hungry. He told her he would stop off at Petry's and then get to bed early for a change.

He drove slowly down Bridge Street. The night was perfect; no one would leave their homes on a night like this unless on some important appointment, an appointment such as the one waiting for Joseph Flynn.

The streets and sidewalks were deserted. He drove across streets and avenues, until finally stopping his car in an alleyway behind the Conroy's empty home. Joe looked out of the window. A thicket of woods was all that separated him from Gena's back yard. He waited. The snow moved in gusts past the car. There wasn't a house in the area except for the one on the end of the alley, and it was well out of sight. He pulled his car into a wide space in the thicket. Now, even if someone went by, they wouldn't notice it. He sat for a moment after turning off the engine, and considered what lay before him. He'd have to move quickly.

He got out of the car and opened the back door. He removed the jacket that camouflaged the can. As he picked it up, the sharp odor of gasoline filled his nostrils. He half-ran through the trees and bushes, easily following a path he knew well, for he had spent countless days and years of his childhood in this very thicket, and he knew every inch of it. Not even the shadows of night could form an obstacle to his movement.

He ran down the concrete steps that led to the cellar entrance.

He pushed open the door and smiled. He knew it wouldn't be locked. Tom and Gena had always left it open. Once inside, he removed a flashlight from his pocket. He cupped the illumination it offered, just allowing him enough light to move with haste. He splashed the gasoline against the electrical wires that were exposed along the low ceiling. Then he rushed up to the kitchen and splashed it over the wallpaper. He walked into the parlor. Joe was just about to soak the parlor couch before his memory recalled the moments he spent there with Gena; those wonderful, forever lost moments. He hesitated before pouring the contents of the can.

"She would understand," he thought. "She would. She'd have to."

With no further hesitation he emptied the can of gasoline; first on the couch and then in a circular motion on the rug. His eyes were adjusted to the dark now. He turned off the flashlight and put it back into his jacket pocket. He walked back into the kitchen and opened the door to the steps that led back to the cellar. He placed the empty can in the small hallway and removed a pack of matches from his pocket and went back to the parlor. Making sure he was far enough away, he struck a match. He watched the orange flame dance in the darkness. With that flame, he lit the remaining matches and threw the pack onto the gas-drenched rug. He heard a whoosh, and suddenly the floor burst open in fire.

The flames drew a quick path to the couch and it too exploded in fire. Joe ran into the kitchen and ignited another pack of matches.

He threw it at the wallpaper. Once again, there was an explosion of fire. He ran into the cellarway, picked up the can, and raced down the steps. Once again he ignited matches and pitched them at the wires. The cellar lit up in heat and light. He didn't wait another second. He raced out into the backyard. As he approached the thicket that led to his car, he turned around. He saw no one. The snow was falling heavier than before. He looked at a window and saw the orange light filling the kitchen. In an instant he turned and disappeared into the woods.

Midway through the bush, he threw the empty, battered can

into a pile of garbage just off the path. It was a favorite dumping ground of the neighborhood residents. He returned to his car and, for a minute, just sat there recounting his movements. He saw the snow falling in blizzard-like proportions and thanked God for the blessing. By the time, anything was discovered, the snow would have filled his footprints and tire tracks. "God's on my side," Joe thought. "He's on my side."

Joseph drove directly to Petry's Restaurant. There were parking spaces all along Main Street. Even the lights of the pool hall were out. Everybody had stayed home; even the night owl pool jockeys. But he knew Petry's would be open. Old man Petry wouldn't have it any other way.

As he pulled his car to a stop in front of the restaurant, Joe saw Ray Walton emerging from the building.

"Hey, Joey! Hey, Joey, babe!" Ray screamed.

Joe walked up onto the sidewalk. "What's wrong, Ray?"

"Nothin', fuckin' nothin' is doing. Jesus, you'd swear it was a blizzard in Alaska the way nobody's around."

"Well, it is a lousy night. Only two idiots like you and I would be out in it."

"Hell, baby Joe, we're not idiots, my man. We're livin', we like to live. Nothin' wrong with livin', is there my pretty boy?"

Joe was about to say something but was suddenly stopped by the look of horror on his friend's face.

"Jesus ever lovin' Christ! Look there, Joey! Look there!"

Joseph turned following his friend's eyes. He saw the flames rising into the sky.

"My God, Joey, it looks like it's on Bridge Street. Let's go, c'mon."

They piled into Joe's car and made a U-turn on Main Street.

They drove toward the railroad crossing and Bridge Street beyond. Just as they approached the crossing, the night was filled with the screaming cry of the fire siren.

As the car turned onto Bridge Street, the Conroy house was visible and a blazing fury of flame.

"Holy shit!" Joe said feigning surprise and terror. "It's my Aunt Gena's house! Holy shit!"

A mass of people were already on the sidewalk across the street from the house. In a little while the fire trucks and the Hanway fire volunteers were on the scene. Large groups of men ran wildly about with hoses; attaching them to hydrants, running with them, their voices and actions in committed frenzy. The hose nozzles jerked in their sudden spitting of water and within minutes, long, strong streams of water arced through the blizzard and splashed powerfully against the inferno.

Joseph stood and watched. The house was unsalvageable. Flames roared through the roof. The front porch was even engulfed. The firemen were prepared to fight valiantly, but it was too late.

The house was already well destroyed.

Joseph tried to resist the feeling of pride that almost caused him to smile. At this point, he had to be careful not to give himself away.

"I can't believe it," Joe said, with feigned emotion. "Jesus Christ! How could this happen?"

"I know, my man," Ray replied. "I'm damn sorry. Jesus! It's like a sign or somethin'. Your aunt isn't even dead one day and this happens. Jesus!"

Joseph didn't answer, electing to remain still and say no more. The side walls of the house began to crumple. He felt like leaving the scene. He'd seen enough. And then, he saw his father.

Patrick Flynn was on the street barking orders at the policemen who had arrived on the scene. Police Chief Mullen immediately obeyed Patrick's command, and rushed over to the throng that had moved from the sidewalk to the road for a better glimpse of the fire.

"Back up there! C'mon, get back on the sidewalk! Let the men work. Back up I say! I'm warning all of you, get back on the sidewalk!" The errant bystanders made haste in moving from the roadway. Chief Mullen turned back to Patrick. "They'll stay back now,

Mr. Flynn," he shouted, Patrick shook his head and turned back to the fire. From the crowd, Joseph closely studied him. His father stood on the center of the street, in the middle of the animation. The brightness of the fire illuminated his imposing figure. Patrick's eyes never left the flames. His hair was soaked and matted to his head from the driving wetness of the snow. The curls fell in tight ringlets as they decorated his forehead.

His face was a tight, angered mass as he stuck his hands into the pockets of the drenched, camel hair topcoat. Chief Mullen walked over to Patrick and stood alongside him. "It's only natural," Joseph thought. The suddenness to follow his father's orders, the careful obedience. The chief was only another soldier in Patrick's army. Every member of the police force was beholden to Joseph's father; for their jobs, for their measly, occasional raises in pay. They all had no choice but to pay homage to their master.

As Joseph watched Patrick, drenched in snow and flame on Bridge Street, he knew everything was worth it. He could almost hear his father's cash register brain ringing up the loss. There would be insurance, but nothing to match the loss. Joseph knew his father's sick plans. Being sure that Tom Conroy's family had long ago died off, Patrick had figured out he'd get everything— the furniture, the whole works. He could've rented out the house for a healthy sum; but his son had fooled him. All Patrick had left was Gena's property, and if he intended to build something there, it would cost big dollars and a brand new inconvenience. His son had fooled him.

Joseph had no fear concerning any investigation. Hanway was not yet that sophisticated. The fire would be written off as a pitiful accident and that's all there would be to it. No one in Hanway, not even the poisoned mind of Patrick Flynn, would ever suspect it was done on purpose. Joe was in the clear.

"C'mon, Ray! I've had enough. Let's go!" Joe said.

"Okay, babe," Ray replied. "Drive me back to my car. It's up on Main Street."

The two boys walked back to Joe's car, parked near the corner where they had left it. As Joe opened the car to get in, he looked back at the scene. He saw Patrick silhouetted in the night. Joseph smiled to himself and brushed the wet snow from his eyes to get a better look. Patrick's shoulders were hunched and forlorn, and Joseph was thrilled to know that this was one battle that he had finally won.

BOOK
THREE

1

THE YOUNG WOMAN lay on the table, unable to look at Doctor Benson. He studied her soft, fine features. He hadn't asked her name; it was unimportant. She couldn't have been more than twenty. Her hair was blonde and piled into an upsweep. Her eyes were a startling blue and moved quickly from one part of the room to another, as if they belonged to a frightened cat. A sheet covered her naked body as it moved nervously on the examining table.

"Just try to relax," Benson said.

The girl didn't reply.

Benson was amazed at how Patrick Flynn, time and again, could be responsible for such errant, pathetic pregnancies involving such young women, and treat each event with such disdain. As always, Benson knew that Patrick wouldn't even check on the outcome of the abortion. He would just accept it as something taken care of and forget about it as if it weren't the murder it was, as if the young life of the erstwhile mother would go unaffected by the event. It was so cruel, so pitiless. The thought of what lay raced ahead through Benson's mind. Small beads of perspiration began to form on his forehead and his heart palpitated with guilt and revulsion.

"It won't hurt very much, Miss," he said. "These are stirrups," he said, pointing to the small structures mounted to the both sides at the bottom of the table. "I want you to bend your knees, place your feet here."

The girl began to cry softly, dabbing at her nose and eyes with a handkerchief. Benson moved his instrument table closer to him. He firmly placed his hand on the woman's abdomen. He closed his eyes and said a silent prayer. While he prayed he cringed at the blatant hypocrisy, asking God for help as he murdered. He pulled the sterile gloves onto his hands and once again looked at the woman. "Don't worry," he said in a soft voice. "Don't worry, honey. Everything will be all right. Don't worry."

The phone in Patrick Flynn's real estate office rang loudly. Patrick was busy studying a pile of papers on his desk so Bill lifted himself from his own desk and walked over and lifted the receiver. "Flynn's Real Estate," he muttered. He listened to the hysterical voice on the other end. In a moment he discerned what was being said and a wave of panic swept through him, but he did not flinch. Patrick was looking up at him and Manley did not want to give the situation away, not yet. "I'll get back to you. Stay where you are. I'll get back to you in a few minutes."

Bill slowly replaced the phone into its cradle.

"Who was it?" Patrick asked.

Manley looked at the door as it suddenly opened. The secretary rushed into the office. "Oh my God, Mr. Flynn, I'm sorry I'm late but my bus was held up. I couldn't help it, honest!"

"That's okay," Flynn said, forgetting about the phone call. "But there's a pile of things here I want you to look at." He got up and walked over to her desk, placing the papers he had previously studied on her blotter.

He turned and looked at Manley. "Let's go in and have a drink, Billy."

Patrick pushed through the door leading to the lounge room and Manley followed. Patrick poured a double shot of scotch into a glass. He handed it to Bill. He poured the same for himself and drank it quickly. "What was that phone call about?"

"Yeah, we've gotta talk about it," Manley replied.

"I knew it. I could tell. What's so important?"

"Boss, this is really important."

"What?"

174

"That was Benson on the phone."

"And?"

"It's about the broad you sent over."

"Yeah, the abortion, yeah. I knew she was going over today. What about it?"

Manley felt his hand shake as he placed the glass back on the bar. Patrick was calmly staring at him. For a moment Bill couldn't find his voice. He cleared his throat, but the words came out hoarse and rasping. "The girl's dead."

Patrick's eyes opened into a wild stare. "Dead!"

"Yeah, something went wrong in the office. I guess she bled too much or something. Benson was saying something about shock. He was hysterical. I couldn't understand him that well."

"Get him back on the phone!" Patrick screamed. As Bill dialed the number, Patrick paced wildly about the room.

"Hello, Doc?" Bill said. "Pat's here. He wants to talk to you."

Patrick grabbed the phone from Manley's hand.

"What happened? Goddammit, what the fuck happened?" Pat held the phone to his ear and listened. He tapped his fingers on the wall and his eyes blinked continuously. The back of his grey, starched shirt was suddenly soaked with perspiration. Bill walked over and handed him another double of scotch. Patrick swallowed it as he listened to the hysterical doctor on the other end.

"Okay! Okay!" Patrick finally said. "Nobody knows you're in the office, right? Okay. Just stay there! I'll figure something. Bill will be over." For a moment he stopped talking and once again listened to Benson.

"All right, for Christ sake. Calm down. Make sure everything there is locked up. Don't touch the girl. Just wait until Bill gets over there. Do you hear me, goddammit? Do you hear me?" Patrick waited. Manley could hear Benson's incoherent voice from the other side of the room.

"Okay, Doc. Okay. Don't worry. Just sit tight, all right?" Patrick laid the phone back onto the receiver. He walked over to the couch and sat down, placing his hands over his face. "Jesus, Jesus Christ," he muttered.

Bill Manley stood stark still with his back against the bar.

He pulled his tie loose and unbuttoned his collar. His gigantic chest was heaving and his beet-red, Irish face formed a rigid scowl. Bill wasn't necessarily an ugly man, just menacing; his nose was wide and swollen from too much whiskey. His eyes were small and heavily circled, staring out from a hood of grey-black brows that perfectly matched his wiry, abundant hair. He was as massive as his boss; easily six feet, with no girth or unnecessary fat. Two hundred and twenty pounds of muscle, but nevertheless he looked much older than his fifty years, and now, his frown made him ugly and fearsome.

"What the hell is going on?" Manley said. "Are we under some kind of cloud or what? First your sister dyin', then the house burning down, now this. What the hell is going on?"

"Oh, forget her and the house. What the hell. But this, Jesus, this is something else." Patrick pressed his knuckles against his temples.

"What are we goin' to do, Boss?"

"Wait a minute. Let me think," Patrick said, as he got up and went to the door. He walked very calmly into the other room and smiled at his secretary. "Millie, honey, if I got any calls, have them call back, will you? I've got something I want to check on and I don't want to be disturbed for a while."

Millie Morris looked up and smiled. "Sure Mr. Flynn," she said.

Patrick walked over and rubbed the back of her neck. "Now you do a good job, you hear?" he said in a friendly voice.

"Oh, yes sir. Don't worry. No calls until you say so."

Patrick squeezed her neck and walked back to the lounge.

Her eyes followed him admiringly. She brushed back the dark hair from her forehead and removed a small mirror from her purse. She checked her makeup; the lipstick perfectly lined the lush lips.

The dainty features satisfied her. She fluttered her long, dark lashes and looked down at her chest. Her breasts set enticingly in the tight red sweater; pointed and full. She looked to where Patrick had disappeared into the lounge and smiled, satisfied that her appearance might have impressed him.

"Do you think she heard anything?" Bill asked.

"Who, Millie? No. She's only interested in me rubbing her neck or feeling her tits. She has no idea what went on."

"Well, what are we going to do?" Manley said, his voice filled with urgency.

Pat walked over and poured himself another drink. He then walked to the window that overlooked the city. He slowly rubbed his fist against his chin and narrowed his eyes. "No question, Bill, We've got trouble here. Benson is a fuckin' weasel. He'll never handle this."

"I agree," Manley replied.

"Ya know," Patrick laughed sarcastically, "he'd rob anybody blind, but deep down he's a sanctimonious bastard."

"You're tellin' me, I had a hell of a time havin' him agree to this abortion. I'm tellin' you, Boss, even if we can get rid of the broad's body, Benson won't hold up. He'll fall apart and blow everything," Manley said. "He'll tell, I know it."

Patrick downed the scotch in one swallow. Bill walked over to Flynn and placed his large hand on his shoulder. "Boss, is there any way they might trace the girl back to you?"

"No. There's no way at all. She was just a little slut from down in Georgia, I think. I set her up pretty well. Paid all her bills. She kept her mouth shut. She was street wise. She wouldn't throw away a good deal like that. She never told anyone about me. No one ever saw us together. I'd go to her hotel. That was it. I was never in public with her. She probably fucked around with some other guys, I have no way of knowing. But she didn't mention me to anybody. I'm sure."

"Okay. I'll find some way to dump her. You'll have to straighten out Benson," Manley said.

Patrick turned and smiled at Bill. He reached over and grabbed his arm. "Billy," Patrick said softly, "this isn't twenty years ago. Things are more tough now. You can't go and just dump her. It's not that easy."

"I'll find a way."

"No," Patrick said. "I've got an idea. It's the only way," Flynn punched his fist into his palm. "Goddammit, if only Benson wasn't such a creep. I know damn well he'll spill everything. Let one person, his wife for instance, look at him the wrong way and he'll blurt out the whole story."

"Well, what should we do then?" Bill asked.

"How long would it take you to drive up to the cabin and back?"

"Where? The cabin up in Perch County?"

"Yes. How long?"

"I'll be up and back in two hours."

"All right, call back Doc and tell him again to stay put and don't answer his phone, Tell him you'll be there in two hours. Tell him we've got something figured out."

2

BILL MANLEY pulled into the reserved parking space alongside the Clarkson Hotel. He checked his watch. It was a few minutes past noon. The trip to the cabin and back had taken approximately two hours, exactly as planned. Before getting out of the car, he looked up at the second story level of the hotel.

The entire floor was reserved for office space and Patrick's suite faced the parking lot. The Venetian blind over the window of Patrick's lounge was drawn tight. Manley had expected to see his boss peering out, awaiting his return, but he should have known better. Patrick Flynn was confident that the matter lay in capable hands. He knew there was nothing to worry about. Manley felt the rush of pride surge through his skin, "Relax, Boss," he thought. "Old Bill will take care of everything."

Bill got out of the car and walked quickly down Susquehanna Avenue. Although it was Saturday afternoon, with many of the stores and shops closed between the holidays, the streets were crowded with people. It was very cold and the wind blew in great gusts up the avenue. As he walked, Manley rubbed his glove covered hands together and squinted as the frigid wind laced his face.

When he reached the corner of Susquehanna and Spruce Street, he jogged across the intersection. He stopped for a moment and lit a cigarette. He looked across the street and. saw the enormous plate glass window bearing the words: Patrick Flynn Enterprises. It was in that ground floor office, where twenty people worked full time, attending to the Flynn empire of real estate and beer distribution, as well as county politics. Nevertheless, Patrick spent little time there. He chose to remain, for the most part, at the hotel suite, where he overlooked the main office and entertained business associates. All day long, runners from the building on Spruce Street would bring messages and portfolios to him, filled with papers that he would study and make decisions over.

The main office was closed and quiet on that wintry afternoon.

Manley stood on the corner, in the wind, until he finished the cigarette. He pushed his hands into the pockets of his camel hair top coat and once again began to walk toward his destination. The Medical Arts Building was less than a block away.

Bill entered the huge lobby of the building, instantly relieved by its warmth. He stood for a second to collect himself, and then proceeded to the stairway and slowly climbed the three flights that led to Benson's floor. All of the offices on the floor were locked, and the halls were barren and still. As he approached Benson's door, he read the sign attached to its windows: Doctor William J. Benson, M.D.

Bill knocked three times on the door. It opened slowly, and the ravaged face of Doctor Benson peered out. "Oh, Bill, thank God," Benson said. "Come in. Hurry before someone comes."

Manley entered the waiting room and closed the door behind him. Benson waved him into the office. When Manley saw the white, still body on the examining table, he stopped short. The girl was young. Her eyes were open and staring, unseeing at the ceiling.

Her feet were still in the stirrups and there was blood everywhere. Benson looked at Manley. "She hemorrhaged, Billy. I couldn't stop it. Jesus, I tried. I tried." Benson sat down on the chair near his desk. Manley was startled at his appearance. The usually graceful figure was hunched and sagging. His eyes were horror stricken and sunk deep into his face. The stately exterior and manner were all gone now. Benson looked like a tired, frightened old man. His face and bald head were shiny with perspiration, and his hands shook as they rubbed against his face. "Good God, Bill, what are we going to do? What did Patrick say? How are we going to get out of this?" The doctor covered his face and began to cry, cutting the air with harsh sobs. "I tried, I tried," he said over and over.

Manley, without uttering a word, quickly walked over to him.

For a moment, he just looked down at the crying, trembling form.

Bill took a deep breath and simultaneously withdrew his right hand from his overcoat pocket. The metal of the thirty-eight glinted under the fluorescent light. Manley fired just once. There was a loud popping sound and Benson jerked to his right, and fell to the floor.

Manley calmly surveyed his work. Benson lay twisted and dead. The flowered wall paper was stained with dots and splashes of blood, like hideous graffiti. The dark stain under the doctor's head grew larger and larger as it soaked into the carpet. Bill checked himself closely, making sure none of the blood had touched him. Except for Manley's quickening breath, the room was deathly quiet. He dropped the gun, exactly as he imagined Benson would have dropped it, had he fired it himself. He walked from the office, leaving the ghastly scene behind him. He slowly opened the main door and looked out into the hallway. As before, it was empty and quiet. Manley rushed through the corridor and down the stairs. Before emerging into the lobby, he checked himself once more for bloodstains. Finding none, he squared his shoulders and walked out into the crowd of people. They were entering and leaving the numerous first floor offices that remained open on every Saturday—dentists, optometrists and optical shops, available to weekend trade. He unobtrusively walked from the lobby to Spruce Street and back to Patrick Flynn.

From the lounge, Patrick heard the office door open. He looked at the clock as Manley walked in.

"I need a drink," Manley said walking toward the bar.

Patrick walked over and leaned against the bar. He tried to appear calm, but the excitement in his eyes betrayed him. "How did it go?" he asked.

"Perfect, Honest to God, Pat, if we planned this for six months, it couldn't have gone so well."

"Tell me what happened. "

"I shot him. He's dead, just the way you wanted it."

"Did you see anyone?"

"Nobody. I told you. It went perfect."

Manley swallowed the scotch and poured another. "Do you want one?" he asked.

"No, not now," Patrick said. "Was the silencer up there in the cabin?"

"Yeah, attached to the gun just like you said."

"Where did you find it?" Patrick asked.

"In Benson's bureau where you said it would be."

"Jesus, how did you put it all together so quickly? It's not even one o'clock."

"There wasn't much traffic, I made good time up and back."

"Was anyone around the cabin?"

"Naw, nobody. I went to Benson's room and found the gun," Bill said.

"I remember putting it there the last time he and I went up for target practice," Patrick said. "Before we left, I had to go back to the cabin for my jacket and he asked me to put his gun in his bureau drawer. I knew damn well the silencer was still attached."

"It came in handy today," Bill said,

Patrick walked behind the bar and poured himself a drink.

"Doc always insisted on using it. The gunfire bothered his ears."

"Well, it won't bother him anymore," Manley said,

"No, I guess it won't," Patrick said thoughtfully. "It's too bad it had to end like this, Billy, but there was no other way."

Patrick became quiet as he remembered all the years he and Benson had spent together; the political intrigue and the shared secrets. The innumerable all night poker games and the happy, drunken weekends at the hunting cabin. His mind swept over all the memories. Finally he said, "He was with me from the beginning. I'm going to miss him."

"Miss him! You've got to be kiddin', Boss. He wasn't worth a shit," Manley said.

Patrick studied the empty glass in his hand, "Yeah, Billy, that was the trouble with Doc. No matter how you measured it, he wasn't worth a shit. But he came in handy, you know."

"C'mon, Boss," Bill said. "You're not tellin' me you're sorry."

Patrick laughed. "No, Bill, he's out of our hair once and for all. This is the way I wanted it. It was a smart decision."

"Well, it went perfect. There's nothin' to worry about," Manley said.

Patrick threw his arm around Bill's shoulder. With his free hand he playfully squeezed Manley's face. "Goddamn, I knew you could do it, pal, I knew it."

"They'll think it was a suicide for sure," Bill said. "I dropped that gun just perfect."

"Yeah, there won't be any problems," Patrick said.

"I hope not. I'm sure I didn't overlook anything."

"Don't worry about it," Patrick said.

"The cops'll probably investigate the shit out of this," Manley grumbled.

"Don't be silly," Patrick said in an amused voice. "Investigate what? The doc was aborting a young kid and she bled to death. He got panicky and shot himself. What's there to investigate? Don't make me laugh. There's nothin' to trace. The girl never told anyone about me. Benson didn't talk to anyone but us about the abortion." Patrick paced the floor pleased with himself. "It's his gun they're going to find on the floor. No one saw you. We're in the clear."

"What now?" Manley asked.

"We just relax," Patrick answered. "This'll be a big deal in the newspapers for a while, and then it'll blow over. I'll give it two weeks. I've got a young guy lined up to replace Benson as coroner. This kid'll work out perfect. Everything's beautiful."

"What about Benson's wife?" Bill asked.

"She'll head for Florida to live with her son," Patrick replied. "She'll be gone the day after the funeral. I know her pretty well and she's not going to spend much time mourning Doc."

"That's good," Manley said.

Patrick walked over to Bill and shook his hand. "Thanks, buddy," Flynn said.

"Thanks for what?"

"Billy, you're the only man in the world I can depend on."

"Jesus, Boss, you know I'd do anything. Just say it and I'll do it. You know that. Without you I'd be nothin'." Manley placed both his hands on Patrick's shoulders. "You gave me everything I have-my house, money in the bank, a lot of power, and respect. I owe you, Pat, I'll always owe you."

Flynn smiled and looked down at the floor. "C'mon, Billy," he said, smiling. "You're embarrassing the hell out of me."

Manley laughed and punched Patrick's shoulder. "Okay," he said. "Enough of the violins and flowers. What are we doin' tonight?"

"You go home. You deserve a rest," Patrick said. "I'll be in touch with you later."

"What are you goin' to do?"

"I'll stick around here for a while. I'll call you later."

"Who'll take you home?" Bill asked,

"I'll manage. You go on home."

"Look, give me a time and I'll come back for you."

"No. I'll take care of it."

"Well, what the hell are you goin' to do hangin' around here?" Bill asked.

Patrick laughed and ran his tongue across his upper lip. "When Millie gets back from lunch, I'm going to invite her back here for a drink. The broad's been beggin' for some action."

Manley's eyes opened wide. "Jesus, at a time like this, you're thinkin' about ass. I don't believe it."

"Why not?" Patrick said. "She's been askin' for it long enough, so I'll give her a little action."

"Do you have any rubbers available?" Manley asked. He began to laugh.

"Nothing to fear," Patrick chuckled. "There's other doctors in the world besides Benson, you know."

Bill Manley continued to laugh as he left the room.

3

May 1959

THE HORRENDOUS WINTER had finally passed, and Hanway stretched its muscles in the face of spring. It was mid May and the sun was well into its northward journey. The ice and snow had melted away; the days were a splendid mixture of cool breezes and delicious warmth. The crack of baseballs echoed from the field and the old men were in their back yards, tending to their early, sprouting gardens. The Appalachian highlands that surrounded Hanway were already deep green and saturated with mountain laurel. After supper, the families drifted out to their front porches. They inhaled the friendly aroma that came from the lavender lilacs huddling in clusters on the bushes in the yard. The mornings ware filled with the beauty of crocuses and lilies of the valley. The woodland was alive with the yellow of daffodils. It was the hour for men to stand in front of saloons and on street corners to discuss baseball. It was the hour of rebirth and laughter; to watch the orange flash of robins in the backyard and the crowd of starlings along the wires of Main Street. It was a time to await the arrival of roses and the intense heat of summer.

Patrick Flynn had proved to be a prophet of sorts. Indeed the matter of Doctor Benson's death had quickly passed. Mrs. Benson departed for Florida soon afterwards and everything fell perfectly into place. Patrick appointed a young doctor, Myron Royal, to complete Benson's term as coroner. He was a young man, interested in a fast reputation and a fast dollar, and ideally suited to function under the direction of Pat Flynn.

Joseph made good use of the weather. He was spending almost all of his time with Carol. After leaving Mickey's station, he would rush home to shower, have something to eat and race back to the Granahan home. Mr. Granahan's job still hadn't come through. It was becoming more and more likely that it would never materialize. Joseph reveled in knowing that Carol would remain with him in Hanway.

He and Carol had spent the whole evening driving through the mountain roads above town. Joe pulled his Chevy off the main road. He negotiated the car over the bumpy road that led to an abandoned coal breaker. The dust moved in swirls before the car's headlights. Here and there cars were nestled in open areas of the woods alongside the roadway. Joseph pulled into one of them. He turned off the motor and looked over at Carol sitting next to him. Her face was covered by shadows, but its magic still reached out to him. He could barely stand being near her without touching her, without having her close to him. She filled his thoughts and dreams. She was rapidly becoming his whole life.

"I love you, babe," he whispered.

Carol smiled and moved close to him. Joseph hungrily kissed as his hands expertly explored her body.

"Joey," she gasped. "I love you. I love you."

They fell back onto the seat and lost themselves in their passion. They made love in a wild combination of animal lust and tenderness. For what seemed like hours, their bodies responded to each other in spasms of desire.

Later, Joe slipped back behind the wheel and rested his head against the window. His body was satiated and relaxed.

"Jesus, I hate taking you home," he said.

Carol straightened her dress and smiled. "We only have a year to wait."

"I can't wait a year. I'd like you to quit school right now. Honest to God, I'd like to get married right now."

"Oh, Joey, I know. Don't you think I feel the same way?"

"Listen. I'm not saying this for the good of my health. I really mean it."

"I know you do, honey. But we've got to wait until after I graduate. You know that."

"Yeah, I know it. I know I've got to find another job too. Mickey can't afford to pay me any more, and it's just not enough. I've got to find something else."

"Well, you're working on that."

"Yeah, I check the papers every day. I ask around, but there doesn't seem to be anything available."

"Why do you refuse to ask your father about it? He's bound to have something for you."

"I told you to forget about him, dammit," Joe said, his voice edged in anger. The thought of his father was enough to disturb Joseph's sense of relaxation.

"Let's go," he said.

Carol turned her head and looked out the window. She was instantly disgusted with herself for mentioning Patrick Flynn. The outcome was always predictable in Joseph's presence. It was always the same, deep, burning hostility and hate.

"I'm sorry, hon," she finally said.

"That's okay. Don't worry about it." Joe replied. The bitterness in his voice said otherwise.

He started up the car and loudly revved the engine. He quickly drove the car back onto the dusty trail. The rear wheels spun furiously sending back a burst of dust and dirt. The car bolted forward to the highway and back to Hanway .

4

JOSEPH thought he was dreaming. The voice, filled with alarm and urgency, drifted through his brain. It sounded like his mother's voice. Something in his sleep-dulled mind assured him it was too early to get up, but the annoying persistence of the voice refused to abate. Suddenly, his body jostled to life. His eyes opened and Anna was pulling and tugging at him. Her voice was screeching and babbled. Her eyes were wide and filled with terror.

Joseph leaped from the bed and grabbed her shoulders. "Ma, what's wrong? What's going on?"

Anna was crying and trying to speak in the same breath.

Joseph sat her down on the bed. "Ma, what the hell is wrong?"

Anna continued her crying and incoherent screaming. Joseph lightly slapped her face and her body froze. The crying stopped.

"Ma, what's wrong?" Joseph said.

Anna collapsed against him. "Joe, help me. Come downstairs and help me." She jumped from her sitting position on the bed and raced to the stairs. Joseph ran behind her and grabbed her as she began to descend the steps.

"What is going on?" he screamed.

His mother turned and looked at him. "It's your brother. It's Larry. Help him, please."

Joe half carried his mother down the stairs and through the dining room.

"He's in there, in the kitchen. Do something, Joey. Please help him," she cried.

Joseph hurried into the kitchen and saw Larry sitting at the table. He appeared to be in a trance. His eyes were open and staring. He sat bolt upright and it seemed as though he were paralyzed.

Joe grabbed Larry's shoulders and shook him. "Come on, Larry. What are you doing?"

Larry never blinked. He didn't move or speak.

Anna's voice rang with fright. "One minute he was talking, and then he went silent. I thought he fooling at first, but then I knew something was wrong. I'm scared, Joey. What should we do?"

"Where's Father?"

"He called yesterday evening and told me he was staying over in town."

"Jesus Christ!"

"I can call him at the office. He had some business. He probably slept over there. I'll call him now." Anna was trembling and her voice shook with emotion.

"Call him, goddammit! Call him now!"

Anna rushed toward the parlor. Joe continued to shake Larry but there was still no response.

"Jesus, man," Joseph said. "What's wrong with you? Snap out of it." Larry's face remained expressionless.

Joseph felt the strangling grip of panic. "C'mon, Larry!" he screamed. "Jesus Christ you're scarin' Ma. What the fuck are you tryin' to prove?" Even as Joseph yelled into his brother's face, he knew he was deceiving himself. Larry wasn't playing any game. This was no call for attention. There was something terribly wrong.

Anna ran back into the kitchen. "He was there, Joe. He's coming right home. He'll have a doctor with him."

"All right, Ma. I'm going to put Larry on the couch."

"No! Don't move him! "

"It's all right, Ma. It won't hurt him, I'm just going to lie him down."

Joe carried him into the parlor and lay him full length on the couch. Larry's eyes stared at the ceiling and his mouth remained fixed and tight. Joe shook him a few more times, but it was useless. Larry's body was rigid and unresponsive,

"Just let him there. We'll just let him alone," Joe said, in a low voice. "I want you to go back in the kitchen. Go ahead, Ma. Go in the kitchen and sit down. C'mon."

Joe sat Anna at the table. Larry's untouched breakfast rested on its plate. Anna leaned forward and rested her forehead on her fist. "My God! My God!" she whimpered.

Joseph went to the stove and poured her a cup of coffee. He rushed back to her and set it in front of her. "Drink this, Ma, please."

Anna looked up at her son. "I knew something like this was coming, Joey, I knew it. Larry hasn't been right for a long time. The way he was staying home all the time. He didn't care about school anymore. He didn't want to talk to anybody. He didn't want to see anybody. You were right, Joe. We should have given him more help. The poor baby." Once again, she began to cry.

Joseph went back into the parlor. He knelt down alongside Larry. Joseph could hear his brother breathing, and it brought him a strong measure of relief. When he earlier had laid him on the couch, he wasn't sure that Larry was alive. Joseph studied the rigid figure, and felt no pain or torture. Instead, he was filled with revulsion at his brother's pathetic weakness. Larry's condition was very real and reflected a life immersed in dependence and belly-crawling to be his father's favorite. "This is his reward," Joseph thought, "and he deserves every bit of it."

Joseph returned to the kitchen and realized that his mother was near collapse. He carried her upstairs and lay her on her bed. He pulled the bedspread up over her shoulders and softly ran his hand along the side of her head. "It'll be okay, Ma. Just stay here until the doctor gets here. Larry'll be all right. Don't worry."

Anna's eyelids fluttered. Her voice was weak and strangled. "Oh, Joey, honey, I hope so. He will be okay, won't he?"

Joseph fought desperately to remove the doubt from his eyes. "Sure he will. Just wait and see."

From the bottom of the stairs, Joe once again looked at Larry. He still hadn't moved a muscle. Joseph walked over and fell into the chair near the fireplace. The first signs of morning were at the window. The house was as still as death. Joseph couldn't resist smiling as he leaned his head back into the cushion. There was nothing to do now, but wait for the arrival of Patrick Flynn.

5

Mrs. Davis entered the kitchen through the hack door. She knew Anna had been feeling poorly and had decided to start on the housecleaning a little earlier than usual. More and more, of late, Anna allowed her to do most of the housework. She saw Joseph and Anna sitting at the table. The looks on their faces immediately told her something was wrong.

"Hello, Anna. Good morning, Joe," she said.

Joseph was relieved to see her. By now, he had become accustomed to seeing her around the house. She was a kind, decent, hardworking woman and proved to be a major help and close companion to his mother, filling the void left by Gena's death. She stood near the door unsure of her next move.

She addressed Joseph. "Is there something wrong?"

Joe explained the prior events of the morning. Anna slowly drank her coffee and said nothing.

"My father and Doctor Royal are with Larry in the parlor," Joe said.

Mrs. Davis removed her cloth coat. Her tall figure walked across the kitchen and into the hallway. She momentarily returned and sat down next to Anna.

"Why don't you go upstairs for a while, Anna?" she said.

"No, Marion, I want to talk to the doctor," Anna replied.

"Well now, don't you worry. Everything will be fine."

Mrs. Davis spoke with such authority, Joseph almost believed her. But he had first hand knowledge of the situation which told him otherwise. Joseph looked across the table and studied her kindly countenance; she was a handsome woman, with a finely sculptured face and a well-kept, firm body. She was a lifelong friend of Anna's and approximately the same age. Her hair was severely pulled into a bun and liberally streaked with grey. A long, perfect blade of a nose was the dominant feature on her expressive face. Her eyes had the attractive ability to underscore every word that emanated past her thin lips.

"Larry's just nervous," she said. "That's all it is. I'm sure."

At that moment Doctor Royal appeared in the kitchen. "Mrs. Flynn," he said. "I'd like to speak to you for a minute."

Mrs. Davis cleared her throat and stood up. "I'll get upstairs and start straightening things, Anna," she said. Her eyes locked on Joseph's face. "If there's anything at all you might need me for, just yell." For several seconds after she left the room, there was an uncomfortable silence. Finally, Doctor Royal's voice, deep and powerful, broke the stillness. "Mrs. Flynn, your husband explained most of the facts surrounding Larry's behavior, but perhaps you might inform me further." The doctor was standing over Anna. His figure was somewhat unimpressive. He was of medium height with narrow shoulders. Nevertheless, he possessed tremendous presence. His voice, with its deep, intelligent tone and unusual inflections, combined with eyes that moved slowly and missed nothing, commanded instant attention. His face was youthful; he couldn't have been more than thirty. His blond hair was considerably long and pushed back from his face. His entire demeanor contained a message of self assuredness.

Mrs. Flynn offered him a chair and he sat down next to her. "I'll tell you anything I can," Anna said.

"Well, Mr. Flynn has put things pretty well into perspective," he said. "According to him, Larry has been acting strangely for some time."

"We thought it would pass," Anna said.

"Yes, I understand. But unfortunately some things don't pass and this appears to be one of them,"

Anna looked at the doctor, and spoke in a halting voice.

"What caused him to become paralyzed like that?"

"In medicine we refer to it as a catatonic state. It usually reflects a serious mental disorder."

Anna's hand moved suddenly to her face, "Mental disorder," she said in a stunned voice. "What mental disorder? What do you mean?"

Doctor Royal reached out and carefully squeezed her hand.

Joe walked around the table and came to his mother's side and rested his hand on her neck.

"Take it easy, Ma," Joseph said tenderly.

"Yes, Mrs. Flynn," Royal said. "There is no need to become alarmed about this. We'll do everything possible to relieve Larry. But it will take time."

Anna attempted to get up from the chair, "How is he? How is he now? I want to see him."

Joseph held her in the chair. "He'll be okay, Ma. Talk to the doctor. You can see Larry later."

"Yes, Larry's fine now," Doctor Royal said. "I gave him a sedative and he's quite relaxed."

"Can he talk?" Anna asked.

"No, Mrs. Flynn, not right now. He'll sleep for a long while. We can all talk to him later on." The doctor leaned forward in the chair and placed his face close to Anna's. "Tell me, Mrs. Flynn, has anything like this happened before? Was there any previous suggestion of this type of reaction in your son?"

"What do you mean?"

"Did he ever show such non-communication before? Perhaps for even a brief period of time?"

"No, nothing like this," Anna replied. "He might've stayed in his room a lot and keep to himself, but never anything like this."

"Did he ever have sudden moments of hilarity?" Royal said.

"What?"

"Did he ever act unusually happy or active, jumping from a morose state into one of exuberance?"

"Yes, he did" Joseph interrupted. "You're damn right he did.

He'd talk to himself and laugh and carry on. It was spooky."

"During such times, did your brother converse with you?"

"Naw, he never said much to me or anyone else. It was as if he were in his own private world or somethin', mumbling, whispering, and carrying on like a crazy man."

"Did you ever experience such moments with your son, Mrs. Flynn?"

Joseph interrupted again. "Yeah, she did. We all did. But we were all pretending it would go away."

"Doctor Benson said Larry'd be okay. He said things like this would eventually clear up on its own," Anna said.

"He didn't know what he was talking about," Joseph said.

Anna looked up at her son. "Maybe so, Joey, but God rest his soul. He meant well."

"Yeah, sure he meant well," Joseph replied sarcastically.

Doctor Royal's voice politely broke, back into the conversation. "What we've got to be concerned with at the moment is Larry's present situation. He needs vigorous care."

"What should we do?" Anna asked.

"I've already made the necessary arrangements. I'm going to admit him to a hospital." Doctor hesitated. "A sanitarium really."

"A sanitarium! My God!" Anna said.

The doctor squeezed and patted her hand. "It's not so terrible, Mrs. Flynn. A sanitarium is a place where Larry can rest and recover,"

"A sanitarium is for crazy people," Anna said.

"No, no," Royal smiled. "You're expanding this way out of proportion. We'll treat him there and try to help him come to grips with his problems."

"What problems?" Anna cried. "He doesn't have any problems. He's just nervous, that's all. He's not crazy."

"No one is saying he's crazy, Mrs. Flynn. Let me try to explain." Doctor Royal stood up and walked over to the window. Joseph followed his every move.

"Mrs. Flynn," the doctor said as he turned around, "your son is exhibiting classic symptoms of schizophrenia."

"What is that?" Anna said.

"It's a derangement of the thinking process. We're not entirely sure what creates the condition, but we have a good idea. It's a combination of many factors and we have ways to investigate them and alleviate them. There are forms of counseling and medication we can offer. Whatever it was that precipitated this condition in your son will have to be explored. And a sanitarium is the best place to do it."

"I don't want him going there," Anna said,

"Oh, for Christ sake, Ma!" Joseph said, "What're you trying to prove. The doctor's right." Joseph was about to continue but he abruptly stopped when his father walked into the kitchen.

"The ambulance will be here any minute," Patrick said. "Is there any way we should get him ready?"

Joseph looked at his father out of the corner of his eye.

He looked tired and worn out. His sleeves were carelessly rolled up and his tie was pulled loose from his neck.

"Mrs. Flynn isn't sure she wants Larry to go," Doctor Royal said.

Patrick grunted. "Never mind what she thinks." He walked over and spoke directly to Anna. "Jesus Almighty Christ! What's wrong with you? What are we going to do keep him here? We can't handle this. For Christ's sake, wake up!"

Anna forlornly looked up at him. Her voice was shaking and strained. "But Pat, our son's not crazy."

Patrick banged his forehead in disgust. "Jesus, what do you call it then?" he said loudly. "He's crazy as far as I can see and he's going to that sanitarium and that's all there is to it."

Anna bowed her head and began to cry.

Patrick walked over and rested his hand on Doctor Royal's shoulder. "We'll ride out together. We'll follow the ambulance."

"Yes, Pat, that will be fine," the doctor replied.

Patrick turned to Joseph. "You get your mother upstairs and

have Mrs. Davis help her change. I called Bill. He'll be around in a while and he'll drive you and your mother out to the hospital."

Joseph looked away and said nothing.

"Answer me, you bastard!" Patrick said.

"Answer you how? What do you want me to say?" Joseph replied in an annoyed voice.

The doctor walked over to Joseph. "Go ahead, Joe. Take your mom upstairs. Your dad and I will get things ready."

Joe walked over and helped his mother out of the chair. "C'mon, Ma. Let's get going."

Joseph returned downstairs and walked past the attendants as they prepared Larry for the ambulance. He stopped for a moment and watched them as they wrapped his brother in a blanket. Larry rested in a peaceful sleep. His father and the doctor were talking as they put on their coats. Joe walked out onto the back porch.

A breeze gently quivered against his face. He looked out over the terrain. The grass and trees were already a summer green and flowers were blossoming everywhere. For a moment Joseph didn't move or think. He just stood there in the coolness of the morning enjoying the breeze and the brightness. Although he desperately tried to keep his mind dormant, the effort was in vain; he wondered how long Larry would be away. Doctor Royal had given no real hint of the time involved. Joe fervently wished for a long duration. His most hidden thoughts saw the whole situation as an opportunity, once and for all, to finally reach his father. Regardless of the years of terror and punishment behind him, he knew it was the communion his heart continually longed for; to be his father's son again, to walk and laugh with him. He knew that all the hate and vengeance that filled his soul could be erased in a moment with a kind gesture or smile from his father. If it were ever to happen, the time must be now and Joseph knew it.

He took a great, deep breath of the morning's freshness before going in to get ready for Bill Manley's arrival.

6

THE LONG, sleek Continental moved slowly over the narrow, country road. Myron Royal adeptly worked the automobile around the considerable bumps and turns.

"Mount Rose is a beautiful place, Pat."

"Is it?" Patrick's voice was uninspired'.

"Yes, really. It's the best sanitarium of its type within two hundred miles. It has an extraordinary staff and admirable program. I'm sure you'll be very satisfied with it."

Patrick cleared his throat. "Tell me, Doc," he said. "Can Larry's condition be cleared up or what?"

"Yes, we can clear it up somewhat."

"I'm not talking about somewhat. Can you clear him up permanently?"

"That's difficult to predict, Pat. I don't know."

"Well then, I want something made clear."

What is it?"

"Do I mean anything to you?"

Doctor Royal turned toward Patrick. "Of course you do," he said.

"Have I helped you? Have I been good to you?"

"Yes, you know that," Royal replied.

"You also know that I'll be good to you in the future. Don't you?"

"Yes."

"You know what's waiting for you. You're no dummy. I hand-picked you for the coroner's job. That alone increased your practice three-fold. I've offered you plenty of stock investments you'd otherwise never see. There's also some of the best property in the county waiting for you, you know that."

"Well, I..."

"Well shit. You know I can hand you a fortune. You don't have to bust your ass on house calls as long as we're tied up."

"All right, Pat. Yes, I do know that."

"All right then, I want you to promise me something."

Doctor Royal remained quiet and waited for Pat to continue.

"I want you to guarantee me, unless my kid is a hundred percent cured, he'll remain in this sanitarium."

"Remain!"

"Yes, remain. I don't want him home or around the streets calling attention to his condition. It's embarrassing and goddamn bad for business. I don't like any weaknesses staring people in the face. When people see weakness, they see opportunity, and I don't need that kinda bullshit. You understand me?"

"Well Pat, I'm not sure."

"Well, be fuckin' sure! What I'm sayin' is that I want the kid kept there unless he's a hundred percent. You follow me? I've got enough cash to keep him there forever. That's no problem."

"It's very difficult to clear this type of illness permanently," Doctor Royal said.

"Then he stays there. It's very simple."

"There is an excellent psychiatrist I'm acquainted with that I'm going to consult. He's on the permanent staff of Mount Rose and he'll give your son immediate attention."

"Will he cure him?"

"I told you, Patrick, I don't know."

"What if he sees an improvement and wants to discharge him? Will you step in?"

"I'll explain the situation to him."

"Is he going to understand the way you do?"

"I think so."

"I don't want any mistakes, Doc. I don't want any fuckin' shrink goin' around talkin' about my attitude."

"No, you can be sure he won't."

Patrick reached over and grabbed Royal's shoulder. "You make it clear to him that if he does it my way, it'll be well worth it. I can set him up pretty good. He might have a few bucks but I never met anybody that wasn't interested in a few more."

"He'll understand."

"Make goddamn sure, because if there's anything said about any of this, there's goin' to be some broken heads layin' around."

"That won't be necessary, Patrick," Royal said.

"You guarantee it?" Patrick asked.

"I'm sure my psychiatrist friend will be very interested."

"Will you guarantee he'll go along?"

"I guarantee it," Doctor Royal smiled.

Patrick stretched back into the seat. "Now that's real fine," he said, "That's really, really fine." He looked at Royal. "I'll see to it that you get an extra payday too."

Mount Rose Sanitarium was fifty miles north of Clarkson.

It was a complex of three immense white buildings with beautifully tended grounds covering many acres. There were flower gardens everywhere, Along the labyrinth of cemented sidewalks were fountains and various colored benches. Many of the patients were walking about, all of them escorted by hospital aides. The hills and dales seemed to reach as far as the eye could see.

The Flynn group was led into a large, elegantly furnished waiting room on the main floor. Doctor Royal attended to Larry's admission. It was a long, tense wait and Joseph grew increasingly restless. By ten a.m. he could no longer sit and wait. He walked over to his mother. "Ma," he said, "I'm goin' to go outside and walk around a while."

Anna reached up and gently squeezed his hand, "Okay, Joey," she replied. "We'll call you as soon as the doctor comes back."

Joe walked out to the front sidewalk and languidly stretched his arms. He wondered if Mrs. Davis had known enough to call Mickey and inform him that Joe would be late for work. In the excitement of the early morning, Joseph had completely forgotten about his job. Joe felt reasonably sure that the always responsible Mrs. Davis had taken care of it.

He slowly walked about the grounds for a long while engrossed in the chattering and animation of the patients as they passed him. He looked at their shuffling gaits and empty eyes. He was amazed at their vast number; never before seeing so many mentally disturbed people at one time, in one place. If felt odd to imagine his brother as one of the sad assembly.

Eventually, he returned to the waiting room. He wasn't there a minute when Doctor Royal and another man entered the room. The tall, bearded gentleman was obviously a physician of some sort; a long, white coat hung to below his knees. His white shirt was stiffly starched and his mannerisms were quick and confident. He followed Doctor Royal to where Pat Flynn sat reading a book. When he saw them approaching, Patrick stood up.

"Patrick," Doctor Royal said. "I'd like you to meet Doctor Malcolm Brogan."

Doctor Brogan extended his hand to Patrick. Joseph was stunned to see how much the doctor towered over his father. Brogan was at least six-feet-five and splendidly built. Although his face was almost totally covered by the chestnut colored beard, his handsomeness was easily discernible. In contrast to the severe neatness of Doctor Royal's hair, Brogan's was a wild bush of curls. His eyes were dark and alert over a patrician nose and a mouth that seemed permanently fixed in a slight smile.

After general introductions and greetings, Brogan turned his attention to Patrick, "I examined your son, Mr. Flynn, and although I can't confirm it at this moment, I believe his is suffering from extreme schizophrenia." The doctor turned slightly and looked at Anna. "I'm afraid that he's going to be with us for quite a while."

Anna sat quietly, desperately trying to maintain her composure.

"We understand, Doc," Patrick said. "We sorta expected it."

Brogan turned his smiling face back to Patrick.

"It won't be so terrible really," he said, "It's for the best. Mount Rose is ideal for the type of treatment your son's condition necessitates."

"I'm sure," Patrick said.

"I'll keep the family informed of Larry's progress," Brogan said.

Doctor Royal stepped forward and addressed the group, "I think we should allow Doctor Brogan to get back to work."

Brogan patted his shoulder and continued smiling. "If there's anything anyone wants to know, I'm here eight hours a day and Doctor Royal has my home phone number,"

"I'll clarify everything for them," Royal said.

Patrick walked over and once again shook Brogan's hand.

"You'll be hearing from me."

"I'm looking forward to it."

Anna stood up and put on her coat. Joseph rushed over to help her. Her face was a mask of pain and confusion,

"Everything'll be okay, Ma. Just relax," Joe said.

Anna didn't reply. She was having a difficult time restraining the tears from spilling over.

Doctor Brogan walked to the doorway that led to the corridor. "Remember," he said, "anytime anyone needs me, just call. Feel free." He smiled and gave a slight wave as he left the room.

Doctor Royal walked over to where Joseph and Anna were standing. "Would you like to drive my car back, Joe?" he said.

"Yeah, that'd be fine."

Royal turned to Bill Manley. "I'll drive back with you and Pat."

"Sure," Bill said.

As Doctor Royal opened the car's door to allow Patrick in, he tapped him to gain his attention. Patrick looked up.

"Doctor Brogan understands the situation," Royal said.

Patrick smiled, "I sorta got that feeling."

As the car pulled forward, Patrick turned to Doctor Royal. "Incidentally," Patrick said. "You can speak freely in front of Billy. He understands the situation too."

Royal looked past Patrick to the immense figure of Bill Manley sitting behind the steering wheel. "I didn't mean to..."

"Forget it," Manley said without looking at him.

"What does the kid's condition look like, Doc? Can he get better?" Patrick asked.

"Perhaps."

"I don't know. He's been acting real goofy. I think he'd be happy here."

"Permanently?" Royal asked.

"Well, he'll be around people like himself. That should make him less nervous."

"You don't think he'd resent staying here permanently?"

"Resent? What do you mean resent? If he's sick this is where he belongs. And if he doesn't clear up all the way, I want him to stay."

"We'll see."

"Whadaya mean, we'll see? I thought it was understood."

Royal's face assumed a morose expression. "It is understood. I just don't want to belabor the point."

"Professional ethics, eh?" Patrick smiled. Doctor Royal didn't answer.

7

ANNA FLYNN was rarely home all through the spring and early summer. Almost every day Mrs. Davis would drive her out to the sanitarium where they would spend the entire day with Larry. Occasionally, Joe would drive, as Anna and Mrs. Davis softly chattered on the back seat. Nevertheless, Joe resolutely refused to see Larry or speak to him, offering the excuse that it bothered him too much to witness the condition of his brother. Of course, Anna knew better. She was well aware of her youngest son's true feelings. Joseph could easily discern that his mother saw through his deception, but it was just as well; he couldn't tolerate the thought of Larry any longer, regardless of his sickness or predicament.

Larry's condition showed no improvement. There were intermittent periods when he appeared perfectly normal, only to return to strange silences or abnormally raucous behavior. Anna began to resign herself to the fact that it would be a long time before her son would come home.

Patrick and Bill Manley infrequently drove out to Mount Rose for short visits with Larry. Patrick's lack of enthusiasm for seeing Larry made Joseph furious; absolutely convincing him that his father couldn't bear to see his adored son in such a frightful condition.

The situation had failed to close the gap between Joseph and Patrick, creating a higher level of hostility in Joe's attitude. As always, he seldom saw his father. When they were in each other's company, little or nothing was said.

Joseph devoted practically all of his time to Carol. He knew that he should he spending more time with his mother and offering encouragement, hut he had no stomach for it; at the slightest provocation he would become annoyed at her disconsolateness and tears. He had no inclination or desire to attune himself to her pain over Larry. He could offer no sympathy, so he chose to avoid being near her. Carol's constant recriminations concerning his attitude did nothing to alleviate the great burden of his guilt.

She would say, over and over, "You should spend more time with your mother ..."

Carol was unaware that her words drummed against Joseph's brain like a jackhammer, but he refused to relent. He had enough of Larry and was deliberate in his attempt to sever all remnants of his relationship with the brother he hated. He had made up his mind; his mother was enmeshed with Larry's illness to the point that it remained the only element of her conversations and activity. Joseph wanted none of it. Therefore, Anna would have to endure her great trial without him.

It was the hottest July Joe had ever experienced. The heat came off the pavements in waves, as day after day the sun battered Hanway. Joe saw Ray Walton's car pull up to the gas pump. He slammed down the hood of the car he was walking on and walked outside. Ray stuck his head out of the window. "Jeeeeesus Holy Keeeerist, it's hot," he said.

"You know it," Joe replied, as he ran his handkerchief across his forehead. Ray got out of the car.

"How much gas?" Joe asked,

"By Jeeesus, fill 'er up, boy. Fill the fucker up."

Joe looked at him and laughed. "Crazy bastard."

"Hey, what are you doin' tonight?" Ray asked.

"I'm probably goin' over to Carol's. Why?"

"Well, man, I thought you'd like to take an excursion into the city with me."

"For what?"

"There's a nice place I've found that doesn't mind serving minors, ya know," Ray said, as he bumped his elbow against Joseph's side.

"Naw, I can't."

Ray spread his arms and looked at the sky. "Good God, what's happening to this boy?" He looked back at Joe.

"What's your problem?" Joe said.

Ray's eyes opened wide. "Well, what the hell are ya doin', gettin' married or what? You're like an old man anymore."

Joe set the pump into the gas tank and turned to Ray. "What am I going to do in Clarkson. There's nothin' there to interest me."

"Shit man, we could have a drink, find some cunt, you know."

"Naw, I'm sorry, Ray. No dice."

"Ah, you're like a fuckin' queer. Why doncha wise up?"

"Kiss my ass."

Ray started to laugh as he messed Joe's hair. "Baby, if those hot broads get a look at you, we'll be on easy street."

"Sorry buddy, you'll have to do it without me," Joe smiled. "Do you think you can manage?"

"I'll manage, I'll manage. I've been doin' okay. I'm tellin' you. You don't know what you're missin'."

"Maybe some other time," Joe said.

"Maybe my ass."

"Well what the hell, Ray. I've got a girl, I like seein' her."

Ray let out a whoop as he jumped back into the car. "You do whatever you like, but I'm goin' to screw my ass off."

Joe walked over to the window. "Watch yourself. You might get yourself beat up messin' with the big boys."

Ray looked up at him, his face beaming. "Honest to God, Joe, it's the fuckin' end. You don't know what you're missin'."

"I'll live without it," Joe smiled.

"Okay," Ray said, as he started the car. "But let me know if you change your mind."

"Yeah, I will,"

Joseph watched Ray's car until it made the turn on Bridge Street. "Crazy bastard," he said to himself.

8

THE MAILMAN laboriously made his way up the Granahan front steps to the porch. He knocked on the door.

Momentarily, Elaine Granahan appeared at the door's screen and looked out. "What is it, Harry?" she said.

The elderly man pulled an envelope out of the large pouch and opened the door. He playfully held the envelope against his chest. The full, white moustache lifted as his mouth split into a wide grin. "I think I've got something you've been waiting for."

Mrs. Granahan felt her heart skip. "C'mon, Harry," she whispered. "Don't kid me."

"Would I kid you?" The old man laughed, exposing his toothless mouth. "It's postmarked Ohio."

She looked at him standing there, his face, filled with a thousand wrinkles, his eyes glinting with happiness. "You're serious," she whispered.

"Darn right I am."

Her hand darted out and pulled the letter away from him. She looked at the postmark. "Ohio," she said in a breathless voice. "Ohio, I can't believe it!"

She grabbed the old man around the waist and they bounced around the front porch in an impromptu dance. "Ohio, Ohio," she sang.

"Is Mr. Granahan home?" the old man asked.

"Yes, he is. Oh, thank God. He'll be so happy."

The mailman patted her face. "You better get in there and tell him the news."

She grabbed his hands and kissed him softly on the cheek.

"Oh bless you, Harry. Bless you."

The smile left the man's face, replaced by a look of sadness.

"Everybody'll miss you," he said, in a quiet voice. "But I'm sure it'll be for the best. Frank's been feelin' real low."

Elaine Granahan held the letter up. "Not anymore he won't. Not when he sees this." She kissed the man again and ran into the house.

Frank Granahan sat quietly on the back porch, his eyes fixed on the back yard, looking at nothing in particular. He heard the squeak of the screen door and turned around. His wife stood above him, her body trembling.

"Frank, honey, you're not going to believe this."

"What?"

Her small, trim body looked as though it was ready to leap from the porch. Her grey hair was pulled back in a careless up-sweep. Her forehead was damp with perspiration. Her blue eyes sparkled with joy.

"You're not going to believe this."

He saw the envelope in her hand and jumped up.

"What's that?" he said.

"What do you think it is?" she answered, barely able to contain herself.

"No."

"Yes."

He grabbed it from her hand. He read the contents, his lips moving silently.

Elaine examined her husband's face. The features she loved so dearly had aged and grown haggard over the past year. The joy had long ago left her husband's eyes. He had lived listlessly, filled with doubt and fear. The old freshness had turned stale and the strength of his personality had all but vanished.

But now, before her eyes, a transformation was taking place. His body seemed to fill with energy. His eyes danced.

"Jesus Christ!" he shouted.

They stepped toward each other and embraced. "Oh thank

God, Frank," she said, as the tears filled her eyes.

He pulled back and waved his arms in happiness.

"I knew Mr. Rupp would come through."

"Did you?" She smiled, knowing in fact, that he'd long ago given up the possibility of the job.

"Well, let's pretend," he laughed.

Once again, they embraced. "We've gotta be there by Monday, The letter says the movers will be here this weekend."

"He said he wants you to call him."

"Yeah, there's a lotta things he's got to tell me about—the new house, the salary, but the letter pretty well tells me everything I've gotta know."

"I know," she smiled. "I read it."

"Will Carol be ready to leave at such short notice?"

"Oh, Frank, don't worry about Carol. She has no other choice."

"But, I mean about Joe and everything."

"I'll tell her when she gets home," Mrs. Granahan said.

"She'll get over it," he said.

"Sure she will. If nothing else, she'll be happy for our sake."

He crushed the letter under his fist. "I hope so," he said. "God Almighty, I hope she understands."

Elaine walked over and held his face in her hands. "Of course she'll understand. That's already been taken care of. Now why don't you start getting things together?"

Joe pushed open the screen door and walked into the kitchen. His presence in the Granahan home had become so routine, he no longer found it necessary to knock on the. door. The kitchen was empty. The porcelain sink gleamed in the evening's shadows. A vase, filled with red and white artificial flowers, sat in the middle of the kitchen table. Blue carpets that matched the color of the wallpaper lay neat and straight over the shining linoleum.

"Anybody home?" he yelled.

Joe heard Carol's voice as she approached from the parlor.

"Coming, Joe."

The second he saw her he knew something was wrong. He pretended to ignore the look on her face. "Where's everybody?" he asked.

"In the parlor. Please sit down a minute, hon."

He obeyed without question, intensely interested in Carol's expression and his own growing feeling of dread. He pulled back a chair and sat at the table. "What's up?"

Carol just looked at him as she idly ran her fingers over the bright red neckerchief around her neck. She bit hard against her lower lip, unable to meet his eyes. She pressed the vividly colored skirt against her backside before sitting down. She tried to say something but the words wouldn't come.

"What's wrong?" Joe said.

Her voice was a whisper. "Joey, my dad got that job. They wrote him today."

He was caught totally unexpected by her statement, and for a moment, it failed to register. Finally, his lips moved. "What are you talking about? What job?"

"Oh, Joe, you know what job."

"Not that Ohio thing?"

"Yes, that job."

The sound of Joseph's heart turned to thunder. His mouth went dry. Carol saw the pallor replace the color in his face.

"What are we going to do now?" she said, her voice on the verge of breaking.

Joseph abruptly stood up. "I'll talk to them," he said.

"About what? What can you talk to them about? They have no choice. My father needs the job. We've got to go."

"You don't have to do anything," he said, his voice snarling.

"Joe, please… They're so upset the way it is. They know how we feel about each other, but there's no choice."

"That's it then? That's all you have to say about it?"

"What can I say? What can I do?"

214

"You can stay, goddammit! That's what!" Joe said, desperately trying to keep himself from shouting.

"Stay where?"

"We can figure something out."

Carol felt the sobs catching her, throat. "Oh, Joe, we've talked all about that a million times. You know I've got to go with them."

Joseph paced about the kitchen. "I don't believe this," he said. "How could this happen?" He walked over to where Carol was sitting and roughly tugged at her shoulder. "There's got to be a job around here."

"It's been a whole year, Joe. There is no job. He tried."

"Oh, fuck," Joe said disgustedly.

Carol stood up and put her hands on his waist. "Let's go for a drive. I've got to get out of here. We've got to talk."

"You're staying."

"Joe, I'm not! I can't!"

Joseph viciously grabbed her chin, "Is that all you can say? Is that all you think about it? You've got to go, it's as simple as that," he said, mocking her, "Is that all there is to it?"

"There isn't anything I can say. Don't you understand? I've put them through hell the last couple of hours and I'm ashamed. They don't deserve that. I've screamed and cursed at them. I've been miserable, but they can't change anything, It's the only chance they've got."

"And what about me?"

"They're upset about you too. They're sick about it. They don't know what to say to you."

"They don't have to say anything to me."

"Joe, please go in the parlor and talk to them. They want to explain and make you understand."

"Fuck it. I understand perfect."

Carol sat back down and began to cry.

Joseph looked down at her, feeling himself turn to ice. He didn't want to hold her or kiss her now; instead, he wanted to kill her.

His voice was dry and hard. "I'm asking you one more time. Are you staying?"

Carol didn't answer as she continued crying.

"That's it then!" he said.

She leaped up from the chair and threw her arms around him. "Joe, Joe," she sobbed. "I love you so much. Please, please, understand."

Joe pushed her away. "Yeah, I told you I understand," he said icily.

"We'll manage something," she sobbed. "You'll see. It won't be so bad."

Joe continued to push her away from him as he answered. "We won't manage anything. I'm finished with you."

"Oh, no. Don't say that, please."

Joseph turned and rushed toward the door. Carol quickly followed pulling at his shoulders. Just as he reached the door, he turned around and roughly shoved at her arms. "You fuckin' pig, keep your hands off me," he said through clenched teeth.

Carol was stunned at the epithet, but continued to grab at him. He viciously slapped her across the face, driving her back toward the table.

Suddenly, Frank and Elaine Granahan appeared in the room.

"What in the hell is going on?" Mr. Granahan shouted.

Mrs. Granahan ran toward Carol. She tenderly held her daughter's shoulders as she turned toward Joseph. "You get out of here," she hissed.

Frank Granahan rushed toward Joseph and Carol screamed. "Daddy, don't!" Her harsh scream stopped him in his tracks. His eyes blazed, as he wildly stared at Joseph.

"I'll kill you, you bastard!"

"You'd better hold it right there, old man, or I'll bust you in half."

Carol broke loose from her mother's grip and ran to her father. "Daddy, Daddy, please," she cried. "He's crazy. He doesn't know what he's saying."

Joe's voice was mean and sarcastic. "I know what I'm saying, and if any of you ever come near me again, I'll tear you apart."

He slammed the door loudly behind him as he left the house.

Joseph aimlessly drove his car for hours. His mind continued to be a seething, raging hell. He proceeded to drive into Clarkson where he vainly searched out Ray Walton's car. Ultimately, he returned to Hanway, parked his car on Main Street and walked the streets for a long time, trying to pull himself into some semblance of order.

When he finally returned home, it was almost midnight and his mother was standing in front of the mansion waiting for him.

He got out of the car and walked toward her.

"What are you doing up this late, Ma?"

"Waiting for you, son."

Joseph searched her eyes. "What's wrong now?" he said,

"Carol's been calling and calling,"

"I don't want to talk about her."

Anna walked over to him and crossed her arms in a gesture of annoyance.

"How could you have hit her?"

Joseph laughed derisively. "Oh, so she told you, huh. What are they going to do, arrest me?"

"Don't be so mean and ignorant, Joe. She and her parents are very upset."

"Is that so?"

"Yes, that's so. They're not angry with you. They feel bad the way you're taking all this."

Joseph laughed again, "Wow, that's a change. A coupla hours ago, old man Granahan wanted to kill me."

"He was just upset. You can't blame him for that. You had no business hitting Carol but they do understand you were upset. Carol explained how hurt you were. They want you to go over and talk to them. They'd like to straighten everything out."

"I'm not going anywhere, and I'm not talking to anybody."

Anna reached out and touched his arm. "Oh, Joey, make some sense. Carol told me they have to move away. I'm sorry for you. Everybody involved is. But think of Carol and how hurt and upset she must be."

"Nobody has to be sorry for me."

"Joe, you love that girl and you know it. Now, for God's sake, act your age and go over and see those people in the morning."

Joe turned away. "I told you I'm not."

"For God's sake, Joey, They're leaving on Saturday, The day after tomorrow. You don't have too much time to make up."

Joe's jaws worked furiously over the wad of gum in his mouth. "Look, I know one goddamn thing for sure, I don't want to ever see that little whore again."

Anna instinctively slapped his mouth. She disdainfully looked at him. "Well, with your stubborn, wise guy attitude, I can see there's no point in talking to you!"

"That's right. Go to bed."

"I will. That's exactly what I'll do."

"Right. Fine."

Anna walked up the high concrete steps and disappeared into the house. Joe walked over to the giant oaks that stood just off the driveway. He slowly sat down in the damp grass and rested his back against one of the large, gnarled trunks. His head ached and his body felt numb. He sat there, wide awake, until morning.

On Friday, the phone rang all day and night. Carol tried desperately to reach Joseph. She visited the Flynn mansion several times during the day, begging Anna to try and locate him, but he couldn't be found. He hadn't shown up at Clark's gas station for work. Knowing the volatile nature of her son, Anna wasn't worried; she knew he was all right and just making himself scarce, refusing to communicate with anyone because of Carol. His mother didn't expect him to reappear, until after Carol and her family's departure.

Joseph Flynn sat disconsolately alongside the shoreline of the huge dam. He was certain no one, not even Carol, would think of searching him out at such a location. He absently threw small pebbles into the shimmering water, and watched the circles of tiny waves interrupt the stillness of the scene. The birds in the thicket surrounding him emitted their varying calls. Occasionally there was a whisper of leaves as a soft, summer wind moved across the watershed high above the heat of Hanway.

Although he tried, sleep was impossible. His car was littered with the wrappings of cold sandwiches he had picked up at Petry's Restaurant. He felt lost and alone.

Bill Manley shifted into a comfortable position on the stool alongside Patrick. Mulrooney's Bar was a favorite drinking place for the larks on County politicians, and Patrick and Bill made it a daily after-dinner stop.

"Did Anna hear anything about Joe?" Bill asked.

"No, nothing," Patrick answered,

"Where in the hell could he be?" Bill said.

"Who knows? Anna said he had a problem with his girl."

"About what?"

"She's moving away or something. Some kind of nonsense."

"Oh, yeah, that's right. I heard something about Frank Granahan getting a job somewhere. Illinois, I think."

"Ohio. Anna told me."

"Joe musta been stuck on the daughter pretty bad."

"Yeah, he's off sulking somewhere. He's a real strange kid."

"Anna must be worried as hell."

"Naw, not really. She knows he'll turn up. He's just hiding until she goes," Patrick laughed.

"Kids are real goofy."

"Yeah, especially him, the little bastard." Patrick's sarcastic laughter drained away. "Ya know, Billy, I've got a problem here."

"About what?"

"Well, with Larry in the nuthouse, it leaves me in a rotten situation."

"How?"

Patrick slowly sipped at the scotch and water, staring at his reflection in the mirror behind the bar. "Neither one of us are getting' any younger," he said.

"I guess not," Bill laughed.

"No, I mean it. You know the way I feel. I always thought Larry would run the business when I gave it up."

"But you always wanted him to be a doctor."

"Yeah, sure. I wanted to show that crummy town that a Flynn could have the best education in the world, and the brains to handle it, but the fuckin' kid washed out. I was always afraid that might happen."

"But if he was a doctor ..."

"Oh shit, Bill. So Larry'd be a doctor. That wouldn't mean he couldn't handle my businesses ... The doctor thing would just make him nice and legitimate. He'd make ten times the money and have ten times the power taking over what I was going to leave him."

"Well, how do you know? He might shape up."

"That's impossible. He's a liability to me now. He always will be." Patrick slammed the glass down on the bar. "Jesus Christ!" he muttered, "How could this happen? How could he crack up? All my fuckin' plans turned into an embarrassment." He turned and looked at Manley. That's why I've gotta keep him in that sanitarium, to try and make everyone forget about him. I want them to forget any of my sons have a weakness."

"There's nothin' weak about Joe."

Patrick rubbed his hands across his eyes. "No, there's not, He's a tough bastard. It's funny the way everything worked out. I always despised the kid, now I need him."

"You don't need anybody," Manley said.

"In this case I do. I want one of my sons to keep what I built up. I don't want anyone to forget the name of Flynn. It's gotta be a thing that passes from one generation to the other. It can't be no other way."

"What are you gonna do?"

"I'm not sure."

"Why don't you just go to the kid? I think he's been waiting for you all his life."

Patrick laughed again. "Are you kiddin'? The fuckin' kid hates me. I don't think we passed three civil words between us."

"That doesn't matter, Boss. He's still your kid, and I got the feelin' he really wants you to care for him."

"You're wrong."

"Well, it's a feelin' I always had."

"Don't misunderstand me, Billy. I don't give a fuck if I ever see him again, or any of them for that matter. But under the present circumstances, I'm in a bind."

"How are you goin' to work it out?" Bill asked.

"I don't know. I've gotta figure something, hut I don't know how to approach him. I don't know how he'll handle it, hut I've gotta come up with something."

"Is it really that important?"

"Is what that important?" Pat asked,

"That one of your kids gotta handle things. I mean, you're goin' to he around for quite a while yet."

Patrick laughed and slapped Bill's shoulder. "Yeah, that's right. I am, hut not forever. When I'm too old to do it, I want another Flynn to be doin' it, and Joe's the only Flynn I know."

"Well then, if it's that important, you'll handle it. You always do."

Patrick smiled as he counted the hills he put on the bar. "Yeah, that's right. I always do. I'll have to swallow a little pride." He turned and looked sideways at Manley. "Ya know what I mean, Billy?"

"Yeah, Boss, I understand what you mean. You'll figure out something."

Patrick dropped the last leaf of green onto the mahogany. "You bet your ass I will," he smiled. "Let's go."

9

FRIDAY NIGHT was always the busiest time at Riverio's Supper Club. Well-dressed families filled the numerous tables, enjoying, with relish, the specialties of macaroni and meat balls. The expensively decorated restaurant presented a high priced menu, allowing only the well-heeled to dine there. Lila Walton walked into the large kitchen. She approached a heavy-set, Italian-looking man who was surveying the kitchen workers' activity.

"Armond," she called, as she pulled loose her apron, "I'm leaving."

The man twisted his neck at the sound of her voice, "Okay, Lila," he smiled. "You have a nice night."

"You bet, honey,"

The heat of the July night was sickening. She walked quickly along the sidewalk, looking forward to the air conditioned coolness of her room. Three blocks from Riverio's she entered a small hotel. She passed the attendant at the desk, with a smile and a wave. She took the elevator to the fourth floor. Minutes later she was enjoying a drink in her cool and beautifully furnished apartment. Patrick Flynn had been good to her. He set her up with a job at Riverio's, full knowing the benefits involved.

Flynn was Armond Riverio's landlord, and the arrangement was simple. Lila was a waitress in name only; appearing at, and leaving the restaurant only as she desired, for it was Patrick Flynn who paid her salary. The so-called job gave her a perfect excuse to spend almost all of her time in Clarkson, allowing everyone, including her son Ray, to believe she was working double shifts to keep her life going. In fact, she was Patrick's well-paid mistress. She would arrive in Clarkson by bus at mid-morning, and spend most of the afternoon relaxing in her apartment, away from the responsibility of caring for her son. She had always felt burdened by Ray and paid little or no attention to his needs. They had no semblance of a mother-son relationship. She treated him as she treated all men, as objects to admire and desire her. Ray recognized that quality in her but desperately pretended not to see it. She'd ask him embarrassing questions about his sex life and laugh huskily at his confusion. She often walked nude around the house and was aroused by her son's furtive glaces. She had never kissed him or held him. She had never considered any of his problems; she saw him simply, as just another man, something to be teased and used. She left him orders to clean the house, as well as leaving him a few dollars for restaurant meals. But she would buy him anything to amuse himself. Anything to keep him from asking too many questions. Nevertheless, often the questions would come, and she'd beat him and tell him to mind his own business. After a while, her plan worked. It had been many years since Ray cared to know Lila's habits, content with his aloneness and freedom from her.

Patrick Flynn was the only man to ever win her respect.

In his presence she was a dependent, hungry animal, desiring his overpowering sensuality from the first time she saw him. It was after he had returned home a hero. Somehow, prior to that time, she had failed to cross paths with him. Patrick had never finished school, and had gone his own way as a child, always working and scratching to keep ahead. Then he met Anna, and was removed totally from the usual Hanway social scene. It was during a chance meeting at a political rally when Patrick and Lila first came together. Both of them were instantly galvanized by the sexual currents they discharged. Patrick arranged everything—the job at Riverio's, the apartment, as well as the permanent removal of the husband who stifled her. She was always there for his asking, spending almost every night in the lounge of his real estate office, loving him, satisfying him. Lila was well aware that Patrick was involved with other women, and tried not to be annoyed by the realization. She knew that she alone couldn't quench his insatiable sexual appetite. But she was satisfied to know she was his main woman. Long ago, she stopped pleading with him to divorce Anna. Whatever his reasons, he refused to do it. She finally acquiesced to the fact, reluctantly settling for the role of his mistress.

She sat, completely nude, in the large chair, and looked out the window at the traffic that moved through the late city.

She would rest for a while before going to his office. She was not seeing Pat as much as she'd like to, and it was causing her a growing concern; but she assured herself he would never tire of her. She would keep herself young and vital, and love him more wildly than the whores he bothered with. But if all else failed, she would hold him with the chain of her husband's murder. She looked forward to a wonderful night.

Ray Walton felt ill at ease as he shifted about on the bar stool. Although he had pretended to Joe that a night on the town was a familiar thing to him, he was still a rank amateur in the arena of saloons and women. On Friday night, he chose to try his luck in the Pink Swan Bar, directly across the street from the Clarkson Hotel. Many transients stayed at the hotel and would often leave the confines of the hotel's elaborate dining room and bar to wander over to the bright lights of the Swan.

He pulled the blue, striped tie slightly away from his neck. He was wearing his best suit. It was a blue gabardine with narrow, long lapels. He was certain he looked dashing. The freckled young face and the wild red hair did not fit the suave appearance he was desperately trying to project. The bartender slid the third Tom Collins toward Ray and looked suspiciously at the youngster. Ray knew that the little man with the starched, white shirt and black bow tie was contemplating whether or not he should demand identification.

Ray managed to inconspicuously slide away from the bar and

huddled into one of the corner booths. He sipped at the drink while he watched the activity near the bar. Several women, none of them having the slightest notion that Ray was alive, sidled up to some of the customers along the bar. The women were dressed for a big time; expensive dresses clung to their bodies and all of them were well on their way to intoxication. The entire room was dimly lit, with most of the furniture done up in pink vinyl. Over the bar was an enormous painting of a pink swan. "What symbolism," Ray thought to himself, as he suppressed a chuckle.

His gaze moved away from the women to the window at his left, which gave him a panorama of the city's lights. It was just past nine o'clock, and Clarkson was well into its weekend hustle. People scurried along the streets, intent on their individual rendezvous. Neon was everywhere, lighting up the night places of Susquehanna Avenue. Suddenly, he jolted to attention. He squinted to ascertain the figure across the street. Lila Walton walked quickly along the sidewalk in front of the hotel.

Ray noticed how the exquisite dress outlined her body contours as she walked up the steps and entered the hotel. He instinctively drew back in the booth, not wanting her to see him. He finished the drink quickly and left the bar. His first thought was to go around the corner, get into his car and get out of the city, but something in his brain told him otherwise, His mother was supposed to be working. Instead, she was in the lobby of the Clarkson Hotel, dressed to the teeth. With no further thought or consideration, Ray ran across the busy street and entered the building. As he moved through the revolving door, Lila was stepping onto the elevator at the far end of the lobby. He watched the arrow as it stopped, indicating the second floor. He saw the stairway to his right and raced up the steps. When he reached the second story level, he stopped and peeked around the corner of the wall. His mother was slowly opening a door midway down the hall. He waited until she closed the door behind her before he silently approached the spot where she had been standing. He saw Patrick Flynn's name on the opaque window. Ray caught his breath. Lila had used a key to get in and Ray suspected that she was in there alone.

He walked back to the stairway and leaned against the wall, wiping the perspiration from his forehead and face with the back of his hand. He stood quietly for almost a half hour before he heard the elevator door open down the hall. Once again, he peeked from the corner. It was Patrick Flynn. The tall, handsome figure moved jauntily toward his office. Once again, Ray heard the door click open and slam shut. He sat down on the top step and covered his face with his hands. There was nothing to do but wait.

Ray had always suspected this kind of situation. But the dark swirling of his mind had never conjured the image of Patrick Flynn. He was sickened by the obvious reality he faced; his mother and his best friend's father were lovers. He waited in silence for a long time. Finally, he heard the clicking of the door.

He looked at his watch and realized that they had been together for almost three hours. Once again, he peered from the corner. Lila's hips swayed as she moved toward the elevator. Patrick stood in the doorway and watched her. Ray raced back down into the lobby and quickly made an exit to the street. Once outside, he ran to his car. Along the way he bumped against an elderly couple, knocking the man to the ground. Ray didn't stop to offer assistance. His mind was in an awful, spinning ferment. He gunned the engine of the old Ford and headed for home.

10

JOSEPH drove directly from the mountain to Clarkson. He arrived in the city at six a.m. It was a Saturday morning and Clarkson was quieter than usual. Although he had fought diligently against it, Joe finally gave way to the compulsion to see Carol one final time. He knew Mr. Granahan's mentality and was certain they'd be on the first bus out of the Greyhound Terminal. He walked into the bus station and approached the woman at the ticket counter.

"Pardon me, ma'am," he said.

The woman sleepily looked toward the voice. Joseph stood in a total disarray. His unshaven face was heavily shadowed. His eyes were red and filled with nervous fire. As he scratched his shoulder he muttered, "What time does the first bus leave for Dayton?"

The woman adjusted her glasses and lazily leafed through some papers. "Seven o'clock," she said without looking up.

"Yeah, right," Joe said, as he made his way to the exit. Across the street and about thirty yards down the terminal, he saw the open door of a diner.

Once inside, he collapsed in a booth. The man behind the counter looked over at him. "Whadaya havin'?" the man asked in a loud voice.

"Coffee."

"Anything to eat?" the man said.

"No."

"Then come over here and sit at the counter."

Joe got out of the booth. Several men, sitting at the counter, were totally unaware of the words that passed between Joe and the counterman. They simply hunched over their morning coffee, dressed in their work clothes, contemplating another day at their jobs. Joe sat down alongside them and sipped at the steaming liquid.

The voice came from behind the counter. "Ya look like ya had a rough night, kid."

Joe looked up at the man standing across from him. Despite his loud, authoritative voice, his face was kind; it was a large, round face, freshly shaved and washed, shining and rosy around the fat cheeks.

"Naw," Joe said. "I'm just a little tired."

"What were you on, a drunk?"

Joe smiled. "No, really, I'm just tired."

"The coffee'll do ya good."

"Yeah."

The man slowly wiped his hands with a small rag. "Whatsa matter? Don'tcha have the cash for a meal?"

"I'm not hungry."

"How about a slice a toast or sumpin?"

"No, thank you."

"Oh, c'mon, kid, it won't cost ya."

Joe offered his hand. The man reached out and grabbed it.

Joseph vigorously shook the hand. "Thanks for your kindness, but I'm really not hungry. I'd just like to sit around for a while and drink some coffee."

The man nodded his head and smiled. "Okay, but you're welcome to it." He turned around and went back to shining the coffee urn. Joe returned to the sipping of his coffee,

Joseph was standing at the diner window a half hour later, when the Hanway commuter bus pulled alongside the Greyhound Terminal. The Granahans alighted from the bus and disappeared inside. Joe had barely caught a glimpse of Carol. His eyes shifted to the departure platform on the side of the terminal. From his vantage point, he would see her clearly when she left the station.

Carol looked at her face in the ladies' room mirror. It was swollen and bleary eyed from her recent crying.

Her mother wrapped her arm around her, "Please, please, honey, stop it. Please. You're making Daddy a nervous wreck."

"I can't help it," Carol sobbed, as fresh tears began to fill her eyes.

Mrs. Granahan desperately tried to maintain her composure. "Good God, Carol, is it worth it? What kind of boy is he? Why didn't he try to see you before we left? What kind of boy is he to waste your tears on?"

Carol turned to her angrily. "Can't you understand? He's hurt, Mother. That's why no one can find him. He's hurt and torn up. Can't anybody understand that?"

Mrs. Granahan's voice was just as angry. "I'll tell you what I understand," she said. "Your father is outside this door with his heart breaking in half on account of you, and he doesn't deserve it."

Carol understood the truth of her mother's words. She didn't reply.

Mrs. Granahan's voice softened. "Oh honey, I do understand but nothing can be done. Joe was wrong in what he did."

Carol splashed cold water on her face and reapplied a small amount of makeup. She grabbed her mother and squeezed her. "Oh, Mommy," she said. "I do know I'm being unreasonable and I'm sorry but it hurts so much to leave him, especially like this."

"I know. I know," Mrs. Granahan said in a sympathetic voice. "But later on things'll work out. Wait and see. You'll write to him or call him. When he adjusts to the circumstances he will understand. Somehow the two of you will get together again."

"How?"

"Maybe Daddy can find him a job in Dayton. You never know."

Carol managed a smile. "Really Mother, do you think he will?"

"Of course he will. Your father has forgiven Joe for what happened. He understands too."

Carol kissed her mother's cheek. Her eyes brightened up.

There was a knock on the door. When Mrs. Granahan opened it, her husband faced them, looking nervous and forlorn. "Didn't you hear the loudspeaker?" he asked hesitantly. "They want us to board the bus."

Carol ran to him and wrapped her arms around his slight shoulders. She kissed him several times on the face. "Yes, Daddy," she smiled lovingly. "Let's go."

Frank Granahan looked past his daughter to his wife. "What?"

Mrs. Granahan smiled, tears filling her eyes. "It's all right, Frank. It really is," she said.

Frank grabbed Carol and lifted her up. "Everything's okay? You really want to go, baby?"

"Not really," Carol smiled, as she pinched his cheek. "But under the circumstances, I'll go happily."

"Well, let's not miss the bus." He laughed as he picked up the luggage. "Let's go."

Carol was immediately grateful for the glint of life she put into her father's eyes. She slipped her arm into her mother's and hurried with them to the departure platform. She continued to force her smile as the small contingent boarded the bus to Ohio.

Joe leaned against the curtain rod of the diner window. When he saw the small group approach the departure platform, his eyes opened wide, and his jaw locked shut. His gaze focused on Carol as she walked between her parents toward the bus. Once she moved away from the shadows of the terminal, the early sun caught the auburn glint of her hair. Joseph saw her breasts swelling through the blue cashmere of her sweater and the strong contours of her thighs moving under the dark, straight skirt.

He felt his stomach tumble over and nausea fill his throat. He waited until the bus moved out onto the street and turned from him. He left the diner. From the sidewalk, he heard the noise of the machine's air brakes as it slowed to negotiate the corner that led to the turnpike. When the bus disappeared from sight, Joseph ran to the corner. He got there just in time to see the bus turn toward the turnpike entrance. In a moment it was gone, leaving a floating cloud of white exhaust in its wake. It was too early for traffic and no one was on the sidewalks. Joseph stood alone on the city corner. He felt as though his heart had shattered, leaving a thousand sharp fragments to tear and bite at his chest. He felt the tears welling in his eyes and a gurgle of sobs building in his throat. He leaned against a mail box and cried unashamedly. He cried and cried until his hurt finally abated and was slowly replaced with a burning, consuming anger. He stood up straight and looked around to see if anyone had been watching him. He saw no one. He wiped the tears away and ran his hand over the stubble of beard. He once again looked at the location where the bus had disappeared. The tears were replaced with a cold gaze of hatred. At that moment, the message from the belly of his brain came through to him. There would be no more tears over the loss of Carol Granahan. There would be no more tears over the loss of marriage and children and such sweetness. Destiny had long ago seen to it, that such tenderness was not to be a realized for Joseph Flynn. On that awful city street, he acknowledged the inevitable. Suddenly, he felt hungry. He began to walk slowly back to the diner.

11

AT APPROXIMATELY the same time Joseph Flynn was arriving in Clarkson on that Saturday morning, Ray Walton was slowly awakening from a troubled sleep. On the night before he had decided not to challenge his mother with his recently acquired knowledge. He was too sick, too weary. Instead, he fell into his bed and fitfully slept through the night.

A clatter of dishware had awoken him. He went downstairs and into the kitchen. His mother was pouring coffee into a cup. She looked up at her son. Her blonde hair was tangled. Without makeup, her face was more sensual than beautiful,

"What are you looking at?" she said, in an annoyed voice.

Ray cleared his throat. He tried to speak but the words froze in his throat.

"What's wrong with you, Ray?"

He cleared his throat once again. "Nothing," he said, in a barely audible voice.

Lila's face assumed a mask of disinterest. "Ya want some coffee?" she asked.

Ray sat down at the table. "Ma," he said, "I saw you last night."

Lila was walking back toward the sink. When he spoke, she abruptly turned. "You saw what?"

The words poured out of Ray in a torrent. He told her everything. Lila remained silent until he had finished. She was about to say something, when Ray bolted from his chair and ran back upstairs. Lila sat down at the table. Her mind wandered over everything her son had said, and her main consideration was Patrick Flynn. She knew that if he ever became informed of Ray's knowledge, it would be all over. He would make Ray believe some implausible story, and then proceed to rip Lila from his life, in spite of the nature of her husband's death. Patrick would somehow face up to her challenge. Lila knew that Pat Flynn would somehow meet that challenge and defeat her. He would do anything to maintain his reputation. She had always known it. Regardless of her conscious efforts to pretend otherwise, there was no other solution. She had to keep her son quiet.

Ray was lying on his bed when she entered his room. "Ray, honey," she said, in a quiet loving voice. "Ray!"

Ray lay face down and didn't answer. She walked over and sat next to him on the bed. She patted the back of his head. He reached back and roughly pushed her hand away.

Lila pretended to sob. "Ray, sweetheart, please. Talk to me."

As Ray lay there, he was astounded at the measure of softness and caring in her voice. He turned over. He leaned on his elbow as he looked at her. "What can you say, Ma? What can you possibly say?"

Lila bent her head and softly squeezed his arm. "I've been lonely, Ray. Awful lonely. You couldn't understand." She placed the palm of her hand against his face. "Oh Ray, forgive me. Please forgive me." Ray had never seen his mother like this. He pulled her close to him. "Ma, it's all right. It's all right," he said.

Lila's face nestled against the side of his face. She wondered if her feigned attempt at contrition would keep Ray quiet.

She thought of what he possibly might say another time, in another place. Because of his closeness to Joseph Flynn, she couldn't be sure of what might be said later on. As her face pressed against him, she made her decision.

She got up from the bed. "Wait here, honey," she said smiling.

"Where are you going?"

"Downstairs, I'll be a minute."

She went downstairs and quickly returned. When she reentered the room, she carried a bottle of wine and two glasses.

"What the hell?" Ray said.

Lila smiled. "Don't you understand?" she said. "We've got something to celebrate about."

"What...?"

"It took something like this to finally bring us together as a mother and son," she said. "Isn't that reason for celebration?"

Ray blinked and smiled. "Oh."

She handed him a glass. "Let me pour," she said graciously.

Ray laughed. "Jesus, Ma, it's a little early."

"Not for an occasion like this," she said. "It's time we had a talk and a drink together."

Ray held up the glass. He smiled happily. Lila poured until his glass was filled. She began to talk, as she sat back down on the bed. Ray listened, somewhat confused. Her conversation rambled disjointedly over her early marriage and childhood. She talked about her parents and growing up in Hanway. She talked about her husband. Never once did she mention the name of Patrick Flynn.

As she talked, Ray sipped at the wine. She continually refilled the glass. After consuming almost the entire contents of the bottle, he finally raised his hand. "Wow! Hold it, Ma. I'm gettin' dizzy with all of this grape," he laughed. Lila had barely drunk anything, She watched as Ray laughed and rubbed his eyes. She remembered the many times she caught his eyes stealing glances at her as she left the shower or moved about the house in various stages of undress. She never before had offered him a parental relationship and she knew he sometimes desired her in spite of himself.

She carefully pushed him back onto the bed until he was lying down, "Relax, honey," she smiled. "You look so tired."

Ray felt giddy. He closed his eyes. "I am tired, Ma," he said with a smile. "I'm very tired."

"Well, sleep. Sleep now," she said as her hand rubbed along his leg. Ray wasn't aware of her hand until he felt it press along his thigh. He opened his eyes. Lila had removed her bathrobe with her free hand and she wore nothing underneath. Ray saw the full, firmness of her breasts and the smooth softness of her naked torso.

Ray's voice was tinged with shock. "Jesus Christ, Ma! What in the hell are you doin'?"

Lila continued to press her hand against his tense thigh. "Doesn't it feel good, baby? Doesn't it relax you? I want to relax you."

Ray reached down to push her away. Lila saw the beads of sweat form a line above his upper lip, "Whatsa matter, honey? Don't you like that?" she said in a sultry, alluring voice.

Ray could hardly breathe. With growing horror, he felt the swell of pleasure coming from his groin. Breathing heavily, he attempted to get up. Lila pushed him back onto the bed and covered him with her body. Ray felt the pressure of her naked breasts against his chest. His body went numb. She bent her head and kissed his mouth. At that moment, he wanted to die.

She gripped his ears as she forced her tongue between his teeth.

It was then, due to a lifetime of programming, that the resistance slowly crept from Ray Walton's body. She slipped her hand through the opening of his pajama bottoms and chuckled at the rigid hardness of his excitement. She felt a wave of lust envelop her. She tore at his clothes until he was as naked as she. His mind was dazed and spinning. She pulled him on top of her, placing his trembling hands on her breasts. At first he remained still, his hands unmoving. Through her urging and caressing he finally relaxed. He carefully rubbed his fingers over her rigid nipples. His mouth hungrily returned her devouring kisses, and then he penetrated the lushness of her sensuality.

Afterwards, Lila, still nude, leaned against the bureau and looked at Ray. He lay motionless on the bed staring at the ceiling.

Her laughter was deep and low, "Well, now we've both got a story to tell," she said, as she slowly rubbed her breasts and abdomen. "All you have to do," she said menacingly, "is utter one word about me and Pat, and I'll tell the whole fuckin' town what you did."

Ray didn't answer,

"Did you hear me?" she said loudly. "One goddamn word and I'll tell them how you made love to me, I'll say it. You know I will."

Ray slowly got up from the bed, covering his nakedness with his pajama top.

"Everybody'll believe me. When they see your face, they'll see your guilt," she said. He walked past her towards the bathroom. "They'll believe me when they see your face. One word, one lousy goddamn word from you, and I swear this whole town'll know what you just did to me."

Ray knelt down before the bowl and felt the vomit rise in his neck. He bent forward and violently threw up. The sweet smell of wine filled his nostrils. Lila walked over to the bathroom doorway. "That's your shame you're throwin' up, baby. Don't forget it. One word and I'll make you the talk of the town. They'll forget about me and Pat."

Ray held onto the sink as he heard the muffled sound of her bare feet on the steps as she returned to the kitchen. He went back to his room. As he dressed, his body felt as though it was wounded and bleeding. The bedroom still smelled of her perfume.

He walked to the closet and removed some clothing. He pulled several changes of underwear from his bureau drawer. Reaching under his bed, he slid a large, well-worn suitcase toward him. He lifted it up to the bed. When he finally locked it shut, it was filled to capacity. He walked over to his bookcase and pulled out a large, black covered box. Opening it, he removed a thick wad of money.

It was every dollar he had ever managed to save. He counted out twelve hundred and nine dollars. He didn't know how far it would take him. He knew it was enough to go somewhere. Anywhere. Some place away from his mother and Hanway. He put the money into both front pockets of his worn out jeans and pulled the heavy suitcase off the bed. He practically stumbled down the stairs and into the kitchen.

Lila had put her robe back on. The sash was tied carelessly allowing most of her breasts to protrude. She sat at the table idly stirring her coffee with her index finger. "Where are you off to?" she smiled.

Ray stood in the doorway. His lustreless eyes looked at her. "I'm leaving, Ma," he said in a dull monotone.

"Leaving!"

"Yeah, leaving."

"Well, now," she said sarcastically. "That's all right. This whole thing is workin' out better than I figured."

The side of Ray's mouth twitched as he set the suitcase down. "I'd like to kill you," he whispered.

"Kill me! Don't make me laugh. You wouldn't have the guts. You're too much like your old man," she said in a loud, angry voice. "Get out! Get the fuck out! Do me a favor. I've been praying for this moment for years. Get outta here. Once and for all, get out of my life."

Ray looked at her contemptuously, but felt the coiled anger slip from his gut. "Don't worry. I'm going."

With a broad, defiant smile, she looked directly at his eyes. "Then go," she said.

Without another look or word, Ray picked up the suitcase.

As Lila heard the front door close behind him she smiled, "Good," she whispered. "Good. Good."

12

RAY drove to a small motel on the outskirts of Clarkson. He stayed locked up and alone for two days trying to work out his plight. After what seemed like an eternity, he arrived at a decision. He would drive to New York state and enlist into the Army, where he might find something to offer a new direction to his life. Except for one final time, he would never speak or think of Lila Walton or Hanway ever again. At nine o'clock on Monday morning he went into the bathroom. He showered and shaved. He dressed himself carefully, before going to his car in the hotel parking lot. There was only one person to talk to now. By this time, Joseph Flynn would be at work and as usual, Patrick Flynn wouldn't be at home. Ray turned over the car's engine and moved out onto the highway, back toward Hanway and Anna Flynn.

At eleven a.m. on that July morning, it was already hot and sticky. The old Ford moved up the long, Main Street hill toward Jessup Avenue. Ray looked into the rear view mirror and saw a small group of people leaving Petry's diner; except for them, the street was relatively quiet as Ray examined its wide, grey stripe of macadam stretching back to the rise of the railroad tracks.

The gate leading to the Flynn driveway was open. Ray drove through. He parked his car behind the cement fountain. Before getting out of the car, Ray watched the refreshing sprinkle of water rush up toward the cloudless sky, return in an arc and softly splash in the water that edged against the lip of the fountain's cradle. As he walked toward the house, he ran his hand through the water, enjoying the feel of its clean coolness against his skin.

Ray leaned against the button alongside the huge, ornately decorated mahogany door. Simultaneously, he heard the melodious sound of chimes coming from within the mansion. In a moment Mrs. Davis appeared in the doorway.

"Why, Raymond, good morning."

"Morning, ma'am."

"What can I do for you?" she smiled.

Ray looked past her toward the empty foyer, "Is Joe home?" he asked.

"Why no, he's at work,"

"How about Mr. Flynn?"

"I'm sorry but he's not in either. He left the house about two hours ago."

Ray was relieved at hearing her expected reply, "Is Mrs. Flynn in?" he asked,

A thoughtful expression passed over Mrs. Davis' face. "Yes," she said. "She's in. Is there something wrong, Ray?"

Ray tried very hard to pretend everything was fine, "Oh, no," he said smiling. "Nothing's wrong at all. I just need some information and I think Mrs. Flynn might be able to help me out."

Mrs. Davis turned her head and looked over her shoulder. Her eyes studied the second floor balcony. "She hasn't been feeling too well," she said in a lowered voice. "She hasn't been feeling well at all."

Suddenly, Ray felt like an interloper on Anna's privacy. "Look, never mind then," he said in a soft voice, "It's really not that important. Don't even mention that I stopped by," he said.

Mrs. Davis' intuition told her that Ray's morning visit was much more significant that he pretended it to be. She reached out and gently touched his hand. "No, I'm sure it'll be all right, Anna would be very disappointed if you didn't speak to her," she smiled. "I'm sure she'd be very annoyed with me if I didn't tell her you were here right this minute."

Ray smiled, "Thanks, Mrs. Davis, I appreciate it."

Mrs. Davis waved him in. "Come on and sit down. Anna's upstairs in her room. I'll run up and tell her you're here."

Ray remained standing. He watched the woman scurry up the stairs. In a short time, she emerged from one of the rooms and leaned against the balcony railing. "Mrs. Flynn'll be right down, Ray," Mrs. Davis said in a pleasant, singsong voice. "She said to go into the kitchen and help yourself to something to eat. The refrigerator is filled. I've got things to do up here, so have a nice chat."

Ray smiled nervously. He looked up at her and waved, "Okay, Mrs. Davis. Thanks."

"You're welcome, honey," she replied, smiling broadly. She gingerly grabbed a dust mop that was leaning against the balcony railing. "I'll see you," she called. She quickly moved through the hallway.

Ray felt himself sink into the plushness of the carpets as he slowly made his way through the large rooms. He had been in the mansion on several occasions and was always awed by its splendor. He sat down at the kitchen table and waited for Anna.

He had planned no logistical approach for his conversation with her; he would simply allow his instincts to be his guide. As he sat there waiting, his mind was blank. He softly drummed his fingertips against the white linen tabletop covering the porcelain surface.

His ear caught the rustle of Anna's housedress as she approached. When she entered the kitchen, Ray was taken back by her appearance; the areas under her eyes were black, and her large, dark eyes were sunken deep into her face. Her color was so pale she seemed almost transparent. Her body, always slight and fragile, was now incredibly thin. Smiling wanly, she walked over to Ray and looked down at him. "Well, hello, Ray," she said, in a voice barely above a whisper.

Ray stood up, "I'm sorry if I've bothered you, Mrs. Flynn. Maybe—"

Anna interrupted, "No, honey, you're not bothering me. I'm very happy to see you," she said, in the same sad voice. "What is it?"

Ray pulled a chair over and set it alongside the one he had been sitting on. "Here, ma'am, sit down."

Anna sat down and Ray pulled his chair close to her. "Mrs. Davis said you haven't been feeling well."

"I suppose that's obvious," she smiled.

"Well, you look a little down " Ray said. "Have you seen a doctor?"

"No. No doctors. I've seen enough doctors for a while."

"Hasn't Joe or Mr. Flynn said anything?"

Anna smiled. "Joe and Patrick are involved in other things. I guess they haven't noticed, but I do feel lousy." She ran her thin fingers across her eyebrow. "I've been sick and tired before, I got over it and I'll get over this. But I suppose if things don't start looking up soon, I'll call Doctor Royal."

Ray, aside from his troubles, was sincerely concerned with Mrs. Flynn's appearance. "I think that'd be a good idea."

Anna feigned unconcern, but she was truly alarmed at her condition— the difficulty in breathing, the ominous, heavy pain that almost continually filled her chest, the dizziness and general weakness of her body. She feared a checkup from Doctor Royal, knowing she would wind up in a hospital bed. Then she would be unable to visit Larry, who so desperately needed her company and attention.

"Well, enough about me," she said. "I know you didn't come here to talk about me."

Immediately upon hearing her words, Ray forgot about the problem of Anna's health. The burden of his own predicament shrouded him.

"What is it, Ray? You look concerned," Anna said.

"Are we alone?" Ray asked in a whisper. "Is Mrs. Davis still upstairs?"

Anna leaned over and grasped his hand. "Yes, Ray, of course we're alone. Mrs. Davis will be upstairs for a while. She wouldn't interrupt us or try to listen in."

"I-I-I know. I kn-know," Ray replied, in an anguished voice.

"What is it then? Go ahead, honey. Tell me."

In a choking, sobbing voice Ray proceeded with his story.

He told her about discovering his mother and Patrick. He graphically described the bedroom event with his mother, choosing to leave nothing out. He wanted desperately to define Lila's evil, to show her corruption and debauchery. When he finished, he began to cry openly. Anna held him against her, crooning to him, comforting him. She tried to tell him things would be all right. And then, she also began to cry, crying for the awful horror perpetrated on such a fine, young man. Crying for the lost luster and life of Ray Walton's eyes. Crying for the lost, happy innocence that was replaced by the shamed, sobbing wreck she held in her arms. She cried too, for her own loss; to finally have all her worries and fears about her husband confirmed by the honest, stinging grief of Ray Walton. After a while, both Anna and Ray grew still in each other's arms. Anna carefully drew back, and her gaze formed a stricken union with Ray's.

"What are we going to do?" she whispered.

"I don't know," Ray said, in a lifeless voice. "Whatever is goin' to be done, you're gonna hafta do it, Mrs. Flynn. I can't."

Anna reassuringly patted his hand. "I know. I know, honey. You've been through enough."

"I'm goin' away," he said. "I'm not stayin' here anymore."

"But where, Ray? Where can you go?"

"I've got plans, Mrs. Flynn. I'll be okay."

"Please, Ray. Stay. We'll work something out."

"No. No, I can't. I won't. I'm trustin' you, Mrs. Flynn. Don't say anything about me goin'. Just leave it out somehow. Whatever you say or do, leave it out."

"Yes, Ray," she said quietly. "Don't fear. I'll leave it out, I won't tell anyone about your involvement."

"I don't want anyone but you to know what happened between me and my mother. Promise me."

"I promise, Ray. It's our secret."

"But she knows. My mother knows. It's not a secret."

"I'm sure she'll never tell a soul. She wouldn't dare. She only did that to you to keep you quiet."

"But if she knew I told you about her and your husband, she'll tell. I know her. She'll do it."

"I'll confront Patrick in a way that won't involve you."

"Don't say I was here. Don't tell anyone I told you I was goin' away. My mother thinks I'm gone already."

"No one will know."

"What about Mrs. Davis?"

"You leave Mrs. Davis to me. I'll take care of her."

Ray stood up, rubbing his eyes with his open palms. He then looked at Anna. "I'm sorry, Mrs. Flynn, Honest to God, I'm sorry. I had to tell you, I had to tell somebody. I just couldn't let her get away with it, or him either."

Anna placed her hands against the sides of his tortured face. "Don't be sorry. You did what you had to do. I'm glad you told me." She knew she was lying. She would rather live unaware of Patrick's infidelity. She would prefer to pretend that things were all right, even though her heart and mind always knew otherwise.

She craned her neck and kissed his cheek. "Go ahead, Ray. You go on out there and find yourself a life. Maybe your leaving is the best thing for you. There's no life left for you in this town. I understand that. I won't lie and pretend otherwise, and neither should you. My life is built on pretending and self deception. I know what it is, and I don't want you to have any part of it."

Ray smiled sadly. "Thanks, Mrs. Flynn. You're a fine woman. I knew you were the one I had to talk to." For a moment he was silent. "I'm goin' to miss Joe. I really am," he said.

"I know you will, honey. But I'm sure you'll get together again sometime."

"I hope so."

"You will."

"I hope he never finds out about this."

"If I can manage it, he won't," Anna said. "But if I can't, he'll have to know the kind of man his father is."

"I think he already knows, Mrs. Flynn."

"Yes, I guess he might know better than all of us."

Ray swept her into his arms and held her tight, "Thank you. Thank you. I'll never forget you."

Anna felt the tears once again welling in her eyes. Her throat grew tight with emotion. "Go, Ray. Go quickly, and God bless you."

Ray released his hold on her and walked to the back doorway.

He opened the door and turned around. He smiled at Anna, and gave her a slight wave. "Goodbye," he whispered.

"Goodbye, Ray," she said.

Standing alone in the kitchen, Anna wasn't sure how to contend with the problem. She would have to think about it, devise some sort of plan by which she would trap Patrick and Lila. Beyond that, she wasn't sure what might happen. She didn't know if she could ever leave Patrick. She didn't know what to do about Larry or Joe or how either of them would respond. She would have to think about it. But it couldn't be now; she was too tired and sick, too shocked and stunned to put all of her wits together.

She'd deal with it in the evening, or the next morning, but not now.

She laboriously made her way back to the top of the stairway. Anna was eager to return to the relative comfort of her bed. Never before had she felt so tired. She was about to proceed toward her room, when the pain struck her like a knife, ripping and tearing as it filled her chest. A tremendous, vise-like pressure cut off her breath; she gasped as she reached for the balcony railing.

The pain grew to an unbearable level, and Anna fell. Her body, almost noiselessly, collided with the lush carpet. Unyielding, the pain continued to pierce her chest. At that moment, Anna knew she was dying. She rested her cheek against the soft carpet, her brain reeling; disjointed images of her husband and sons moved past her half-opened eyes. And then, the pain that had contorted her body seemed to be apart from her. She heard her own gasping, but there was no longer a desperate need tor air. She closed her eyes and gladly allowed her body to melt into a new reality. Anna Flynn, without reluctance, gave her life away.

13

MRS. DAVIS never heard Anna fall. Completely unaware of her dear friend's final breath, she hummed and sang along with the radio as she busied herself with getting Joseph's bedroom in order. She didn't see or hear the long, black automobile slow to a halt in the Flynn's front driveway. The grandfather clock in the downstairs foyer showed the time to be quarter past one.

"I'll be out in a minute," Patrick Flynn said as he lifted himself out of the car's front seat.

Bill Manley grunted a reply. He rested his broad chest against the steering wheel.

Patrick had no idea of what awaited him. He was concerned with the business file he had earlier forgotten, almost certain he had left it on the nightstand in the master bedroom.

When he entered the house, he heard the soft music and the trace of Mrs. Davis' melodious voice coming from the upstairs. He rushed up the stairway. When he reached the second floor landing, he abruptly stopped, his eyes freezing on the inert figure lying on the floor. He ran toward Anna and fell to his knees alongside her. He rolled her over on her back. Her jerked away from the open, unseeing eyes, A grotesque, cottony saliva filled the corners of her mouth. Her body was stiff and unresponsive. Patrick wildly shook her shoulders, praying silently for some show of life. His heart refused to accept his brain's certainty that she was gone. He attempted to cry out for Mrs. Davis. His throat rebelled and no words would come. He released his grip from her shoulders and knelt quietly alongside her. A thousand thoughts rolled through his mind. Finally, he carefully lifted her from the floor and carried her into their bedroom, laying her down on the bed and setting a pillow beneath her head. After covering her torso with the blue bedspread, he once again looked at the silent, composed face. He bit his teeth against his bottom lip as he reached over and closed her eyelids.

Mrs. Davis was startled from her pleasant humming when she saw Patrick enter Joe's room. "My God, Patrick, you scared me."

Then she saw his face and the hollow, stricken look in his eyes. "What's wrong?" she exclaimed,

Patrick didn't look at her. The dull monotone of his voice seemed to be directed to someone else. "We've lost Anna," he said. Mrs. Davis screamed. "What! Where? Where?"

"I put her in our bedroom."

She ran crazily out of the room, and began to cry and ramble incoherently when she saw Anna's body on the bed. Patrick appeared alongside Mrs. Davis and rested his large hand on her shoulder, drawing her toward his chest,

"Is she dead, Patrick?" she cried. "Is she dead? How do you know? Are you sure?"

"Yes, she's dead."

Mrs. Davis knew it was true; the hardness and finality of Patrick's voice, the unmoving body on the bed, all the ugly evidence told her it was true. Patrick strongly held her grief against him, until her trembling body went slack and quiet in his arms. Afterwards, he held her away from him and spoke in a quiet, authoritative voice. "Go downstairs and tell Bill to come up here. Then I want you to call Doctor Royal. He'll he at his office."

Mrs. Davis wiped her tears away and squared her shoulders. She knew there was much to attend to and she had to be strong. Without saying another word, she left Patrick and walked toward the stairs.

Before Manley reached the upstairs, he knew what had happened. Mrs. Davis almost unintelligibly delivered the message of Anna's death. After managing to decipher the woman's words, he sat, stunned, on the front seat of the car. It took him only seconds to regain his composure and race to Patrick's side.

As Mrs. Davis dialed the downstairs phone in the hope of reaching Doctor Royal, Patrick instructed Bill to go to Clark's Service Station and pick up Joseph. Following Bill's departure, Patrick returned downstairs and found Marion Davis sitting disconsolately on the parlor couch. He walked over to her and gently held her hand.

"Didn't you hear anything, Marion?" he said softly. "Didn't you hear her fall?"

Mrs. Davis's sullen voice revealed her deep feeling of guilt.

"No, Pat," she half sobbed, "Not a sound. Nothing. It was that damn radio. If only ..."

"Shhhhh," Patrick interrupted. "Don't blame yourself now. It just happened. There's nothing you or anybody else could have done."

"I'll never forgive myself," she said, as she wrung her fingers over her soaked handkerchief.

"Did she give any sign that this might happen?" he asked.

"No, not really. She was listless, but she wasn't feeling well. We all knew that." Mrs. Davis began to sob once again, "Oh, poor, poor Anna. She should have seen a doctor. We should have forced her."

Patrick blinked several times against the burning of his eyes, "She'd been sick so many times before and she always got over it," he said. "Who would have thought this could happen? I knew she looked terrible, but with Larry being away and all, I figured it was mostly that. I thought it would pass."

Mrs. Davis sat quietly, allowing her mind to reflect on the tender and beautiful relationship she had known with Anna Flynn. After a few silent minutes, she dabbed at her eyes with a handkerchief and said, "She was so good, so kind."

Patrick sat forward on the chair, his elbows resting on his knees. "I can't understand it. I didn't think she was that sick. Was she out of bed today?"

"Yes."

"When?"

"Young Ray Walton stopped by. He was looking for Joseph. He asked for you. I don't know what he wanted, but he seemed upset. He talked to Anna for a while."

"About what?"

"I don't know. I was upstairs. I didn't even hear him leave. Anna must have come upstairs right after Ray left."

"What could he have wanted?"

"Oh, I'm sure it was nothing that serious. Probably some simple thing that he might have thought was important. You know how kids are."

"Well, maybe when she climbed the stairs, the strain..."

"I believe that's what it was, Pat, She was sicker than we thought. It must have been her heart."

Patrick sat heavily back into the chair. "Jesus Christ," he whispered.

Mrs. Davis listened for the sound of Bill Manley's return. "Bill and Joe should be getting here any minute," she said. "How are you going to tell Joe?"

"I told Bill to break the news to him."

"Oh."

Patrick stood up and walked to the window. "I wanted him to know before he got here."

"Maybe it would have been better if you told him," she said.

"No," Patrick said, as he peered out the window. "You know Joe and I have a problem talking. I wanted Bill to do it,"

The woman nodded her head. "Yes. Maybe you're right."

Patrick's eyes scanned the length of the driveway. There was still no sign of the car. "I'm going to wait upstairs," he said. "You wait here for them."

Marion Davis stood up. "Yes, Pat. Don't leave her up there alone, I'll make some coffee."

Patrick slowly walked toward the stairway.

14

WHEN THE CAR finally arrived, Mrs. Davis was standing nervously on the front porch. Joseph bolted out of the car and ran toward her. His face was blank and pallid, but his terror-filled eyes told a different story.

Mrs. Davis, once more, began to cry. "Joe, Joseph," she whimpered.

Unhearing, Joseph rushed past her, nearly knocking the woman over in his agitation. Every nerve in Joseph's body was alert and receptive. Never before were his senses so keen. Everything around him registered in his screaming brain. The smell of fresh coffee, coming from the kitchen. The early afternoon shaft of sunlight that lit up the parlor's far wall. The chirping of birds heard through the open front door. The sounds of Mrs. Davis's sobs and the grunting of Bill Manley's breath a few yards behind him.

As he reached the door of his parents' bedroom, he saw his father's back. Patrick was standing just inside the doorway and his large body practically obscured the still figure lying on the bed. Up until that moment, Joe had not thought about his father. Seeing him just an arm's distance away, sent Joseph's heart into fury. For a second, Joe stopped all movement, allowing his rage to fill him with the violence of murder. And then, just as he prepared to pounce on him, he saw Patrick's shoulders shake and heard the low, pitiful sound of grief escape from his father's lips.

Patrick was unaware his son was behind him, and Joseph knew it. Joe wanted to kill him for all the wrong he had heaped on his mother. He wanted to kill him; but his body wouldn't move.

It remained frozen in position. He watched, in a kind of shock, as Patrick, overcome with harsh, rasping sobs, collapsed to his knees.

It was that second when the form of his mother came completely into view; she lay lifelessly on the bed. Her dark, tortured eyes were hidden behind closed lids. All of the nervousness of her once mobile face was quieted. All of her fears and heartaches were finally disconnected; no longer biting at her heels in their ugly pursuit.

Looking at her, Joseph became oblivious to the presence of his father. He rushed to the bedside. He crouched alongside her and tenderly touched her cheek. Her face was still warm; as if her heart continued to beat and sent the blush of life through her skin, Joseph prayed it was all a mistake. He watched and listened in vain for a sound of breath or a blink from her eyelids. But the stillness remained. Tears silently ran down his face as he removed the sheet covering her body. He pressed his ear against her chest. Desperately, he listened for a flutter of heartbeat.

But there was nothing; no breath, no sound, not a whisper of life.

He began to softly call to her. "Mom. Mom. Please talk to me. Please." He held his breath and listened as something in his soul defiantly lashed out against the evidence of her death. He grabbed her face and began to scream; but he knew there would not be an answer; not now. Not ever. He crawled onto the bed and lay next to her; he softly ran his hand over her glistening black hair. He brokenly cried, over and over, "Mom. Mom."

Mrs. Davis lifted him to a sitting position on the bed. Through a veil of grief, he saw his father and Bill Manley standing near the doorway. Mrs. Davis was speaking to him, but he couldn't hear. The sounds of all his life filled his ears instead: his mother's voice, her laughter, her cries. He could hear nothing else. He bolted from the bed and ran to his room.

Patrick looked over at Mrs. Davis. "Let him alone!" he said, "Let him be for a minute."

Mrs. Davis nodded in agreement.

Bill tapped Pat's shoulder and beckoned him out of the room.

In the hallway where Mrs. Davis couldn't hear them, Bill whispered, "What are we goin' to do when the kid comes out of this,

Pat? You know how he is. You know the way he must be feelin' about you. He's goin' to be tough to handle."

Patrick's eyes looked toward his son's room. "No, I don't think so. I know him well enough. If he was goin' to pull anything, like comin' after me, he would've done it the minute he hit the room."

"I don't figure it," Bill said.

"I do," Pat replied, "When he came in there, he found me cryin'. I didn't know he was there. My cryin' musta' shook him up. That has to be it."

"But why?" Bill asked,

"I don't know," Patrick replied in a rasping whisper. "Maybe my cryin' got to him. I don't know."

Bill continued to whisper, but Patrick didn't hear him. Instead, he kept his eyes locked on Joseph's door. The crying was past. Patrick Flynn's mind was lucid and working fast. He had been trying to devise a way to get Joseph into his business. He was even willing to swallow some of his pride in approaching Joe.

But now, he was sure it was no longer necessary. With Anna dead, Joseph was vulnerable, and Patrick knew it. "Maybe Bill had been right after all," Patrick thought, "Maybe the kid has been waitin' for me all his life." He turned toward Manley. "That's it!" Patrick whispered as he slapped Bill's shoulder. "That's it!"

"What?"

"It was my cryin', Bill. That's what stopped him from comin' at me. He never expected to see me like that and it got to him." Patrick's whisper shook with excitement. "If I'm ever going to get to him, Billy, it's right now."

Manley looked at Joe's door. "Are you goin' in there, Boss?" he asked.

"Yeah, Yeah, I think so. I'd better make my move now."

Joseph sat huddled in the loneliness of his room. His body shook violently, the tears and sobs continuing unabated. He could see all of his years in that loneliness; all of his years with her; he visualized his mother smiling at him and touching his face with her special tenderness. He remembered the joy in her eyes whenever he was happy, and the tears and pain whenever he suffered. She would have died for him, and maybe she did. Now there was no way to thank her, no way to tell her about all of the love and loss he was feeling. He enveloped himself in guilt as his mind burned with accusations. *Why didn't I stay with her more? Why didn't I help her more? Why didn't I make things easier? Why? Why? Why?* He thought about how he had always blamed his father for his mother's pain. But Patrick had cried on his knees at her bedside. He must have loved her. He must have cared. Joseph remembered his Aunt Gena and how she tried to make him understand. The words came, like a spectre, out of the past. "Maybe you can bring your parents back together and give your dad the kind of help he needs. Your mama still loves him. Your mama still loves him. Your mama still loves him." The words came over and over, cascaded through his memory. "She did love him," Joseph thought, "And he loved her, otherwise why would he have broken down the way he did. She loved him. Oh God, why didn't I make it easier? Why didn't I understand? Why didn't I listen to Gena?"

The sound at his door caught Joseph's attention. He looked up and saw his father in the doorway.

"Joe, son, please let me talk to you," Patrick said in a quiet, unsure voice.

"Dad?" Joseph sobbed.

They both moved toward one another at the same instant. Joe wrapped his arms around Patrick and pressed his face against his neck. He tried to speak but his words, mixed with sobs, were unintelligible .

"Easy son, easy," Patrick said in a soft voice. He held tightly to Joseph as his son's grief quivered in his arms

"Dad, I'm sorry. I'm sorry," Joseph cried.

Patrick walked Joseph over to a chair and sat him down. "There's nothin' you've got to he sorry about, Joe. Don't blame anybody for this."

His father's words offered Joseph a welcome measure of relief, lifting away some of the horrendous guilt.

"It was me, Dad. I killed her. I never understood anything. It was me."

"Nobody killed your mama, Joe. It was her time, that's all. It was her time to die. Nobody killed her, not you, not me. There's nobody to blame. You were a good son, a darn good son. You have nothin' to be ashamed of."

Joe tightly squeezed his father's hands, silently thanking God to have someone near him, someone of his own flesh and blood, who didn't blame him. Joe squeezed and squeezed Patrick's hands,

"If I did do wrong, I didn't mean to hurt Ma. I loved her so much. I didn't mean to hurt her."

"You didn't hurt her, son," Patrick whispered. "You only did good. You were a good boy." Patrick carefully measured his words in trying to win Joseph over. "You were the best son she could have ever had."

Joe looked up. "Do you mean it? Do you really mean it?"

"Of course I do."

"You mean Larry and I were the best."

"No, it was you. You were the best. I'm sorry for everything." Patrick spoke carefully trying not to reveal his deception, "I'm sorry for always taking your brother's side. I was wrong, but I thought you hated me and I resented it, I see everything now and I'm sorry. You were the best son. You always were. I see that now. Do you forgive me? I was wrong, I'm sorry."

"Do I forgive you?" Joseph said. "Of course I forgive you. I love you. I've always loved you."

Patrick lifted Joe from the chair and hugged him. Joseph hadn't been that close to him in a long time. His father smelled of that same fresh manliness. Joe felt the strength of his father's arms, the same arms that held him so long ago. He pulled back his head and for the first time in many years he really looked at Patrick's face. Except for the increased lines and the shocks of grey that highlighted the curls on his forehead, it was the same face he had seen in that long ago driveway almost two decades before, the face that had stayed within his mind and dreams for every moment of his life.

Patrick whispered into Joseph's ear, "We'll get through this, son. We'll make each other strong. We're all either of us has left. We've got to make up for a lot of lost time."

Joseph's voice was a grateful whisper. "Yes, Father. Yes, yes."

15

JOSEPH, totally exhausted, lay asleep in his bedroom. Mrs. Davis sat alongside Anna's bedside; her lips moved soundlessly, as her fingers traced over her rosary beads. She heard the knocking on the front door. Bill Manley got up from where he and Pat were sitting, near the parlor window, and walked to the front door. He opened it. Dr. Royal entered. His face was flushed with excitement.

"Don't rush, Doc," Patrick said quietly. "She's dead."

"Where is she?"

"Upstairs in our bedroom," Patrick replied. He looked at Manley. "Show him the way."

Manley waved Royal toward the stairs.

When both men returned downstairs, they were followed by a sobbing Mrs. Davis.

"I'm certain it was a coronary," Royal said. "If you desire an autopsy, Pat, we can confirm it."

Patrick waved away the suggestion. "No. Forget it. What difference does it make now?"

"I'm sure it was a coronary," Royal repeated. "How long was she ill? I don't recall hearing you mention anything about it."

"Yeah, she wasn't feeling well," Patrick said, "But I didn't think it was anything that serious, you know."

Royal dropped his satchel to the floor and sat down. Manley offered him a drink.

"No. No thanks, Bill. I don't think so."

"How about some coffee then?" Patrick said. "There's some fresh stuff in the kitchen."

"No, thank you," Royal said. "I'll call a funeral director unless you want to."

"No. That's all right. You take care of it."

"Is there anyone special you want me to contact?" Royal asked.

Patrick looked at Manley and Mrs. Davis. He shrugged his shoulders. "Frank Kearney took care of Gena and Tom. We might as well as call him. Bill, find the phone number."

As Manley headed for the phone book, Royal looked at Patrick. "How did Joe take it?"

"Pretty bad."

"Where is he?"

"Asleep upstairs. Me and Mrs. Davis had him lie down for a minute and he conked right out."

"It was the shock," Royal said, "He'll sleep for a while."

"It'll do him good," Mrs. Davis said.

"One minute he was excited and wide awake, and then he just dropped off like he was dead himself," Patrick said.

"Sometimes it proves to be a valuable reaction," Royal said,

Manley found the number and called Royal over to the phone, Patrick looked at Mrs. Davis. "You'll have to tell Larry."

"Oh, Patrick," she said, "I think that's your place."

"Marion, for Christ sake, I haven't seen him in I don't know when. I can't look at him in that place. You'll have to do it."

The woman sighed,, "All right then, I will. I'll go down there later today."

"Good. I appreciate it."

Doctor Royal spoke quietly into the phone. Finally, he hung up and walked back toward Patrick,

"It's taken care of, Pat," Royal said softly. "Mr. Kearney will take care of everything."

Patrick nodded. "Thanks," he said. "That'll he fine."

Within an hour, Anna's body was removed from the Flynn mansion.

Bill drove Mrs. Davis home, allowing her to change her clothes for her visit with Larry. Bill returned directly. Patrick was still sitting in the same chair. Manley filled a glass with scotch and handed it to him.

"No, Bill," Patrick said, "You drink it, I'm not in the mood."

Manley sat down next to him. "I'll tell you, Boss. You're taking this a lot worse than I expected,"

"Why?"

"Well, Jesus, it's obvious. You were crying up there, That's not a usual thing with you. I can understand why Joe was surprised. I was surprised myself,"

"Oh yeah?"

"Shit. Look at you. You look like the life's gone out of you sitting here. I mean I don't blame you. She was a good lady. But knowing the way it was between the two of you, I'm surprised."

Patrick's eyes moved toward the upstairs. "Keep your voice down. If the kid wakes up I don't want him to hear."

Patrick took the glass from Manley's hand and swallowed a large amount of scotch. He wiped his mouth and looked at Bill. "I was cryin' all right," he said in a hoarse whisper, "But not because she died. As far as I was concerned, she died a helluva long time ago. Fuck, man, I don't love her, not now. That was over long ago." He rubbed his hand across his forehead. "But seeing her up there, I mean really seeing her dead, it brought back a lot of memories. You know there had been a lot of good times. I was thinking about the way it was, the way it mighta been, if not for those fuckin' sons of mine, especially that guy upstairs. Don't kid yourself. There's no life gone of out me. I'm just thinking. My friggin' mind is workin' overtime."

"Oh Jesus, Boss," Manley said in a low voice. "Don't start on that. You wanted to make up with Joe. It seems to be okay. But if he hears you talking like this, it'll fuck it up."

Patrick's eyes squinted. "I wanted to make up with him for one reason only. He's got to get into the business. A Flynn has got to keep his hands in it when I'm not able to. I think the kid has the moxie to handle it. That's the only fuckin' reason I'll have anything to do with him, the little punk."

261

"Jesus, Boss," Manley said. "He might pick up on it. He might figure out the way you really feel."

Patrick smiled. "No, he won't. I'm a pretty good goddamn actor. I handled things pretty damn good up there. He fell for it like a ton of bricks. I can keep doing it."

"Do you think it's all that important?" Manley asked.

"Is what important?"

"That one of your kids gotta run your business. I mean when you're dead you won't really give a shit."

Patrick laughed. "You'll never understand. No matter what happens, no matter where I am, I'll always give a shit when it comes to the name of Flynn." His eyes flashed with anger, "There'll always be a Flynn sticking up Hanway's ass. I'll teach Joe well. I'll make him like me. Maybe I'll even get to like the kid."

"You really hate this town," Manley said.

"Yeah, I do. For the way they fucked me over when I was a kid," Patrick let his mind wander back to his childhood, "I was seven years old, a fuckin' baby, shinin' shoes in saloons and listenin' to all that fuckin' shit. It was always work, shinin' shoes, runnin' errands for the big shots at the coal breaker, always workin', workin'. Nobody ever gave me anything."

"But, Boss," Manley said softly. "It was tough for everybody back then. Nobody had nothin'."

"At least you had a mother and father," Patrick said.

"Yeah, I know, Boss. I know it was tough on you. But you weren't an orphan. You had Gena. She was good."

"She didn't do enough."

"She watched out for you. I remember."

"Yeah, and she got married and didn't give a damn about me. What did she care?"

"Maybe she thought it would help."

"Help!" Patrick laughed. "Help. What a fuckin' joke. When my old man died I was six years old, and my mother might as well have died too. She was no good without him. She was always sick, always in bed. When she died, I was ten years old, but she was always useless to me."

"Yeah, Boss, but that's what I'm sayin'. Gena hung in there and took care of you. She tried."

"She couldn't wait two fuckin' minutes to get married. Right after I turned sixteen and quit school to work full time, she married that prick. She would have married him sooner, but she thought I would've been a burden to Tom. I know damn well that's how she saw it."

"Maybe she thought it was the best thing for you."

"Bullshit. She was lookin' out for herself. When she turned the house over to me, I woulda thrown them the hell out, but Tom's salary made it easier to keep the house up. I just charged them rent and got the fuck out, I went on my own. And the rest, as they say, is history."

"If she didn't care," Bill said, "Why should she turn the house over to you?"

"Who knows?" Patrick shrugged. "She must've had some plan."

"Ah, Boss, you're being too hard on her. Too hard on the town."

"The town," Patrick said, "Fuck the town. Where was it when I needed it? Nobody gave me nothin'."

"But, Boss," Manley said, "Back then nobody had nothin'."

"Fuck it," Pat said. "I never had any use for none of them, Gena or the rest. I never will and I'll never let them forget it."

"Joe'll never feel that way," Manley said.

"When I'm finished with him, he will."

"I don't think so. The kid seems to really like the place and the people."

"We'll see," Patrick smiled. "And by the way, your speeches are gettin' to be a pain in the ass. I don't need any sermons from you about this town or what I think."

Manley smiled apologetically. "Pat, I'm only concerned about you. I don't care about anything else. You're the only one I owe. Not this town, not nobody else. Just you,"

"Well, shut up then."

"Okay, I will. Just remember, I'm only worried about you being happy, I'm just tryin' to relieve your mind about some things. That's all."

Patrick laughed, "All right, Father Manley, you tried. Now forget it."

Bill laughed in return and squeezed Patrick's arm. "Amen, Boss. Amen."

Patrick looked at Manley. "In a way, you were halfway right about the way I feel about her."

"Yeah."

"For a second up there," Patrick said. "I thought my fuckin' heart was going to crack."

Manley looked down at the floor.

Patrick slapped him lightly on the shoulder, "But it didn't," he said, "I'm still here. I'm still Patrick Flynn, And honest to God, Bill, now that it's over, I'm glad she's out of my way."

Manley still didn't answer. After a while both men were quiet, as the rays of the afternoon sun poured through the drawn drapes, lighting up the room in an eerie crimson glow.

Mrs. Davis used carefully chosen words in explaining Anna's death to Larry. When she finished, she sat, trembling, in the stiff-backed chair, looking at the young man's face for some sign of emotion. Throughout her sad explanation, Doctor Brogan had supportively stood at Larry's bedside.

Larry sat back on his bed and looked at the vast vista of countryside beyond his window,

Brogan walked over and whispered to Mrs. Davis. "He'll be all right. I think it's best to leave him alone now. He won't do anything rash. Between the medication and his condition, he's not able to recognize the significance of the situation."

The woman stood up and walked over to the bed. "I'll come in to see you regularly, Larry," she said, fighting to maintain her composure. "We'll go for walks like we always did. Wait and see. It'll be just like it always was."

Brogan walked over and took her arm. He smiled sympathetically. "Come on. It's best we leave now."

"Goodbye, Larry," she said softly.

As she and Doctor Brogan walked down the long, sterile corridor toward the exit, Marion Davis was demoralized by the hollow, limbo-like world that was left to Larry Flynn.

"He's too sick to care about anything," she thought sadly. "God love him. He'll never be able to know or care about anything." From his window, Larry saw Mrs. Davis get into the long, dark car. He watched it move through the narrow roadway until it went far beyond the sanitarium gate. He watched until it was lost from sight. Long after it disappeared, he continued to forlornly sit at the window, allowing the tears to drench his face. inundating him with a sense of loss only he could understand.

While Mrs. Davis and Bill Manley drove out to the sanitarium, Patrick remained behind in the mansion. He called Lila and told her of Anna's death. Lila saw it all as an unexpected blessing.

She almost screamed with joy at the news. Patrick ignored her exuberance and asked her about her son. "Ray was over here today. Just before Anna died. He had a talk with her and he left. Do you have any idea what he wanted?"

Lila didn't consider for a moment the actual reason for his visit, so sure was she of her son's shame. "Ray made up his mind the other night to go away and see about getting a job," she said. Her mind was working quickly, "I got into an argument with him about it and he left the house. He told me he'd never bother with me or the town again. I don't know what got into him. I don't know what the hell to expect from him. He just might mean it." She dropped her voice, feigning concern. "I might not see him again."

"Well, whatever will be," Pat said.

"Yes," Lila said. "Whatever happens, happens."

265

"Anyway, he did stop by here today. What could he have wanted?" Pat said.

"Maybe he came back to say goodbye to Joe. You know how close they are."

"Why didn't he stop by Clark's station? It's Monday. He knew Joe'd be at work."

"Well, Jesus, Pat, I don't know," Lila said unconcerned.

"Okay, forget about it," Pat said. "I just wondered."

Patrick and Lila never again discussed Ray's visit to the Flynn mansion. Marion Davis would eventually forget about the incident. It would be a long time before anyone would know the importance of Ray Walton's discussion with Anna Flynn.

BOOK
FOUR

1

JOSEPH wandered disconnected through his mother's wake and funeral. Afterwards, he was never able to form any mental associations with those three horrible days in July; as if his mind, rebelling against what would have been a debilitating memory, disallowed its inclusion into the mysterious labyrinth of his psyche. Nevertheless, he was tortured and pursued by a hounding guilt. Time and again, his body was rocked by the recurring recollections; the voice of Carol hammering at him. "Joey, you should spend more time with your mother." Time and again, her words came back to him haunting him with their truth. More than ever he was certain that his Aunt Gena was right. He could have made the difference; if he had been less selfish, he could have saved his parents' relationship. He could have saved his mother's life. He remembered Larry's accusations. "You're selfish, Joe. You're hurting Ma... You're hurting her." Grudgingly, he admitted to himself that his brother had been right. Although such recollections failed to taint his revered memories of Gena, they caused him to hate Larry and Carol with even greater intensity. He refused to even consider visiting his brother at the sanitarium, and Carol's letters were thrown, unopened, into the daily garbage.

Joseph's terrible guilt was assuaged, somewhat, by his new experience with his father. They were getting along well. He saw Patrick as a kind of savior, as an exit from the dungeon of his self-inflicted punishment. His father seemed to push the past aside, forgiving his wayward son for everything, for Joseph's refusal to redirect the natural flow of Anna's love to her husband, and forgiving him, as well, for the cruelty he showed Larry. Because, regardless of what his father had said during that reunion moment in Joseph's bedroom, Joe continued to believe that Larry was the favorite son; his father was just being kind during that unforgettable afternoon, and Joseph was positive that all the years of Larry's clever sycophancy had permanently endeared him to his father. It was on that point only, that Joseph saw his Aunt Gena's deductions as illogical; she might have been right about everything else, but she was incorrect in assuming that Larry didn't own a special place in Patrick Flynn's heart. It didn't matter that Pat never visited Larry; Joseph simply accounted it to the fact that Patrick was unable to see or talk to Larry in the milieu of Mount Rose, that dreary, sad, mentally disturbed world. But, although Joe's resentment of his brother remained at fever pitch, it no longer mattered who was the favorite son. In Joseph Flynn's new, confused perspective, his father's forgiveness was enough; it gave him new breath, new life. The only thing that mattered now, was that Joseph, at long last, was indeed his father's son.

He would offer contrition at Patrick Flynn's altar and serve his penance gladly.

Just prior to the fall semester, Joseph enrolled into Clarkson University's evening school. Through his father's persuasion, he had quit his job at Mickey's and took his first step into the business world. By day he was indoctrinated into the myriad aspects of his father's enterprises, and by night, he was a diligent and highly motivated student at the university. With Patrick's agreement, he chose not to pursue a degree. Instead, he devoted his efforts to courses aligned with the family businesses. Joseph had no trouble with his studies, using his intrinsic intelligence to garner the same academic success he had known in high school. Joseph Flynn had always possessed wondrous gifts—physical beauty, a charismatic personality that endowed him with great, personal presence. Most important, he had a brilliant and incisive mind that absorbed everything. Now he was pulling all his gifts to the surface, allowing them to give him a new direction. For a young man, still in his late teens, his adjustment was remarkable. Patrick was seriously impressed by the maturity and confidence of his son.

Of all the new vistas open to him, Joe was surprised to find himself especially enamored with the hustle and fast-talking atmosphere of politics. As a child, it was that part of his father's life that he hated most of all: the ugly wheeling and dealing; the political hacks, during hot, sweaty parlor discussions, kneeling like subjects at his father's feet. But now he saw it all differently. He saw the conniving, contradictions and hypocrisy as a kind of perverted art. Inordinately, he was drawn into it. At first, he stood on the fringes of Patrick's political army, listening, watching, learning. And then, by and by, he began to make contributions. He offered proposals and solutions. They indulged him in the beginning, but eventually they listened. Everyone was impressed by his political proclivity and were eager to accept the solid common sense he presented. He motivated them with his stirring of new excitement. Before long, next to Patrick himself, he was the group's most aggressive member. Patrick wasn't threatened by Joseph's encroachment onto his stage; to the contrary, he was pleasantly surprised at Joseph's expertise in such things as ward and county politics.

But there needn't have been any surprises; for Joseph was, after all, the son of Patrick. He was the natural flesh and blood heir to all of the necessary, inner workings that made that perverted art possible.

In time, Joseph ceased wondering about Ray Walton's mysterious exit from Hanway. He even stopped wondering why he never heard from his lost friend. Joe's long hatred of his father was behind him and he was eager and happy in their new relationship. The only distasteful remnants left to him from the past were his expanding hatred for Carol and his resentment toward the letters that continued to come and harass him. The haunting spiritual presence of Larry also remained. He was still incarcerated in that countryside asylum and Joseph dreaded his possible return. But, above all else, although he was slowly reconciling himself to his mother's death, her face and tenderness remained. She was constantly with him. There were no such environments or excitements that could successfully isolate Joseph from that lingering knowledge. He had failed the person who had loved him most of all.

2

June 1962

THE YEARS that intervened between his mother's death and Joseph Flynn's twenty first birthday were an exhilarating period of change and adjustment in his life. During the autumn of 1959, an evolutionary process was set into motion that was to sculpt and mold his personality into an altered state. His thought processes and behavior, slowly but surely, assumed the mantle of Patrick Flynn. In the summer of 1962, the metamorphosis was almost complete.

Almost everything that was a source of dissatisfaction was behind him now. Carol Granahan's desperate entreaties had finally faded away; years before, the letters gave way to phone calls. She cried and pleaded, but to no avail. The poison had set too deeply into Joseph's soul and forgiveness was out of his reach.

He responded to her desperation with a scathing verbal brutality that eventually wore her down. Finally, she stopped calling and writing, terminating all contact with the man she had hoped to marry and cherish, to love and have his children. With burning resignation, she accepted the obvious; his destiny was different than that of most men. He was never meant to be the recipient of such common, lovely things, As if she knew that the design of Joe Flynn's life had been indelibly drawn many long years before, during the harrowing, formative years of his childhood, and were well beyond any changes that might have been wrought by his own hand.

Not a day passed when Joseph didn't think of Anna and his commitment to redeem himself in her memory. But now he was totally confident that she would be as happy as he was in his new, strong, communion with his father. However, there was no way for him to earn any justification from her memory in his unrelenting attitude toward Larry. So he chose to think about that situation as sparingly as possible, as if, for the most part, his brother didn't exist.

Although the passing time had caused startling tidal shifts in his personality, Joseph managed to keep a tight rein over some of his former realities. During the year before, he had departed from the university scene, inherent brilliance notwithstanding.

He was never content in a classroom atmosphere. He rebelled against the necessary regimentation and the restrictions that smothered him. He stayed within the school walls just long enough for his receptive mind to capture all the material he needed and then he returned, fulltime, to the energy of the streets.

He still loved Hanway, as if his flesh and the town's soil were mystically intertwined in some inexhaustible alliance. Everything about it still managed to provide him with a continuing reserve of strength. Like a bellows, it expanded him with hope.

More so than anyone, Mickey Clark was a main line to that strength and hope. Both men saw their respect and allegiance for the other grow more and more with each passing year.

Joseph Flynn began to feel comfortable at the right hand of his father. Since that faraway springtime in 1946, he had traveled an arduous journey, a journey that might have destroyed most men.

But now, the way ahead seemed clear and easy. He moved into each new day with a fresh sense of purpose. His machine was in high gear and he was elated with the beauty and motion of his flight.

For early June, the weather was unusually hot. Patrick got up from his desk and walked into the lounge. He went over to the air conditioner and switched it on. He stood against it until the cool air rushed against his chest, causing the front of his shirt to ruffle in the artificial breeze. "Hello, Bill," he called.

Bills' voice, filled with exasperation from the heat, came through the open lounge door. "Yeah, Pat, what is it?"

Against the grumble of the air conditioner, Pat could barely hear him. "Come on in here," he said.

Bill, pulling his tie and starched collar away from his thick neck, walked slowly into the room. "Yeah," he said.

"Sit down for a minute," Pat said. "Let's take a break."

Pat rolled up his shirt sleeves and walked behind the bar. "Scotch?" he asked, as he pulled the caramel-colored bottle from one of the shelves.

"Yeah, that'll be fine."

"Jesus, it's hot," Pat said. He poured a triple shot into a large tumbler. "I'll leave enough room for some ice," he said smiling.

Bill downed the drink in one large swallow. As he placed the glass down on the bar, he grimaced as the alcohol delivered its heat to his throat and belly. "Wow," he smiled. "That hits the spot."

Patrick leaned against the bar and sipped slowly at his drink. Bill walked over to the couch and sat down. Millie, busy about her office work, walked past the open door. Pat made a gesture with his head, and Bill got up and slowly closed the door. As he returned to the couch he looked over at Patrick. "How're you doin' with her?"

"Who?"

"Millie. How're things goin'?"

"Good. Pretty good," Patrick said.

"You don't say much about her."

"What's to say?" Pat asked.

Bill kicked off his shoes and stretched back onto the couch.

"I think you really like the broad."

Patrick stopped sipping the drink and watched the ice cube as it bobbed about the liquid. Slowly, he shook the glass, his eyes never leaving the cube. "Yeah, she's nice," he said.

Bill let out a low chuckle. "I think she's startin' to tie you up. Ya better watch yourself."

Pat smiled and downed a large mouthful of scotch.

"I don't know how you manage to keep it from old Lila," Bill said.

"Old Lila is right."

"I know," Bill smiled. "Lila is falling against the competition. I can't blame you. Millie's a knockout."

Patrick didn't answer.

"C'mon, Boss. How do you keep it from her?"

"That's no problem," Patrick answered. "I manage to see a lot of her."

"Yeah, but Lila's wise, real fuckin' wise," Bill said. "I don't know how you do it."

"I guess I've been lucky so far," Pat said.

Bill quickly moved into a sitting position. "Yeah, Pat," he said. "But now you're keepin' real regular time with Millie. Before it was only once in a while. I mean, Lila's gotta' find out sooner or later."

"Screw her then," Pat said. "Let her find out."

Manley laughed out loud, "Don't give me that bullshit," he said. "When she gets wind of this, she'll tear your eyes out." Bill leaned back, continuing to laugh.

Patrick looked over at the laughing face of Manley and smiled. "You bastard," he said.

"Oh, Jesus," Manley said, still laughing. "She'll tear your goddamn eyes out."

"I'll take care of her when the time comes."

"You better," Manley said smiling.

Patrick walked out from behind the bar. "I just keep givin' her some regular lovin'. That's all old Lila needs."

"You hope," Manley said.

"Ah, how can she find out? What the hell, not too many people know about me and Lila anyway. How can she find out? I just gotta' keep makin' sure we never all wind up at the same place at the same time."

Bill shifted his position to make room for Patrick to sit down. "How about Millie?" he asked. "Does she know anything?"

"Whadaya mean?" Pat said.

"Does she know about Lila?"

276

"No," Pat said. "I've never mentioned it. No point in it."

Patrick got up and walked over to stand, once again, in front of the air conditioner. "Lila doesn't give me much of a pick up anymore, Billy," he said, with his back to Manley. "She's old stuff, you know. The old fire's gone."

Bill rubbed his hands together looking at the immense, knotted knuckles. "Yeah, Lila's lost a lot of her looks over the last coupla years. She was a hell of a broad in the old days."

"Yeah, but it's not the old days anymore," Pat said as he turned around. "I'm goin' to eventually shake her loose."

"It won't be easy, Boss," Bill said.

"I suppose not, but I'll manage it somehow."

Manley walked over to the bar and began fixing another drink. "Joey certainly doesn't have your problems," he said.

Patrick looked at him with a perplexed squint. "How's that?" Pat said.

"Man, he doesn't bother with any broads at all. I can't understand it. He's a great lookin' kid," Manley said.

Patrick nodded. "Yeah, Joe'd never have any trouble with women. He's just not too interested."

"But why? It's sorta strange."

"Well, a coupla years ago, he had a problem with Frank Granahan's daughter. I remember that," Patrick said.

"What kinda problem?"

"Oh Christ, you know. Frank moved the family out to Ohio. Joe got all upset about their daughter. He was going with her at the time."

"Oh yeah, right. I remember," Bill said. "Wasn't Joe missing for a coupla days or somethin'? I remember Anna callin' you about it."

"Yeah, that was the time," Pat said. "I guess Granahan did all right. He never did come back."

Manley took a long drink of the scotch, wiping his mouth as he set the glass down. "Ya mean it bothered Joe that much, to the point he won't bother with any broads at all?"

"I guess so. He doesn't have much use for them. At least it seems that way," Patrick said. "Then, you gotta consider that he keeps himself real busy around here. He's really up to his neck in my businesses, you know. Maybe the kid doesn't have time for women."

Manley smiled. "C'mon, Boss, there's always time for women."

"Well, he'll get around to them soon enough. In the meantime we don't have to worry about anybody callin' him a queer."

Manley laughed. "Jesus, that's for sure. He's a tough sonofabitch. Nobody'll ever doubt he's a man, and for all we know he's screwin' regular."

"Naw, he's not," Patrick said. "I know where he is almost all the time. The kid's all business. That's all that's on his mind."

"Does he keep in touch at all with that Granahan kid?"

"Nope. Not as far as I know."

Patrick exposed his massive forearms, as he slowly rolled up his shirt sleeves.. "In a coupla years, Joe'll be ready for anything. I can see it comin'. I can groom him for anything, especially in politics. He'd be a real good candidate, you know. He's got everything, good brain, good looks. He's goin' to be a real power. Wait and see."

Manley leaned his weight against the bar. "I don't have to wait," he said. "I can see it right now, the same way you do. You sure didn't make any mistake bringin' Joe in. He worked out just like you expected. I always figured it would be Larry."

"Nah," Patrick said, derisively. "Larry's finished, all through. He's still looney. That's not gonna change,"

"What does Royal and Brogan have to say about it?" Manley asked.

"Not much. They take their piece of the payroll and keep their mouths shut," Patrick said, "But anybody can see the kid's doin' lousy. It's just as well. It's better he stays there. If he comes out, he might take another breakdown and it'd look like hell. Who needs that shit. We have no use for the kid here. Anyway, he's better off where he is. He's gettin' used to it up there."

"They don't see any improvement in him at all?" Bill asked.

Patrick rubbed his hands together and looked at the floor.

"I told them not to look for any improvement. I said he's better off where he is."

Manley discerned a note of annoyance in Patrick's voice.

"Yeah, Boss, yeah, you're right," he said.

"There's only one thing," Patrick said. "I should get up there a little more often. It looks like shit that I never visit him."

Manley remained still.

Patrick continued. "Not that I think anybody notices, but they might start noticin', ya know."

"Well what of it," Bill said. "Nobody up in that area knows who you are or anything. We're outta touch with that area. So why worry about it."

"I suppose," Pat said. "But then there's the people around town."

"Ah shit, they don't pay any attention."

Patrick's voice was filled with exasperation. "Well, Mrs. Davis and Mickey Clark go up there all the time. They probably know damn well I'm never there."

Bill Manley waved his hand in unconcern. "Don't worry about it. If they wonder about anything, it's why Joe never goes up."

"Nah. They don't wonder about that. Joe makes it pretty clear about the way he feels about Larry."

"Joe never goes up at all, does he?" Manley asked.

"Never."

"What's the matter there?" Manley asked. "Two brothers. That's a hell of a thing."

Patrick Flynn had never really thought about the estrangement between his sons, totally unaware that he was the catalyst in the changing wind of their relationship.

"I don't know," Patrick said, "They never were on the same level. I think they hated each other from when they were kids."

Manley walked over and stood near him. "Well what the hell," he said. "No point at all in worryin' about it. Fuck it. You have enough on your mind."

Patrick walked over and studied himself in the mirror behind the bar. He brushed back the curls that lay on his forehead. His brow was damp with perspiration. The droning hum of the air conditioner filled the room, unable to fully neutralize the stifling heat.

"Damn, it's hot," Patrick said.

At last, the image in the mirror was beginning to show undeniable signs of age. Patrick studied the crevassed laugh lines that ran from the sides of his nose to the level of his lower lip. His eyes, bloodshot and weary, showed a need for rest. They were further emphasized by the pouched sacs underneath. The cheekbones were still strong and proud, but the facial muscles were sagged, obscuring the once powerful jaw line. He squeezed the flesh under his jaw. "I'm gettin' a double chin," he said. "It's rotten to get old."

Manley slapped him on the back. "Old! Who're you kiddin', you look great. Look at me. I'm your age and look twice as old."

Patrick looked at his longtime friend. Bill Manley was, indeed, getting old. The powerful figure was more girth than muscle. His face, always full, was now swollen with years of scotch and undisciplined living. Manley ran his hand through his short cropped hair. "Look at this," he said. "I'm practically white."

Patrick laughed as he rubbed Bill's head. "Ah shaddap. You'll live to be a hundred, for Christ's sake. You're too goddamn mean to get old."

Bill patted his hand against his huge belly. "Naw, no shit, Boss, look at this," he said, gesturing toward his abdomen. "I've got a bay window here. We're both gettin' old, baby."

Bill sat down on the couch and began to put on his shoes. Patrick watched as his friend strained in bending over to tie the laces. He remembered the young Billy Manley of decades past. As if it were yesterday, he recalled both of them wrestling and punching on that far away bar room floor, when they were both young and vital; unconcerned with age and time, in a time when wrinkles and white hair were unimaginable. He was a different Manley then, rippling with muscle, unlined and arrogant with the youth-filled sense of his own immortality. Patrick could almost recall every hour that had passed between that night and this moment. He watched his friend struggle against girth and age, to tie his shoes. In spite of his distaste for sentimentality, Patrick could not deny the twinge that filled his chest.

"Billy," he said.

Manley, grunting, looked up.

"Go somewhere. Take the rest of the day off," Patrick said.

Manley, his shoes finally laced, sat up straight. "Why?" he asked.

"Because it's too goddamn hot. That's why. Now get movin' before I change my mind."

Manley smiled. "Okay, I won't turn down an offer like that. There's a movie downtown I'd like to see." He looked over at the groaning air conditioner. "At least the movie house has a conditioner that works." He got up and walked toward the door.

As he opened it, he turned hack to Patrick. "Boss," he said.

Patrick was about to pour himself another drink. He looked at Bill. "What?"

"When do you want me back?"

"Don't bother comin' back. It's okay. Joe's comin' over later, I'll wait for him. I'm goin' to explain that draft thing to him."

"Well, what about after that?" Bill asked.

"Nothin'. Joe'll drive me home. I'm goin' to get some sleep tonight. You just go and have a good time. I'll see you in the morning."

Manley hesitated another moment before leaving. "Boss!" he said.

"What in the hell is it now?" Patrick answered in an annoyed voice.

Manley smiled. "You're gettin' soft."

"Get outta here," Patrick laughed. "You sonofabitch."

3

JOSEPH FLYNN stood on Mickey Clark's front porch. He examined his watch. It was almost six o'clock. The day's heat had somewhat retreated, and a breeze ruffled the leaves on the branches of the elm trees in the front yard. Joe felt relaxed as he rested his seersucker jacket on his shoulder and leaned against the porch post watching the cotton clouds drifting through the early evening sky. The screen door opened and Joseph turned to see Mickey walking toward him.

"Thanks for the supper, Mick," he said. "It was delicious."

"Don't tell me, tell Mary," Mickey laughed.

"Oh, I did. I already did. You don't think I'd forget to do that."

"She enjoys praise for her cooking more than anything," Mickey said. "She'd rather cook than eat."

Joe smiled, "She's a hell of a cook. No wonder you look so well fed all the time."

Mickey laughed and grabbed his belly. "She treats me good," he said.

"She damn well better," Joe smiled. "You're the best." Joe yawned and stretched his lean body. "I eat here so much I'm going to have to start sendin' Mary a weekly check."

Mickey put his arm around Joseph's shoulder. "The more you're here, the better we like it, and you know it, ya clown."

Mickey sat down on the step, gesturing to Joe to do the same. Joe sat down.

"It turned into a beautiful day," Joe said.

"It was hot this afternoon," Mickey said.

"Yeah."

"Too damn hot for this early," Mickey said.

"Well, get ready for it. It's goin' to be a long summer."

"I was up to see Lobo the other day."

"How's he doin?" Joe asked.

"Not too good."

"What's the matter?"

"He might lose the other leg."

"Oh shit!"

"Yeah. The doctor up there said that Lobo was lucky he didn't lose both legs right after the accident. But now it looks like he's goin' to lose the other one after all."

Joseph looked down and watched a tiny ant struggling with a crumb. Time and again, as it tried to make its way across the long step, the ant would drop the crumb, only to persist in retrieving it and continuing on in its journey.

"I never did write that letter to Lobo," Joe said,

"Why not? I thought you told me you did."

"I was lyin', Mick. I couldn't do it. I don't hold anything against the poor guy, but I just couldn't write him that letter."

"I thought you did," Mickey said sadly.

"Oh, well, what's the difference? Lobo doesn't know how to read anyway. Does he?"

"He did once," Mickey said.

"Yeah, but he probably doesn't now, so what's the difference?"

"Well, I can't blame you, kid. Losin' Gena and Tom was tough to take. I can understand how you feel."

Joe clenched his teeth as he looked at Mickey. "I really do forgive Lobo, Mick, but writing him a letter, I can't do it. I just can't do that. I can't tell him I forgive him. I can tell you, that's okay, but I just can't admit it openly to him."

"I understand."

"You get up to that hospital quite a bit, don't you?" Joe asked.

"Yeah, yeah, quite a bit. There's no one else since his mother died, so I feel sorta obligated, you know,"

"You're a good man, Mick."

"Ah, being good has nothin' to do with it. Lobo used to be a good, good friend. He woulda done the same for me."

"I know that you get out to see Larry a lot too," Joe said.

"Yeah, pretty often."

For a moment, both men remained quiet. Joseph watched the ant carry its bounty over the edge of the step and disappear.

"Go ahead, Mick. Say it," Joseph said, in an irritated voice.

"I'm not goin' to say anything, nothin' at all," Mickey answered.

"I know damn well it bugs the shit outta you that I never get to see Larry. I know it does." He looked over at Mickey.

"Well, doesn't it?" Joe asked, "Goddammit, doesn't it?"

Mickey smiled and softly punched Joe's thigh. "I don't think much about it, kid,"

Joe smiled sarcastically,

"Well, I'm tellin' you, Joe, I really don't think about it that much. The trouble with you is that you feel damn guilty about it, and you're imaginin' all kinds of shit. If you don't want to see Larry, that's your business. Nobody else has a right to preach to you. Do what you think is right."

"You don't think it's right."

"Well, now that you're mentionin' it, no I don't, but it's none of my business, so forget about it."

Joseph knew that the conversation threatened to destroy an otherwise perfect evening. "You're right, Mick. Let's forget about it."

They got up off the step and slowly walked to Joseph's car. Joe put on the striped seersucker and stretched once again. "I really enjoyed the meal," he said lazily. "Mary's fantastic, and tell her I said so."

Mickey laughed, "All of these compliments'll spoil the hell out of her."

Joe slapped him on the back and got into his car. Mickey waved and turned back to the house.

"I'll be in touch with you tomorrow or the day after," Joe said through the open window.

Mickey smiled and waved once again.

The long, blue Oldsmobile pulled away from the curb and slowly made its way down the quiet street.

Patrick turned the knob of the office door to ascertain that it was locked. It was secure. He pressed Millie against the wall alongside the door, and slid his engorged organ deep inside her. He began to rhythmically pound his groin into hers. He heard her catch her breath and groan, sensuously, into his ear.

He reached down behind her and squeezed her high, soft buttocks. Millie smiled against his neck, as she listened triumphantly to his panting whispers of pleasure. It was over in less than a minute. The violent thrusts relaxed into a slow, delicious cadence. Finally, he eased to a stop and pressed his full weight against her. Millie pulled his head back and smiled at him,

"Is it all okay now, honey?" she smiled.

"I'm sorry it had to be so quick," Patrick whispered.

Millie emitted a slow, sexy laugh, "That's okay," she whispered. "Tomorrow night it'll be a lot slower,"

"And a lot better," Patrick smiled, "at least for you."

Millie continued her low laughter. "Well, I can't really get the kind of satisfaction I'm used to with quickies like this."

Patrick smoothed back her hair. "I know. I'll make it up to you tomorrow," he whispered.

She carefully pushed him back away from her. She turned and looked at the door, "C'mon, now," she smiled. "Joe might be here any minute. We'd better pull ourselves together."

Patrick pushed his shirt back into his pants and quickly zipped his fly. As he tightened his belt, he studied his lover. Millie snapped her panties back into place and straightened her skirt. She saw him watching her. She moved against him and kissed him softly on the mouth. Her lips, under Patrick's, were soft and full.

"I think you'd better go into the lounge before I open the door. Someone might be walking by out there." She gestured toward the hall. She unlocked the door and glanced up and down the corridor. She turned around and smiled at Patrick, "Nope, nobody," she said. From where he was standing in the lounge doorway, Patrick blew her a kiss.

She waved. "Bye," she said, as she closed the door behind her.

Patrick watched from the window until Millie Morris's car disappeared in the boulevard's traffic. He pulled the blinds tight and checked his watch. It was fifteen minutes before seven. Joe was expected any minute. There were two major items he had to discuss with his son, and he was uncertain how Joseph would respond to them. He paced continuously over the heavily carpeted floor. Finally, he heard the office door open. Moments later, Joe walked into the lounge.

"Hi," Joseph said, as he came into the room.,

"What's up, Joe?" Patrick said,

Joe walked toward the bar. "May I have a drink?" he said.

Patrick smiled. "Help yourself."

Joe filled a glass with scotch over ice and handed it to his father. "Age before beauty," he laughed.

Joe's statement, in the aftermath of the discussion with Manley, struck Patrick with its irony. He laughed out loud, shaking his head back and forth. "Dammit. If I think or hear anything else today concerning my age, I'll spit."

Joe swallowed several mouthfuls of scotch. "What's that about age?" he asked.

"Nothin'. Really nothin'. Joe, Listen. We've got some things to talk about, you know."

"Yeah, I figured. What's up?"

Patrick rested himself on one of the high stools. Joe absent-mindedly tapped his fingertips on the bar. The illumination from the lamp hanging above him caught the side of his face, its glare of light defining his profile. It was near perfect. The cheekbones jutted out under the thick-lashed eyes, moving into a sculpted hollow in his lower face. His nose was straight and long. His full black hair was brushed back over the top of his ear, and the razored angle of his jaw completed the overall image of strength and confidence. Patrick watched him; Joe was movie star handsome, and his body was practically a duplicate of Patrick's own body when he was his son's age, the same beam-like shoulders and powerful chest. Under the thin jacket sleeve, Joseph's arms bulged with muscular power. There wasn't a pound on his body that was in excess, every ounce falling into a perfectly proportioned symmetry.

"Well, are you going to pay attention or not?" Patrick asked. Joe turned toward him and smiled. "Oh, I'm sorry, Dad. Go ahead. I was just drifting. Go ahead." Joseph let his thoughts of Mickey Clark and their conversation about Larry slip away.

"I'm sorry," he said. "Go ahead."

Both men sat down on the stools facing each other. The incessant humming of the air conditioner drowned out the traffic sounds of the street. Patrick lit a cigar, and deeply inhaled it. As he began to speak, the swirling clouds of smoke drifted above his head.

"I was talkin' to Matt Royal earlier this morning," Patrick said.

"Oh, yeah, about what?"

Patrick's movements suddenly became agitated. He jumped from the stool and began walking across the room. Roughly, he turned the off button of the air conditioner. "Goddamn. Ya can't hear yourself think with this friggin' thing."

Joseph didn't utter a sound.

"Well, like I said, I was talkin' to him," Patrick continued. "Ya know, this Vietnam thing is gettin' to be a pain in the ass. From all the inside information I'm getting, we're goin' to be in a war before long."

Joe's eyes widened in surprise. "No kiddin'?" he said.

"Yeah. That's right."

"I thought the government was only going to send military advisers."

"Oh, you're keepin' track of it, huh?" Pat said.

Joseph smiled. "Well, I read the papers, Dad," he said. "And

I happen to he right at the age of jeopardy if there is a war. You know what I mean?"

"Well, that's one of the things I want to discuss. You're not in jeopardy, war or no war."

Joe's eyebrows elevated. "Oh, how's that?" he asked.

"Look, Joe. Just listen to me. Okay?" Patrick said, expecting opposition to what he was about to say.

"Yeah, okay. I'm listenin'."

"Well, all right," Pat said, gesturing with his hands, "By sixty-four or sixty-five, this situation is going to be a bastard. Believe me. I've been talkin' to some important guys and they know what they're talkin' about. I mean these guys have inside lines with the Pentagon. Before long, every guy your age is goin' to be drafted." Pat walked over and nervously poured a drink. He looked out of the corner of his eye at Joe.

"What'd you do, fix it for me?" Joe asked.

"Yeah, I did."

"How?"

"I've got friends on the draft board and they owe me. Between them and Royal, they're goin' to take care of it."

"How?" Joe repeated.

"Matt told me this mornin' that he's goin' to falsify your medical records somehow. He'll make it legal. I've already straightened it out with the rest of the people involved. By the time your name comes up, there won't be a thing to worry about."

"How do you expect the people around here to fall for it?"

"Fuck the people around here. Anyway Matt said when the time comes, nobody'll have any reason to question it. I dunno, he's goin' to make it seem like you have high blood pressure or somethin'. There's not goin' to be any problem."

"Nobody'll believe it," Joe said sarcastically.

Patrick's response was in a voice loud and angry. "Jesus Christ! I expected somethin' like this from you. Get over that high school shit about war and country. It's no fuckin' picnic. I was there already. It's goddamn ugly. Whadaya' think it's like, the movies? Ya'll shit in your pants when the time comes, but that time is not goin' to come, ya' hear me?"

Joe sucked an ice cube into his mouth and rolled it around with his tongue. His eyes were expressionless, and Patrick was unable to discern his son's feelings.

"Look, Joe," Patrick said in a soft voice. "Listen to me. I've got big plans for you, big. You're goin' to be a county commissioner in a coupla' years and after that maybe a congressman or senator. You know I've got the connections to pull it off, and besides you've got everything goin' for you. You're smart, good lookin', and in the next coupla years, you're gonna make big contacts of your own. I can see already that you've got big ideas. You know you're goin' to be somebody. Everybody knows you're goin' to be somebody, and we're not goin' to let any fuckin' war screw it up."

As his father spoke, Joe listened to every word. His mind simultaneously analyzed every sentence, breaking down every possibility, as if the entire situation was an equation, leading to an irrefutable, scientific answer.

Patrick continued in his oration as he paced the floor, avoiding his son's eyes. "The sky's the limit for you, Joey," he said. "Believe me. Listen to what I'm sayin'. It's the best thing for you."

"Okay, Dad. Okay. Relax," Joe finally said. "No problem. Do whatever you have to do, I don't want any part of bullets or bombs or any of the rest of that shit. I'd rather stay right where I'm at."

Patrick almost staggered at his son's reply, "Jesus! Jesus!" he said exuberantly. "Goddamn, I should've known better," He laughed and heartily slapped Joe on the back. "You're smart! You're smart! I should've known you wouldn't disagree," he said, as he happily squeezed Joe's neck with his forearm.

Joseph grabbed his father's arm and shook it gratefully. "I appreciate what you're doin', Dad. Aunt Gena said that you did enough for your country for one family, and I agree with her."

Remembering Gena, Patrick smiled, "She did, huh?" he said.

"Yeah, she did, a long time ago,"

"Well, she was right," Patrick said.

Joe thought of the conversation he had with his aunt, so many years before. This was the perfect time to validate her premise. "Dad," Joseph said quietly, "why In the hell did you enlist when you did? Gena said you could've stayed out of it."

Patrick laughed. "Stay out of it for what? I was really into gamblin' back then, you know. Man, I was sharp with cards and dice. I knew I could take those punks for a bundle, and I did. They didn't know their ass from a hole in the ground. I made a pile of bucks in the army."

Joe smiled to himself as he recalled his aunt's wisdom.

"All in all," Patrick said, "the war turned out to be a good thing for me. I won that medal and became a hero. What the hell, it set me up good when I got backk and I had a lot of thousands in my pocket to do what I had to do."

"God," Joseph said, "how did you take over everything the way you did? Money or not, medal or not, it must have been tough."

"Naw, not really. The right time spent, the right investments, the right contacts. All it took was a little common sense and a lot of muscle. I'm goin' to do the same for you. Just the same, you listen to me."

Joseph was quiet for a moment. Then he asked the question that was thumping against his head, "You did the same for Larry too, didn't you?"

"What?"

"You made the arrangements that kept him out of Korea. There wasn't anything wrong with his ear, was there?"

Patrick hesitated for a moment, "Yeah, I did," he finally said. "I did. Why not? He was my son, and at the time I had plans for him too."

Hearing his father talk about Larry made Joseph wince.

"But I shoulda known the kid was always meant to be a fuckin' washout."

Joe barely heard his father's last statement, as his brain busily spun around his next question. "Did he know?"

"Whadaya mean?" Patrick asked. "Ya mean, did he know that I kept him out?"

Joe was almost breathless, but in the deep confines of his heart he already knew the answer.

Patrick hesitated again. "No," he said finally. "He didn't know. We actually had him believe it was legitimate," Patrick laughed, "Doc Benson convinced him that the kind of ear problem he had could only be detected by a doctor. The kid actually believed it, I really don't think he was pretending. He really fell for it." Patrick continued to laugh. "I really think the kid would've been pissed if he knew the truth."

"Yeah, I think he would too," Joe said solemnly.

Patrick quickly turned toward his son. "That's because he was thick. He was a dummy. He always was. You're smart. That's the difference. That's the difference between you and your brother. That's why you're where you are and he's in the nut house. Remember that."

Joe slid off the stool. "Yeah, that's right," he said quietly, without looking at his father. "Do whatever is necessary. I don't want any part of that thing in Vietnam."

Patrick smiled and shook his head affirmatively.

"Is there anything else?" Joseph said.

Patrick was ecstatic about Joseph's attitude to the draft fixing. His face was lit up in a broad smile, "Oh yeah, yeah," he said. "There is something else," He walked over and playfully grabbed Joe's face. "I'm proud of ya, boy. Real proud."

Joseph laughed and grasped both his father's hands. "All right. Now what else do you have to tell me?"

Patrick suddenly grew serious once again. "This is almost as important, Joey, It's real important to me."

"All right then. What is it?"

"We need a new real estate office in Hanway, don't we?"

"Yeah, I suppose."

"Suppose nothin'. The other one's way too small. We need a new place and it's gotta be big enough for more than real estate transactions."

"Big enough for what?"

Patrick elaborately spread open his arms. "It's gotta be big enough to handle all of the county political business."

"What's the matter with the office in town? I mean you use it strictly for your chairman operation. It seems big enough to handle everything."

"Look, I want to establish a place to run all the operations involving the boroughs. The old place'll be just involved with city affairs. I'm goin' to transfer a few guys from the city headquarters up to Hanway, but you'll run the operation. You'll run the local real estate business as well."

Joe smiled. "All right. That sounds okay."

"There's only one thing," Patrick said.

"What?"

"I want Petry's place for the office."

Joe looked shocked. "What for? There's plenty of other places."

"Yeah. Well maybe there is," Patrick said. "But that's the place I want."

Joe's voice was edged with disgust. "But why? Why Petry's?"

"Because that's the place I want."

"Oh shit man, Mr. Petry's restaurant is a landmark. Jesus."

"Oh it really bothers you, doesn't it?" Patrick said sarcastically.

"Well, sure. I mean what's the old man gonna' do?"

"Don't worry about that old wop. There's other diners in town. After a while nobody'll miss him."

Joe's own Italian heritage bristled at his father's ethnic slur. "Ya know, Dad, you ought to get over that wop stuff. Mom was Italian, and I'm half Italian and there's plenty of Italian people in this county. They've always been good to all of us. You shouldn't have that kind of attitude."

Patrick laughed at his son's obvious anger. "Oh my, now he's insulted."

"I'm not insulted but it's time you stopped with that bullshit. You and Bill pull that stuff all the time. It seems that all the politicians in this county see everybody as wops or kikes or hunkies. It sounds like hell."

Patrick laughed. "That's because all the politicians and sharpies are Irish, boy. All the guys with the bread are Irish. They built this county, politically and otherwise and don't you forget it. We've got our rights to call them whatever we want. If it wasn't for our people, the rest of them wouldn't have a job, y'know."

Joseph rolled his eyes and looked at the ceiling. "That's a pile of garbage and you know it. They'd get along damn well on their own. They handle all the tough jobs. Some of your buddies don't know what a shovel's used for."

"The wops and the rest of them wouldn't have a pot to piss in, if it wasn't for me and my buddies."

Joseph knew there was no point in arguing with his father. Patrick's core of ethic prejudice ran much too deep. Joe was also well aware that his father wasn't alone in his attitudes. Such hostilities moved like a snake through the proud heritages of each group; Irish, Italian, Jew, and Eastern Middle European alike. It was one of the few and enduring indictments that were ingrained in the perspectives of Manway's melting pot of people; no matter how many years passed, the provincial attitudes of ethnic pride continued to be maintained by the ugly breath of bigotry.

"Just try and remember," Joe said with a smile. "I happen to be part Italian, so give me a break."

"You're Irish," Patrick said scowling. "You're no more Italian than the man in the moon."

"Oh, yeah," Joe said continuing to smile. "Look at this dark skin." He ran his hand over his face. "Look at this Roman nose."

Patrick looked at his son and smiled. He couldn't deny his wife's image was in Joseph's face. "Well, you might look like one, but you don't act that way. You weren't brought up like one."

Joe's eyes grew sad as he remembered his mother. "Ma never missed a chance to tell me about grandma and grandpa. She told me stories and stories about Rome and all the things her parents told her."

"Yeah, well never mind that. Just remember you never saw any sauce on our table, and you and Larry went to St. James Church. You always belonged to the Irish parish, I personally saw to things like that. I knew what was best for you."

Joe suddenly grew bored and somewhat nauseous with the direction of the conversation. "Yeah, let's forget it," Joe said. "Now what about Petry's place?"

Patrick immediately forgot about the ethnic discussion.

"Well, Joey," he said, "This is what I want you to do. I've already bought the building. We went through the closing yesterday. All you have to do is tell Petry he's finished by the end of the month. He doesn't have a lease, you know. The old man just rents month by month."

"How'd you get the place? What was the price?"

"I paid way over its head. John Mangan owned the building. He couldn't turn the offer down."

"Shit, Dad, Petry's too old to start up anywhere else. This'll break his heart."

Patrick laughed. "Don't be so sentimental. The guy's almost seventy. It's about time he retired."

"What's he gonna do?"

"What do I care what he does. Maybe he'll take his old lady on a trip to Italy," Patrick laughed derisively.

"Yeah, well you didn't tell me what you want me to do," Joe said in an annoyed voice.

"I want you to tell the old man he's got two weeks to get out."

"Why me? Tell Bill to do it."

"No, that's just it, Joe. I expressly want you to do it. It'll help you get over this shit about Hanway."

"What shit?"

"Oh, c'mon. You've always thought the town was some kind of Shangri-la. I've heard a hundred people say that. Well now you're gonna prove you care more about the Flynn interests than you do about the friggin' town."

"I don't see how..."

"You don't see how," Patrick interrupted. "Well, I see how. If you do this, if you grab this old guy Petry by the balls and tell him to get movin', you'll be showin' me you're a man."

Joe looked confused, "But what does this have to do with the town?" he asked.

"Because Petry is the town, that's why. He's an institution there, just like you said. All right then, I want you to throw him out. He'll beg. I know damn well he will, but you're goin' to tell him there's no other way out. He's got to go."

Joseph just sat there and said nothing.

"Well, are you going to do it or not?" Patrick said in a loud voice,.

Joseph twisted his lip in disgust and rested his elbows on the bar. He dejectedly bowed his head.

"Well c'mon, c'mon. Are you going to give me an answer? Whadaya care about a rummy like Petry or any of the rest of them? We can buy and sell them any day of the week. No one'll open their mouths or we'll jam our fists down their throats. What's there to worry about?"

Joe drummed his knuckle against his teeth and remained silent.

Patrick walked over and placed his hands on his son's shoulders. "Look, Joe," he said. "You're either with me or with them. I've got a lotta plans that concern Hanway, We're gonna buy up a lot more properties. There's gonna be a lotta cryin' and it's not gonna matter a damn. If any of them get in my way I'll trample them. I don't need any of them anymore. Now you're either with me or against me."

Joe remained silent and in deep thought.

Patrick was becoming more and more agitated, "Jesus, can't

you see anything at all?" he said. "This is only the beginning. I just want you to prove to me you can handle it. You gotta prove to me that I matter more than they do."

Patrick waited for Joe to reply, but his son remained silent.

Patrick's voice was low and hard. "Jesus Christ, what'd they ever do for you? They only want to take, take." He leaned over and whispered slowly into Joseph's ear. "What'd they ever do for you?"

Joe's mind was filled with what they had always done for him. All the kindnesses and decency. All the tenderness and friendships. In desperation, he pushed all of it out of his mind. He turned around and faced his father. "Okay," he said. "I'll tell him."

Patrick smiled triumphantly. "Goddamn it, don't listen to any sob stories. I want you to be hard on him if you have to." Patrick smiled knowingly. "You'll have to if I know Petry. He's an emotional bastard. They all are."

Joseph smiled and stood up. He softly grabbed his father's elbow. "I'll do what I have to do."

"All right, all right," Patrick said happily.

"I'm with you, now and always, Dad. Don't ever doubt that."

"Not now, I won't."

Joseph poured a shot of scotch and swallowed it quickly. "Is that all then?" he asked.

"Yeah, that's it," Patrick replied.

"Good. Okay then," Joe said, "Everything's settled."

"It will be when you take care of Petry."

Joe started to walk to the door. "I'll take care of it," he answered without turning around,

"Wait a minute. Wait a minute," Patrick shouted to his departing son, "I'll walk out with you.

Joe turned around with a look of concern. "Oh, do you need a ride home?" he asked.

"No, I'm going across the street to Mulrooney's. Some of the hoys will he around. You got me in a good mood. I feel like talkin'."

"How're you gonna get home? Where's Bill?" Joe asked.

"I gave him the day off. Don't worry. There'll he a thousand rides."

"You sure?"

"Yeah, yeah, let's go." Patrick snapped off the lounge lamp and walked alongside Joseph to the office door. Before following Joseph out into the hallway, he looked at the wall. Just a short time before, Millie Morris' body squirmed under his. "It's been a beautiful day," he whispered.

Joe turned around, "What's that?" he said.

"Oh, nothing, Joe. Nothing," he smiled as he turned the lock and slammed the door behind him.

PATRICK and Joe emerged from the hotel, and, for a short while stood on the sidewalk talking in hushed tones. On that summer night, Susquehanna Avenue was quiet; its lonely stretch of asphalt extending blocks and blocks past each quiet intersecting avenue. An occasional vehicle drifted by. A large, unshaven man sat alone on the sidewalk. His back comfortably rested against the cement facade of the building. His filthy, ragged shirt was open down the front, exposing a bloated, hairy belly that he absentmindedly scratched with one hand. The other hand pressed a small radio to his ear. He was oblivious to everything but the cacophony blaring into his head. Joseph caught the man's eye and smiled at him.

"Hey, man!" Joe called.

The figure looked over at Joe, simultaneously moving his hand from his belly to his unshaven face. He began to scratch through his beard. He smiled back at Joe.

Joseph flipped a fifty cent piece. It bounced alongside the man, who reached out and grasped it. He smiled and waved.

Joseph turned his attention back to his father, "Well then, I'll see you," he said.

"Right. Okay, we'll get together tomorrow," Patrick said. Pat watched his son walk toward the parking lot. Joseph's stride was sure and easy, reminiscent of a confident animal; his shoulders were straight and intimidating, his hips and arms moved in a sure unison, as if each and every muscle were in some secret, special communication. Looking at Joe, it was as if Patrick were watching himself in a time, long past, before the years tampered with his own grace and arrogance. Also, it was as if certain other elements in the past never existed. The father had finally forgiven the son. At last the gap seemed to be closing. He took a deep breath of the late evening air, and jauntily crossed the street toward Mulrooney's Bar.

Joseph swiftly moved his car through the silent city. Within minutes after leaving the suburbs, the car moved onto the open highway, leading back to Hanway. Through force of habit, he switched on the radio, but his concentration was enmeshed within his own grinding thoughts, impeding all else, as they pushed and plowed their way through to his mind's surface. He was embarrassed by his agreement to his father's Vietnam solution. He cringed, thinking of how he had condemned Larry for a similar conspiracy.

But his brother had never been a part of it, which made Joseph's action all the more despicable. He had judged Larry wrongly in that case, and perhaps in many others. For the first time in many years, he thought of his brother with a stirring of remorse. But it was the thought of a defenseless Mr. Petry that bothered him. Driving through the countryside, he called on every source of possible justification to ease his guilt-laden mind. Finally, he measured everything against one priority, the Flynn dynasty, its money and power. He wanted to believe his father's concept, that it didn't matter who suffered or what means were implemented to keep his influence intact. It only mattered that Patrick and Joseph Flynn remained on the top of their own special world.

Joe managed to breathe easier. He held all of his actions accountable to a set of convictions he desperately wanted to believe in.

Within a half hour, his car was on the Hanway streets. Children were everywhere, running in heedless herds along the sidewalks and over the road. Shirtless and grinning, they filled the atmosphere with sound and motion. Joe smiled as he caught a glimpse of an old man, impervious to the noise. He lay, fast asleep, stretched out on his front porch glider. His straw hat was carelessly pulled down over his forehead. It was a familiar vista, women in housedresses and aprons, leaning against porch railings and fences as they chattered out their daily gossip. The lowered sun cast an unreal pinkish glow through the lush trees, blanketing the well-kept front lawns and reflecting from windows. As the car approached the railway crossing that led to Main Street, another band of kids were running and stumbling down the embankment that sloped away from the railroad tracks. A straggling few were jumping over the smooth, steel rails in their efforts to catch up.

Main Street was alive—an assortment of men dressed in their spare uniforms of summer, sitting on the weather beaten wooden benches in front of the saloons. Others leaned against parking meters or gestured wildly as they argued about something or other. The open barroom doors led to more men lining the bars. They wiped away sweat as they hovered over games of poker. A large fan turned endlessly overhead, in a losing battle against the heat and foul stench of whiskey and tobacco. They would sit at the card tables all night, with stogies firmly clenched between their teeth, taking occasional breathers only to down great schooners of foaming draft beer. In a kind of profane security, they would drink and swear and laugh their hours away, utterly unconcerned with the bloated bellies and hairy backs that pushed through their open-shouldered undershirts.

Joseph knew them all. As he drove past, he waved and honked his horn. Some of them waved back, while others remained inanimate and watched him with questioning eyes. The storefront neon was already blinking. Clusters of teenagers stood in front of Petry's.

Joseph accelerated his machine in its climb up the long hill. He was very much aware of the men who didn't wave. More and more, the townspeople were associating him with his father; and in Hanway, in that time and place, any alignment with Patrick Flynn was suspect. Once, these streets and all the people on them were Joseph's champions. But now, things were changing. In the face of it, Joe held no self recriminations; changes were a fact of life, to be used, if possible, as supports for one's best interests. If he was no longer a child of Hanway, so be it. He would be its owner instead.

He turned off Main Street onto Jessup Avenue, roaring eagerly toward the mansion he once abhorred, resolutely prepared to assume his new role of beguiling himself into believing he was someone he wasn't. For Joseph Flynn, regardless of his imaginings and self deception, would never be far removed from the town he loved, or the child he was born to be.

5

THE MOUNT ROSE residents always found summer to be the best time of the year. The grounds were like a huge park with acres and acres of green extending out in all directions. Along the flowered pathways, birds would splash in the small, gurgling fountains and the quick running brook glistened like crystal.

Most of the patients, with watchful attendants nearby, spent almost the entire day reclining on the colorful lawn chairs that were scattered about the area. Others walked about enjoying the weather and scenery.

Doctor Brogan stood at his office window. His eyes followed the thin, young man pacing back and forth on the sidewalk.

Behind Brogan, Matthew Royal sat hunched in a chair.

"That's funny," Brogan said, as he turned toward Royal. "Here we are discussing Larry Flynn, and there he is right outside my window."

"You're kidding," Royal said.

"No. Take a look."

Royal got up and went to the window. "God, he looks terrible, doesn't he?" Royal said.

Brogan sat down at his desk. "Yes, he does. He looks worse every day."

"He's lost a great deal of weight," Royal said.

"It's no wonder," Brogan said quietly, "We almost have to force feed him."

Royal watched as the nurse, standing near Larry tried to talk to him. Larry, his eyes blank, ignored her and continued in his pacing.

"Have you established any kind of communication with him?" Royal asked.

"Not really," Brogan answered.

Royal turned away from the window and watched Brogan shuffling through the papers that littered his desk.

"What's the matter, Malcolm? You seem a little edgy," Royal said.

Brogan rotated his swivel chair, enabling him to look better at his friend. "Well, as I was explaining to you, Matt, this situation with Pat Flynn is getting on my nerves."

"Why? What's wrong?"

"I feel like a goddamn thief taking his money."

"A thief!" Royal laughed. "If anyone is a thief, it's Flynn."

"I don't think I can tolerate it any longer," Brogan said disgustedly. "On the first of every month, that thug is knocking on my front door."

"Not Patrick," Royal said,

"No. No, it's that other goon."

"Who? Manley?"

"Yeah," Brogan said, "He's always there like clockwork with his wad of bills," Brogan pressed his knuckles against his forehead. "And I'm no better than they are. Neither of us are. We're on the take, like two common crooks."

"I don't see it that way," Royal said. "Of course nobody's knocking at my door."

"Where do you do your collecting?" Brogan asked sarcastically. "At his office?"

Royal laughed. "Yes, I do all my collecting there."

"How can you stand it?" Brogan asked.

"I manage," Royal answered. "And you manage, too, so cut the pontificating."

"I'm serious, Matt," Brogan said. "I want to end this."

"Well, end it then!" Royal said in an annoyed voice. "But I'm warning you, Malcolm, you'd better not let that kid out of here. You know as well as I do that there's no way we can offer Pat a guarantee on Larry's future."

"Or what?" Brogan said angrily.

"Or Manley will tear you in half. Patrick will see to it. I'm warning you."

"He wouldn't dare."

"Oh, wouldn't he now," Royal laughed, "Well, you've got a lot to learn about Patrick Flynn."

"He'll get his ass hauled off to jail. I'm not one of his barroom punks, I've got my own connections. I don't have any reason to be afraid of that hoodlum."

"Connections!" Royal said incredulously, "Are you kidding? You're not in his league, my friend, He'd chew the two of us up."

"I think you're exaggerating his power."

"For Christ's sake, it's not a question of power. It's a question of violence."

"Oh, c'mon, Matt," Brogan said.

"Listen to me," Royal said in a voice filled with concern. "If you take a step against Flynn, you'll never take another one. Believe me, Malcolm. I'm telling you this for your own good."

"What can he possibly do?"

"For starters, you'll wind up with broken legs and a rearranged face, and then he'll find a way to destroy your practice."

"You make it sound easy."

"For him, it is easy. You're not really aware of the kinds of power he has access to. He'll ruin you. I mean it."

Brogan's face twitched nervously, knowing that Matthew Royal was privy to the inner workings of Patrick Flynn. "Well, Jesus, Matt, what am I to do here? I can't operate this way. I just can't. It's bothering the hell out of me. There must be some way to stop it."

"There is no way," Royal said. "You've got to keep the kid here."

"It's not a question of keeping Larry here," Brogan said. "It's the money. It makes me feel dirty."

Matthew Royal broke out into laughter. "Then what's the problem?" he says. "If Larry stays, there isn't any problem. I'll explain to Pat that you feel guilty about taking a payoff."

"How will he accept that?"

"He'll accept it just fine, as long as you assure him that Larry stays."

"The fact is," Brogan said quietly, "Larry wouldn't survive five minutes out of here. The boy is really sick."

"Then just keep him here and forget about the money. Pat will understand."

Malcolm Brogan, preoccupied with his thoughts, paid no atten\ tion to Royal. "I've really tried, Matt," he said. "I've used every form of therapy imaginable, but his condition continues to deteriorate."

Royal's face grew serious. "I'm surprised," he said. "His overall picture didn't imply as much in the beginning."

"He's much worse now."

"But why?" Royal asked,

"I'm aware of one significant factor," Brogan replied.

"What's that?"

"Since Mrs. Flynn died, not one member of his family has visited the boy and he's cognizant of that fact. Except for a few older friends, absolutely nobody comes to see him."

"Yeah, I know," Royal said.

Brogan's eyes were clouded. "My God, what kind of family would do such a thing? From Larry's past history, I can't see where he's ever harmed anyone. What kind of animals are they? It's as if his father and brother are pretending he doesn't exist."

"I don't see where that's so difficult to understand," Royal said. "I mean, the old man's paying you to keep Larry locked up. That indicates how little he cares."

"What's wrong with the brother?"

"I don't know. I do my best to avoid Patrick Flynn's family affairs.

"How does the other boy get along with Flynn?"

"Fabulously, or at least it seems that way."

Brogan's thoughts went back to Larry. "I can't understand it," he said thoughtfully.

"Well, listen to me," Royal said. "Stop trying to be the fine and honorable physician and keep Larry here. Do whatever you can for him. But, by all means, keep him here. You gave your word."

Brogan's face was a mask of anger. "I didn't know what I was getting into. I should never have listened to you."

"But you did," Royal said angrily. "You did because you liked the idea of a fat payday every month for doing nothing. It's a little late to be playing a sanctimonious role."

Brogan nodded his head. "I can't disagree with you there, Matt. That's exactly what I did, and don't misunderstand me, I'm not blaming you. But I'm definitely not going to play this game anymore."

Royal smiled and walked toward the door. He ran his hand over his smooth hair and straightened his tie. "I'll tell Pat you don't want anymore money. He'll understand. I'll see to it. As long as the kid stays, there won't be any reprisals."

Malcolm Brogan's jaw was firmly set. "I'll discharge him in a minute if Larry gives me any chance at all. I'll discharge him in a minute, and Pat Flynn can be damned," Brogan said. "I know right well that there's no way to insure a complete cure for Larry. But if he shows reasonable improvement, I'll allow him the chance to live a normal life."

Royal looked amused. "No, you won't my friend," he said. "You're much too smart for that." He started to walk away. "I'm sorry, Malcolm," he said. "But that's the way it's got to be."

Before Brogan could reply, Royal left the office, closing the door behind him.

For a long time, Brogan sat, brooding, at his desk. Finally, he lifted his long frame out of the leather chair and walked to the window. Larry Flynn was gone.

6

THREE DAYS after his and his father's discussion about Dominick Petry, Joseph took care of the matter. He handled it in the manner Patrick had suggested. He was indeed hard on the old man. Patrick had, once again, proved to be a brilliant prognosticator. The old man did cry and beg but Joseph was every bit as ruthless as he had to be. After almost an hour of pleading and bargaining, Mr. Petry knew he was through. Joseph, with no show of emotion, delivered the ultimatum.

"You've got two weeks then," Joseph said coldly. "Everything'll be out. If there's any equipment left here, we'll junk it."

The old man stood quietly, looking at the floor. He nervously dabbed at his wet eyes.

Joseph Flynn cleared his throat. His manner was extremely businesslike. "Is everything clear then?" he said, "We expect to be in here in two weeks."

Mr. Petry nodded his head, indicating he understood.

"That's fine," Joseph said. Joseph quickly walked past him. "I'll see you."

As he reached the door of the diner, he turned around. Mr. Petry remained in the kitchen. Joseph left the diner and hastily got into his car. His hand trembled as he slipped the key into the ignition. He felt nauseated. As deliberately as he tried, he could not block the echo of the old man's voice—the tearful, heavily accented voice reverberating over and over within his ears. He knew he would never forget the sight of Mr. Petry's defenseless posture or the confusion in his eyes. Since Joseph's early childhood, he had known Dominick Petry. Through those years there had been many words and much laughter. But now, all he had left to remember was the dull, empty stare of a scared and grief-stricken old man.

As Joe walked through the front door of the mansion, Patrick was coming down the stairs. His black, wing-tipped shoes shone from beneath the blue pants cuffs. His torso was naked. "What brings you back here? I thought you were going into the city."

Joe waited for him at the bottom of the stairs. " I decided this morning I'd take care of that Petry thing."

"Oh really," Patrick said smiling. "How'd you make out? Have you seen him yet?"

Joseph looked away. "It's done," he said softly. "It's taken care of."

Patrick arched his eyebrows. "Any problems?" he asked.

"Yeah, there sure was," Joseph answered.

Patrick discerned the irritation in his son's voice. "What happened?" he said.

Joe rested against the banister and ran his fingers through his hair. "Mr. Petry was sick about it. It was terrible."

Patrick nodded his head. "I told you what it'd be like. Didn't I tell you?" he said emphatically.

"Yeah, you hit it."

"I told you. I knew it. What'd he do? Rant? Rave? Cry?"

Joe nodded.

"There. What'd you expect? I told you. They're all the same." He thought to himself for a moment. "Emotional bastards," he mumbled. He looked at Joe. "Well, how did ya" handle it?"

"Just like you said," Joe answered. "I treated him rough."

"Did you sympathize with him?"

"No," Joe muttered. "I was rotten."

"Good thing. The last thing you wanna do is sympathize with him."

Joe, disconsolately, shook his head, "I really feel lousy about it," he said quietly.

Patrick laughed and slammed his palm against his son's shoulder, "C'mon, c'mon, ya gotta be tough." Patrick waved Joe to follow him. When they entered the kitchen, Patrick walked to the refrigerator and removed a quart of milk. He turned around to his son. "In the mood?" He gestured toward the milk.

"No thanks," Joe said.

As Patrick poured the milk, he began to laugh. "See that? See what I mean? You're learnin', you're catchin' on," he said, in an enthusiastic voice.

Joe slumped onto one of the chairs.

Patrick laughed at him. "Don't look so downcast, boy. Ya did the right thing. You'll be doin' it a lot more in the future so get used to it. In the next coupla months, there's gonna be big changes in this town, and you're gonna handle most of the action from now on."

"I didn't think I was goin' to be. able to get through it," Joe said.

"But you said you were hard on him."

"I was. Goddamn it, I was. It was the only way I could get through it."

Patrick looked perplexed,

Joe attempted to explain himself. "I wanted to be nice, Dad. But when Mr. Petry started to cry and carry on, I hadda get tough or I woulda given in to him. I just hardened up, that's all. I had to pretend that I didn't care. There was nothin' else I could do. Otherwise I'd never be able to tell him to get out."

"Whadaya mean, pretend?"

"I was pretending. I didn't want to be cruel to him. I thought I was goin' to throw up right in the place, I felt so sick."

Patrick waved his finger in emphasis. "But ya didn't throw up, and you were hard. Ya proved ya could do it. Next time it'll be easier,"

"Anything'll be easier," Joe said.

Patrick wiped away some droplets of milk from the corners of his mouth. He was freshly shaved and had slept well. He felt strong and happy. "It'll get easier, Joe, Don't worry," he said. "Just remember, don't go callin' the old guy. Just let him be. He'll be outta there in two weeks, and that's all we care about. Right?"

Joseph's head was bowed as he answered his father. He chose

not to lift it up. "Right," he said drearily. "You're right."

The new Hanway real estate office was functioning the first of July. The old restaurant and kitchen areas had been partitioned off into four medium sized offices. Joseph's office was off by itself in the rear of the building. It was opulently furnished with wall to wall carpeting and expensive drapes. In comparison, the other offices prepared for functional purposes only were sparsely furnished.

Patrick sat in a high-backed leather chair as he admired the room's appearance. "Very nice, Joe, Very nice," he said.

Joseph, sitting behind the large mahogany desk, smiled. "Yeah," he said, "I like it."

"It's real nice."

"This room cost enough," Joe said.

Patrick laughed, "Don't worry about cost. A Flynn's gotta have the best."

"Did you hear about Mr. Petry?" Joe asked.

"Yeah," Patrick said in an unconcerned voice, "I heard he left town."

"I heard that too," Joseph said softly. "It looks as though you were right again."

Patrick looked at him, and laughed. "I told you, didn't I? See? We did him a favor. He took his old lady to Italy, The vacation'll do them good."

Joseph was well aware that his father couldn't care less about the Petry's welfare. "Jeez, I'm really surprised though," Joseph said. "I mean he really didn't waste much time leaving."

"That's for sure," Patrick said, as his eyes continued to survey the room.

"Do you think he'll stay?" Joe asked.

"Who cares?"

"Well, I mean, did you hear anything? Did he sell his house or what?"

"I don't know," Patrick said laughing. "I don't own the property."

"Well, did you hear anything?"

"I'm only concerned with what happens to my properties," Patrick said.

"Well, did you hear anything about whether he's comin' back or not?"

Pat knew his attitude was agitating Joe. "Look, Joey, don't worry about the Petrys or what the hell they're goin' to do. A good businessman isn't concerned with that kind of bullshit."

Joe, rubbing his hands nervously together, leaned back in his chair.

"Yeah, yeah, I did hear," Patrick said in a resigned voice. "They did go to Italy. Rome, I think. I heard the house is in the process of being sold. One of his nephews or somebody is takin' care of it." Patrick grew quiet for a moment. He smiled. "I'd try to buy it myself," he said, "but I don't think they'll negotiate with me." He began to laugh.

"No, I don't think so," Joseph said, without smiling. For days, he had thought about the good-natured old man. Because it upset him so much, Joseph tried not to contemplate the Petrys' fate, but time and again, thoughts of the old man would drift back to him, "I hope everything turns out okay for them," he said.

"Yeah, yeah," Patrick said. "Don't worry about it." He walked over and ran his hand over the plastered wall. "This place is built real well, I like it. We should do a nice business here. It'll attract people."

Joe smiled. "We don't need a good-lookin' office to attract people. Anyone interested in buyin' property in this town would have to see us anyway. It wouldn't matter if we were in a tent."

"No. A nice place always helps," Patrick said.

Patrick looked at his son. Except for the lack of gray, Joe's brushed-back hair, with several idle curls falling on his forehead, was identical to his own. Even the effect of Joe's clothes—the conservatively colored vested suits, the buttoned down shirt collars and striped ties, reflected Patrick's style of dress. Joe even sounded like him. He used Patrick's inflections and rapid-fire style of speaking. He walked and moved like him, and Patrick was confident that, slowly but surely, Joe was beginning to think like him.

"You remind me of me," Patrick said proudly.

Joe smiled. "Do I?" he asked.

"Yeah," Patrick said with a smile. "Ya oughta be proud to look like me."

"I am."

Patrick grinned, "It's a great honor, ya know."

Joe's smile grew broader. He arched his brows. "Oh, I know," he said. " I know."

Patrick reached inside his coat pocket. "I've got somethin' for you," he said.

Joseph watched as his father pulled a gun from the inside of his jacket.

"What's that for?" Joseph said in surprise.

"It's a thirty-eight."

"What the hell is it for?"

Patrick placed it on the desk. "It's loaded. Except for the chamber, it's set on. Keep it in one of your drawers."

"For what?"

"Look," Patrick smiled. "We're in a tough business. You'll never know when you might need it."

Joe picked up the gun and moved it around in his hand.

"Do you know how to use it?" Patrick asked.

"Oh, yeah," Joe replied. "Ray Walton and I took a course in handling guns down at the youth center."

"When?"

Joseph thought for a moment, "I think it was in our sophomore or junior year."

"Ya can handle it then?"

"Oh, yeah," Joseph said confidently.

"That's good then. It's licensed and registered under your name. I took care of it."

"Oh, Jesus, what am I goin' to do with it?"

Patrick's eyes grew serious. "Like I told you," he said, "ya never know."

Joseph opened the top drawer and carefully set the gun down. He looked at his father. "You never had to use one, did you?"

Patrick laughed. "I'll tell you some time."

Something told Joe to he quiet. The room was suddenly filled with an ominous aura, causing a quickening of his pulse. He didn't pursue the conversation.

"Well, I'll never get any work done like this," Joe said.

"Neither will I," Patrick said laughing. He stood up and rearranged his suit coat. "I'll see you tonight."

Joseph walked him out to the sidewalk. Manley was sitting in the limousine. When he saw Joe, he smiled and waved. Joe waved hack. After his father and Bill left, Joe stood on the sidewalk for a long while. It was going to he a busy summer. He looked up and down Main Street. It was early, and things were quiet. He took a long, deep breath and reentered the building,

7

JOSEPH FLYNN reclined on the bed as he watched the young woman undress. She smiled brazenly as she unhooked her bra and let it fall to the floor. Her face was more sexy than beautiful, but it was definitely her body that served as her best asset.

As if she were performing a striptease, she slowly removed her panties and held them delicately with her fingertips. She smiled at Joe as she set them on the back of a chair. The bureau lamp offered a soft light to the room, exposing the voluptuous proportions of her naked body.

She walked over and sat beside him. She was obviously excited. Her heaving chest caused her breasts to move enticingly above Joseph's face. She moved her hand to his belt and began to unfasten it. Joseph grabbed her wrist. "Never mind," he said.

Her eyes widened in disbelief. "What?"

"You heard me," he mumbled. "I said never mind."

She thought he was kidding and began to laugh. "C'mon," she said. "What are you tryin' to do?"

In a sudden move, he quickly turned and sat up, resting his elbows on his knees. He felt the perspiration forming on his forehead.

She reached over and carefully touched his shirtless back. It was damp and clammy, "What's wrong?" she asked softly.

He didn't answer.

Her voice remained soft and gentle, "C'mon," she said. "Just relax a little."

Joseph stood up and began to put on his shirt. She haplessly sat on the bed watching him.

"What in the hell are you doin'?" she said.

Joseph's hands shook as they fumbled over the buttons. "No

questions, okay?" he said, "We're getting' outta here."

She knew it wasn't a joke. She began to snicker. "And you looked like such a stud," she said, her voice filled with a mocking sarcasm.

Joseph tried to ignore her snickering. He grabbed her clothes and threw them onto the bed. "Get dressed!" he said.

She ran over to him and grabbed him around the waist, pressing her enormous breasts against him. She was still laughing. "You can't mean it," she said.

Joseph tried to push her away, but she struggled and held on to him. He tried to be calm. "Look," he said gently. "I said never mind. I mean it. Get dressed."

She suddenly grew angry. "Why you rotten bastard!" she shouted. "Who the hell do you think you are?"

"Don't yell," Joe said. "Just get dressed."

Her eyes glinted with resentment. "What is it with you?" she said. "You came on like gangbusters in that bar. All swagger and bullshit, lookin' like a real stallion. And now you're pullin' this. You fuckin' crumb."

Joe walked toward the door. "I'll wait in the car," he said.

"Just wait a goddamn minute!" she shouted. "This was all your idea. You were on the make, not me. I didn't have any plans for screwin' tonight. I was out for a coupla' drinks and dancin'. You come on real heavy with the make, and you turn into a friggin' queer."

Joe turned around and glared at her.

"Well, listen, sonny boy," she said sarcastically. "You owe me twenty bucks. You knew the price. Give it to me or I'll make a lotta noise."

Joe pulled some bills out of his pocket. He quickly counted them. "Here's fifty," he said angrily, throwing them at her. "Now goddammit, get dressed."

She picked up the money and counted it. She viciously looked at him. "I deserve the bonus," she said. She snapped her bra back on. As she pulled up her panties, she couldn't resist another insult.

"Ya friggin' queer," she said.

Before she could catch her breath, Joe was beside her. He roughly grabbed her arm. "I'm warnin' you," he said, his voice barely above a whisper. "You'd better shut up."

"I'm not afraid of you," she hissed. "You goddamn girl."

Joseph smashed her across the face and sent her reeling back onto the bed. He picked her up and threw her to the floor. "You lousy pig," he said, as he pulled her to her feet. He slapped her again.

The woman's heart almost stopped. She thought he was going to kill her. His face was contorted with rage and his eyes were wide and threatening.

She began to cry. "Okay, mister. Okay please," she whimpered. "Honest to God I'm sorry. I didn't mean it."

For several, long seconds he held her in dangerous silence, and then the violence in his grip receded. He let her go and turned away. "Please get dressed," he whispered.

The woman, clumsy in her haste, put on the remainder of her things. Joe walked over to her and extended his arm. His fist was holding more bills, "Here's fifty more," he said softly. "I'm sorry."

Her eyes were filled with a mixture of fear and understanding. "That's okay," she said gently. "I'm not worth that much." She rubbed her reddened face and smiled. "The slaps were my fault, I'm the one who's sorry."

He placed the bills into her hand. "Take it," he said. "It'll make me feel better."

She held the money and looked at him. "There'll be another time. We'll get things to work out better. Everybody has a bad night."

Joe tried to smile. "I don't think so," he said,

"Is there somethin' wrong with me? Maybe that's it," she said.

"No, baby, it's not you. Like you said, it's a bad night."

She looked at her fistful of money. "It wasn't that bad a night," She touched his cheek and smiled,

"I'm sorry I hit you," he said.

"Don't mention it," she said laughing, "You heard about the

whore with the heart of gold, didn't you? You're forgiven."

Joseph smiled and tenderly gripped her arm. "Let's go," he said.

Hours after Joe took the woman back to the bar, he lay, wide awake, in his bedroom. It had happened again; no matter how alluring the woman, he was unable to respond. He knew it was because of Carol. He didn't need any psychiatrist to tell him that. He compared every woman to her and was unable to function against that comparison. Over the past year he couldn't stop thinking about her. Just when he thought he had finally exorcised her from his brain, the memories of her returned with a frightening force, haunting him once again. As determinedly as he tried, he couldn't shake free from her. She no longer wrote or called, but it made no difference. His need for her continued. He got out of bed and from his window, he looked out into the darkness. He knew that all he had to do was pick up a phone, and she'd return to him in a minute. She'd beg him to go to her. Against the raging torrent of his desire, he wouldn't do it; the price of his pride being too high, the weight of his revenge, being much too devastating.

Joseph let his mind wander as he studied the stars, sitting like tiny gems in the dark sky. All of the old guilts and questions had, insidiously, found their way back to him. He longed for the old companionship of Ray Walton and the wonderful, carefree respite he had always offered. Why did he leave? Where was he? Joseph found the old interrogations as enigmatic as ever. For a time, his new life had successfully camouflaged his interest in the mystery, but now the image of Ray Walton had once again surfaced. Joe had talked to Lila Walton soon after her son's disappearance and received little satisfaction. Nothing made sense. Joe couldn't determine any sensible reason for him to leave. But, beyond the thoughts of Ray and Carol, one image loomed with far greater significance—the torturing, overwhelming presence of Larry.

Joe feverishly tried to maintain the old hate that was, undeniably, beginning to ebb. He still feared his brother's return and what its impact might be—the possible relegation to a lesser tier in his father's hierarchy. After all of his amazing gains, he wasn't prepared to accept any losses. Nevertheless, his hate was receding. He found himself analyzing his past perspectives on Larry. He knew that the long-ago words of his Aunt Gena were starting to make sense. Maybe Larry did get the roughest deal of all. Maybe Larry, in his own way, was really trying to hold the family together. His breakdown and incarceration in an asylum might not have been the reward he deserved. Joe couldn't escape the recollections of the early years, when Larry was his protector and closest friend; the early years, when they laughed and played, two united brothers, loving and caring for each other. Such thoughts made Joseph ill, but he couldn't deny them. It had been many years since he had seen Larry's face...the serious, concerned eyes, the freckles that formed a path over the perfectly straight nose, the wide split of a smile, the curled, reddish hair that rode in waves at the sides of his head. As he watched the stars, Joseph thought of the old habits, the nervous tapping of his fingers, his tongue between his teeth when he concentrated, the excited motion of his thin arms when he was happy. Although the old visions were blurred, they reached out and touched Joseph's soul, imparting to him the sinking and degrading feeling that he might have been wrong. After all the years gone, after all the ugliness and hatred, he might have been wrong. But, what was left to him? All that happened couldn't be changed. At least, now it was Joseph who was at his father's side. Joseph's brain spun and tumbled in the twists and swirls of the changing tide. The sharp delineation of the stars outside his window dulled in the descending veil. He pressed his forehead against the cool pane. Very softly, he began to cry.

8

THE HANWAY real estate purge had begun. By mid-autumn, at least thirty properties had changed hands. It started with Petry's Restaurant, followed by a number of other business places and finally invading houses where families had dwelled for many years. Patrick had owned each of the properties. He simply moved people out, renovated structures, and sold or rented them to the highest bidders at amazing profits. He shrewdly managed to keep ownership control of most of them. One-time denizens of the city began their exodus to the safety and peace of the small towns beyond the suburbs. The Flynn Real Estate Company presented an attractive offer; the old houses were repolished and modernized. The rents were relatively extravagant but nothing the city people weren't used to. Patrick pumped his advertising into the metropolitan newspapers and the prospects came in droves, eager to leave the threatening shadows of the concrete canyons. He transformed the larger buildings which once contained business establishments into reasonably appealing apartment houses. Everything was moving extremely well. The transactions were quick and profitable, and Joseph, almost singlehandedly, managed it all.

Patrick watched as the builders went through the process of dismantling what was once Palumbo's Saloon. The old and familiar facade had been ripped away leaving a gaping hole where a large rectangular window and its neon beer advertisement used to be.

The inside was already gutted. The building was large enough to contain four good-sized apartments and Patrick had them all rented in advance. It wouldn't be long before the imposing structure would be ready and Patrick was delighted. Joseph stood alongside him. His mind was filled with thoughts of another substance; in a staggeringly short period of time, he and his father changed the face of Hanway and its heart as well. Landmark establishments like Petry's and Palumbo's were gone. New faces filled the town. All of the faces and figures that had once moved over the streets and sidewalks were instantly familiar. But now, the scenario was different. Strange, new children were seen making their morning journey to school. People with unrecognizable faces passed through the shops and stores of Main Street. Hanway was the most provincial of places and found it difficult to adjust to the intrusion of new families. Who were they? Where did they come from? The townspeople were secure and satisfied with their long-time knowledge of each other, and were immediately put off by such interlopers.

Hanway was a bastion of Catholicism and certain traditions that were indigenous to the community, and such a combination provided an atmosphere that did not retreat easily to strangers. They were also the most decent and generous of people, and Joseph was certain that the adjustment would come. He hoped they would finally extend their arms in welcome. In time, it would be different; attitudes would change and it would broaden the opportunities of the town. There would be new input. New ideas and possibilities. Joe knew the future was no place for narrow viewpoints and provincialism. He knew that traditions would have to change. Still, he understood their resentment; he and his father had moved too quickly. They had devised wise and fruitful advertising. They had made all the right moves. But it was too sudden, the town was left breathless and angry, Joseph witnessed old friends avoiding him in the same way they had always avoided his father. He was now considered one with Patrick Flynn. Whenever he appeared in a local situation, the tension was so thick he could bite it. In the face of it, Joseph was filled more with regret than hostility. He understood their feelings, honed and polished by generations of habit. Being one of them made it very easy to understand. He wasn't happy with what he had done, but if it came to a face off between

Hanway and the Flynn fortune, his reluctant decision had been made. He would stand with his father.

"Looks good, doesn't it?" Patrick said.

"Yeah."

Patrick turned toward his son. "I didn't tell you," he said, "I bought this guy out."

"Who?"

Patrick pointed toward the bustle of carpenters. "The guy who owned this outfit. He's got about forty guys workin' for him." His face lit up in a smile. "I mean us."

Joe raised his eyebrows in confusion. "Why?" he asked.

"Well, what the hell. No use payin' someone for doin' your work. I figure we come out way ahead with our own builders, you know, I've got a lot of work planned."

"Jesus, how much more can we do?"

Patrick laughed. "You'd be surprised, boy. Wait and see."

"I don't think it's setting too well in town here."

"Fuck them."

"Dad," Joe said, "I didn't have time to keep track of a lot of this. We've moved out a lot of families. Where in hell are they going?"

"I rented out to most of them. I had some places available."

"Not all of them."

"No, not all of them, but most of them. The rest hadda get outta town. But they'll be back."

"What makes you think they'll be back?"

Patrick looked at Joe with a sly expression. "The poor jerks have no choice. For them, livin' anywhere but here is like prison. I talked to all of them. That's one of my reasons for buyin' out this company, I'm developin' that big piece of land down by the river. I'll throw up a pile of row houses, and all of them'll be back in a minute."

"Are you sure?"

Patrick's eyes filled with annoyance. "Am I sure. Goddammit, of course I'm sure. I don't make foolish investments. Everyone of

325

those boobs've been callin' me steady. They can hardly wait to get back. I made the rent somethin' they can afford. We stand to make a big profit. Don't worry."

"I'm not worryin'," Joseph said. He walked to his car. He turned back to his father. "I've gotta get moving, I've got a lot to do."

Patrick smiled. "Okay, kid, I'll see ya."

As Joseph drove to his office he thought once again of his old friends and their exposure to an invasion of strangers. There was no doubt in his mind that would eventually forgive the newcomers for their trespasses; but whether they'd forgive him or not, was an unresolved question.

9

SOON after her son left Hanway Lila Walton permanently moved into Clarkson. She sold her home to Patrick for practically nothing, and he reciprocated by setting her up in a new modern three-room apartment in the city. It was far more elaborate than her old, one room hideaway, and it was more convenient. She was approximately one block from the Clarkson Hotel. Patrick saw to it that all the cash she needed arrived in the mail every week.

The job at Riverio's was no longer necessary. She spent most of her time drinking and relaxing in the apartment or shopping in the numerous city stores. Everything would have been fine, except for the absence of Patrick Flynn. Lila was hardly seeing him at all. He offered a hundred excuses and Lila found each of them suspect. She was beginning to drink constantly, alleviating her loneliness with nightly drunken stupors.

She parted her curtains and looked out at the street. The city traffic was at its evening halt. Brisk wind blew along the street and men leaving their places of business held onto their hats as their overcoats flapped in the rush of air. Lila dejectedly walked over to the small liquor cabinet and pulled out a half bottle of whiskey. She screwed off the cap and put the mouth of the bottle to her lips, taking several large swallows. She lit a cigarette and walked back to the window. There was a gnawing fear biting at her insides. Since the onset of her relationship with Patrick, she had always been supremely confident of her hold over him. Of course, there had always been his occasional dalliance with prostitutes, but she felt that she was the one woman who could hold him fast. Their affair had been seriously altered over the past several months. It had started insidiously; he had always trusted her and told her everything, even the episode concerning Doctor Benson. But it was after Benson's death when things started to change. Now he barely saw her or talked to her at all. Even their delicious trysts had stopped. Following Anna's heart attack, she begged Patrick to bring their relationship out in the open; there was nothing in their way now. Anna was dead.

Ray had gone away. There were no obstacles left. However, Patrick refused; he used his son Joe as an excuse, claiming that he would sum everything up if he saw his father and Lila together. "In time," Patrick promised. "In time." As far as Lila was concerned, several years was time enough. She would go no further with his lame excuses. Perhaps she was wrong. Maybe her grip on him was not nearly as tight as she imagined. She walked over to the mirror and pushed the loose, blonde hair back with her hand. Without makeup, her face looked haggard and pale. She tapped her abdomen and winced at its lack of firmness. Her breasts, the chief ornaments of her figure, were beginning to noticeably sag. All of her doubts began to overwhelm her. "He couldn't," she thought. "He couldn't. He wouldn't do this to me."

She sat down before the mirror. Her hands shook as she applied her makeup. It was Saturday night, but once again Patrick begged off from seeing her. Her life was turning into a tired and inexcusable monotony.

When she finished dressing, Lila picked up her phone and nervously began to dial. It seemed like an eternity before she heard a voice on the other end. "Oh, hello," she said. "Will you please send a taxi to the corner of Wyoming and Kennedy Street?"

She waited for the reply, "Yes. Ten minutes," she said. "That'll be fine." She hung up and picked up her purse. She looked in the mirror one more time, and dabbed at her lipstick. She snapped off the lights and left the apartment.

When the taxi reached the outskirts of Hanway, the evening had grown dark. Finally, it pulled to a halt in front of a tiny, well-kept house. Lila paid the driver and told him to leave. She walked quickly along the cement pathway that led to the porch.

She hesitated for a moment before knocking on the door. In a few moments the door opened and Bill Manley looked out.

Bill's voice was edged with surprise. "Lila!" he said. "What's up?"

"May I come in?" said. "I've gotta' talk to you."

Bill waved her inside. "Sit down," he said. "D'ya want a drink?"

She refused the offer of the drink, but quickly walked into the small parlor and sat down. Her legs felt weak.

"What's goin' on?" Bill said, as he sat down next to her.

Lila desperately tried to hold her composure, but as she began to speak, her bottom lip started to quiver and her eyes brimmed with tears. Manley was surprised by her state. He had always known Lila Walton as a hard, self-sufficient woman who seldom showed emotion.

"What the hell is wrong?" he asked. He was well prepared for her reply. From the moment he saw her in his doorway, intuition told him the reason for her visit. She began to cry.

"Easy now, Lila," Bill said uncomfortably. "Take it easy now."

"What's he tryin' to do to me?" she said, her voice interrupted by sobs.

"Who?"

"You know who!" she said angrily.

Bill knew his words had to be carefully measured, "No, I don't know."

Lila looked at him sarcastically. "You're all dressed up," she said. "Where are the two of you going?"

"I was on my way to get Pat. I think he's got a meeting or sumthin' downtown."

"Meeting my ass," she said.

"Look, Lila, I mean you better explain what the hell is goin' on."

"I want to talk to him right now."

"Who? Pat?"

Her eyes flashed in anger, "Yeah! Pat," she said mockingly. "I want to talk to him now. I'm not waitin' and I mean it."

"Why did you come here?"

"You know fuckin' well why. I can't go to his place. He'd kill me. I want you to call him up and get him over here."

Manley stood up. "Okay, I'll get him."

"Call him up."

Manley cleared his throat. "No, I don't think I should call. I'll just go over and get him."

Lila's voice was harsh and ugly. "I'm tellin' you. There'd better be no fast tricks. I'll get to see him, one way or the other."

"Don't worry," Bill said. "I'll bring him back here."

"You damn well better," she said threateningly.

Bill slipped on his jacket. "I'll be right back," he said. "Make yourself comfortable.

"I'll just sit and wait."

Manley walked toward the door. "There's some liquor on the table in the other room," he said, pointing past her. "Just help yourself."

Lila sullenly looked at him. She didn't answer.

Manley entered the mansion without knocking. Patrick was standing near the fireplace.

"Hey, Bill," Patrick smiled. "I'm ready. You shoulda blown the horn."

"Wait a minute, Boss," Manley said, "I wanna talk a second."

Patrick noticed Bill's agitation, "What's wrong?" he asked.

"Lila's over at my house."

"What!" Patrick exclaimed.

Bill told him everything she had said. Patrick tapped his fingers on the stone mantle.

"Whadaya think it's about?" Patrick asked.

"Oh, c'mon, Boss," Manley replied. "You know fuckin' well what it's about."

"Ya think she's on to me and Millie?"

"She's on to somethin',"Manley said.

"She'd hafta catch on sooner or later," Patrick said quietly.

"Whadaya goin' to do?" Bill asked.

Patrick set his jaw. "I'm gonna' tell her the truth, that's what I'm gonna' do. I'm finished with this bullshit."

"You don't hafta tell her. You can fake it."

Patrick waved his hands in disgust. "No, no more, Bill. I'm tellin' her the truth. I want her outta my way."

"But, Jesus, Boss. She's dangerous."

Patrick smiled. "You mean you're afraid she might talk out loud about some things."

"Damn right," Bill answered. "She knows enough to hang the both of us."

"Don't worry about it," Patrick said. "She won't talk."

He walked over and pulled his overcoat from the coat rack in the foyer. "Let's go," he said.

As Patrick rode toward Manley's house, he thought of what Bill suggested. Lila could, in fact, be put off. He could make up some type of story that she'd swallow, but it was no use.

Millie Morris had become too important a force. Patrick thought of her constantly. He wanted her with him all the time. He was even contemplating explaining the whole situation to Joe, who was only vaguely aware of Patrick and Millie's relationship.

Keeping the situation from Lila was becoming a nuisance. He would straighten it out once and for all.

Bill parked the car and Patrick quickly got out and went into the house. Manley excitedly followed. When Patrick entered the parlor, Lila started to get up from the chair.

"Sit down!" Patrick ordered.

Lila looked at him and her heart began to race. She wanted him so bad she could taste him. "Oh, Pat, Pat," she sobbed.

"Shut up and don't move," he said.

Lila saw the violence in his eyes, She knew him only too well, and he was obviously on the verge of inflicting damage.

He removed his overcoat and threw it on a chair. "Did anyone see you come here?" he muttered.

"No," she said quietly. "I don't think so."

"Well, you said you wanted to talk, so talk," he said.

She looked at Manley. "Can we be alone?" she asked.

Patrick turned to Bill, "Stay where you are," he said, "Whadaya hafta say?" he said, turning back to Lila. "What's so fuckin' important?"

"Pat, I know there's somethin' goin' on. I wanna know, that's all."

"Is that all?" he said sarcastically.

Lila began to cry. "Why are you avoidin' me?" she whined. "Why? Why?"

"I think you can figure it out."

"I want you to tell me," she said,

Patrick looked at her with contempt. "All right, I'll tell you," he said. "I'm sick of you. It's that simple."

"But why, baby? What did I do?"

"Ya didn't do anything. The whole thing just wore out. That's all."

"But I don't understand. Is there somebody else that special? Why can't you see me?"

"Yeah. There's somebody special, real special. I'm not gonna see you at all, I'm not gonna see anybody but her."

Lila's eyes flashed dangerously. "Who is it?" she asked, her voice trembling in a building anger.

"Watch your tone of voice," Patrick warned,

Lila immediately settled down. Although she had always pretended otherwise, she was always frightened in the presence of Patrick's anger. "Just tell me who it is," she begged.

Patrick sneered, "Yeah, I'll tell you," he said. "I'll tell you and if you know what's good for you, you won't do one goddamn thing about it." He walked over and stood directly above her, "I have this secretary and she's pretty special. I wanna be with her all the time."

"Not that Morris kid?" Lila said incredulously.

"Yeah, that's right. You've got it. That's the way it is."

"But she's young enough to be your daughter. She's a baby."

"Whatever she is," he said. "She's mine."

332

"Did you tell her about me?" Lila asked.

"No, I didn't. Very few people know about you and me and that's the way it's gonna stay."

Even in the face of obvious danger, Lila could no longer hold back her venom. "Why you lousy four-flushing prick!" she shouted. "I'll fix your ass. I'll make you sorry for this."

Patrick smashed her across the face. The blow jerked her back in the chair. She tried to say something and he smashed her twice more. Manley moved toward him. "Easy, Boss," he said.

Roughly he shoved Bill away. "Stay outta this, buddy," he said in a menacing voice.

Bill's face reddened. "Okay, Boss. Okay. I just don't want you to get carried away, that's all."

"Just stand still," Patrick said. "I know what I'm doin'."

Lila sat speechless, rubbing her face. Patrick reached down and grabbed her neck, lifting her off the chair. He half-threw her across the room. She stumbled and fell to the floor.

He walked over and yanked her to her feet, pulling her face close to his. "You listen to me, bitch," he hissed. "For two cents I'd kill ya. D'ya understand that?"

Lila, her eyes filled with fear, nodded her head.

"All right then," Patrick smiled. He pushed her back into the chair. Lila was crying softly,

"Now, while we're at it, let's get a few more things straight. You know a lot about me, and if you ever utter one word, one fuckin' word, I'll kill you."

Lila stared up at him, knowing he meant every word.

"You can stay in that apartment and I'll keep sendin' you the money. Do whatever the fuck ya want, but lay off me. If I ever want you I'll call you, but don't count on it."

Lila sat stark still.

He reached down and violently grabbed her hair.

"C'mon, Boss, wait a minute," Manley said.

"I told you to shut up!" Patrick shouted. "One more fuckin' word outta you, and I'll put you through the fuckin' door."

Manley stood still as Pat turned back to Lila. Patrick's eyes were glinting with anger.

"Now, bitch," he said. "Do ya understand me?"

Lila was so frightened, her voice was imprisoned in her throat.

"Good. Good," Patrick smiled. "I'm glad you understand. One word outta' you about anything and you're dead."

Patrick straightened his shoulders and walked away. He looked at Manley. "Get her the fuck outta here!" he said. "I'll wait here until you get back."

Bill gestured to Lila. Without a word she got up and walked to the door. Patrick never looked at her.

All the way back to Clarkson Lila was silent. Manley stared through the windshield and said nothing. Her jaw where Patrick had struck her was stiff and painful. But, at that moment, she suffered from a greater hurt; her heart felt as if it had ruptured. Never before had she known such pain and humiliation. Lila couldn't imagine living without Patrick Flynn.

He was the only person in her entire life that she ever wanted.

She bit down on her lip and tried not to cry. She had been made to look foolish in front of Bill, She would not show him any further emotion. All she could do was think about Patrick and how desperately she needed him. She would wait and see what the outcome of his fling with Millie Morris would turn into. She was only a kid. Lila was certain that a kid couldn't hold on for too long with a man like Patrick. She would wait and see. She would remain quiet and still until he returned to her. She would contain her hurt and her anger. She would wait. But if he didn't come back, she would even the score, and the hell with everything.

10

Joseph Flynn's rise to prominence was phenomenal. He was not yet twenty-two, and already his grip on the reins of power was firm. His father's cronies, recognizing Joe's breathtaking faculties of acquiring knowledge and turning it into dollars and success, treated him with the greatest deference. They almost placed him on the same level of his father. His amazing development rivaled the legendary ascension of Patrick Flynn.

The hills and valleys of the son's existence had. allowed him to mature well. In so many ways, he displayed the perspectives and deportment of an old man; serious, hard, wise to the disappointments and triumphs of a fickle world. There seemed to be no end to his abilities and foresight.

Prior to and during the local election activity in November, he operated with zeal and perfection. Patrick included him in every significant situation, constantly conferring with him on political matters and acting on his counsel. Joseph Flynn's future expanded with each passing day. Patrick couldn't have been more proud. He eagerly anticipated the election year of 1964; Joseph's public, political career would begin in earnest. First, it would be the county commissioner's office and then the state senate. The possibilities were boundless.

Joseph was approaching what should have been the zenith of his life. Everything he had ever longed for was coming to fruition.

But nothing seemed to be falling into a predictable order. Although he tried to remove the persistent doubts, he remained troubled.

He lost himself in his work, allowing his instincts for survival to carry him through many situations that his conscience rebelled against. But work and success didn't offer him the peace he had hoped for. He was afflicted by doubts and self-recrimination.

The first Sunday in December was frigid and blustery. There was a hint of snow. The expansive chunk of land around the Flynn mansion had grown cold and hard. Mounds of white, left in the wake of the late November snowfalls, dotted the yellowed grounds of the estate.

Joseph finished his coffee and set the cup down on the table. "Very good, Mrs. Davis," he said with a smile.

Her face brightened at the compliment, "Why thank you, Joe," she said.

Since Anna's death, Marion Davis took over the complete housekeeping duties of the house. She practically spent all of her time within the confines of the mansion.

"You're doin' a great job here," Joe said.

"I'd better," she replied. "I'm paid pretty well."

"You deserve every dime."

"Do you think I should call your dad?" she asked. "If he doesn't get up, he'll miss Mass."

"Give him a coupla more minutes. When I passed his room, he was sleepin' like a baby."

"Well, if I know Bill Manley, he'll be here at ten. Right on the dot. Pat might not be ready."

Joe smiled, "Give him a coupla more minutes."

Mrs. Davis rolled her eyes, "My, you men love to sleep."

"Not me," Joseph said. "I'm up every morning at six, right?"

She laughed. "Well, you're about the only one."

Joseph had already been to early Mass, returning home to change his clothes and consume a large breakfast. He was dressed casually, in a sport shirt and jeans, happy to be out of his usual workday attire of suit and tie,

"Well, I've got to be off," Joe said, as he slipped into a fur-lined leather jacket.

"I hope you're warm enough," she said.

"Oh, yeah," he said. "This jacket does the trick." He waved to her as he opened the back door.

She called to him. "You better be sure. It's freezing out there."

Marion Davis, over the years, had developed a strong affection for Joseph. She saw him as the son she always longed for. Under his seriousness, she discerned the picture of doubt and confusion. In spite of his tremendous prestige, the influence of frustration and pain was still in his eyes. She wiped her hands on her apron as she watched him back his car out onto the driveway. He was a chameleon, changing moods and colors in a weird regularity. On the outside, in the whirl and competitive pressures of business, he was the embodiment of his father. But in his private moments that she so often saw, his periods of silence and contemplation were the remnants of another story.

She saw so much of his mother in him it was uncanny. Whenever Mrs. Davis passed him in the parlor, observing him as he stared through the window or at the orange licking flames in the fireplace, lost in some intangible concentration, she thought of Anna. Such moments offered confirmation that regardless of what the world believed, the real Joseph Flynn, the blood and soul of Joseph Flynn, belonged more to the mother than to the father.

In the past, whenever Marion carefully mentioned the name of his brother, Joe would turn stiff with anger and resentment. But now the rigidity of that reaction had altered into a specific kind of torment. She was not surprised at the change for she had always felt that she knew and understood the inner workings that controlled Joseph. Therefore, she had always known that this moment in time would somehow arrive.

Joseph stood on the windblown hill and looked at his mother's headstone. Sunday mornings were a habitual pattern. He would attend early Mass. Following breakfast, he would drive to the cemetery and then spend the rest of the morning at Mickey Clark's home where he'd relax and have dinner. He used the rest of the day to pour over business matters in the quiet of his office.

Joe knelt down on the damp ground. The moisture soaked through his jeans until his knees were wet. He closed his eyes and sighed. He wanted so badly to once again hear his mother's voice. He missed her terribly. It almost seemed as though her soulful, black eyes and tenderness had existed in another world. Ho matter how often he knelt on the ground that contained her, it drove him to tears and longing. Had she lived, she would have been ecstatic about the relationship between her husband and son. At least Joseph was certain of that. Things would've been so different. He made himself believe that she was aware of it and swollen with pride and satisfaction. His eyes moved a few yards past Anna's grave and rested on another headstone. Gena and Tom's names were carved into the granite. Except for the wind and Joseph's breath, everything was still. He fought against the whisper of his brain as he avoided thinking about the stillness and ugly prison that surrounded them. All he wanted to think about was how much he loved them. How much he was a part of them. Time and the hand of death would never wither that bond. As always, he searched for the precise words in his prayer for their souls.

11

AFTER dinner, Mickey called Joe into the parlor. Mickey was sipping at some wine. He looked out into the front yard and waved Joe over to the window. "Look at this," he smiled.

Joe looked out and watched Mickey's two young sons, laughing hysterically, as they wrestled on the ground.

"It's nice to he a kid. Isn't it?" Mickey said.

"Yeah, it sure is."

Mickey turned to him and laughed. "I remember when you were that age. You were a goddamn devil."

Joe smiled and sat down on the sofa,

"What's the matter with you, kid?" Mickey said. "Is there somethin' on your mind or what?"

"Why?" Joe asked.

"I don't know. You're too quiet to suit me. It seems as though somethin's bothering you."

Joe leaned back into the cushion and sighed. "You know," he said. "It's a little of this, a little of that."

"Jesus, you're on top of the world," Mickey said. "You shouldn't worry about anything."

"I'm gettin' a hard time around town."

"How?" Mickey asked. "In what way?"

"Ah, you know. A lotta them are pissed off about the sellin' we did."

"Oh that. Look, kid, they'll get over it. It'll take some time but it'll pass. Don't let it getcha down."

"But it does. It bothers me."

"It'll pass," Mickey said, "They'll come around. If they're the friends you think they are."

"Ah shit, Mick. They have a right to be pissed off. We knocked a lot of them down. We cut the legs right off them."

"Look, Joe, I know a lot of them are mad. You're right, they have good reason. But they'll get over it. Eventually they'll understand it was just good business on your part."

"Would you understand if you were in their place?"

"Sure I would. Not right away maybe, but in time. Yeah, I'd understand. You sold a few houses, so what?"

"Well, I sure hope so."

Mickey reached over and squeezed Joe's shoulder. "Look, kid," he said. "I know how you feel. All right, they are pretty well pissed off, I know that. I have eyes and ears like you. But there's no point in worryin' now. What's done is done."

Joe smiled sadly. "I guess I screwed up the neighborhood."

"The neighborhood'll survive," Mickey said,

"Yeah, I guess so."

"Well, then c'mon. Don't look so goddamn miserable. Shape up."

Joe smiled. "You're a good morale builder. Thanks Mick, I need the support."

"Shit man, you don't need anything. You're an important guy right now and you're gonna get a lot more important. Everybody knows that. You don't need anything."

"You're wrong, buddy," Joe said. "I need this town. I always did."

"Well, you've got the town. The bullshit'll pass. Wait and see."

"It'll never be like before."

"Sure it will. Sure it will," Mickey said. "One day you'll be in a position to make everything up. You'll be in a position to help a lotta people."

"I haven't helped them much so far."

"But you will."

Joe grew silent. He stared at the floor. After a while he looked at Mickey. "How's Larry?" he asked in a strained voice.

Mickey was jolted by the question. For a moment he just looked at Joe. "What makes you ask that?" Mickey said.

"Ah, I don't know," Joe replied, "I was just wonderin'."

Mickey took a deep breath. "Jesus, it does me good to hear you ask about him. C'mon, what brought it on?"

"I've been thinkin' about him a lot lately," Joe said.

"Look, we can take a trip out to the sanitarium right now," Mickey said happily. "Whadaya say?"

"No, no I don't think so," Joseph said.

"Why not? You oughta see him. It's about time."

"Not just yet," Joe said.

Mickey was elated. "Jesus, this is somethin'. Last time I was down there, Marion Davis and I were talkin'. She mentioned that she thought you were feelin' different about Larry."

Knowing the keen intuition of Mrs. Davis made Joe smile.

"She did, did she?" he said,

"Yeah, isn't that somethin'. Jesus, that's great, kid. Why the change of heart?"

"I'm not sure myself. It's all just been botherin' me, you know. I think I oughta see him, that's all."

"When?"

"Oh, look, Mick, I don't know yet. I expect to get around to it in time. I know the way you are. Don't make an issue out of it,"

Mickey laughed out loud, "Yipee!" he exclaimed, "I almost gave up hope."

"Well, hold on, Mick. I don't know when I'll get there. It's been a long time. I'm gonna have to work my way up to it."

"Work up to it, shit. He's your brother. The kid'll be happy to see you. You oughta go right down there."

"Does he ever say anything?"

"About what?"

"About me."

"To be honest, kid, Larry doesn't say much. I know he appreciates me and Mrs. Davis being there, but he doesn't say much at all. Just generalities."

"Does he ever mention the family?"

"No, never. But I know he'd wanta see you. He was always crazy about you. You know that."

"Does he ever mention my father?"

"No."

"He goes down there once in a while, you know."

"Yeah, I know, about once a year. He should be ashamed of himself. I think he only goes for the show of it so people won't have too much to say. It's a friggin' shame the way he cut that kid off."

"I don't think he likes seein' him there," Joe said.

Mickey's eyes blazed. "You're wrong there. That has nothin' at all to do with it. He just doesn't give a shit."

Joseph knew that Mickey couldn't understand Patrick's feelings for Larry. He didn't want to talk about it any further. He stood up. "Well, pal, I've gotta get goin'."

"Stick around," Mickey said, "What's the rush?"

"No, really, I've gotta go."

Mickey knew that the conversation about Larry had upset Joe. "All right, when will I see you?"

"Oh, I'll drop around during the week."

"Fine."

Joe walked back into the kitchen and said goodbye to Mrs. Clark. She walked back with him to the front door. Mickey joined them as they went out onto the porch. The two youngsters were still wrestling. "Here now!" Mrs. Clark shouted. "The two of you stop that!"

The boys, unhearing, continued on with their game.

Joe smiled as he looked at the Clarks. "Let them go," he said. "They're havin' a good time." He squeezed the woman's hand and patted Mickey on the shoulder. "Thanks for everything," he said, "I'll see you."

The Clarks stood on the porch until Joe's car disappeared around the corner.

Mary Clark turned to her husband, "Joe doesn't seem happy," she said. "Is there something wrong?"

Mickey's voice was very low. "Yeah, there's somethin' wrong."

"Can't we help?" she asked.

Mickey smiled at the sincerity of his wife's face. "No, we can't. He can only help himself. He's gotta do it himself. There's no way anybody can help." He looked to where the car had turned the corner. "The poor bastard," he said.

About six o'clock in the evening, Joseph was working in his office. He heard the front door open. He left the desk and walked into the hallway. His father was walking toward him.

"What brings you here?" Joseph asked in surprise. "I thought you and Bill were goin' downtown to play some cards."

Patrick took off his overcoat. "Changed my mind," he said. "Listen, I told Bill you'd drive me home. You're not gonna be too late here, are you?"

"No, I was getting ready to leave any minute. But why didn't Bill drive you home?"

"I have to talk to you."

"About what?"

Patrick threw his arm around Joe. "C'mon into the office here where it'll be comfortable." Joe went behind the desk and sat down. Patrick slid a chair over to where he could face him.

"First off," Pat said, "I've spent most of the day at my lawyer's office. I hadda get certain things straightened away."

"Like what?" Joe said.

Patrick pushed a manila envelope across the desk. "Take a look," he said.

Joe opened it and looked through the papers. His head jerked in surprise. "What'd you do?" he said. "Did you make me a partner here?"

Patrick laughed. "Sure, don't you think it's about time? Me and Bill figured we needed a third man."

"Bill didn't mind?" Joe asked.

"Mind?" Patrick exclaimed. "He knows you carry your weight in gold. Anyway, if he didn't like it, I'd throw him out. I'm the senior man." He began to laugh, "Don't worry about Bill. What I say, he does."

Joe reached his hand to his father. Patrick shook it vigorously.

"There's a few more things," Patrick said. "How much do you think you're worth?"

"Shit. I don't know."

"Well, I've been payin' you pretty good the last coupla years. What's your bank account look like?"

Joseph tried to remember the figure.

"C'mon," Patrick said with a broad smile. "I know you've been stashin' it away."

"About ten thousand, I think. In round figures."

"Well, I've got news for you," Patrick said. "I had all those stocks I gave you checked over and updated. That, combined with your new interest in this business pushes that figure up a little." Patrick smiled eagerly. "D'ya wanna know how much?"

"How much?" Joe said,

"A little over a half million. That's how much. Of course, that includes half of the beer business, but those papers won't be ready until tomorrow."

Joseph was stunned, "Are you kiddin' me?"

"That's it, my boy. That's the figure. There's a hell of a lot more comin'. I also decided on makin' a will."

"Why?"

"Look I'm gettin older. I've gotta take care of things. I want you to know that you're the heir to the whole bundle."

Joseph, speechless, just sat and stared at him.

"Do you have any idea of what that amounts to?" Patrick said, his eyes gleaming. Before Joe could answer, Patrick said, "Somewhere in the neighborhood of four million."

"My God!" Joseph exclaimed. "I never imagined."

"Whadaya think I've been doin' these many years?" Patrick said laughing. "Playing tiddlywinks?"

"My God!" Joseph repeated, "I didn't know it added up to that much."

"Well you know now," Patrick said as he squeezed Joe's hand. "And when I'm gone it's all yours."

Joe hesitated before asking his next question. "What about Larry?" he said.

Patrick looked unconcerned. "Well, when I'm gone, he'll be your responsibility. Do whatever you want."

Joe was taken aback by the cold hardness of his father's voice. He got up and walked around the side of the desk. "Are you serious, Dad?" he asked.

"Of course I'm serious," his father replied, "It'll be your problem then."

"But I thought..."

Patrick interrupted. "Look, there's no point in goin' over the problem. This is the way I want it."

Joe nodded, "Okay, if that's what you want."

"That's what I want."

Patrick got up and placed his hands on Joe's shoulders. "We've got big things ahead of us, kid," he said.

Joe nodded and smiled, but his thoughts were somewhere else. This should have been his moment of greatest triumph; he had finally won his father completely away from Larry, or so it seemed. But the moment of victory dissipated under a nagging cloud of uncertainty.

Patrick banged him hard on the shoulder. "Well, whadaya think, boy?"

Joseph pretended to he much happier than he actually was. He wrapped his arms around his father's wide shoulders and hugged him tightly. "Sounds good, Dad," Joseph said. "Sounds real good."

12

MATTHEW ROYAL walked vigorously through the corridor. Christmas decorations were strung along the walls. They offered a breath of gaiety to the usual forlorn atmosphere of the sanitarium. He walked into Doctor Brogan's office.

"Howya doin'?" Royal said.

Brogan's eyes didn't leave the papers on his desk. He grunted a reply.

Royal walked over to a mirror and began combing his hair. "How's the Christmas shopping coming along?" he asked.

Brogan sat back in the chair, watching Royal admiring himself. "Are you finished with rounds?" Brogan said.

Royal walked over and leaned against the desk. "Yeah," he said nonchalantly. "I expedited things a little, I've got quite a bit to do."

"There's a couple of patients on second floor exhibiting signs of the flu. Did you notice?" Brogan said.

"No, I didn't. I skipped the second floor."

"Well, you better take a look."

"What the hell, I'll just prescribe something."

"No, I think you'd better take a good look."

"Jesus, c'mon. If it's only the flu, I'll just write some medication orders."

"I'd rather you go down there."

"Oh, Jesus," Royal said. "Have a heart. It's the holidays."

"Goddammit, Royal, I said go down there," Brogan said, his voice rising in anger.

Royal was surprised at Brogan's reaction. "Okay, doctor, okay. Don't get so nervous for Christ's sake."

"When you're finished, take a minute to write your resigna-

347

tion from the staff."

"What?"

"That's right," Brogan said. "Your resignation. I was going to wait until the end of the week to inform you, but this is as good a time as any."

"What in the hell are you talking about?"

Brogan got up. "I want you out of here, Matt. It's as simple as that."

"It doesn't make any sense," Royal said. "What's going on?"

Brogan spoke in a quiet, even voice. "I want your resignation on my desk before you leave today. I want you to understand that."

Royal's eyes were masked in confusion. "But why?" he asked.

"You don't belong here, Matt. You never did. You don't belong in medicine."

Royal's eyes looked up and down the long, lean figure. "Why, you bastard," he said contemptuously.

Brogan walked over to the window. "Just make it simple," he said quietly.

Royal grabbed his shoulder and turned him around. "I know what this is all about," he said angrily. "It's about the Flynn kid, isn't it?" Royal, his eyes flashing, didn't wait for Brogan's response. "Goddamn, who do you think you are? When I first told you about the situation, you went for it pretty damn quick."

"We've already discussed that."

"Well, okay," Royal said. "Then what's this stuff about resigning? I thought the problem was settled."

"The fact is," Brogan said, "every time I look at you, I think about what I did."

Royal laughed sarcastically. "Oh shit, here comes the hearts and flowers."

Brogan could no longer control his anger. "I don't like associating with you. You degrade me. I won't allow any more of your dirt to rub off on me."

"You bastard," Royal said. "I have no reason to pay any attention to you. You don't run this place."

"If you don't write that letter," Brogan warned, "I'll go to Pat Flynn and tell him the whole thing was a sham, that we knew all along that Larry would never leave here."

"He'll break your head."

"Maybe he will. But where does that leave you?"

"He won't believe that about me."

Brogan laughed. "I think you know better."

"You're lying. You wouldn't do it."

"Oh yes I would, and you know it," Brogan said. "Now, I think we've talked enough. Do us both a favor and leave."

Royal's eyes narrowed. "I'll get you for this."

"You won't get me for anything," Brogan said. "You don't have the guts." Brogan began to walk back toward his desk. He turned around. "And you might as well forget about anymore paydays at Larry Flynn's expense. I'm calling Pat Flynn today to inform him that Larry's condition is such that payoffs are no longer required. I think he'll appreciate that."

"I don't care what you do," Royal said defiantly.

"Of course you do. People like you regret every filthy dollar you lose," Brogan said. "You and Pat Flynn deserve each other."

"You're not getting away with this," Royal said.

"I'm going to do what I can to help Larry," Brogan said. "If it's possible, one day he'll be well and out of here."

"Flynn doesn't tolerate people going back on their word," Royal warned.

"I'll worry about that when the time comes."

"Who do you think you are?" Royal shouted. "I'm warning you. Don't fuck with me."

Brogan suddenly reached out and grabbed Royal's throat. He pushed him toward the doorway, "Don't go near the second floor," Brogan hissed, "I'll have someone else take care of it. I don't want your hands on my patients." Brogan's hand slid from Royal's neck to the front of his silk shirt. He gripped his fingers around the smooth material and roughly jerked Royal back and forth. "Don't bother coming back here with your letter. Leave it at the front desk, I don't want your stench in here again."

"Malcolm," Royal said imploringly. "For Christ's sake wait a minute."

Brogan, with his free hand, opened the door. He shoved Royal out into the corridor. "If you know what's good for you, Matt, you'll write that letter goddamn fast."

"If you'll just wait a minute," Royal said.

Brogan slammed the door shut. Royal stood confused and alone in the hallway. After a few thoughtful moments, he walked to the front desk and asked for a sheet of paper and an envelope.

He quickly scribbled his resignation. He walked over to the woman behind the desk, "See that the administrator gets this," he said, his lips trembling.

The woman took the envelope. "Of course, Doctor Royal. I'll see to it right away." The woman looked at him strangely.

He tried to conceal his embarrassment. Royal didn't look back as he hastily walked toward the exit.

Doctor Malcolm Brogan stood at his office window, allowing his eyes to drift over the sprawling grounds of Mount Rose. A great amount of snow had fallen. It covered the small hills and valleys like a cloak of fine white linen, stretching many miles to the horizon and its rendezvous with the sky. It had been a long time since he felt so good.

13

AFTER that ugly evening in Bill Manley's house, Lila Walton made a concerned effort to win Lack Patrick Flynn. She didn't hesitate for very long; within days, she barraged his office and home with phone calls. She tried to bump into him on the streets and at his usual haunts. But everything failed. He hung up whenever he heard her voice on the phone. He cleverly managed to avoid her attempts to see him. She avoided bursting into his office, for she knew that such an action might result in severe consequences. There was one last plan for her to follow. She prepared to put it into action.

Bill Manley got up from his desk and walked into the lounge. "Do you want me to pick up some sandwiches from Mulrooney's?"

Patrick was lying down on the couch. His forearm hooded his face. "No," he said.

"It's just about lunch time."

Patrick got up into a sitting position. "I don't feel like eating."

"Was that phone call from Doc Brogan bad news or what?" Manley asked.

"No, it was good news. He told me there's no longer any reason to worry about Larry gettin' outta that joint. Accordin' to him the kid's really gone."

"Oh," Manley said. "And what about it?"

Patrick began to laugh, "If you can believe it, he told me it wasn't necessary to give Royal any more money. Isn't that somethin'?"

"Money for what?"

"He knew I was slippin' Matthew a little extra, as a bonus for helpin' to keep Larry there. I guess he didn't think it was right."

"He's a regular boy scout."

"Yeah, I guess that's why he stopped takin' his payoff when he. did. He musta figured Larry was in tough shape then."

"Were you surprised to hear about the kid's condition?"

"Naw, the coupla times I saw him, I knew he was in tough shape. He doesn't have a chance." Patrick stood up. "Anyway, I already knew about it before Brogan called."

"How?"

"Royal called me yesterday and told me all about it. As a matter a' fact, he resigned from the staff. He said there was no point in stayin' on."

Manley smiled. "Are you going to kill his bonus?"

"Of course not," Patrick said. "I'm going to increase it. It'll keep him happy and crooked, just the way we want him."

"That's right," Manley smiled.

"If it wasn't for that friggin' Lila, everything'd be fine," Patrick said.

"Is she still buggin' ya?"

"Yeah."

"I knew she'd be tough to shake," Manley said.

Patrick got up and walked behind the bar. He pulled a letter from one of the shelves. "Here," he said. "Read this. She mailed it to the house."

"When?"

"I found it in yesterday's mail."

Manley read the letter's contents. He looked at Pat. "She says she's gonna do some talkin', huh?"

"Yeah, that's what she says."

"Do you believe her?"

"Well, I'm not takin' any chances," Patrick said, "I called her right after I read it. I'm goin' over her place tonight."

Manley frowned, "Jeez, I don't know. Do you think that's the right thing?"

Patrick's eyes turned cold. "Oh yeah, I think it's the right thing. If she thought I was kiddin' that night at your house, I'll give her somethin' else to think about tonight."

"What are you gonna do? Ya better watch yourself."

"Don't worry. I'm just goin' to straighten her out, that's all."

"What if she doesn't listen?" Manley said, "What if she does talk?"

"After tonight, she'll forget about talkin'. You can bet on it."

"You sure?"

"Oh, I'm sure," Patrick said.

Lila Walton walked into the kitchen and once again checked the clock. She walked to the mirror and began fidgeting with her makeup. Time and again she went over her planned speech. Patrick would be arriving at any minute. She. couldn't let the opportunity to retrieve him slip away.

She turned up the radio, allowing the room to be filled with Christmas music. Unable to sit still, she walked to the window and parted the curtains. The empty street showed no sign of him. She checked the clock again; it was nine-thirty. He was an hour late, Lila leaned against the wall alongside the window and stared into the quiet night. Snow was beginning to fall. She would plead and beg to him one final time.

Her throat choked with despair, knowing her plight was almost hopeless. If it was the only thing left to her, she would use an alternate plan. She was well aware that Pat was considering the possibility that she might talk, and he was right. She would speak out, but not to the parties he expected. She would hit him where he lived, his son Joseph. Through Patrick's own words, she knew that Joe had no idea about certain past events—her affair with his father, the murder of her husband and Doctor Benson, the reason for her son's leaving Hanway. Whether or not he would remain in darkness was now in the unknowing hands of his father.

A familiar figure made his way down the sidewalk. When Lila saw him she practically ran across the room. She picked up the tape recorder from the chair. She checked the tape one last time.

She turned the volume up to loud. Carefully, she placed it underneath the chair near the window and ran the cord back to a receptacle and plugged it in. The chair blocked the cord from visibility. She stood and waited.

Almost immediately, there was a loud knocking. "Just a minute!" she shouted. "I'll be right there." She bent down and reached under the chair. She felt for the button and pressed down. Before she opened the door, she straightened her skirt and checked herself in the mirror. She went over and turned the lock. Patrick pushed open the door and walked into the room. Lila backed away.

His hair was wet from the snow, and his face was flushed. "Well, I'm here," he growled.

"Take your coat off, honey," she said.

He began to unbutton his topcoat. He glared at her. She took it from him and draped it carefully over the back of the couch.

She smiled nervously. She gestured toward the couch. "Sit down," she said.

"So you're gonna talk. You're gonna do a little squealin'," he said.

Lila's eyes began to twitch. "Ah, c'mon, honey. You knew I didn't mean that."

"Didn't you?" he said.

"No, I didn't," she lied. "I didn't mean it." She began to cry.

"Oh, cut the shit, Lila." Patrick said. "Don't give me your cryin' routine."

"Pat, please," she sobbed. "Honest to God, I can't live like this. I need you. Please."

He stood there unmoved. "Look, baby, it's no use. I'm not goin' to lie to you. It's finished."

"Why?"

"I told you why," he said angrily. "It won't work anymore. I'm stuck on this other girl."

"Can't you give me some time? I think you owe me that," she pleaded.

"No, I'm not playin' that game. It's finished, and that's it."

354

"How can you do this? You know what we've been through."

Patrick pulled a cigar from his pocket. He bit off a small piece of the end and spit it onto the floor. He took his time lighting it. He took a deep drag. He blew the grey, curling smoke toward the ceiling. "No," he said. "It's finished."

"I know a lot, Pat," she said.

"I know you do," he smiled.

Her eyes grew angry. "I will talk! I'm not afraid of you!"

Patrick laughed. "Nobody'd believe you and if they did, I'd get to them and hush it up. It'd be pretty simple."

"Oh, you think so?" '

"I know so. It'd hafta wind up with the cops one way or the other. I own them. They'd make you out a liar, and I'd convince them you were."

"You wouldn't convince everyone," she said.

"I think I would," he said. He reached for his coat.

She grabbed at his arm. "Wait a friggin' minute!" she said. Patrick laughed.

She stood up and tried to kiss him. He shoved her back onto the couch. "Get away from me," he said.

Tears ran down her face as she looked up at him. "Please, baby, please don't do this," she whimpered.

He began to put on his coat. She stood up and reached for him again. He shoved her away.

"Do you know what you're doing?" she screamed. "Do you?"

"What am I doin'?" he smiled.

"I'll tell. I will. You killed my husband. You killed Benson. You pay to keep your kid locked up. I'll tell, I swear."

"If you do," he said quietly, "I'll kill you too."

She tried to control her voice. "But Pat, you loved me. You know you did. All those years we hid it, so Anna wouldn't find out. I went along with everything. Is this the way I'm rewarded? Please don't do it."

Patrick set the cigar in an ashtray alongside of him. "Yeah, you're right," he said, "You do know a lot but you're a little screwed up in your story. I didn't kill anybody. Bill did."

"You're the one who ordered everything. You're just as guilty."

"So are you," he smiled, "withholding all that information for so long. You'd be in a lotta trouble yourself."

"I don't care about me. It doesn't matter."

"So, what's the point?" he said. "I don't care about you either." He walked toward the door. "Anyway, you're not gonna talk," he said turning around. "Because if you do, I'll still get away with it. And when I get finished with you, you'll wish you were never born."

She moved quickly and blocked the doorway. "Get outta the way!" he warned.

Slowly, she reached for his groin. "Please, baby," she begged. "Let me touch you. Let me love you. I'll change your mind."

He slapped her hand away. "I'm tellin ya, ya fuckin' slut. Get outta the way."

She knew it was final. With all her strength, she moved her arm in a wide arc, and smashed the side of his face. His head twisted sharply. For a moment, he stood stark still, staring at her. Then he began to hit her. Over and over, he struck at her, until she fell onto her knees. He drove his knee against her chest, knocking her back against the door. He crouched down in front of her, grabbing her hair and pulling her head back.

"Did you like that?" he smiled. Viciously he slapped her several more times. She moaned softly. Her mouth filled up with blood. Once again, he pulled back her head. For a second he smiled at her. Then he spit in her face. Patrick stood up and kicked her out of his way. He opened the door. "Goodbye, pig," he said.

The Christmas music played on.

Patrick walked up the street toward the car parked near the corner. He got in. Bill Manley turned on the ignition. "How did it go, Boss?" he asked.

"Just get outta here!" Flynn replied.

Bill drove the car around the corner. As he passed Lila's apartment, he looked at Patrick. "Was it bad?"

Patrick blew into his hands and rubbed them together.

"It wasn't good," he said.

"What happened?"

"I hadda knock her around a little bit."

'Well, is it gonna be okay or what?"

"I don't know, Bill, I really don't know."

"Well, Jesus Christ, do you think she'll say somethin'?"

"I don't know."

"What are you goin' to do?"

"Goddamn, I don't know," Patrick said.

"Okay, relax," Bill said.

Patrick turned to him, "We might hafta do somethin', Billy. I don't know if she'll clam up."

"We're gonna do what?" Bill asked.

"I've gotta think," Patrick said quietly, "I've gotta think."

"Well, if you think she's gonna start blabbin', we better figure somethin' fast."

"We'll wait until after the holidays. I'll figure somethin' out by then."

"Are we gonna do her in or what?" Bill asked calmly.

"Yeah," Patrick replied, "If we hafta."

"How will we do it?"

"I said I'll think about it."

"But what if she says somethin' right away?"

Patrick shrugged, "For all we know, she might not say anything. Maybe I scared her tonight. We'll hafta wait and see."

"Wait and see!" Bill exclaimed.

"Look, Bill, the broad might not talk. Who's she gonna go to? She's afraid of the cops. She knows damn well they won't do anything. Anyway I told her she was implicated."

"She doesn't care about that,"

"Yeah, she said the same thing. But when the time comes, everybody's scared."

"I hope so."

"I told her I'd make her regret it," Patrick said. He sat, thoughtfully, for a moment. "Naw," he said, "I don't think she'll do any talking."

"But we've gotta stop her before she says anything. There's not much we can do afterwards. They'll pin it on us for sure."

"Pin what on us?"

"There's not gonna be any way we could wipe her out. They'll know who it was. Payoffs or not they'll grab us."

"I'll arrange it to look like an accident. Don't worry. Nobody'll blame us."

"You're the one who said we'll hafta do somethin'," Bill said.

"I know. I know, and we will. If she utters a word, she's dead."

14

ON THE FOLLOWING morning, Joseph Flynn had awakened early. It was Christmas eve and he had a long day ahead of him. Since Gena's and Tom's death, Joseph had grown to detest the holidays. They no longer contained the old, soft throb of excitement.

He hated winter. He hated snow. He hated the entire season, and its echoes of voices no longer heard and images of faces no longer seen.

Since the evening his father told him about the will, Joe had tried his best to avoid thoughts of Larry; the guilt and questions had become too great. But in recent days he couldn't hold them off; they surrounded and swallowed him. Finally, he decided to see his brother.

Joseph dressed carefully, wanting to look his best. He chose to wear his pinstriped suit and selected a tie that matched perfectly. He thought about how fastidious Larry was about such things. Joseph hoped that Larry would notice his recently acquired good taste in clothes and tried to imagine his brother laughing at the surprising change in his style.

It was so early Mrs. Davis hadn't yet arrived at the house. Joseph grabbed a quart of milk out of the refrigerator and walked over to the table. He sat staring quietly at the bottle, knowing he couldn't drink it–he was too nervous. His stomach churned and his head ached. He hadn't told anyone that he was going to see Larry, for he was barely able to deal with the anticipation himself.

He found it impossible to tell anyone. He put the milk back and slipped into his overcoat. In a few minutes, he got into his car and drove away from the mansion.

As he traveled down the Hanway streets, his brain was occupied with many memories. Everything around him reflected the warm, wonderful days that were gone. Days when he and Larry laughed and played together; racing over sidewalks in games of tag and their childish glee, when they invaded the stores along Main Street. He thought of the snow huts near the railroad and the enjoyment that had filled every hour. At last, the fires of Joseph's hostility and hate had died away. Now, he wanted to remember the good times and feelings the way they once were, times and feelings that should have been eternal. He knew now that he had been wrong about his brother. There was no longer any point in avoiding it or denying it. He had to make his peace.

He parked his car in the lot directly in front of the sanitarium and he checked his watch. It was eight o'clock. As he walked from his car to the building, his eyes studied the huge edifice. It was well taken care of; the paint that covered what seemed like miles of wood, was as white as snow. Massive columns stood side by side on the wide, open porch. When he got to it, he took a deep breath of the fresh air and slowly ascended the concrete steps.

He approached the desk in the lobby, A woman, sitting at the switchboard, got to her feet when she saw him coming, "Hello," she said smiling. "What can I do for you?"

Joseph was so nervous he could barely speak. He coughed and cleared his throat. "I'm here to visit one of the patients," he said quietly.

"Oh, I'm sorry." she said. "But I'm afraid it's much too early. We don't allow visitors until after lunch."

Joe's pulse was racing. "I've got to see this patient now," he said. "He's my brother."

"Well, that really doesn't matter," she said. "The rules hold for everyone."

Joseph couldn't wait. "I've got to see him now," he said. "I'm sure it'd be okay."

"Well, I'll see what I can do," she said. "Doctor Brogan usually arrives early. He should be here any minute. I'll check with him."

"Yes, I think he's taking care of my brother," Joseph said.

The woman pointed toward a chair. "Why don't you sit down a minute?"

Joseph was walking toward the chair when the front door opened. He recognized the man immediately. Seeing Joseph, the man stopped, "Don't I know you?" he said.

"I'm Joe Flynn."

"Yes, of course," the man said. "I'm Doctor Brogan. Do you remember me?"

Joseph felt a flush of embarrassment, "Yes," he said softly, "I remember."

"It's been a long time."

Joseph didn't answer.

Brogan broke out into a wide smile. "I'm glad to see you. I hear you've done pretty well for yourself."

Joe shrugged.

"My God," he continued, "the last time I saw you, you were a boy. You've certainly changed some."

"I'd like to see Larry," Joseph said. "The lady says it's too early."

Brogan smiled, "It is early, but I think we can bend the rules a little." He looked at the woman and winked.

She smiled, "It's okay with me, doctor."

"Fine," Brogan said, turning back to Joe. "Would you like to come into my office for a minute?"

Joe followed the doctor down a long corridor. Brogan opened a door and waved him inside.

The doctor hung up his coat and asked Joe to sit down.

"No, I don't think so, I'd really like to see Larry."

"Okay, Joe, just sit down for a minute. I'd like to talk to you."

Joe walked over and sat down. Brogan lit a cigarette and held out the pack.

"No, thanks," Joe said.

"I really am very glad to see you," Brogan said. Joe nodded.

Doctor Brogan wasn't exaggerating. He was genuinely enthusiastic about Joseph's visit. "What took you so long?"

Joseph stood up, "It's a long story, doc. I don't feel like getting into it right now."

"Oh, I understand. I understand," Brogan said. "Please don't be angry, I didn't mean to pry."

"Yeah, I know that. But you've probably been condemning me for never coming here."

"Yes, I suppose I did," Brogan said softly. "But I'm sure you had your reasons."

"It's a long story."

Brogan smiled ruefully, "We all have our stories, Joe. Me, you, everybody. I had no right to condemn you."

Joe nervously rubbed his cheek. "I don't know," he said, "Everything's such a goddamn mess,"

Brogan got up and walked over to him, putting his hand on Joe's shoulder. "I just want to prepare you before you see him."

"Prepare me for what?"

"Well," Brogan said, "Larry looks quite a bit different than the last time you saw him. How long has it been, exactly?"

"Three years," Joseph answered, without hesitation.

"Well, there's been a lot of changes in three years."

"What kind of changes?"

"We have a difficult time getting your brother to eat. He's very thin. When you see him, don't get upset. He's otherwise in fine health."

"He is?"

"Well, I'm talking about his physical health. Mentally, he's no better. But we keep trying." Brogan bowed his head, "One day, things might be different. We'll just keep trying."

"I'd like to see him now."

"Don't expect him to jump with joy. He doesn't respond well to conversation. Over the past two weeks, he's been unusually disoriented."

"Maybe when he sees me."

"I hope so, but don't bank on it. He's very depressed," Brogan said. "He might not show you any reaction at all. He might not even recognize you."

Joseph frowned. "I'll believe that when I see it."

"Well, you've got to realize it's a combination of his condition and the medication we have him on."

"Well, for Christ's sake, take him off the medication."

"We can't. Without it, we'd lose him entirely. Would you like me to come along?"

"No, I don't think so, I'd rather be alone."

Brogan held the door open and nodded in understanding. "Good luck," he said. "His room is the last one on the right, at the end of the hall."

Joe walked out into the corridor. "Which way?" he asked nervously.

Brogan pointed to Joseph's right. "Down there."

He walked to the end of the hall. There was a slot on the front of the door that held a small white card with his brother's name on it. Like a series of punches, it hit him over and over again. Larry Flynn! Larry Flynn! Larry Flynn! Joseph felt the stirrings of panic. He rested his back against the door and tried to catch his breath. His heart was pounding.

Finally, he turned the doorknob. The inside of the room was dark and still. In the shadows, Joe was hardly able to see the figure lying, fast asleep, on the bed. The room smelled of antiseptic, and at its far end there was a lone window. He walked over and raised the shade, allowing the early sun to light up the room. He went over to the bed and looked at his brother's face. Joseph recoiled in shock. He couldn't believe it; in repose, it was the image of an old man. Larry's countenance had aged beyond all limits of imagination; deep furrows traversed his forehead, and lines traced their way, like a hideous map, over the shrunken, bony face. Joseph almost screamed. He backed away from the bed and bit deeply into his hand.

"Oh good God," he whispered as tears sprang to his eyes. "Oh good lovin' Jesus Christ."

Joe waited until he gained some control over his emotions, and walked back to the bed. He tenderly tapped Larry's shoulder. His brother stirred.

"Are you awake?" Joseph whispered.

He didn't respond. Joe shook his shoulder more vigorously.

"Larry, Larry," he said loudly, "It's me, Joe. Are you awake?"

His eyelids began to flutter. Finally, he opened them completely and stared at Joseph. Joe tried to smile. Larry mumbled something, but Joe wasn't able to interpret it.

"What?" Joe whispered, "What did you say? Do you know me?"

Larry, his lips unmoving, stared directly into his brother's eyes.

"It's me. Joseph. Don't you know who I am?"

Larry pulled back the covers and sat up on the side of the bed. The white hospital gown hung on him like an oversized sheet. His exposed arms and legs looked like flesh covered pipes.

Joe's lips began to tremble. The room was as quiet as death, as the two men stared silently at one another. Larry emitted a soft, unintelligible sound as he agitatedly moved his fingers over the gown. Joe reached out and grasped his brother's hand.

"Do you know who I am?" he asked, his voice, hoarse and rasping. "It's Joe! It's me, your brother."

Once again, Larry's eyelids went into a rapid blinking. He pressed two fingers against his lips, and gestured to Joe.

"What? What is it? What do you want?" Joe asked.

"Smoke," Larry said, as he tapped his fingers against his lips, "You want a cigarette?" Joseph said, "I don't…"

"Smoke," Larry repeated.

"Wait a minute. Just a minute," Joe said, as he quickly walked to the door, "I'll be right back. Wait." He raced down the corridor toward Brogan's office. The doctor was startled when Joe burst into the room. "What's wrong?" Brogan said, his voice ringing in alarm.

Joe rushed over to the desk. "He wants a cigarette. Give me your pack, please."

Brogan's hand went to his shirt pocket. "Yes, sure," he said. Joseph grabbed his pack and turned back to the door.

"It's all right," Brogan said. "We allow him to—"

Joseph paid no attention as he rushed out of the office. He picked up the pack of matches that he had noticed on Larry's bedstand and carefully lit the cigarette. Larry took several fast puffs, blowing the smoke into Joseph's face.

"Is that better?"

Larry, concentrating on drawing the smoke into his lungs, didn't answer.

"For Christ's sake, Larry," Joe said. "Say somethin'. Talk to me."

He remained silent as he continued to puff on the cigarette. Joseph carefully removed it from his lips and stamped it out on the floor. He looked at Larry. "Do you know who I am? Do you know me?"

Larry looked at him strangely.

"Do you?" Joseph said desperately.

Larry whispered something.

"What?" Joseph asked.

The voice grew somewhat louder. "I know Ma." Larry said. Joseph's heart was about to burst. "Oh God, please, Larry, please. It's Joe!" he said, his voice wavering with pain. "It's not Ma. It's Joe."

Larry offered a faint smile. "I know Ma," he said again. Although his brother's staring eyes bore a hole through him, Joseph knew that it was something far away that Larry was attending to, as if Joseph were not even in the room.

He reached his arms around Larry's emaciated back and gently pulled him close. The stubble of short, auburn hair rubbed against Joseph's cheek. "Oh, no," Joe whimpered, "Oh, God, what have I done? What have I done?"

Larry pushed him away, and once again began to press his fingers against his lips. He looked eagerly at the cigarette pack on the bed stand.

Joe picked it up and handed it to him. Larry, in an extravagant motion, struck a match and put it to the cigarette.

As tears coursed down Joseph's face, he watched his brother. "Aren't you going to say anything to me?" Joseph said softly. Larry offered a wan smile and raised the cigarette.

"You've gotta know me," Joseph begged, "you've gotta."

Larry, continuing to smile, remained silent. He looked toward the window, squinting in the face of the sun. A sick feeling grew in Joe's stomach. The scene before him became too much to bear.

In a world filled with thieves and animals, Larry had been an innocent, reaping an unjust and terrible harvest. Joseph knew that it was he who was responsible for his brother's destruction. He walked over and placed his mouth near Larry's ear. "I'm sorry," he whispered. "Forgive me." He tenderly kissed the cold, bony cheek, allowing his lips to linger for long, precious moments.

"I love you, Larry," he cried softly. "I love you." One last time, he squeezed his brother's shoulder and walked to the door. Quietly, he closed it behind him.

Joseph leaned his forehead against the wall in the corridor, nearly collapsing in his grief; he cried helplessly, the tears filling his mouth with the taste of salt. His throat choked in harsh sobs of guilt and sorrow. Suddenly, he was aware of a presence. Turning around, he saw the tall figure of Doctor Brogan.

"Easy, Joe, easy," Brogan said sympathetically, "Things'll improve. You've got to believe that."

Joe's gut was starting to rebel against the nausea. He felt as though he would faint.

Brogan continued talking, "You did right by coming here. I know it's hard, but you'll—"

Joseph rushed past him and ran down the hall. He wanted to be in his car and driving away from the terror that enveloped him; to drive away, to escape to home and the revival of Hanway.

Doctor Brogan entered the room and walked over to Larry.

Larry, sitting on the bed, seemed not to notice.

"Here, let me take that," Brogan said softly, as he took away the cigarette and crushed it into the ashtray. "Did you recognize that fellow?" he asked.

Larry watched a slow drift of smoke arise from the ashtray and tiredly stretched his arms.

"It was your brother, Joe. Did you talk to him?"

Larry yawned and scratched at his shoulder.

"Okay," Brogan whispered, "We'll talk later. You're tired."

He walked back across the room. "Get some sleep," he said, without turning around. "We'll talk later."

Larry continued to scratch his shoulder as the doctor made a quiet exit. After a while, he got up and went to the window.

The light annoyed him. He pulled down the shade and returned to his bed. Climbing into it, he covered himself with the sheet and closed his eyes. Once again, the room was dark and still. Larry sighed contentedly and almost instantly fell off into a deep sleep.

15

FOLLOWING their well-established Christmas Eve tradition, Pat Flynn and Bill Manley arrived very early at the Clarkson Courthouse. they delivered bottles of liquor and boxes of candy to the large offices and work rooms that acted as the hub of county business. The women, young and old alike, giggled like school girls in Patrick's presence. He laughingly stood before them, his white teeth gleaming, grandly accepting the innumerable kisses that pecked at his cheek. As always, Manley tagged along basking in the power and glory of his idol. Important-looking men left their desks to take the opportunity to shake Flynn's hand and perhaps gain a point by saying the correct thing to the master. The atmosphere was one in which Patrick thrived, surrounded by sycophants stumbling over themselves in their efforts to pay him homage for his clever generosity. Patrick had long before learned the significance of simple gifts. They maintained the respect of the rank and file workers, the army that made his political power grow to staggering proportions.

Later on in the morning, Pat and Bill retreated to the second floor office reserved for the Democratic chairman. They planned on spending the rest of the day drinking and laughing with their cronies. By noontime, the office was in a din of noise, with almost every politician in the county stuffing himself into the thick camaraderie of the room. They lurched drunkenly about, singing and laughing as they offered salutes to their leader.

Patrick sat comfortably on his desk savoring everything. He heard Manley's voice. He turned to see Bill calling to him from the hallway. Pat moved through the throng finally making his way to the open door.

"What's up?" Flynn said.

Bill gestured to him and walked further down the hall. Patrick followed him until they were alone in an alcove near the elevator. "You can't hear yourself think in that noise," Bill said.

Patrick laughed, "Yeah, they're as drunk as skunks." He looked questioningly at Bill. "What's so important?"

"I was just wondering," Bill said, "Joe hasn't shown up yet."

"So what?"

"Well, I mean this party won't last forever. He oughta be around. There's a lotta people he could meet."

"What the hell, he knows most of them."

"Yeah, I know, but not alla them."

"He'll get to know them. Don't worry. Haffa them are in a daze anyway. They're drunk. They don't know what's goin' on anyhow."

"Well, I thought..."

"Look, he'll know alla them in time. This isn't the right place for business anyway. It's party time," Patrick laughed.

"Was Joe supposed to be here?" Bill asked.

"Yeah," Patrick said. "He knew we were all getting together. I don't know where he is."

"That's funny."

"He probably had somethin' to do. You know how he is."

"Yeah, Pat, I know," Bill said, "but sometimes I wonder if the kid's right for politics."

"What makes you say that?"

"Well, I dunno. He's a funny guy. He doesn't go for all a this shit."

"Don't you worry, " Patrick said, "He'll be a master. Just give him time."

Patrick walked to a window and looked out. He called Bill over to him. Grabbing Manley's shoulder, he pointed at the bustling city. "We own it, Bill boy," he smiled.

Manley patted him on the back. "You own it, Pat, Not me. This is your city and your county. You did it all yourself."

"Bullshit," Patrick said. "You were with me all the way."

"It was you, Pat. Without you I'd be nobody."

"Well, any which way, it's all ours. You know that," Patrick said.

"Yeah, I know that," Bill said humbly, as he grabbed Patrick's arm. "You've been my whole life. God knows where I'd be if not for you."

"Don't worry about Joe," Pat smiled. "When we're gone, he'll be right up their ass. A Flynn'll be always around to give them orders. You and I will see to it."

"You bet," Bill said. "We damn well will see to it."

Patrick smiled confidently as he looked out the window.

"Any news on Lila?" Bill asked quietly.

Patrick turned around. "I think she's gonna be okay," he said, "If she stays still until after New Years, that'll be it."

"Whadaya mean?" Bill asked.

"Well, she'll be feelin' pretty low durin' the holidays. If she's gonna say anything, now'll be the time she'll do it."

"Well, Jesus, what if she does?"

"I'll handle it then. It won't take much to make her out a liar."

"Yeah, but if she says it loud and long enough, somebody'll start listenin'."

"She'll only say it once," Patrick said, "and that'll be the end of her. Don't worry. Nobody'll suspect us."

"If anything has to be done with her," Manley said angrily, "I wanna be the one to do it,"

Patrick laughed. "Of course it'll be you. Who else would it be?"

The pulse in Manley's neck throbbed. "The fuckin' pig," he said. "I'll break her bones."

Patrick smiled and punched Bill's shoulder. "Okay, okay, let forget about it now. If it becomes necessary, I'll work somethin' out."

"Just say the word, Boss."

Patrick smiled, "I think it's gonna be a great year, Billy."

"Sure it will, Boss. Sure it will."

"Let's get back to the party," Patrick said.

Bill threw his arm around Patrick's shoulder. "Merry Christmas, Boss," he said.

Flynn reached over and playfully slapped Manley's cheek. "Merry Christmas, ya lug," he said.

As both men made their way back to the hilarity, the winter wind rattled the window that looked out over the city. Dark clouds began to fill the cold December sky.

16

ALL THE WAY home, Joseph Flynn drove in a dazed state. He crossed the Hanway boundary and went directly to his office. The moment he walked through the door, his secretary noticed his red, swollen eyes. "Good morning," she said. "You just missed a call from your father."

"Did he say what he wanted?"

"They're having a party down at the courthouse. He was wondering where you were."

"What time is it?"

She looked at her watch. "Twenty to one," she said.

Joe had driven aimlessly for hours, lost in thoughts of his brother. He was stunned to realize so much time had passed.

"My God, I didn't realize it was so late," he said.

"Mr. Flynn said it was going to go on for a while."

"What's gonna go on?"

"The party."

"Oh, that," Joe said, "Well never mind about it. I'm not in the mood."

"Is something wrong?"

"Why?"

"You don't look very well."

Joe blinked. "I've got a cold," he said. "I feel lousy."

He bent over and looked at her memo pad. "Were there any other messages?" he asked.

"Oh, yes, " she said, rolling her eyes. "A Mrs. Walton has been calling all morning. She wants to see you."

"Did you give her an appointment?"

"I tried, but she insisted that she wanted to see you as soon as possible."

"Well, is she coming here or what?"

"No, she wants you to go to her. She said it was extremely important."

It has to be news about Ray, Joseph thought. Maybe it's good news. He walked around the desk. "She doesn't live in town anymore. Did she leave an address?"

"Yes," the woman replied, "I wrote it down here, along with her phone number. Would you like me to call her?"

Joe pulled the sheet of paper from her hand. Something told him not to call. "No, never mind," he said. "I think I'd better see her." He rushed out of the building.

Joe knocked softly on the apartment door. When Lila opened it, he couldn't believe his eyes. Her face was a mass of welts and bruises. Her right eye was discolored and almost closed.

"Don't I look pretty?" she said.

"What in God's name happened?" he asked in alarm.

"Come on in," she said, "I'll tell you all about it."

She led him into the tiny kitchen and took a pot of coffee off the stove. "Would you like some?" she said.

"Yes, please," Joseph replied.

He sat down at the table as Lila reached into the cupboard. She filled two cups, set them on the table and sat down.

"What happened, Mrs. Walton?" he asked with concern. She sipped at her coffee and stared at him.

"Are you all right?" he asked,

"Yeah, I'm okay," she muttered.

"Will you please tell me what happened?"

"Just give me a second," she said.

"How'd ya do that to your face?"

"I didn't do it," she hissed.

"What's goin' on?" Joe asked.

Lila looked at him sarcastically. "I'll bet you thought I had some news about Ray."

"Yeah, I did," Joe said expectantly, "I was hopin' it was good news, I could use some."

"Well, prepare yourself, sonny boy," she said. "Amongst other things, I do have somethin' to tell you concerning Ray. But it's not good news, so brace up."

Joseph was dismayed by Lila's brazen attitude, "What's this about?" he asked.

"It's about your daddy," she said smiling.

"My father. What about my father?"

Lila pushed her coffee cup away, "Frig that," she said, as she got up and went into the parlor. Joseph followed her.

She pulled a bottle of whiskey from a cabinet and poured some of it into a glass. She offered it to Joe.

"No, thanks," he said.

She quickly drank it and poured another.

"Mrs. Walton, what were you sayin' about my father?"

Lila laughed. "This goddamn world is a joke. I've been screwin' Patrick for over ten years and nobody, goddamn nobody knows about it."

Joe, disbelievingly, stared at her.

"The whole friggin' world is blind," she said.

"What are you saying?" he said,

"You heard me. Your old man and I have been a lovin' twosome for quite a while."

"You're a liar."

Lila laughed hysterically. "No, no," she mocked, "I used to be a liar, but now I'm sworn to the truth."

"I don't believe you," Joe said.

"Oh, you will. You will," she laughed. "Your old man is pretty foxy, keepin' me under wraps the way he did. Only a few, select few ever knew about old Lila, but now you're gonna be one of them."

Joseph's disbelief suddenly transformed into a great interest. He sat down in a chair, "Go ahead," he said. "I'm waitin'."

"Well," she said, "like I told you, he's been screwin' me for years.

How do you like that?"

Joseph had always believed his father was capable of infidelity. But Lila Walton had never fit into that region of his imagination. "How long did you say?" he asked.

"For ten years, sonny boy. That includes the years your mother was alive."

Joe had to fight back a compulsion to kill her but he let her go on.

"I was his paramour," she laughed, "and your mother was his fool."

Joseph gripped the arms of the chair. "You'd better watch your mouth," he whispered dangerously.

"Well, now, sonny boy is gettin' mad. Isn't that too bad?"

Joe knew he had to allow her to continue. "Keep talkin'," he said.

"Do you know what happened to my hubby?" she asked. "No you don't, do you? It's one of the great mysteries." She gulped down several more swallows of whiskey. "Well, let me tell ya," she said. "You're old daddy wanted me so bad that he had Bill Manley kill him. How do you like that?"

"You're crazy," Joe said.

"Why am I crazy?" Lila laughed. "Because I'm callin' Pat Flynn a murderer. It's too bad old Doc Benson wasn't around to tell ya about it."

"What do you mean?" Joseph said,

"I mean that your old man had him murdered too."

"How?"

"He had Bill Manley blow his head off, that's how." She began to laugh again. "A suicide, what a joke. I told you kid, the friggin' world is blind, and deaf on top of it,"

Joseph allowed her to continue.

"I suppose you're dyin' to know why he had Benson wiped out. I'll tell you why. Because the old man killed a young girl while he was abortin' Patrick's baby, that's why," She walked over to the bottle and refilled the glass. "Oh, yeah, I knew about all the scum he played around with but I tolerated it. Your old man has an incurable itch for snatch, ya know." She turned around and looked at the astonished expression on Joseph's face. "Are ya surprised, sweetheart? Well, here's another one for ya. Ray found out about me and your father and I was afraid he was gonna tell somebody, like you for instance, so I concocted a little plan."

Lila went on to tell Joe about her incestuous encounter with Ray. She included every detail. When she finished, Joe leaned back into the chair and closed his eyes. He felt as though he were hit by a truck.

"Oh wait a minute, sonny boy," she said angrily, "I'm not finished yet. There's one more murder to talk about." She poured herself another drink, "The day Ray left, I happen to know it's a fact that he visited your mother, and it happens to be a fact that she died the same day. The minute he left the house, or so I understand." An evil smile played on her lips as she continued, "The way I figure it, Ray told her everything. At the time, she was real sick and couldn't handle it, so she conked out. That's murder in my book, and your sweet daddy had his hands in that one too. And there's somethin' else. He's been payin' doctors to keep Larry locked up. He wants him away for good so he won't embarrass him."

Joseph stood up slowly.

"Oh, what are you gonna do? Beat me up the way your old man did?" She pointed to her face, "Yeah, he did it... You wanted to know so bad. Well I'm tellin' ya. He did it! Do ya wanna know why?" she screamed.

Joe clamped his teeth and pressed his fist against his hand, "You lousy bastard," he whispered.

"No, I'm not the bastard," she shouted, "your father is! He thought he was gonna throw me over like one of his whores, so I told him I would tell everything I knew. This is what he did to me."

She began to cry, "He'll kill me when he finds out I told you. But I don't care, I'm glad! I'm glad!" She ran to the tape recorder that was placed on one of the end tables, "Here!" she screamed, as she pressed down the button, "you think I'm crazy, do you? Listen to this."

Joseph stood speechless as he heard his father's voice roll off the tape. He listened until it ended with Lila's cries and the violence of his father. Lila collapsed into a chair. Joseph walked out of the room. He left the door open behind him. Gagging and crying, Lila reached for the bottle. Her hands were shaking so badly she was hardly able to hold onto it.

18

B Y THE TIME Joseph hit the street, his body was practically
convulsed with rage. He looked at his watch. It was almost
two-thirty. He jumped in his car and drove crazily through
the traffic. He headed for the courthouse. When he pulled into
the large parking lot, he leaped from the car and raced toward
the building.

By now the office was almost empty. Patrick and Manley along
with two other men were conversing quietly near the massive oak
desk. Joseph burst into the room. His face was contorted, his eyes
burning.

He pointed at his father, "I want to talk to you!" he screamed.

"What the hell is goin' on?" Patrick yelled. "What's wrong
with you?"

"Get them outta here!" Joseph shouted.

The two men ran past Joseph and out of the room.

"Him too!" Joseph screamed pointing at Manley. "Get him
outta here!"

Patrick was stunned. "Jesus Christ, Joe, what's wrong?" he said.

"Get him out, I said."

"I'll wait in the hall, Boss," Manley said.

"No you won't," Pat said. "Stay right here. Don't move."

Joe's voice dropped to a dangerous whisper. "All right, let him
stay. He's in on it, the son of a bitch."

"What the hell is wrong with you?" Patrick said in alarm.

"Do you know where I just was?" Joseph said, his eyes wide
and blazing.

"Where were you? Where?"

"Lila Walton just told me a story."

Manley's body went stiff. "Oh Jesus, Pat. Jesus Christ Almighty. I knew it."

Patrick gestured for quiet. "What story?" he said. "What'd she tell you?"

Joseph, almost incoherently, told him everything.

When his son finished speaking, Patrick smiled nervously.

"Oh c'mon, Joe. You don't believe that."

"I believe it."

"The broad's a goddamned liar."

"She's got it on tape!" Joe shouted. "The night you went there and beat her up, she's got it on tape! Everything you said! I heard your voice! I heard you!"

Patrick felt the edge of panic, "She fixed somethin' up," he said, his lips trembling. "She fixed somethin' up. The tape's a phony."

Joe pointed at Manley. "What'd he just say? He knew what?"

"I didn't mean nothin', Joe," Manley said,

"Fuck you didn't!" Joe screamed, "What'd you mean when you said you knew it?"

The anger slowly grew in Patrick's body. "Hey kid," he said. "Keep your fuckin' voice down. The whole building can hear ya."

"You better do some fast talkin'," Joe said. "And you'd better do it fast."

"Hey, boy, d'ya know who you're talkin' to?" Patrick said.

"Yeah, I think I know," Joe said, "a fuckin' whore master killin' bastard. That's who."

Patrick turned to Manley. "Close that door," he said.

"Don't worry, Boss. I think everybody's gone. Everybody left early."

"Check and see," Patrick ordered.

Manley rushed out of the room.

Joseph, even in his anger, prayed that his father might prove Lila a liar. In his heart he prayed. "Well," Joseph said angrily, "what d'ya have to say? You can't deny it, can ya?"

Patrick glared at him. "Just a minute, I'm gonna explain everything."

"I'm waitin'. You better have an explanation," Joe warned.

"Wait, I want Bill here," Patrick said.

After a few moments, Manley returned. "Everybody's gone," he said with relief.

"What about the two clowns that were here?" Patrick asked.

"They flew right outta the building."

"All right," Patrick said as he turned to Joseph, "Now, you want an explanation."

"Yeah, that's right. C'mon, I'm waitin'."

"I'm not gonna play games with you, Joe. I don't need your shit. Believe what you wanna believe."

"You did do all those things! You did!" Joe screamed.

"I did whatever I hadda do, and if you don't like it, get outta here. Nobody's stoppin' ya."

At that moment Joseph knew that the whole ugly story was true, horribly true. "You killed those people and you did that to Mama and Larry, didn't you? Didn't you?"

"Your mama," Patrick laughed bitterly, "she was a first class pain in the ass."

Joseph bolted toward him. Before he was able to reach Patrick, Manley grabbed him and held him in a vise-like grip.

Patrick looked at Joseph and laughed. "I've been blessed with two pissers," he said. "Two sons and they're made of butter."

He walked over to Joe and roughly squeezed his face. "I hafta keep that other idiot locked up so he won't embarrass me, and you're no better." He looked at Manley, "I've got two idiots on my hands and they're not worth a shit."

Manley continued to hold tightly on to Joseph.

"Ya come in here yellin' like a friggin' lunatic," Patrick shouted, "after all I did for ya. I don't care what I did. Ya oughta kiss my ass for the way I took care of ya." He waved his finger in Joe's face. "But don't kid yourself, kid, I'll throw ya out in a fuckin' minute. I don't need you or anybody else. I've got your brother locked in the looney bin for keeps, and I'll find somethin' just as nice for you, if you push me too far."

"I'll kill you, you filthy bastard!" Joe said. "I'll kill you!"

Patrick looked at Manley. "Let him go, Bill," he said. "He thinks he's tough," Patrick smiled. "Let's see how tough he is. "

Bill, very slowly, set Joseph free and backed away. Joseph raised his fists and looked at his father.

"Well, c'mon, tough guy," Patrick mocked. "Come on."

Joseph went at him in a fury. Patrick stepped quickly aside and threw him against the desk. Before Joe could turn, his father smashed two punches to the back of his head. For a moment Joe's eyes blurred. Several more punches dug into his kidneys. Joe, barely able to catch his breath, swung around and held onto his father's shoulders. Patrick threw devastating punches into his belly. Joe began to crumple, and Patrick drove his knee into his son's chest. Joseph pushed Patrick backwards. Manley watched astonished to see Joseph still on his feet. Joe charged at Patrick and threw a wild right fist; it connected on his father's jaw and drove him back against the wall. In an instant, Joseph was on top of him, Patrick grunted as Joseph's fists banged against his body. He reached up and grabbed Joe's throat, but his son twisted away and struck him flush on the face with three fast punches. Patrick, his eyes and mouth bleeding, fell to his knees. Joseph drew back his powerful fist and measured him.

But before he could finish it, Manley sprang to defense; Bill struck a tremendous blow to the side of Joe's head. Joseph reeled sideways. Bill lifted him off his feet and threw him against the wall. Joe bounced back toward him and Manley threw a crushing punch to Joseph's chest. Joe grunted in pain, and Manley stepped back waiting for him to fall. Joe swayed but somehow managed to stay erect. Bill couldn't believe it. "Why, you punk," Manley growled as he moved forward. Joseph saw an open target and fired at it; he struck Manley's chin with two fast, ferocious punches. Bill staggered and Joe went into a feverish attack; he knocked Bill from one end of the room to the other. Finally, he landed several paralyzing blows to Manley's belly.

Bill staggered backward and collapsed to the floor. Joe, breathing heavily, stood triumphantly over him.

Patrick lifted himself from the floor and approached Joe from behind. Quietly, he picked up a wooden chair and raised it above his head; without warning, he brought it down and crashed it over his son's skull.

Patrick struggled to get Manley to his feet. Bill tried to shake away the blur that covered his eyes. "Jesus Christ," he said.

"Are you okay?" Patrick asked.

"Yeah, Jesus, Boss, the kid's tough." Patrick looked down at the inert figure on the floor.

Bill rubbed his jaw. "Man," he mumbled. "The kid hits friggin' hard."

"Never mind," Patrick said, "What're we goin' to do with him?"

"How'd ya stop him?" Bill asked.

Patrick pointed to the broken chair. "I busted that over his head."

"Maybe ya killed him,"

"Nah, he's just knocked out. Look at him. He's breathin'."

"What should we do?" Manley asked.

Patrick thought quietly for a moment. "Look," he said, "the side garage opens to the ground floor. We'll carry him down. Where'd ya park the car?"

"It's right out in the lot."

"Okay, when we get him to the basement, pull the car into the garage, and we'll get him outta here without anybody seein'."

"Then what're we gonna do with him?"

"We'll take him back to the house. I'll have to come up with somethin'. I'll think about it then."

They picked Joe up and carried him to the basement. Both men were puffing as they sat Joe against the cement wall.

"Boy, he's really out," Manley said.

"Yeah," Pat said nervously. "Before you get the car, call the house and tell Mrs. Davis to go home. Tell her we're gonna have an important meeting and we want privacy."

Manley stood staring at Joseph.

"Go ahead!" Patrick shouted. "What the hell are ya waitin' for?"

Bill jerked to attention. "Yeah. Right. Okay, Boss," he said. "I'll call her."

"Hurry up!" Patrick said excitedly. "Goddammit, hurry up!"

19

THEY DRAGGED Joe from the car to the mansion. They struggled as they made their way up the staircase toward Joe's bedroom. Both men stared at the unconscious figure on the bed.

"He looks like he's dead," Manley said.

"Oh, Jesus Christ, he's not dead," Patrick said in irritation. "Can't ya see him breathin'?"

"Well, why isn't he comin' to?"

Patrick walked over to Joe and checked the wound on the top of his son's head. "I split his skull open," Patrick said.

"D'ya think he'll make it?" Manley asked.

"I don't know. But he's gonna be out for a helluva long time. That's for sure. "

"D'ya want me to call Doc Royal or what?" Bill said.

"No, not yet," Patrick said. "Not yet. I've gotta think."

"I'll go downstairs and get us a drink," Manley said. "We could use one."

"I'll come down too. "

Manley pointed to Joe. "What about him?" he asked.

"He's not goin' anywhere," Pat said. "If he comes to, he won't be able to get up anyway. Don't worry. "

"What if he dies here?"

"Don't worry," Patrick said, as he walked to the doorway. "Let's go down."

Patrick sat down at the kitchen table while Manley poured the drinks. "How in hell did all this happen?" Patrick said. He rested his elbows on the table. "How? How?"

Manley set the glass of whiskey in front of him. "I'll tell you how," he said angrily. "I told ya we should've killed that fuckin' broad. I told ya, Pat."

"Could ya imagine?" Patrick said. "She told Joe. That was her plan all the time, and we were worried about the stupid cops. Jesus Christ."

"We shoulda killed her," Manley growled.

"A tape recorder, for Christ's sake," Patrick said bitterly. "She used a tape recorder. Could ya imagine that?"

"What if Joe pulls through that crack on the head? What're we gonna do with him?" Bill asked.

Patrick sighed. "I don't know yet. I don't know. I've gotta think."

"Are we gonna call Royal?"

"Wait a minute, Bill." Patrick said patiently. "Let me think."

Patrick swallowed the whiskey. He wiped his mouth and looked at Bill. "Lila's a dead woman," he said.

"Yeah," Manley said, "the sooner the better."

"I'll pick the time and place," Patrick said.

"But what about Joe?" Manley asked.

"Well, I know one thing," Patrick said as he rubbed his swollen eyes. "Everything is really fucked up. Everything's gone."

"Whatta ya mean gone?" Bill asked.

"All my plans for the kid are blown away," he said, as he banged the glass down on the table, "Just like that," he snapped his fingers. "Everything's blown away."

"Maybe you'll be able to straighten it out," Manley said.

"Straighten it out how?" Patrick said angrily. "How the hell can I straighten out a mess like this?"

"Maybe we'll be able to make Joe understand."

Patrick laughed sarcastically, "Make him understand what?" he shouted. "How do ya make a punk like him understand? You saw him, didn't ya? He's a friggin' lunatic."

"Well, Jesus, Boss, things came down pretty hard on him," Manley said. "I mean he really got a strong dose all at once. All in one bundle. He found out about Lila and her kid, about the father, about Benson. He found out about the situation with Larry. I mean what the hell. I guess he had a reason to go haywire."

Patrick thought for a moment. "I never knew about Lila screwin' her own kid," he said finally. "She's capable of a lotta things, but I never figured she'd do somethin' like that."

"Well, ya couldn't expect her to tell you," Manley said.

"God damn," Patrick said, "she's a maniac."

"She musta wanted to hold on to you pretty bad," Manley said.

"I remember her kid comin' here the day Anna died," Patrick said. "Do ya think he told her about seein' me and Lila?"

"Could be," Manley said.

"If he did, it killed her," Patrick said.

"Yeah, Boss, that coulda been it."

"There's no way this is gonna be cleared up with Joe," Patrick said. Manley stared at the floor.

"I don't know what I'm gonna do," Patrick whispered.

"Look, Boss, don't feel bad," Manley said sympathetically. Maybe Larry'll shape up. You can still keep the Flynn power alive. Larry might be okay, ya never know."

"Oh fuck that," Patrick said. "I couldn't care less now. That was just a dumb dream. I shoulda known better. Joe was never any friggin' good. I always knew it. I was kiddin' myself."

"Maybe somethin'll work out."

"Nothin' will work out. Goddamn it, it's finished and done with. I don't give a shit. It doesn't matter. I just gotta figure what I'm gonna do with him. How the hell am I gonna shut him up?"

"I don't know, Boss."

Patrick looked up. "Well, I think I know," he said. "If I hafta, I'll kill him."

"Oh Jesus, Boss, " Manley said.

"No, I mean it, every friggin' word. I'll kill him. I just gotta figure how to do it."

"Maybe we won't hafta."

"Well, I don't see any other way."

Blood began to drip from Patrick's wounded right eye.

"You're startin' to bleed again, Boss," Manley said. He grabbed a towel and dabbed it at Patrick's eyebrow.

"Ow! Watch it!" Patrick said. "Be careful."

"Man oh man," Manley said. "That fuckin' kid hits like a ton a bricks. I've never been hit so hard in my life."

"Yeah, he hits pretty good," Patrick said.

"Hell, man, he whipped both of us."

Patrick ignored the statement. "Easy, Bill," he said. "Go slow on that eye."

"Jesus, your face is a mess."

Patrick looked up at him. "You're not lookin' too good yourself."

Manley ran his hand over his puffed and bruised face. "Yeah, the kid hits good."

Joseph Flynn slowly opened his eyes. Everything around him moved in bizarre contortions. He closed his eyes to stop the weird feeling of spinning and the knot of vomit that crawled in his throat. Hesitantly, he reopened them and squinted to bring his surroundings into focus. It took him a full minute to realize he was in his bedroom. The pain that moved across his forehead was almost unbearable. He tried to sit up, but the top of his head hurt so badly. All movement was an excruciating torture. He slowly moved his hand toward his head. His hair was stiff and matted from the blood. He put his finger into the gaping wound and felt the unmistakable smooth hardness of bone. Visions moved through his brain like a hideous nightmare; he began to groan and tremble. He was running in a vast tunnel. Hundreds of people were beating at him with clubs. His father's loud laughter was deafening. He opened his eyes suddenly and jerked his head.

He was in his bedroom again and Mrs. Davis stood at the bed. He reached for her and she was gone. He heard the softness of his mother's voice and Gena's sweet laughter. "What?" he said. "What, Ma? Gena! Gena!" He turned toward the sounds and a jolt of pain shot through his head like fire. "Ma!" he cried. "Mama, wait!" The room was suddenly still, the only sound his labored breath. "Oh Jesus," he whispered, as tears streamed down his face. "Help me please. Help me."

After long minutes he painfully pulled himself into a sitting position and rested back against the headboard. Once again, he carefully touched his battered skull. It had come full cycle. After all that had gone, all those years of ugliness and desperate waiting, after all the days of fear and hope. He was right back where he started, beaten and bleeding by his father's hand. But there was something missing. A beautiful, sad tenderness lost.

His mother wasn't crouched before him, whispering words of love and comfort, wiping away the blood with a cool cloth and crying because it was her pain as well. There wasn't Larry to help pull him to his feet, his face filled with misery and frustration.

He couldn't run to sweet, decent Gena and the fortress of her strength. They weren't there anymore. They would never be there.

In his torment, Joseph's chest heaved in grief. His mind swerved and tumbled over all the years of his life, all those years lost. All that time, dead and gone. Poor Larry and his frightened imprisoned soul. His eyes, hidden and blinking in confusion, destroyed in the face of all the heartache and injustice that had bludgeoned his sad life, And Mama, what of helpless, grieving Mama and her tortured dreams and killing reality? What of her and her fragile breast and trembling heart forever stilled? What of Carol, forever lost in the spinning torrent of Joseph's brain? What of Carol and all her sweetness, her beauty and caring, rejected by the whirlpool of his misguided and injured psyche. What of poor, helpless Ray, the friend he couldn't locate, crumpled and ruined for the rest of his tortured hours? What of Gena and Tom and all their stolen treasures?

Mama and Tom and Gena, their voices, laughter and hopes, forever locked away in that eternal soil, on that hill for all the time that would ever come. And broken, helpless Larry, dead in life as well. In his want, Joseph cried and whimpered. He yearned for the soft darkness of his mother's eyes to bathe him with love just one more time. He wanted Larry to be next to him in the bed, to hear the soft bedtime songs for just one more time. He wanted to smell the freshness of him and bask in his protection and goodness, to feel his back in his arms, to beg his forgiveness, to tell him how much he loved him. In his own insane way, Joseph had failed all of them. He had turned his back on their hopes and prayers. He yearned to fall on his knees before them and beg their forgiveness But God, they weren't there. They weren't there to cry to, to beg to. He wanted so badly to be with all of them. He leaned back his head and cried. The sobs choked off his breath. His heart pounded as though it would burst.

Struggling against the pain, he moved off the bed and staggered to the window, With a great effort, he opened the window and let the fresh air wash over him. His head was finally beginning to clear. He saw Manley's car parked in the driveway. His brain almost exploded. "They're in the house," he thought wildly.

"The pigs are in the house." The image of Patrick Flynn drifted through Joseph's brain. His father had destroyed everything he touched. Joseph had always known it. His body flinched in revulsion at the recognition of his own great guilt, the destruction his own hand had wrought. For the love and acceptance of his father, he had betrayed himself. He had acted out a great drama in masquerade, trampling all of the standards he wanted to live by, hurting and crushing all of the people who really cared. He had acted in treachery against the family and town he loved; acting in the ugly guise of expediency, for the love and smiles of a man who was never worth it, a father who was evil incarnate. The horror was that Joseph had always known it. In the deepest corners of his soul, he had always known it. The great question pursued him; what was the poison that coursed through his own veins? What was it that made him turn away from all things right and decent? He searched for the answer, but it would not come.

His head throbbed as he slowly made his way to the desk along-side his nightstand. He opened a drawer and pushed aside sheets of paper until he saw the gun and its bluish tint of steel. Weeks before he had removed it from his office and placed it here, not knowing why, as if the hand of destiny had subtly acted in prepa-ration for this moment, Joseph trembled slightly as he picked it up. The thirty-eight felt heavy in his hand. He knew that five of the chambers were already loaded waiting to wreak out his final bid for salvation.

He had fleeting moments of dizziness as he made his way to the upstairs hallway. He leaned against the banister and looked down into the empty parlor. He held tightly onto the rail as he slowly and quietly descended the staircase, When he reached the main floor, he pressed his back against the wall, afraid he was going to fall. He called on a last reserve of strength, and once again began to stagger forward. He heard and saw nothing.

For a moment he thought that he was wrong, that he might be alone in the house; and just then, he heard his father's voice coming from the kitchen, followed by the rushing sound of running water.

When he finally reached the kitchen archway, he saw them. Their backs were to him. Patrick stood at the sink, splashing water onto his face. Manley, holding a glass of whiskey, sat at the table.

Manley was about to raise the glass, when a deafening roar filled the room. The front of Manley's face exploded. His torso jerked forward against the table, and the glass dropped from his hand. The gun's loud report caused Patrick to turn around in shock. Manley's head crashed down onto the table top. His blood was splattered all over the formica. Patrick, as if hypnotized, watched the glass roll along the table until it went off the edge and broke on the floor. He looked at Joseph, behind the barrel of the gun.

Joseph had great difficulty keeping his father in focus.

"What're ya doin'?" Patrick said. "Put the gun down, Joey. Don't do it."

The gun wavered in Joseph's hand.

"Please son, please," Patrick begged. "Just think for a second. Think about what you're doin'."

Once again, the thirty-eight roared,

Patrick's body smashed against the sink. His chest was on fire. He put his hand on his shirt and felt the trickle of blood, "Oh, no," he whimpered, "Oh Jesus Christ."

The thirty-eight roared again.

He grabbed at his abdomen and began to slide to the floor. Joseph walked over and looked down at him. Patrick, his eyes in an insane stare, lay on his back. He tried to say something. Joe fired again. His father's body bounced spasmodically. Joseph watched as the blood formed a crimson trail from the corners of his father's mouth. He watched and waited until all sound and movement ceased.

Finally, Joseph turned and walked away. He stumbled into the parlor and stood before the window. He raised his hand and parted the curtains. It was beginning to get dark. The snow was shining bright and clean. He squinted to make out the trees at the far end of the estate. Then, he closed his eyes to picture what was beyond them; he and Larry were young and laughing. They were running with their sleds bouncing behind them. They were running down the white hills to home. Their noses were red and running, and in the kitchen, Mama would be waiting with the sweet, steaming cocoa. It was all so real, he could smell it it. He could touch it. A smile of resignation crossed Joseph's lips. The gun's barrel was cool and comforting against his temple. Very slowly, he squeezed the trigger.

EPILOGUE

June 1967

Joseph would have been glad to know that Hanway remembered him fondly. The resentments had died right after him. Now, all recollections were filled with a quiet understanding. Finally, they realized that he was their finest son, the very best of all of them. Despite all of Patrick Flynn's schemes and plans, his wealth and power had come to an ironic end. The echoes of his influence had long since disappeared, and the sound of his name carried nothing but grim notoriety. Larry was the heir to everything, but it was a useless fortune. He remained at Mount Rose, too ill and incompetent to deal with any of it.

Mickey Clark knelt on the grass and looked at the grave.

After five sad years, Mickey still found moments when he looked expectantly at his front door, imagining he heard Joseph's footsteps or the sound of his voice, Mickey had to squeeze his eyes shut to recall the laughter and glowing face of the little boy who had happily followed him around his garage. It seemed so long ago. Tears sprang to his eyes and his throat was sore with emotion. Mickey blessed himself and stood up. He walked slowly down the hill to his car.

On his way home, he drove down Jessup Avenue. When he reached the Flynn estate, he stopped the car and got out. He walked onto the sidewalk and leaned against the large metal fence.

It was rusted. Long, unattended grass and bushes pushed carelessly through its openings. He looked at the vast grounds.

Except for the children and their games of football and baseball, nobody went there anymore. The mansion was in disrepair. The executors had tried, unsuccessfully, to sell it. There were no buyers. The price and the ugly memories were too overwhelming. Mickey stood there for a long time. His brain raced over the whole unbelievable mixture of horror and beauty. He thought of the parents and the sons. He thought of Joseph Flynn.

Mickey silently cursed to himself and shook his head.

Finally, he turned around and walked away. Slowly, the car pulled away from the curb and moved down the avenue.

It was green and summer and the birds were stirring in the trees. The good people were on their way to work and the air was sharp and clear. The sun was bright and moving in the sky.

Hanway, in its infinite survival, was breathing with life. The early children's laughter could be heard, drifting past the meadows and the hills, floating over the lovely streets and filling the town with the freshness of dreams. Dreams that own the world. Dreams that fill all yesterdays and tomorrows. Dreams that become memories. Dreams that become joys and sorrows; the heartbeat of the living and the legacy of the dead.

For more information on *Sons of Sorrow,*
or to arrange an appearance by the
author, please contact:

lee@avventurapress.com

CPSIA information can be obtained at www.ICGtesting.com
Printed in the USA
BVOW05s0931160714

359250BV00001B/8/P